BEYOND
TOMORROW

wren

BEYOND TOMORROW

An Anthology of Modern Science Fiction
Edited by Lee Harding
Foreword by ISAAC ASIMOV

wren

WREN PUBLISHING PTY LTD
2 Palmer Street, South Melbourne 3205
© This anthology, Lee Harding 1976
First published 1976
Set by Trade Composition Pty Ltd, Melbourne
Printed and bound by Wilke and Company Limited,
Clayton, Victoria

Jacket design by Michael Payne

National Library of Australia C-I-P data

Harding, Lee J., ed
    Beyond to-morrow: an anthology of modern
    science fiction/edited by Lee Harding;
    foreword by Isaac Asimov.—Melbourne:
    Wren, 1976.
    Published to commemorate the 33rd World
    Science Fiction Convention held in
    Melbourne, August 1975.
    ISBN 0 85885 169 5.

    1. Science fiction. I. Title.
    823.0876

Contents

Also by Lee Harding

a science fiction novel
A World of Shadows

science fiction for young people
The Fallen Spaceman
The Children of Atlantis
The Frozen Sky

The Bad News
and the Good

A foreword
by
Isaac Asimov

I have some bad news for you and some good news.

The bad news is this. You may have missed the Golden Age of Science Fiction during all the twenty years that it was burning up the news-stands in the United States.

The good news is this. You can start having it now.

If any of you who are reading these words happened to have died during the Forties and Fifties (I suppose not many of you have) then the bad news is permanent. You've missed the Golden Age forever. For most of you readers, who are still alive, or have been born since, the good news is permanent. Just gobble up the Golden Age till your reading capacity is so full the stuff starts leaking out at the medulla oblongata.

Here's what happened—

Back in 1926, a magazine called *Amazing Stories* appeared. It was the first periodical ever to be devoted exclusively to science fiction. There had been plenty of science fiction before, even highly regarded science fiction (think of H. G. Wells and Jules Verne), but they had been written by a relatively few authors at irregular intervals.

With the coming of *Amazing Stories* and, after a few years, two or three more such magazines, it became necessary to find enough science fiction *each month* to fill them.

There just wasn't nearly enough really well-written science fiction produced to fill those magazines and that was the luckiest thing in the world—for the magazines were forced to accept whatever they could get. This meant that youngsters, fiendishly interested in the field, had a chance to sell their lame and inexperienced writings, and that odd literary creature, 'the science fiction writer', came into being.

Very often they were not 'authors' in the literary sense,

didn't want to be, couldn't ever be. They only wanted to be science fiction writers. If their stories lacked stylistic polish, they possessed the crude vigour of unbridled and undisciplined imaginations.

That was a fascinating time to live in. I was nine years old when, in 1929, I discovered the field myself.

Yet, however lusty the childhood of the field was, a time came when it had to mature, and for that a master was needed, strong enough and fervent enough to see that this would come to pass.

That master was John W. Campbell, Jr, who had, himself, throughout the early 1930s, been one of the giants of magazine science fiction, writing stories of vast galactic adventure, in a style as unpolished, a vigour as crude, an imagination as unbridled and undisciplined, as could be found anywhere else in the field.

But, largely unknown to the fans, he had been quietly changing. Campbell had a capacity for development and for two or three years he had been publishing thought-provoking mood pieces under the pseudonym of Don A. Stuart, climaxing with the novella *Who Goes There?* which may very well be the best science fiction story ever written.

Then in 1938 Campbell became editor of *Astounding Stories*, which he promptly renamed *Astounding Science Fiction*. It was his intention to make the field grow with him. He was going to force science fiction writers to cease being John W. Campbells and to begin to be Don A. Stuarts.

Out would go the clichés of science fiction, all the stale world of mad scientists and clankingly murderous robots and cardboard monsters from outer space and stultifying lectures on distorted science. In would come scientists and engineers who talked like scientists and engineers, encountering dangers that might just take place in the real world and finding solutions that showed a respect for real science.

Campbell was ruthless. He would not accept the stories of the old sort by men who had hitherto been successful, and many of the big-name writers of the 1930s had to leave the field. He would, on the other hand, accept stories from unknown writers who seemed to be on the right track even if, at first, only distantly and haltingly.

He made it his habit to write long letters (up to ten single-spaced pages) to writers whose stories he was rejecting, but in whom he saw hope—explaining, cajoling, suggesting. He held open house in his editorial office, welcoming any hopeful youngster, overpowering him with the strength of his own personality, and then sending that youngster out to write and try, and write and try again, till he produced what Campbell was determined to have him produce.

I had the treatment in full. Over a period of three years, I was in Campbell's office at least once a month, getting my going-over. I was eighteen when I got there first—a know-nothing as far as science fiction writing was concerned. But Campbell saw something (Heaven only knows what) in my first never-published story and he never let me go. By the time I was twenty-one I could be trusted on my own, as I demonstrated with my story NIGHTFALL, so he simply raised his sights and demanded more.

Campbell treated dozens of writers as he treated me and out of each and every one of them he yanked more than anyone could have believed was in himself. In some ways, though, I was his favourite. I don't think he worked as hard on anyone else as he did on me, and out of no one did he so ruthlessly squeeze so much.

By mid-1939, Campbell had his stable of authors.

The July 1939 issue of *Astounding* contained the first story of an author named A. E. van Vogt. It also contained the first story by Isaac Asimov that Campbell found it worth his while to accept. The August 1939 issue contained the first story of Robert A. Heinlein. In later issues, there came the first efforts of authors such as Arthur C. Clarke, Hal Clement, Alfred Bester, Theodore Sturgeon, Poul Anderson, Gordon Dickson.

Even authors who had published before the Campbell era —Clifford D. Simak, L. Sprague de Camp, Lester del Rey, Jack Williamson—now began to write with new authority and skill, once they were caught in the grip of the remorseless Campbellian fist. (And the real proof of what Campbell did is that now, thirty years after they had been discovered, the various Campbell writers are *still* in the forefront of the field.)

It is no wonder that that July 1939 issue, featuring van

Vogt's BLACK DESTROYER, is considered to have begun the Golden Age.

The Golden Age came to an end in 1960. That is not to say that science fiction has grown worse since then. Not at all. From a literary standpoint, it has been improving steadily and there are authors now who, in terms of the art of writing, stand head and shoulders above the men of the Golden Age.

Since 1960, though, science fiction has grown too large to be encompassed. There are still the magazines, but there are also the paperbacks and the flood of anthologies, both of reprints and original works—to say nothing of the versions of science fiction in the mass magazines, in the movies and on television. All of it is present in so bewildering an array and in so vastly varying a range, that no one can follow it all.

It just isn't and can't be and perhaps never again will be as it was in the 1940s and 1950s, when at first *Astounding* only, and then *Galaxy* and *Fantasy* and *Science Fiction* in addition, contained all of the field that was worth reading and presented it all with startlingly uniform quality, in quantities well within the capacity of each reader to absorb.

But why did Australia miss out on the Golden Age of science fiction? Well, in 1939, only three months after the Golden Age opened, an event of near-second importance occurred—the beginning of World War II. American science fiction magazines, along with other U.S. publications, became prohibited imports in Australia. This was the result not of censorship, of course, but of a dollar imbalance. The policy-makers (dull people) thought that munitions and such-like tiresome items should take precedence. A similar situation arose in Britain.

The embargo was not lifted till 1960, so that the entire twenty-year-long Golden Age passed Australia by as though it had never existed.

It is only since 1960, then, with the reappearance of American publications and the increasing number of British paperback reprints, that Australia has really had the chance to discover American science fiction and only now, I understand, that the tide of enthusiasm in Australia is cresting to a flood—for both readers and writers of the genre. It is appropriate, therefore, that Melbourne was chosen as the venue for the 33rd World Science Fiction Convention. It is also a fitting occasion for the publication of this anthology, representing, in its selection, the work of major American, Australian and British science fiction writers. *Beyond Tomorrow* is a rich sampling from both the Golden Age and the rich variety since then, with its stylistic experimentation, its greater freedom of theme and its leaning towards both realism and surrealism.

What fun it would be for me to go back, somehow, in time and start all over.—But no, I might grow so fascinated by the stories the second time round that I might never get round to writing my own, and I wouldn't want that.

Isaac Asimov
New York 1975

Rainbird

R. A. Lafferty

Would we accomplish something more worthwhile if we could go back in time and correct the mistakes of our past? Would a second chance improve our lives to a significant degree?

The idea has fascinated generations of science fiction writers, but none has explored the possibilities the way R. A. Lafferty does in RAINBIRD; his combination of absurdist notions and madcap writing style is irresistible.

Lafferty arrived on the sf scene in the early Sixties. At first his star burned fitfully; it has since grown into a giant of the first magnitude. Lafferty is unique—as RAINBIRD testifies.

Were scientific firsts truly tabulated, the name of the Yankee inventor, Higgston Rainbird, would surely be without peer. Yet today he is known (and only to a few specialists, at that) for an improved blacksmith's bellows in the year 1785, for a certain modification (not fundamental) in the mouldboard plough about 1805, for a better (but not good) method of reefing the lanteen sail, for a chestnut roaster, for the Devil's Claw Wedge for splitting logs, and for a nutmeg grater embodying a new safety feature; this last was either in the year 1816 or 1817. He is known for such, and for no more.

Were this all that he achieved his name would still be secure. And it *is* secure, in a limited way, to those who hobby in technological history.

But the glory of which history has cheated him, or of which he cheated himself, is otherwise. In a different sense it is without parallel, absolutely unique.

For he pioneered the dynamo, the steam automobile, the steel industry, ferro-concrete construction, the internal combustion engine, electric illumination and power, the wireless, the televox, the petroleum and petro-chemical industries, monorail transportation, air travel, worldwide monitoring, fissionable power, space travel, group telepathy, political and economic balance; he built a retrogressor; and he made great advances towards corporeal immortality and the apotheosis of mankind. It would seem unfair that all this is unknown of him.

Even the once solid facts—that he wired Philadelphia for light and power in 1799, Boston the following year, and New York two years later—are no longer solid. In a sense they are no longer facts.

For all this there must be an explanation; and if not that, then an account at least; and if not that, well—something anyhow.

Higgston Rainbird made a certain decision on a June afternoon in 1779 when he was quite a young man, and by this decision he confirmed his inventive bent.

He was hawking from the top of Devil's Head Mountain. He flew his falcon (actually a tercel hawk) down through the white clouds, and to him it was the highest sport in the world. The bird came back, climbing the blue air, and brought a passenger pigeon from below the clouds. And Higgston was almost perfectly happy as he hooded the hawk.

He could stay there all day and hawk from above the clouds. Or he could go down the mountain and work on his sparker iv his shed. He sighed as he made the decision, for no man can have everything. There was a fascination about hawking. But there was also a fascination about the copper-strip sparker. And he went down the mountain to work on it.

Thereafter he hawked less. After several years he was forced to give it up altogether. He had chosen his life, the dedicated career of an inventor, and he stayed with it for sixty-five years.

His sparker was not a success. It would be expensive, its spark was uncertain and it had almost no advantage over flint. People could always start a fire. If not, they could borrow a brand from a neighbour. There was no market for the sparker. But it was a nice machine, hammered copper strips wrapped around iron teased with lodestone, and the thing turned with a hand crank. He never gave it up entirely. He based other things upon it; and the retrogressor of his last years could not have been built without it.

But the main thing was steam, iron, and tools. He made the finest lathes. He revolutionized smelting and mining. He brought new things to power, and started the smoke to rolling. He made mistakes, he ran into dead ends, he wasted whole decades. But one man can only do so much.

He married a shrew, Audrey, knowing that a man cannot achieve without a goad as well as a goal. But he was without issue or disciple, and this worried him.

He built a steamboat and a steam train. His was the first steam thresher. He cleared the forests with wood-burning giants, and designed towns. He destroyed southern slavery with a steampowered cotton picker, and power and wealth followed him.

For better or worse he brought the country up a long road, so there was hardly a custom of his boyhood that still continued. Probably no one man had ever changed a country so much in his lifetime.

He fathered a true machine-tool industry, and brought rubber from the tropics and plastic from the laboratory. He pumped petroleum, and used natural gas for illumination and steam power. He was honoured and enriched; and, looking back, he had no reason to regard his life as wasted.

'Yes, I've missed so much. I wasted a lot of time. If only I could have avoided the blind alleys, I could have done many times as much. I brought machine tooling to its apex. But I neglected the finest tool of all, the mind. I used it as it is, but I had not time to study it, much less modify it. Others after me will do it all. But I rather wanted to do it all myself. Now it is too late.'

He went back and worked on his old sparker and its descendants, now that he was old. He built toys along the line of it that need not always have remained toys. He made a televox, but the only practical application was that now Audrey could rail at him over a greater distance. He fired up a little steam dynamo in his house, ran wires and made it burn lights in his barn.

And he built a retrogressor.

'I would do much more along this line had I the time. But I'm pepper-bellied pretty near the end of the road. It is like finally coming to a gate and seeing a whole greater world beyond it, and being too old and feeble to enter.'

He kicked a chair and broke it.

'I never even made a better chair. Never got around to it. There are so clod-hopping many things I meant to do. I have maybe pushed the country ahead a couple of decades faster than it would otherwise have gone. But what couldn't I have done if it weren't for the blind alleys! Ten years lost in one of them, twelve in another. If only there had been a way to tell the true from the false, and to leave to others what they could do, and to do myself only what nobody else could do. To see a link (however unlikely) and to go out and get it and set it in its place. Oh, the waste, the wilderness that a talent can wander in! If I had only had a mentor! If I had had a map, a clue, a hatful of clues. I was born shrewd, and I shrewdly cut a path and went a grand ways. But always there was a clearer path and a faster way that I did not see till later. As my name is Rainbird, if I had it to do over, I'd do it infinitely better.'

He began to write a list of the things that he'd have done better. Then he stopped and threw away his pen in disgust.

'Never did even invent a decent ink pen. Never got around to it. Dog-eared damnation, there's so much I didn't do!'

He poured himself a jolt, but he made a face as he drank it.

'Never got around to distilling a really better whisky. Had some good ideas along that line, too. So many things I never did do. Well, I can't improve things by talking to myself here about it.'

Then he sat and thought.

'But I burr-tailed *can* improve things by talking to myself *there* about it.'

He turned on his retrogressor, and went back sixty-five years and up two thousand feet.

Higgston Rainbird was hawking from the top of Devil's Head Mountain one June afternoon in 1779. He flew his bird down through the white fleece clouds, and to him it was sport indeed. Then it came back, climbing the shimmering air, and brought a pigeon to him.

'It's fun', said the old man, 'but the bird is tough, and you have a lot to do. Sit down and listen, Higgston.'

'How do you know the bird is tough? Who are you, and how did an old man like you climb up here without my seeing you? And how in hellpepper did you know that my name was Higgston?'

'I ate the bird and I remember that it was tough. I am just an old man who would tell you a few things to avoid in your life, and I came up here by means of an invention of my own. And I know your name is Higgston, as it is also my name; you being named after me, or I after you, I forget which. Which one of us is the older, anyhow?'

'I had thought that you were, old man. I am a little interested in inventions myself. How does the one that carried you up here work?'

'It begins, well it begins with something like your sparker, Higgston. And as the years go by you adapt and add. But it is all tinkering with a force field till you are able to warp it a little. Now then, you are an ewer-eared galoot and not as handsome as I remember you; but I happen to know that you have the makings of a fine man. Listen now as hard as ever you listened in your life. I doubt that I will be able to repeat. I will save you years and decades; I will tell you the best road to take over a journey which it was once said that a man could travel but once. Man, I'll pave a path for you over the hard places and strew palms before your feet.'

'Talk, you addlepated old gaff. No man ever listened so hard before.'

The old man talked to the young one for five hours. Not a word was wasted; they were neither of them given to wasting words. He told him that steam wasn't everything, this before he knew that it was anything. It was a giant power, but it was limited. Other powers, perhaps, were not. He instructed him to explore the possibilities of amplification and feedback, and to use always the lightest medium of transmission of power; wire rather than mule-drawn coal cart, air rather than wire, ether rather than air. He warned against time wasted in shoring up the obsolete, and of the bottomless quicksand of cliché, both of word and of thought.

He admonished him not to waste precious months in trying to devise the perfect apple corer; there will never be a perfect apple corer. He begged him not to build a battery bobsled. There would be things far swifter than a bobsled.

Let others make the new hide scrapers and tanning salts. Let others aid the carter and the candle moulder and the cooper in their arts. There was need for a better hame, a better horse block, a better stile, a better whetstone. Well, let others fill those needs. If our buttonhooks, our firedogs, our whiffletrees, our bootjacks, our cheese presses are all badly designed and a disgrace, then let someone else remove that disgrace. Let others aid the cordwainer and the cobbler. Let Higgston do only the high work that nobody else would be able to do.

There would come a time when the farrier himself would disappear, as the fletcher had all but disappeared. But new trades would open for a man with an open mind.

Then the old man got specific. He showed young Higgston a design for a lathe dog that would save time. He told him how to draw, rather than hammer wire; and advised him of the virtues of mica as insulator before other material should come to hand.

'And here there are some things that you will have to take on faith,' said the old man, 'things of which we learn the "what" before we fathom the "why".'

He explained to him the shuttle armature and the self-exciting field, and commutation; and the possibilities that alternation carried to its ultimate might open up. He told him a bejammed lot of things about a confounded huge variety of subjects.

'And a little mathematics never hurt a practical man,'

said the old gaffer. 'I was self-taught, and it slowed me down.'

They hunkered down there, and the old man cyphered it all out in the dust on the top of Devil's Head Mountain. He showed him natural logarithms and rotating vectors and the calculi and such; but he didn't push it too far, as even a smart boy can learn only so much in a few minutes. He then gave him a little advice on the treatment of Audrey, knowing it would be useless, for the art of living with a shrew is a thing that cannot be explained to another.

'Now hood your hawk and go down the mountain and go to work', the old man said. And that is what young Higgston Rainbird did.

The career of the Yankee inventor, Higgston Rainbird, was meteoric. The wise men of Greece were little boys to him, the Renaissance giants had only knocked at the door but had not tried the knob. And it was unlocked all the time.

The milestones that Higgston left are breathtaking. He built a short high dam on the flank of Devil's Head Mountain, and had hydroelectric power for his own shop in that same year (1779). He had an arc light burning in Horse-Head Lighthouse in 1781. He read by true incandescent light in 1783, and lighted his native village, Knobknocker, three years later. He drove a charcoal-fuelled motor car in 1787 switched to a distillate of whale oil in 1789, and used true rock oil in 1790. His petrol-powered combination reaper, thresher was in commercial production in 1793, the same year that he wired Centerville for light and power. His first diesel locomotive made its trial run in 1796, in which year he also converted one of his earlier coal-burning steamships to liquid fuel.

In 1799 he had wired Philadelphia for light and power, a major breakthrough, for the big cities had manfully resisted the innovations. On the night of the turn of the century he unhooded a whole clutch of new things, wireless telegraphy, the televox, radio transmission and reception, motile and audible theatrical reproductions, a machine to transmit the human voice into print, and a method of sterilizing and wrapping meat to permit its indefinite preservation at any temperature.

And in the spring of that new year he first flew a heavier-than-air vehicle.

'He has made all the basic inventions,' said the many-tongued people. 'Now there remains only their refinement and proper utilization.'

'Horse hokey,' said Higgston Rainbird. He made a rocket that could carry freight to England in thirteen minutes at seven cents a hundredweight. This was in 1805. He had fissionable power in 1813, and within four years had the price down where it could be used for desalting seawater to the eventual irrigation of five million square miles of remarkably dry land.

He built a Think Machine to work out the problems that he was too busy to solve, and a Prediction Machine to pose him with new problems and new areas of breakthrough.

In 1821, on his birthday, he hit the moon with a marker. He bet a crony that he would be able to go up personally one year later and retrieve it. And he won the bet.

In 1830 he first put on the market his Red Ball Pipe Tobacco, an aromatic and expensive crimp cut made of Martian lichen.

In 1836 he founded the Institute for the Atmospheric Rehabilitation of Venus, for he found that place to be worse than a smokehouse. It was there that he developed that hacking cough that stayed with him till the end of his days.

He synthesized a man of his own age and disrepute who would sit drinking with him in the after-midnight hours and say, 'You're so right, Higgston, so incontestably right.'

His plan for the Simplification and Eventual Elimination of Government was adopted (in modified form) in 1840, a fruit of his Political and Economic Balance Institute.

Yet, for all his seemingly successful penetration of the field, he realized that man was the only truly cantankerous animal, and that Human Engineering would remain one of the never completely resolved fields.

He made a partial breakthrough in telepathy, starting with the personal knowledge that shrews are always able to read the minds of their spouses. He knew that the secret was not in sympathetic reception, but in arrogant break-in. With the polite it is forever impossible, but he disguised this discovery as politely as he could.

And he worked toward corporeal immortality and the apotheosis of mankind, that cantankerous animal.

He designed a fabric that would embulk itself on a temperature drop, and thin to an airy sheen in summery weather. The weather itself he disdained to modify, but he did evolve infallible prediction of exact daily rainfall and temperature for decades in advance.

And he built a retrogressor.

One day he looked in the mirror and frowned.

'I never did get around to making a better mirror. This one is hideous. However (to consider every possibility) let us weigh the thesis that it is the image and not the mirror that is hideous.'

He called up an acquaintance.

'Say, Ulois, what year is this anyhow?'

'1844.'

'Are you sure?'

'Reasonably sure.'

'How old am I?'

'Eighty-five, I think, Higgston.'

'How long have I been an old man?'

'Quite a while, Higgston, quite a while.'

Higgston Rainbird hung up rudely.

'I wonder how I ever let a thing like that slip up on me?' he said to himself. 'I should have gone to work on corporeal immortality a little earlier. I've bungled the whole business now.'

He fiddled with his Prediction Machine and saw that he was to die that very year. He did not seek a finer reading.

'What a saddle-galled splay-footed situation to find myself in! I never got around to a tenth of the things I really wanted to do. Oh, I was smart enough; I just ran up too many blind alleys. Never found the answers to half the old riddles. Should have built the Prediction Machine at the beginning instead of the end. But I didn't know how to build it at the beginning. There ought to be a way to get more done. Never got any advice in my life worth taking except from that nutty old man on the mountain when I was a young man. There's a lot of things I've only started on. Well, every man doesn't hang, but every man does come to the end of his rope. I never did get around to making that rope extensible. And I can't improve things by talking to myself here about it.'

He filled his pipe with Red Ball crimp cut and thought a while.

'But I hill-hopping *can* improve things by talking to myself *there* about it.'

Then he turned on his retrogressor and went back and up.

Young Higgston Rainbird was hawking from the top of Devil's Head Mountain on a June afternoon in 1779. He flew his hawk down through the white clouds, and decided that he was the finest fellow in the world and master of the finest sport. If there was earth below the clouds it was far away and unimportant.

The hunting bird came back, climbing the tall air, with a pigeon from the lower regions.

'Forget the bird,' said the old man, 'and give a listen with those outsized ears of yours. I have a lot to tell you in a very little while, and then you must devote yourself to a concentrated life of work. Hood the bird and clip him to the stake. Is that bridle clip of your own invention? Ah yes, I remember now that it is.'

'I'll just fly him down once more, old man, and then I'll have a look at what you're selling.'

'No. No. Hood him at once. This is your moment of decision. That is a boyishness that you must give up. Listen to me, Higgston, and I will orient your life for you.'

'I rather intended to orient it myself. How did you get up here, old man, without my seeing you? How, in fact, did you get up here at all? It's a hard climb.'

'Yes, I remember that it is. I came up here on the wings of an invention of my own. Now pay attention for a few hours. It will take all your considerable wit.'

'A few hours and a perfect hawking afternoon will be gone. This may be the finest day ever made.'

'I also once felt that it was, but I manfully gave it up. So must you.'

'Let me fly the hawk down again and I will listen to you while it is gone.'

'But you will only be listening with half a mind, and the rest will be with the hawk.'

But young Higgston Rainbird flew the bird down through the shining white clouds, and the old man began his rigmarole sadly. Yet it was a rang-dang-do of a spiel, a mummywhammy of admonition and exposition, and young Higgston listened entranced and almost forgot his hawk. The old man told him that he must stride half a dozen roads at once, and yet never take a wrong one; that he must do some things earlier that on the alternative had been done quite late; that he must point his technique at the Think Machine and the Prediction Machine, and at the unsolved problem of corporeal immortality.

'In no other way can you really acquire elbow room, ample working time. Time runs out and life is too short if you let it take its natural course. Are you listening to me, Higgston?'

But the hawk came back, climbing the steep air, and it had a grey dove. The old man sighed at the interruption, and he knew that his project was in peril.

'Hood the hawk. It's a sport for boys. Now listen to me, you spraddling jack. I am telling you things that nobody else would ever be able to tell you! I will show you how to fly falcons to the stars, not just down to the meadows and birch groves at the foot of this mountain.'

'There is no prey up there,' said young Higgston.

'There *is*. Gamier prey than you ever dreamed of. Hood the bird and snaffle him.'

'I'll just fly him down one more time and listen to you till he comes back.'

The hawk went down through the clouds like a golden bolt of summer lightning.

Then the old man, taking the cosmos, peeled it open layer by layer like an onion, and told young Higgston how it worked. Afterwards he returned to the technological beginning and he lined out the workings of steam and petro- and electromagnetism, and explained that these simple powers must be used for a short interval in the invention of greater

power. He told him of waves and resonance and airy transmission, and fission and flight and over-flight. And that none
of the doors required keys, only a resolute man to turn the
knob and push them open. Young Higgston was impressed.

Then the hawk came back, climbing the towering air,
and it had a rainbird.

The old man had lively eyes, but now they took on a new
light.

'Nobody ever gives up pleasure willingly,' he said, 'and
there is always the sneaking feeling that the bargain may
not have been perfect. This is one of the things I have missed.
I haven't hawked for sixty-five years. Let me fly him this
time, Higgston.'

'You know how?'

'I am adept. And I once intended to make a better gauntlet for hawkers. This hasn't been improved since Nimrod's
time.'

'I have an idea for a better gauntlet myself, old man.'

'Yes. I know what your idea is. Go ahead with it. It's
practical.'

'Fly him if you want to, old man.'

And old Higgston flew the tercel hawk down through the
gleaming clouds, and he and young Higgston watched from
the top of the world. And then young Higgston Rainbird was
standing alone on the top of Devil's Head Mountain, and
the old man was gone.

'I wonder where he went? And where in appleknocker's
heaven did he come from? Or was he ever here at all? That's
a danged funny machine he came in, if he did come in it.
All the wheels are on the inside. But I can use the gears
from it, and the clock, and the copper wire. It must have
taken weeks to hammer that much wire out that fine. I wish
I'd paid more attention to what he was saying, but he
poured it on a little thick. I'd have gone along with him on
it if only he'd have found a good stopping place a little
sooner, and hadn't been so insistent on giving up hawking.
Well, I'll just hawk here till dark, and if it dawns clear I'll
be up again in the morning. And Sunday, if I have a little
time, I may work on my sparker or my chestnut roaster.'

Higgston Rainbird lived a long and successful life. Locally he was known best as a hawker and horse racer. But as an inventor he was recognized as far as Boston.

He is still known, in a limited way, to specialists in the field and period; known as contributor to the development of the mouldboard plough, as the designer of the Nonpareil Nutmeg Grater with the safety feature, for a bellows, for a sparker for starting fires (little used), and for the Devil's Claw Wedge for splitting logs.

He is known for such, and for no more.

Nine Lives

Ursula K. Le Guin

The possible consequences of genetic engineering have seldom been so eloquently depicted as in NINE LIVES. The rather bizarre circumstances portrayed by this distinguished author may seem unlikely, yet before the end of this century we shall have witnessed remarkable advances in the field of human biology that could make the events in this story seem commonplace. After all, our grand-parents would have expressed some disbelief in the idea of organ transplants, yet this and other modern 'miracles' are now an everyday occurrence. It is therefore relatively easy to accept the possibility of 'cloned' human beings.

Ursula K. Le Guin has written such award-winning novels as *The Left Hand of Darkness* and *The Lathe of Heaven*. Her latest book, *The Dispossessed*, has already gathered impressive critical notices. Her trilogy of novels about the world called 'Earthsea', although ostensibly written for teenagers, has achieved a wide popularity; the final book in the series, *The Farthest Shore*, won the prestigious Newberry Award as best children's book of the year.

Mrs Le Guin was asked to be Guest of Honour at the 33rd World Science Fiction Convention in Melbourne in 1975. She was the first lady to be so honoured, and NINE LIVES gives some indication why—such a combination of compassion and intellectual insight, blended with technical mastery, is rare enough in the field to make her work eagerly sought after by editors and readers alike.

She was alive inside, but dead outside, her face a black-and-dun net of wrinkles, tumours, cracks. She was bald and blind. The tremors that crossed Libra's face were mere quiverings of corruption: underneath, in the black corridors, the halls beneath the skin, there were crepitations in darkness, ferments, chemical nightmares that went on for centuries. 'Oh, the damned flatulent planet,' Pugh murmured as the dome shook and a boil burst a kilometre to the southwest, spraying silver pus across the sunset. The sun had been setting for the last two days. 'I'll be glad to see a human face'

'Thanks,' said Martin.

'Yours is human, to be sure,' said Pugh, 'but I've seen it so long I can't see it.'

Radvid signals cluttered the communicator which Martin was operating, faded, returned as face and voice. The face filled the screen, the nose of an Assyrian king, the eyes of a samurai, skin bronze, eyes the colour of iron: young, magnificent. 'Is that what human beings look like?' said Pugh with awe. 'I'd forgotten.'

'Shut up, Owen, we're on.'

'Libra Exploratory Mission Base, come in, please; this is *Passerine* launch.'

'Libra here. Beam fixed. Come on down, launch.'

'Expulsion in seven E-seconds. Hold on.' The screen blanked and sparkled.

'Do they all look like that? Martin, you and I are uglier men than I thought.'

'Shut up, Owen . . .'

For twenty-two minutes Martin followed the landing-craft down by signal and then, through the cleared dome, they saw it, a small star in the blood-coloured east, sinking. It came down neat and quiet, Libra's thin atmosphere carrying little sound. Pugh and Martin closed the headpieces of their imsuits, zipped out of the dome airlocks, and ran with soaring strides, Nijinsky and Nureyev, toward the boat. Three equipment modules came floating down at four-minute intervals from each other and hundred-metre intervals east of the boat. 'Come on out,' Martin said on his suit radio. 'We're waiting at the door.'

'Come on in; the methane's fine,' said Pugh.

The hatch opened. The young man they had seen on the screen came out with one athletic twist and leaped down onto the shaky dust and clinkers of Libra. Martin shook his hand, but Pugh was staring at the hatch, from which another young man emerged with the same neat twist and jump, followed by a young woman who emerged with the same neat twist, ornamented with a wriggle, and a jump. They were all tall, with bronze skin, black hair, high-bridged noses, epicanthic fold, the same face. They all had the same face. The fourth was emerging from the hatch with a neat twist and jump. 'Martin bach,' said Pugh, 'we've got a clone.'

'Right,' said one of them, 'we're a tenclone. John Chow's the name. You're Lieutenant Martin?'

'I'm Owen Pugh.'

'Alvaro Guillen Martin,' said Martin, formal, bowing slightly. Another girl was out, the same beautiful face; Martin stared at her and his eye rolled like a nervous pony's. Evidently he had never given any thought to cloning, and was suffering technological shock. 'Steady,' Pugh said in the Argentine dialect, 'it's only excess twins'. He stood close by Martin's elbow. He was glad himself of the contact.

It is hard to meet a stranger. Even the greatest extravert meeting even the meekest stranger knows a certain dread, though he may not know he knows it. Will he make a fool of me wreck my image of myself invade me destroy me change me? Will he be different from me? Yes, that he will. There's the terrible thing: the strangeness of the stranger.

After two years on a dead planet, and the last half year isolated as a team of two, oneself and one other, after that it's even harder to meet a stranger, however welcome he may be. You're out of the habit of difference, you've lost the touch; and so the fear revives, the primitive anxiety, the old dread.

The clone, five males and five females, had got done in a couple of minutes what a man might have got done in twenty: greeted Pugh and Martin, had a glance at Libra, unloaded the boat, made ready to go. They went, and the dome filled with them, a hive of golden bees. They hummed and buzzed quietly, filled up all silences, all spaces with a honey-brown swarm of human presence. Martin looked bewilderedly at the long-limbed girls, and they smiled at him, three at once. Their smile was gentler than that of the boys, but no less radiantly self-possessed.

'Self-possessed,' Owen Pugh murmured to his friend, 'that's it. Think of it, to be oneself ten times over. Nine seconds for every motion, nine ayes on every vote. It would be glorious!' But Martin was asleep. And the John Chows had all gone to sleep at once. The dome was filled with their quiet breathing. They were young, they didn't snore. Martin sighed and snored, his Hershey-bar-coloured face relaxed in the dim afterglow of Libra's primary, set at last.

23

Pugh had cleared the dome and stars looked in, Sol among them, a great company of lights, a clone of splendours. Pugh slept and dreamed of a one-eyed giant who chased him through the shaking halls of Hell.

From his sleeping-bag Pugh watched the clone's awakening. They all got up within one minute except for one pair, a boy and a girl, who lay snugly tangled and still sleeping in one bag. As Pugh saw this there was a shock like one of Libra's earthquakes inside him, a very deep tremor. He was not aware of this, and in fact thought he was pleased at the sight; there was no other such comfort on this dead hollow world; more power to them, who made love. One of the others stepped on the pair. They woke and the girl sat up flushed and sleepy, with bare golden breasts. One of her sisters murmured something to her; she shot a glance at Pugh and disappeared in the sleeping-bag, followed by a giant giggle, from another direction a fierce stare, from still another direction a voice: 'Christ, we're used to having a room to ourselves. Hope you don't mind, Captain Pugh.'

'It's a pleasure,' Pugh said half-truthfully. He had to stand up then, wearing only the shorts he slept in, and he felt like a plucked rooster, all white scrawn and pimples. He had seldom envied Martin's compact brownness so much. The United Kingdom had come through the Great Famines well, losing less than half its population: a record achieved by rigorous food-control. Black-marketeers and hoarders had been executed. Crumbs had been shared. Where in richer lands most had died and a few had thriven, in Britain fewer died and none throve. They all got lean. Their sons were lean, their grandsons lean, small, brittle-boned, easily infected. When civilization became a matter of standing in lines, the British had kept queue, and so had replaced the survival of the fittest with the survival of the fair-minded. Owen Pugh was a scrawny little man. All the same, he was there.

At the moment he wished he wasn't.

At breakfast a John said, 'Now if you'll brief us, Captain Pugh—'

'Owen, then.'

'Owen, we can work out our schedule. Anything new on

the mine since your last report to your Mission? We saw your reports when *Passerine* was orbiting Planet V, where they are now.'

Martin did not answer, though the mine was his discovery and project, and Pugh had to do his best. It was hard to talk to them. The same faces, each with the same expression of intelligent interest, all leaned toward him across the table at almost the same angle. They all nodded together.

Over the Exploitation Corps insignia on their tunics each had a nameband, first name John and last name Chow, of course, but the middle names different. The men were Aleph, Kaph, Yod, Gimel, and Samedh; the women Sadhe, Daleth, Zayin, Beth, and Resh. Pugh tried to use the names but gave it up at once; he could not even tell sometimes which one had spoken, for the voices were all alike.

Martin buttered and chewed his toast, and finally interrupted: 'You're a team. Is that it?'

'Right,' said two Johns.

'God, what a team! I hadn't seen the point. How much do you each know what the others are thinking?'

'Not at all, properly speaking,' replied one of the girls, Zayin. The others watched her with the proprietary, approving look they had. 'No ESP, nothing fancy. But we think alike. We have exactly the same equipment. Given the same stimulus, the same problem, we're likely to be coming up with the same reactions and solutions at the same time. Explanations are easy—don't even have to make them, usually. We seldom misunderstand each other. It does facilitate our working as a team.'

'Christ, yes,' said Martin. 'Pugh and I have spent seven hours out of ten for six months misunderstanding each other. Like most people. What about emergencies, are you as good at meeting the unexpected problem as a nor— . . . an unrelated team?'

'Statistics so far indicate that we are,' Zayin answered readily. Clones must be trained, Pugh thought, to meet questions, to reassure and reason. All they said had the slightly bland and stilted quality of answers furnished to the Public. 'We can't brainstorm as singletons can; we as a team don't profit from the interplay of varied minds; but

25

we have a compensatory advantage. Clones are drawn from the best human material, individuals of IIQ 99th percentile, Genetic Constitution alpha double A, and so on. We have more to draw on than most individuals do.'

'And it's multiplied by a factor of ten. Who is—who was John Chow?'

'A genius, surely,' Pugh said politely. His interest in cloning was not so new and avid as Martin's.

'Leonardo Complex type,' said Yod. 'Biomath, also a cellist, and an undersea hunter, and interested in structural engineering problems, and so on. Died before he'd worked out his major theories.'

'Then you each represent a different facet of his mind, his talents?'

'No,' said Zayin, shaking her head in time with several others. 'We share the basic equipment and tendencies, of course, but we're all engineers in Planetary Exploitation. A later clone can be trained to develop other aspects of the basic equipment. It's all training; the genetic substance is identical. We *are* John Chow. But we were differently trained.'

Martin looked shell-shocked. 'How old are you?'

'Twenty-three.'

'You say he died young—had they taken germ cells from him beforehand or something?'

Gimel took over: 'He died at twenty-four in an aircar crash. They couldn't save the brain, so they took some intestinal cells and cultured them for cloning. Reproductive cells aren't used for cloning since they have only half the chromosomes. Intestinal cells happen to be easy to despecialize and reprogramme for total growth.'

'All chips off the old block,' Martin said valiantly. 'But how can . . . some of you be women . . . ?'

Beth took over: 'It's easy to programme half the clonal mass back to the female. Just delete the male gene from half the cells and they revert to the basic—that is, the female. It's trickier to go the other way: have to hook in artificial Y chromosomes. So they mostly clone from males, since clones function best bisexually.'

Gimel again: 'They've worked these matters of technique

and function out carefully. The taxpayer wants the best for his money, and of course clones are expensive. With the cell-manipulations, and the incubation in Ngama Placentae, and the maintenance and training of the foster-parent groups, we end up costing about three million apiece.'

'For your next generation,' Martin said, still struggling, 'I suppose you . . . you breed?'

'We females are sterile,' said Beth with perfect equanimity; 'you remember that the Y chromosome was deleted from our original cell. The males can interbreed with approved singletons, if they want to. But to get John Chow again as often as they want, they just reclone a cell from this clone.'

Martin gave up the struggle. He nodded and chewed cold toast. 'Well,' said one of the Johns, and all changed mood, like a flock of starlings that change course in one wingflick, following a leader so fast that no eye can see which leads. They were ready to go. 'How about a look at the mine? Then we'll unload the equipment. Some nice new models in the roboats; you'll want to see them. Right?' Had Pugh or Martin not agreed they might have found it hard to say so. The Johns were polite but unanimous; their decisions carried. Pugh, Commander of Libra Base 2, felt a qualm. Could he boss around this superman-woman-entity-of-ten—and a genius at that? He stuck close to Martin as they suited for outside. Neither said anything.

Four apiece in the three large jetsleds, they slipped off north from the dome, over Libra's dun rugose skin, in starlight.

'Desolate,' one said.

It was a boy and girl with Pugh and Martin. Pugh wondered if these were the two that had shared a sleeping-bag last night. No doubt they wouldn't mind if he asked them. Sex must be as handy as breathing, to them. (Did you two breathe last night?)

'Yes,' he said, 'it is desolate.'

'This is our first time Off, except training on Luna.' The girl's voice was definitely a bit higher and softer.

'How did you take the big hop?'

'They doped us. I wanted to experience it.' That was the boy; he sounded wistful. They seemed to have more

27

personality, only two at a time. Did repetition of the individual negate individuality?

'Don't worry,' said Martin, steering the sled, 'you can't experience no-time because it isn't there.'

'I'd just like to once,' one of them said. 'So we'd know.'

The Mountains of Merioneth showed leprotic in starlight to the east, a plume of freezing gas trailed silvery from a vent-hole to the west, and the sled tilted groundwards. The twins braced for the stop at one moment, each with a slight protective gesture to the other. Your skin is my skin, Pugh thought, but literally, no metaphor. What would it be like, then, to have someone as close to you as that? Always to be answered when you spoke, never to be in pain alone. Love your neighbour as you love yourself . . . That hard old problem was solved. The neighbour was the self: the love was perfect.

And here was Hellmouth, the mine.

Pugh was the Exploratory Mission's ET geologist, and Martin his technician and cartographer; but when in the course of a local survey Martin had discovered the U-mine, Pugh had given him full credit, as well as the onus of prospecting the lode and planning the Exploitation Team's job. These kids had been sent out from Earth years before Martin's reports got there, and had not known what their job would be until they got here. The Exploitation Corps simply sent out teams regularly and blindly as a dandelion sends out its seeds, knowing there would be a job for them on Libra or the next planet out or one they hadn't even heard about yet. The Government wanted uranium too urgently to wait while reports drifted home across the light-years. The stuff was like gold, oldfashioned but essential, worth mining extraterrestrially and shipping interstellar. Worth its weight in people, Pugh thought sourly, watching the tall young men and women go one by one, glimmering in starlight, into the black hole Martin had named Hellmouth.

As they went in, their homeostatic forehead-lamps brightened. Twelve nodding gleams ran along the moist, wrinkled walls. Pugh heard Martin's radiation counter peeping twenty to the dozen up ahead. 'Here's the drop-off,' said Martin's voice in the suit intercom, drowning out the peeping and the dead silence that was around them. 'We're in a side-fissure; this is the main vertical vent in front of us.' The black void gaped, its far side not visible in the headlamp beams. 'Last vulcanism seems to have been a couple of thousand years ago. Nearest fault is twenty-eight kilometres east, in the Trench. This region seems to be as safe seismically as anything in the area. The big basalt-flow overhead stabilizes all these substructures, so long as it remains stable itself. Your central lode is thirty-six metres down and runs in a series of five bubble-caverns northeast. It is a lode, a pipe of very high-grade ore. You saw the percentage figures, right? Extraction's going to be no problem. All you've got to do is get the bubbles topside.'

'Take off the lid and let 'em float up.' A chuckle. Voices began to talk, but they were all the same voice and the suit radio gave them no location in space. 'Open the thing right up—safer that way. But it's a solid basalt roof.—How thick, ten metres here?—Three to twenty, the report said. —Blow good ore all over the lot.—Use this access we're in, straighten it a bit and run slider-rails for the robos.— Import burros.—Have we got enough propping material? —What's your estimate of total payload mass, Martin?'

'Say over five million kilos and under eight.'

'Transport will be here in ten E-months.—It'll have to go pure.—No, they'll have the mass problem in NAFAL shipping licked by now; remember it's been sixteen years since we left Earth last Tuesday.—Right, they'll send the whole lot back and purify it in Earth orbit.—Shall we go down, Martin?'

'Go on. I've been down.'

The first one—Aleph? (Heb., the ox, the leader)— swung onto the ladder and down; the rest followed. Pugh and Martin stood at the chasm's edge. Pugh set his intercom to exchange only with Martin's suit, and noticed Martin doing the same. It was a bit wearing, this listening to one person think aloud in ten voices, or was it one voice speaking the thoughts of ten minds?

'A great gut,' Pugh said, looking down into the black pit, its veined and warted walls catching stray gleams of headlamps far below. 'A cow's bowel. A bloody great constipated intestine.'

Martin's counter peeped like a lost chicken. They stood inside the epileptic planet, breathing oxygen from tanks, wearing suits impermeable to corrosives and harmful radiations, resistant to a two-hundred-degree range of temperatures, tear-proof, and as shock-resistant as possible given the soft vulnerable stuff inside.

'Next hop,' Martin said, 'I'd like to find a planet that has nothing whatever to exploit.'

'You found this.'

'Keep me home next time.'

Pugh was pleased. He had hoped Martin would want to go on working with him, but neither of them was used to talking much about their feelings, and he had hesitated to ask. 'I'll try that,' he said.

'I hate this place. I like caves, you know. It's why I came in here. Just spelunking. But this one's a bitch. Mean. You can't ever let down in here. I guess this lot can handle it, though. They know their stuff.'

'Wave of the future, whatever,' said Pugh.

The wave of the future came swarming up the ladder, swept Martin to the entrance, gabbled at and around him: 'Have we got enough material for supports?—If we convert one of the extractor-servos to anneal, yes.—Sufficient if we miniblast?—Kaph can calculate stress.'

Pugh had switched his intercom back to receive them; he looked at them, so many thoughts jabbering in an eager mind, and at Martin standing silent among them, and at Hellmouth, and the wrinkled plain. 'Settled! How does that strike you as a preliminary schedule, Martin?'

'It's your baby,' Martin said.

Within five E-days, the Johns had all their material and equipment unloaded and operating, and were starting to open up the mine. They worked with total efficiency. Pugh was fascinated and frightened by their effectiveness, their confidence, their independence. He was no use to them at all. A clone, he thought, might indeed be the first truly stable, self-reliant human being. Once adult it would need nobody's help. It would be sufficient to itself physically, sexually, emotionally, intellectually. Whatever he did, any member of it would always receive the support and approval of his peers, his other selves. Nobody else was needed.

Two of the clone stayed in the dome doing calculations and paperwork, with frequent sled-trips to the mine for measurements and tests. They were the mathematicians of the clone, Zayin and Kaph. That is, as Zayin explained, all ten had had thorough mathematical training from age three to twenty-one, but from twenty-one to twenty-three she and Kaph had gone on with maths while the others intensified other specialties—geology, mining engineering, electronic engineering, equipment robotics, applied atomics, and so on. 'Kaph and I feel,' she said, 'that we're the element of the cone closest to what John Chow was in his singleton lifetime. But of course he was principally in biomaths, and they didn't take us far in that.'

'They needed us most in this field,' Kaph said, with the patriotic priggishness they sometimes evinced.

Pugh and Martin soon could distinguish this pair from the others: Zayin by gestalt, Kaph only by a discoloured left fourth fingernail, got from an ill-aimed hammer at the age of six. No doubt there were many such differences, physical and psychological, among them; nature might be identical, nurture could not be. But the differences were hard to find. And part of the difficulty was that they really never talked to Pugh and Martin. They joked with them, were polite, got along fine. They gave nothing. It was nothing one could complain about; they were very pleasant, they had the standardized American friendliness. 'Do you come from Ireland, Owen?'

'Nobody comes from Ireland, Zayin.'

'There are lots of Irish-Americans.'

'To be sure, but no more Irish. A couple of thousand in all the island, the last I knew. They didn't go in for birth-control, you know, so the food ran out. By the Third Famine there were no Irish left at all but the priesthood, and they were all celibate, or nearly all.'

Zayin and Kalph smiled stiffly. They had no experience of either bigotry or irony. 'What are you then, ethnically?'

Kalph asked, and Pugh replied, 'A Welshman.'

'Is it Welsh that you and Martin speak together?'

None of your business, Pugh thought, but said, 'No, it's his dialect, not mine: Argentinean. A descendent of Spanish.'

'You learned it for private communication?'

'Whom had we here to be private from? It's just that sometimes a man likes to speak his native language.'

'Ours is English,' Kaph said unsympathetically. Why should they have sympathy? That's one of the things you give because you need it back.

'Is Wells quaint!' asked Zayin.

'Wells? Oh, Wales, it's called. Yes. Wales is quaint.'

Pugh switched on his rock-cutter, which prevented further conversation by a synapse-destroying whine, and while it whined he turned his back and said a profane word in Welsh.

That night he used the Argentine dialect for private communication. 'Do they pair off in the same couples, or change every night?'

Martin looked surprised. A prudish expression, unsuited to his features, appeared for a moment. It faded. He too was curious. 'I think it's random.'

'Don't whisper, man; it sounds dirty. I think they rotate.'

'On a schedule?'

'So nobody gets omitted.'

Martin gave a vulgar laugh and smothered it. 'What about us? Aren't we omitted?'

'That doesn't occur to them.'

'What if I proposition one of the girls?'

'She'd tell the others and they'd decide as a group.'

'I am not a bull,' Martin said, his dark, heavy face heating up. 'I will not be judged—'

'Down, down, *machismo*,' said Pugh. 'Do you mean to proposition one?'

Martin shrugged, sullen. 'Let 'em have their incest.'

'Incest is it, or masturbation?'

'I don't care, if they'd do it out of earshot!'

The clone's early attempts at modesty had soon worn off, unmotivated by any deep defensiveness of self or awareness of others. Pugh and Martin were daily deeper swamped under the intimacies of its constant emotional-sexual-mental interchange: swamped yet excluded.

'Two months to go,' Martin said one evening.

'To what?' snapped Pugh. He was edgy lately and Martin's sullenness got on his nerves.

'To relief.'

In sixty days the full crew of their Exploratory Mission were due back from their survey of the other planets of the system. Pugh was aware of this.

'Crossing off the days on your calendar?' he jeered.

'Pull yourself together, Owen.'

'What do you mean?'

'What I say.'

They parted in contempt and resentment.

Pugh came in after a day alone on the Pampas, a vast lava-plain the nearest edge of which was two hours south by jet. He was tired, but refreshed by solitude. They were not supposed to take long trips alone, but lately had often done so. Martin stooped under bright lights, drawing one of his elegant, masterly charts: this one was of the whole face of Libra, the cancerous face. The dome was otherwise empty, seeming dim and large as it had before the clone came. 'Where's the golden horde?'

Martin grunted ignorance, cross-hatching. He straightened his back to glance around at the sun, which squatted feebly like a great red toad on the eastern plain, and at the clock, which said 18:45. 'Some big quakes today,' he said, returning to his map. 'Feel them down there? Lots of crates were falling around. Take a look at the seismo.'

The needle jigged and wavered on the roll. It never stopped dancing here. The roll had recorded five quakes of major intensity back in mid-afternoon; twice the needle had hopped off the roll. The attached computer had been activated to emit a slip reading, 'Epicentre 61'N by 4'24"E.'

'Not in the Trench this time.'

'I thought I felt a bit different from usual. Sharper.'

'In Base One I used to lie awake all night feeling the ground jump. Queer how you get used to things.'

'Go spla if you didn't. What's for dinner?'

'I thought you'd have cooked it.'

'Waiting for the clone.'

Feeling put upon, Pugh got out a dozen dinnerboxes, stuck two in the Instobake, pulled them out. 'All right, here's dinner.'

'Been thinking,' Martin said, coming to the table. 'What if some clone cloned itself? Illegally. Made a thousand duplicates—ten thousand. Whole army. They could make a tidy power-grab, couldn't they?'

'But how many millions did this lot cost to rear? Artificial placentae and all that. It would be hard to keep secret, unless they had a planet to themselves . . . Back before the Famines when Earth had national governments, they talked about that: clone your best soldiers, have whole regiments of them. But the food ran out before they could play that game.'

They talked amicably, as they used to do.

'Funny,' Martin said, chewing. 'They left early this morning, didn't they?'

'All but Kaph and Zayin. They thought they'd get the first payload above ground today. What's up?'

'They weren't back for lunch.'

'They won't starve, to be sure.'

'They left at seven.'

'So they did.' Then Pugh saw it. The air-tanks held eight hours' supply.

'Kaph and Zayin carried out spare cans when they left. Or they've got a heap out there.'

'They did, but they brought the whole lot in to recharge.' Martin stood up, pointing to one of the stacks of stuff that cut the dome into rooms and alleys.

'There's an alarm signal on every imsuit.'

'It's not automatic.'

Pugh was tired and still hungry. 'Sit down and eat, man. That lot can look after themselves.'

Martin sat down, but did not eat. 'There was a big quake, Owen. The first one. Big enough, it scared me.'

After a pause Pugh sighed and said, 'All right.'

Unenthusiastically, they got out the two-man sled that was always left for them, and headed it north. The long sunrise covered everything in poisonous red Jell-O. The horizontal light and shadow made it hard to see, raised walls of fake iron ahead of them through which they slid, turned the convex plain beyond Hellmouth into a great dimple full of bloody water. Around the tunnel entrance a wilderness of machinery stood, cranes and cables and servos and wheels and diggers and robocarts and sliders and control-huts, all slanting and bulking incoherently in the red light. Martin jumped from the sled, ran into the mine. He came out again, to Pugh. 'Oh God, Owen, it's down,' he said. Pugh went in and saw, five metres from the entrance, the shiny, moist, black wall that ended the tunnel. Newly exposed to air, it looked organic, like visceral tissue. The tunnel entrance, enlarged by blasting and double-tracked for robocarts, seemed unchanged until he noticed thousands of tiny spiderweb cracks in the walls. The floor was set with some sluggish fluid.

'They were inside,' Martin said.

'They may be still. They surely had extra air-cans—'

'Look, Owen, look at the basalt flow, at the roof; don't you see what the quake did. Look at it.'

The low hump of land that roofed the caves still had the unreal look of an optical illusion. It had reversed itself, sunk down, leaving a vast dimple or pit. When Pugh walked on it he saw that it too was cracked with many tiny fissures. From some a whitish gas was seeping, so that the sunlight on the surface of the gas-pool was shafted as if by the waters of a dim red lake.

'The mine's not on the fault. There's no fault here!'

Pugh came back to him quickly. 'No, there's no fault, Martin. Look, they surely weren't all inside together.'

Martin followed him and searched among the wrecked machines dully, then actively. He spotted the airsled. It had come down heading south, and struck at an angle in a pothole of colloidal dust. It had carried two riders. One was half sunk in the dust, but his suit-meters registered normal functioning; the other hung strapped onto the tilted sled. Her imsuit had burst open on the broken legs, and the body was frozen hard as any rock. That was all they found. As both regulation and custom demanded, they cremated the dead at once with the laser-guns they carried by regulation and had never used before. Pugh, knowing he was going to be sick, wrestled the survivor onto the two-man sled and sent Martin off to the dome with him. Then he vomited, and flushed the waste out of his suit, and finding one four-man sled undamaged followed after Martin, shaking as if the cold of Libra had got through to him.

The survivor was Kaph. He was in deep shock. They found a swelling on the occiput that might mean concussion, but no fracture was visible.

Pugh brought two glasses of food-concentrate and two chasers of aquavit. 'Come on,' he said. Martin obeyed, drinking off the tonic. They sat down on crates near the cot and sipped the aquavit.

Kaph lay immobile, face like beeswax, hair bright black to the shoulders, lips stiffly parted for faintly gasping breaths.

'It must have been the first shock, the big one,' Martin said. 'It must have slid the whole structure sideways. Till it fell in on itself. There must be gas layers in the lateral rocks, like those formations in the Thirty-first Quadrant. But there wasn't any sign—' As he spoke the world slid out from under them. Things leaped and clattered, hopped and jigged, shouted Ha! Ha! Ha! 'It was like this at fourteen hours,' said Reason shakily in Martin's voice, amidst the unfastening and ruin of the world. But Unreason sat up, as the tumult lessened and things ceased dancing, and screamed aloud.

Pugh leaped across his spilled aquavit and held Kaph down. The muscular body flailed him off. Martin pinned the shoulders down. Kaph screamed, struggled, choked; his face blackened. 'Oxy,' Pugh said, and his hand found the right needle in the medical kit as if by homing instinct; while Martin held the mask he stuck the needle home to the vagus nerve, restoring Kaph to life.

'Didn't know you knew that stunt,' Martin said, breathing hard.

'The Lazarus Jab; my father was a doctor. It doesn't often work,' Pugh said. 'I want that drink I spilled. Is the quake over? I can't tell.'

'After-shocks. It's not just you shivering.'

36

'Why did he suffocate?'

'I don't know, Owen. Look in the book.'

Kaph was breathing normally and his colour was restored, only his lips were still darkened. They poured a new shot of courage and sat down by him again with their medical guide. 'Nothing about cyanosis or asphyxiation under "shock" or "concussion". He can't have breathed in anything with his suit on. I don't know. We'd get as much good out of *Mother Mog's Home Herbalist* . . . "Anal Hemorrhoids," fy!' Pugh pitched the book to a crate-table. It fell short, because either Pugh or the table was still unsteady.

'Why didn't he signal?'

'Sorry?'

'The eight inside the mine never had time. But he and the girl must have been outside. Maybe she was in the entrance, and got hit by the first slide. He must have been outside, in the control-hut maybe. He ran in, pulled her out, strapped her onto the sled, started for the dome. And all that time never pushed the panic button in his imsuit. Why not?'

'Well, he'd had that whack on his head. I doubt he ever realized the girl was dead. He wasn't in his senses. But if he had been I don't know if he'd have thought to signal us. They looked to one another for help.'

Martin's face was like an Indian mask, grooves at the mouth-corners, eyes of dull coal. 'That's so. What must he have felt, then, when the quake came and he was outside, alone—'

In answer Kaph screamed.

He came up off the cot in the heaving convulsions of one suffocating, knocked Pugh right down with his flailing arm, staggered into a stack of crates and fell to the floor, lips blue, eyes white. Martin dragged him back onto the cot and gave him a whiff of oxygen, then knelt by Pugh, who was just sitting up, and wiped at his cut cheekbone. 'Owen, are you all right, are you going to be all right, Owen?'

'I think I am,' Pugh said. 'Why are you rubbing that on my face?'

It was a short length of computer-tape, now spotted with Pugh's blood. Martin dropped it. 'Thought it was a towel. You clipped your cheek on that box there.'

'Is he out of it?'

'Seems to be.'

They stared down at Kaph lying stiff, his teeth a white line inside dark parted lips.

'Like epilepsy. Brain damage maybe?'

'What about shooting him full of meprobamate?'

Pugh shook his head. 'I don't know what's in that shot I already gave him for shock. Don't want to overdose him.'

'Maybe he'll sleep it off now.'

'I'd like to myself. Between him and the earthquake I can't seem to keep on my feet.'

'You got a nasty crack there. Go on, I'll sit up a while.'

Pugh cleaned his cut cheek and pulled off his shirt, then paused.

'Is there anything we ought to have done—have tried to do—'

'They're all dead,' Martin said heavily, gently.

Pugh lay down on top of his sleeping-bag, and one instant later was wakened by a hideous, sucking, struggling noise. He staggered up, found the needle, tried three times to jab it in correctly and failed, began to massage over Kaph's heart. 'Mouth-to-mouth,' he said, and Martin obeyed. Presently Kaph drew a harsh breath, his heartbeat steadied, his rigid muscles began to relax.

'How long did I sleep?'

'Half an hour.'

They stood up sweating. The ground shuddered, the fabric of the dome sagged and swayed. Libra was dancing her awful polka again, her Totentanz. The sun, though rising, seemed to have grown larger and redder; gas and dust must have been stirred up in the feeble atmosphere.

'What's wrong with him, Owen?'

'I think he's dying with them.'

'Them—but they're dead, I tell you.'

'Nine of them. They're all dead; they were crushed or suffocated. They were all him, he is all of them. They died, and now he's dying their deaths one by one.'

'Oh, pity of God,' said Martin.

The next time was much the same. The fifth time was worse, for Kaph fought and raved, trying to speak but getting no words out, as if his mouth was stopped with rocks or clay. After that the attacks grew weaker, but so did he. The eighth seizure came at about four-thirty; Pugh and Martin worked till five-thirty doing all they could to keep life in the body that slid without protest into death. They kept him, but Martin said, 'The next will finish him.' And it did; but Pugh breathed his own breath into the inert lungs, until he himself passed out.

He woke. The dome was opaqued and no light on. He listened and heard the breathing of two sleeping men. He slept, and nothing woke him till hunger did.

The sun was well up over the dark plains, and the planet had stopped dancing. Kaph lay asleep. Pugh and Martin drank tea and looked at him with proprietary triumph.

When he woke Martin went to him: 'How do you feel, old man?' There was no answer. Pugh took Martin's place and looked into the brown, dull eyes that gazed toward but not into his own. Like Martin he quickly turned away. He heated food-concentrate and brought it to Kaph. 'Come on, drink.'

He could see the muscles in Kaph's throat tighten. 'Let me die,' the young man said.

'You're not dying.'

Kaph spoke with clarity and precision: 'I am nine-tenths dead. There is not enough of me left alive.'

That precision convinced Pugh, and he fought the conviction. 'No,' he said, peremptorily. 'They are dead. The others. Your brothers and sisters. You're not them, you're alive. You are John Chow. Your life is in your own hands.'

The young man lay still, looking into a darkness that was not there.

Martin and Pugh took turns taking the Exploitation hauler and a spare set of robos over to Hellmouth to salvage equipment and protect it from Libra's sinister atmosphere, for the value of the stuff was, literally, astronomical. It was slow work for one man at a time, but they were unwilling to leave Kaph by himself. The one left in the dome did paperwork, while Kaph sat or lay and stared into his darkness, and never spoke. The days went by silent.

The radio spat and spoke: the Mission calling from ship. 'We'll be down on Libra in five weeks, Owen. Thirty-four E-days nine hours I make it as of now. How's tricks in the old dome?'

'Not good, chief.' The Exploit team were killed, all but one of them, in the mine. Earthquake. Six days ago.'

The radio crackled and sang starsong. Sixteen seconds lag each way; the ship was out around Planet 11 now. 'Killed, all but one? You and Martin were unhurt?'

'We're all right, chief.'

Thirty-two seconds.

'*Passerine* left an Exploit team out here with us. I may put them on the Hellmouth project then, instead of the Quadrant Seven project. We'll settle that when we come down. In any case you and Martin will be relieved at Dome Two. Hold tight. Anything else?'

'Nothing else.'

Thirty-two seconds.

'Right, then. So long, Owen.'

Kaph had heard all this, and later on Pugh said to him, 'The chief may ask you to stay here with the other Exploit team. You know the ropes here.' Knowing the exigencies of Far Out Life, he wanted to warn the young man. Kaph made no answer. Since he had said, 'There is not enough of me left alive,' he had not spoken a word.

'Owen,' Martin said on suit intercom, 'he's spla. Insane. Psycho.'

'He's doing very well for a man who's died nine times.'

'Well? Like a turned-off android is well? The only emotion he has left is hate. Look at his eyes.'

'That's not hate, Martin. Listen, it's true that he has, in a sense, been dead. I cannot imagine what he feels. But it's not hatred. He can't even see us. It's too dark.'

'Throats have been cut in the dark. He hates us because we're not Aleph and Yod and Zayin.'

'Maybe. But I think he's alone. He doesn't see us or hear us, that's the truth. He never had to see anyone else before. He never was alone before. He had himself to see, talk with, live with, nine other selves all his life. He doesn't know how you go it alone. He must learn. Give him time.'

Martin shook his heavy head. 'Spla,' he said. 'Just remember when you're alone with him that he could break your neck one-handed.'

'He could do that,' said Pugh, a short, soft-voiced man with a scarred cheekbone; he smiled. They were just outside the dome airlock, programming one of the servos to repair a damaged hauler. They could see Kaph sitting inside the great half-egg of the dome like a fly in amber.

'Hand me the insert pack there. What makes you think he'll get any better?'

'He has a strong personality, to be sure.'

'Strong? Crippled. Nine-tenths dead, as he put it.'

'But he's not dead. He's a live man: John Kaph Chow. He had a jolly queer upbringing, but after all every boy has got to break free of his family. He will do it.'

'I can't see it.'

'Think a bit, Martin bach. What's this cloning for? To repair the human race. We're in a bad way. Look at me. My IIQ and GC are half this John Chow's. Yet they wanted me so badly for the Far Out Service that when I volunteered they took me and fitted me out with an artificial lung and corrected my myopia. Now if there were enough good sound lads about would they be taking one-lunged, shortsighted Welshmen?'

'Didn't know you had an artificial lung.'

'I do then. Not tin, you know. Human, grown in a tank from a bit of somebody; cloned, if you like. That's how they make replacement-organs, the same general idea as cloning, but bits and pieces instead of whole people. It's my own lung now, whatever. But what I am saying is this: there are too many like me these days and not enough like John Chow. They're trying to raise the level of the human genetic pool, which is a mucky little puddle since the population crash. So then if a man is cloned, he's a strong and clever man. It's only logic, to be sure.'

Martin grunted; the servo began to hum.

Kaph had been eating little; he had trouble swallowing his food, choking on it, so that he would give up trying after a few bites. He had lost eight or ten kilos. After three weeks or so, however, his appetite began to pick up, and

one day he began to look through the clone's possessions,
the sleeping-bags, kits, papers which Pugh had stacked neatly
in a far angle of a packing-crate alley. He sorted, destroyed
a heap of papers and oddments, made a small packet of
what remained, then relapsed into his walking coma.

Two days later he spoke. Pugh was trying to correct a
flutter in the tape-player, and failing; Martin had the jet
out, checking their maps of the Pampas. 'Hell and damnation!' Pugh said, and Kaph said in a toneless voice, 'Do
you want me to do that?'

Pugh jumped, controlled himself, and gave the machine to
Kaph. The young man took it apart, put it back together,
and left it on the table.

'Put on a tape,' Pugh said with careful casualness, busy
at another table.

Kaph put on the topmost tape, a chorale. He lay down
on his cot. The sound of a hundred human voices singing
together filled the dome. He lay still, his face blank.

In the next days he took over several routine jobs, un-
asked. He undertook nothing that wanted initiative, and if
asked to do anything he made no response at all.

'He's doing well,' Pugh said in the dialect of Argentina.

'He's not. He's turning himself into a machine. Does
what he's programmed to do, no reaction to anything else.
He's worse off than when he didn't function at all. He's not
human any more.'

Pugh sighed. 'Well, good night,' he said in English.
'Good night, Kaph.'

'Good night,' Martin said; Kaph did not.

Next morning at breakfast Kaph reached across Martin's
plate for the toast. 'Why don't you ask for it?' Martin said
with the geniality of repressed exasperation. 'I can pass it.'

'I can reach it,' Kaph said in his flat voice.

'Yes, but look. Asking to pass things, saying good night or
hello, they're not important, but all the same when somebody
says something a person ought to answer . . .'

The young man looked indifferently in Martin's direction;
his eyes still did not seem to see clear through to the person
he looked toward. 'Why should I answer?'

'Because somebody has said something to you.'

'Why?'

Martin shrugged and laughed. Pugh jumped up and turned on the rock-cutter.

Later on he said, 'Lay off that, please, Martin.'

'Manners are essential in small isolated crews, some kind of manners, whatever you work out together. He's been taught that, everybody in Far Out knows it. Why does he deliberately flout it?'

'Do you tell yourself good night?'

'So?'

'Don't you see Kaph's never known anyone but himself?'

Martin brooded and then broke out, 'Then, by God, this cloning business is all wrong. It won't do. What are a lot of duplicate geniuses going to do for us when they don't even know we exist?'

Pugh nodded. 'It might be wiser to separate the clones and bring them up with others. But they make such a grand team this way.'

'Do they? I don't know. If this lot had been ten average inefficient ET engineers, would they all have been in the same place at the same time? Would they all have got killed? What if, when the quake came and things started caving in, what if all those kids ran the same way, farther into the mine, maybe, to save the one that was farthest in? Even Kaph was outside and went in . . . It's hypothetical. But, I keep thinking, out of ten ordinary confused guys, more might have got out.'

'I don't know. It's true that identical twins tend to die at about the same time, even when they have never seen each other. Identity and death, it is very strange . . .'

The days went on, the red sun crawling across the dark sky; Kaph did not speak when spoken to; Pugh and Martin snapped at each other more frequently each day. Pugh complained of Martin's snoring. Offended, Martin moved his cot clear across the dome and also ceased speaking to Pugh for some while. Pugh whistled Welsh dirges until Martin complained, and then Pugh stopped speaking for a while.

The day before the Mission ship was due, Martin announced he was going over to Merioneth.

'I thought at least you'd be giving me a hand with the computer to finish the rock analyses,' Pugh said, aggrieved.

'Kaph can do that. I want one more look at the Trench. Have fun,' Martin added in dialect, and laughed, and left.

'What is that language?'

'Argentinean. I told you that once, didn't I?'

'I don't know.' After a while the young man added, 'I have forgotten a lot of things, I think.'

'It wasn't important, to be sure,' Pugh said gently, realizing all at once how important this conversation was' 'Will you give me a hand running the computer, Kaph?'

He nodded.

Pugh had left a lot of loose ends, and the job took them all day. Kaph was a good co-worker, quick and systematic, much more so than Pugh himself. His flat voice, now that he was talking again, got on the nerves; but it didn't matter, there was only this one day left to get through and then the ship would come, the old crew, comrades and friends.

During tea-break Kaph said, 'What will happen if the Explorer ship crashes?'

'They'd be killed.'

'To you, I mean.'

'To us? We'd radio SOS all signals, and live on half rations till the rescue cruiser from Area Three Base came. Four and a half E-years away it is. We have life-support here for three men for, let's see, maybe between four and five years. A bit tight, it would be.'

'Would they send a cruiser for three men?'

'They would.'

Kaph said no more.

'Enough cheerful speculations,' Pugh said cheerfully, rising to get back to work. He slipped sideways and the chair avoided his hand; he did a sort of half-pirouette and fetched up hard against the dome-hide. 'My goodness,' he said, reverting to his native idiom, 'what is it?'

'Quake,' said Kaph

The teacups bounced on the table with a plastic cackle; a litter of papers slid off a box; the skin of the dome swelled and sagged. Underfoot there was a huge noise, half sound, half shaking, a subsonic boom.

Kaph sat unmoved. An earthquake does not frighten a man who died in an earthquake.

Pugh, white-faced, wiry black hair sticking out, a frightened man, said, 'Martin is in the Trench.'

'What trench?'

'The big fault line. The epicentre for the local quakes. Look at the seismograph.' Pugh struggled with the stuck door of a still-jittering locker.

'Where are you going?'

'After him.'

'Martin took the jet. Sleds aren't safe to use during quakes. They go out of control.'

'For God's sake, man, shut up.'

Kaph stood up, speaking in a flat voice as usual. 'It's un-necessary to go out after him now. It's taking an unnecessary risk.'

'If his alarm goes off, radio me,' Pugh said, shut the headpiece of his suit, and ran to the lock. As he went out Libra picked up her ragged skirts and danced a bellydance from under his feet clear to the red horizon.

Inside the dome, Kaph saw the sled go up, tremble like a meteor in the dull red daylight, and vanish to the north-east. The hide of the dome quivered; the earth coughed. A vent south of the dome belched up a slow-flowing bile of black gas.

A bell shrilled and a red light flashed on the central control board. The sign under the light read SUIT TWO and scribbled under that, *A.G.M.* Kaph did not turn the signal off. He tried to radio Martin, then Pugh, but got no reply from either.

When the after-shocks decreased he went back to work, and finished up Pugh's job. It took him about two hours. Every half hour he tried to contact Suit One, and got no reply, then Suit Two and got no reply. The red light had stopped flashing after an hour.

It was dinnertime. Kaph cooked dinner for one, and ate it. He lay down on his cot.

The after-shocks had ceased except for faint rolling tremors at long intervals. The sun hung in the west, oblate, pale-red, immense. It did not sink visibly. There was no sound at all.

45

Kaph got up and began to walk about the messy, half-packed-up, overcrowded, empty dome. The silence continued. He went to the player and put on the first tape that came to hand. It was pure music, electronic, without harmonies. without voices. It ended. The silence continued.

Pugh's uniform tunic, one button missing, hung over a stack of rock samples. Kaph stared at it a while.

The silence continued.

The child's dream: There is no one else alive in the world but me. In all the world.

Low, north of the dome, a meteor flickered.

Kaph's mouth opened as if he were trying to say something, but no sound came. He went hastily to the north wall and peered out into the gelatinous red light.

The little star came in and sank. Two figures blurred the airlock. Kaph stood close beside the lock as they came in. Martin's imsuit was covered with some kind of dust so that he looked raddled and warty like the surface of Libra. Pugh had him by the arm.

'Is he hurt?'

Pugh shucked his suit, helped Martin peel off his. 'Shaken up,' he said, curt.

'A piece of cliff fell onto the jet,' Martin said, sitting down at the table and waving his arms. 'Not while I was in it, though. I was parked, see, and poking about that carbon-dust area when I felt things humping. So I went out onto a nice bit of early igneous I'd noticed from above, good footing and out from under the cliffs. Then I saw this bit of the planet fall off onto the flyer, quite a sight it was, and after a while it occurred to me the spare aircans were in the flyer, so I leaned on the panic button. But I didn't get any radio reception, that's always happening here during quakes, so I didn't know if the signal was getting through either. And things went on jumping around and pieces of the cliff coming off. Little rocks flying around, and so dusty you couldn't see a metre ahead. I was really beginning to wonder what I'd do for breathing in the small hours, you know, when I saw old Owen buzzing up the Trench in all that dust and junk like a big ugly bat—'

'Want to eat?' said Pugh.

'Of course I want to eat. How'd you come through the quake here, Kaph? No damage? It wasn't a big one actually, was it—what's the seismo say? My trouble was I was in the middle of it. Old Epicentre Alvaro. Felt like Richter Fifteen there—total destruction of planet—'

'Sit down,' Pugh said. 'Eat.'

After Martin had eaten a little his spate of talk ran dry. He very soon went off to his cot, still in the remote angle where he had removed it when Pugh complained of his snoring. 'Good night, you one-lunged Welshman,' he said across the dome.

'Good night.'

There was no more out of Martin. Pugh opaqued the dome, turned the lamp down to a yellow glow less than a candle's light, and sat doing nothing, saying nothing, withdrawn.

The silence continued.

'I finished the computations.'

Pugh nodded thanks.

'The signal from Martin came through, but I couldn't contact you or him.'

Pugh said with effort. 'I should not have gone. He had two hours of air left even with only one can. He might have been heading home when I left. This way we were all out of touch with one another. I was scared.'

The silence came back, punctuated now by Martin's long, soft snores.

'Do you love Martin?'

Pugh looked up with angry eyes: 'Martin is my friend. We've worked together; he's a good man.' He stopped. After a while he said, 'Yes, I love him. Why did you ask that?'

Kaph said nothing, but he looked at the other man. His face was changed, as if he were glimpsing something he had not seen before; his voice too was changed. 'How can you . . ? How do you . . ?'

But Pugh could not tell him. 'I don't know,' he said, 'it's practice, partly. I don't know. We're each of us alone, to be sure. What can you do but hold your hand out in the dark?'

Kaph's strange gaze dropped, burned out by its own intensity.

'I'm tired,' Pugh said. 'That was ugly, looking for him in all that black dust and muck, and mouths opening and shutting in the ground . . . I'm going to bed. The ship will be transmitting to us by six or so.' He stood up and stretched.

'It's a clone,' Kaph said. 'The other Exploit team they're bringing with them.'

'Is it, then?'

'A twelveclone. They came out with us on the *Passerine*.'

Kaph sat in the small yellow aura of the lamp, seeming to look past it at what he feared: the new clone, the multiple self of which he was not part. A lost piece of a broken set, a fragment, inexpert at solitude, not knowing even how you go about giving love to another individual, now he must face the absolute, closed self-sufficiency of the clone of twelve; that was a lot to ask of the poor fellow, to be sure. Pugh put a hand on his shoulder in passing. 'The chief won't ask you to stay here with a clone. You can go home. Or since you're Far Out maybe you'll come on farther out with us. We could use you. No hurry deciding. You'll make out all right.'

Pugh's quiet voice trailed off. He stood unbuttoning his coat, stopped a little with fatigue. Kaph looked at him and saw the thing he had never seen before: saw him: Owen Pugh, the other, the stranger who held his hand out in the dark.

'Good night,' Pugh mumbled, crawling into his sleeping-bag and half asleep already, so that he did not hear Kaph reply after a pause, repeating, across darkness, benediction.

Idiot Stick

Damon Knight

Alien invasions have been a sf staple since Wells' *War of the Worlds*. In magazines of the Twenties and Thirties, invaders were mostly typified as destructive and inhuman monsters. As the genre grew more thoughtful and sophisticated, the invasion theme became more complex; it often mirrored human foibles and the follies of politics—the sort of thing that IDIOT STICK does with such ironic wit.

Damon Knight has a considerable reputation as one of the field's most respected anthologists. His activity in this area has been such that for the last decade we have been rather deprived of his stylish short stories, of which the following is a particularly fine example.

Not all conquests are made with fire and sword . . .

The ship came down out of a blue sky to land in a New Jersey meadow. It sank squashily into the turf. It was about a mile long, coloured an iridescent blue-green, like the shell of a beetle.

A door opened, and a thin, stick-bodied man came out to sniff the cool air. The sky overhead was full of fluffy cumulus clouds and crisscrossing con-trails. Across the river, the tall buildings of Greater New York were picturesquely gilded by the early sun.

A dun-coloured Army 'copter came into view, circling the

ship at a cautious distance. The thin man saw it, blinked at it without interest, and looked away.

The river was smooth and silvery in the sunlight. After a long time, the sound of bullhorns came blaring distantly across the marshes. Then there was a clanking and a roaring, and two Army tanks pulled into sight, followed by two more. They deployed to either side, and slewed around with their 90-mm guns pointing at the ship.

The alien watched them calmly. More helicopters appeared, circling and hovering. After a while a grey-painted destroyer steamed slowly into view up the river.

More tanks arrived. There was a ring of them around the spaceship, rumbling and smelling of diesel oil. Finally a staff car pulled up, and three perspiring general officers got out of it.

From his low platform the alien looked down with a patient expression. His voice carried clearly. 'Good morning,' he said. 'This is a ship of the Galactic Federation. We come in peace. Your guns will not fire; please take them away. Now, then. I shall tell you what I am going to do. The Federation wishes to establish a cultural and educational organization upon your continent; and for your land and your co-operation, we will pay you generously. Here, catch these.' He raised his arm, and a cloud of glittery objects came toward them.

One of the officers, white-faced, tugged at the pistol in his belt holster; but the objects dropped harmlessly in and around the car. The senior officer picked one up. It was insubstantial to the touch, more like a soap bubble than anything else. Then it tingled suddenly in his palm. He sat down, glassy-eyed.

The other two shook him. 'Frank! Frank!'

His eyes slowly cleared; he looked from one to the other. 'Are you still here?' he said faintly, and then: 'My God!'

'Frank, what was it? Did it knock you out?'

The senior officer looked down at the glittery thing in his hand. It felt now like nothing in particular—just a piece of plastic, perhaps. There was no more tingle. The zip was gone out of it.

'It was . . . happiness,' he said.

The rest of the objects glittered and gleamed in the rank grass around the car. 'Go on,' called the alien encouragingly, 'take all you want. Tell your superiors, tell your friends. Come one, come all! We bring happiness!'

Within half a day, the word was out. Work stopped in New York offices; by ferry and tube, people poured across the river. The governor flew in from Trenton and was closeted with the aliens for half an hour, after which he emerged with a dazed and disbelieving look on his face, wearing a shoulder bag full of the glittering little capsules.

The crowd, muddy to the knees, milled around the ship. Every hour the thin alien appeared and tossed out another handful of capsules. There were shouts and screams; the crowd clotted briefly where the capsules fell, then spread apart again like filings released from a magnet.

Dull, used-up capsules littered the grass. Everywhere you saw the dazed expression, the transported look of a man who had had one.

Some few of the capsules got carried home to wives and children. The word continued to spread. No one could describe the effect of the capsules satisfactorily. It lasted only a few seconds, yet seemed to take a long time. It left them satiated and shaken. It was not pleasure of any specific kind, they said; it was happiness, and they wanted more.

Expropriation measures passed the state and national legislatures with blinding speed. There was furious debate elsewhere, but nobody who had had one of the capsules was in any doubt that he was getting a bargain. And the kicker was, 'What else can we do?'

The aliens, it appeared, wanted five hundred acres of level ground to put up certain buildings and other structures. Their explanations to the press and public were infrequent and offhand in tone; some people found them unsatisfactory. When asked why the aliens had chosen a site so near heavily populated centres, rather than wasteland which would have been plentiful elsewhere, the spokesman replied (he was either the same stick-thin man who had appeared first, or one just like him), 'But then who would build us our buildings?'

New York, it seemed, represented a source of native labour to the aliens.

The pay would be generous: three capsules a day a man. When the aliens announced they were hiring, half the population of Greater New York tried to get over onto the Jersey flats. Three-quarters of the population of Hoboken, Jersey City, Hackensack and Paterson was already there.

In the queues that eventually formed out of the confusion, the mayor of New York City was seen alongside an upstate senator and two visiting film stars.

Each person, as he reached the head of the line, was handed a light metal or plastic rod, five feet long, with a curved handle and a splayed tip. The lucky workers were then herded out onto the designated acreage. Some of it was marshland, some was a scraggly part of the New Jersey Parks System, some was improved land. The buildings on the site —a few homes, some factories and warehouses—had all been evacuated but not torn down. The workers with their rods were lined up at one edge of this territory, facing the opposite side.

'When the command "Go" is heard,' said the alien's voice clearly, 'you will all proceed directly forward at a slow walking pace, swinging your sticks from side to side.'

The voice stopped. Apparently that was going to be all.

In the middle of the line, young Ted Cooley looked at his neighbour, Eli Baker. They both worked in the same pharmaceuticals house and had come out together to try their luck. Cooley was twenty-five, blonde and brawny; Baker, about the same age, was slight and dark. Their eyes met, and Baker shrugged, as if to say, Don't ask me.

It was a clear, cool day. The long line of men and women stood waiting in the sunlight.

'Go!' said the alien's voice.

The line began to move. Cooley stepped forward and waggled his stick hesitantly. There was no feeling of movement in the stick, but he saw a line of darkness spring out on the ground ahead of him. He paused instinctively, thinking that the stick must be squirting oil or some other liquid.

Up and down the line, other people were stopping, too.

He looked more closely and saw that the ground was not wet at all. It was simply pressed down flat—dirt, stones, weeds, everything all at once—to form one hard, dark surface.

'Keep going,' said the alien's voice.

Several people threw down their sticks and walked away. Others moved forward cautiously. Seeing that nothing happened to them when they stepped on the dark strip, Cooley moved forward also. The dark ground was solid and firm underfoot. As he moved forward, swinging the stick, the dark area spread; and, looking closely now, he could see the uneven ground leap downward and darken as the stick swept over it.

'Get in rhythm,' called the voice. 'Leave no space between one man's work and the next.'

The line moved forward, a little raggedly at first, then faster as they got the hang of it. The dark, hard strip, running the whole length of the area, widened as they moved. It was as if everything under the business end of the stick was instantly compressed and smoothed down. Looking closely, you could see the traces of anything that had been there before, like the patterns in marbled linoleum: stones, sticks, grass and weeds.

'How the heck does it work?' said Baker, awed.

'Search me,' said Cooley. In his hands the tube felt light and empty, like the aluminium shaft of a tank vacuum cleaner. He didn't see how it could possibly have any mechanism inside. There were no controls; he hadn't turned anything on to make it operate.

A few yards ahead, there was a stone wall, overgrown with weeds. 'What's going to happen when we come to that?' Baker asked, pointing.

'Search me.' Cooley felt bewildered; he walked mechanically forward, swinging the stick.

The wall grew nearer. When they were within a few paces of it, a rabbit burst suddenly out of cover. It darted one way, then the other, hind legs pumping hard. Confused by the advancing line, it leaped for the space between Baker and Cooley.

'Look out!' shouted Cooley instinctively. Baker's swinging

stick went directly over the rabbit.

Nothing happened. The rabbit kept on going. Cooley and a few others turned to watch it: it bounded away across the level strip and disappeared into the tall grass on the other side.

Baker and Cooley looked at each other. 'Selective,' said Cooley through dry lips. 'Listen, if I—' He shortened his grip on the stick, moving the splayed end toward himself.

'Better not,' said Baker nervously.

'Just to see—' Cooley slowly brought the stick nearer, slowly thrusting the tip of one shoe under it.

Nothing happened. He moved the stick nearer. Bolder, he ran it over his leg, his other foot. Nothing. 'Selective!' he repeated. 'But how?'

The weeds were dried vegetable fibre. The stick compressed them without hesitation, stamping them down flat like everything else. His trousers were dried vegetable fibre, part of them, anyhow—cotton. His socks, his shoelaces— how did the stick know the difference?

They kept on going. When they came to the stone wall, Cooley waved his stick at it. A section of the wall slumped, as if a giant had taken a bite out of it. He waved it again. The rest of the wall fell.

Somebody laughed hysterically. The line was advancing. The wall was just a lighter stripe in the smooth floor over which they walked.

The sun crept higher. Behind the line of men and women stretched a level, gleaming floor. 'Listen,' said Cooley nervously to Baker, 'how bad do you want those happiness gadgets?'

Baker looked at him curiously. 'I don't know. What do you mean?'

Cooley moistened his lips. 'I'm thinking. We get the gadgets, we use them up—'

'Or sell them,' Baker interrupted.

'Or sell them, but then, either way, they're gone. Suppose we walked off with *these*.' He hefted his stick. 'If we could find out what makes it do what it does—'

'Are you kidding?' said Baker. His dark face was flushed; beads of sweat stood out on his forehead. He waved his stick. 'You know what this is? A shovel. An idiot stick.'

'How's that?' said Cooley.

'A shovel,' Baker told him patiently, 'is a stick with some dirt on one end and an idiot on the other. Old joke. Didn't you ever do any common labour?'

'No,' said Cooley.

'Well, you're doing some now. This thing that looks so wonderful to us—that's just a shovel, to them. An idiot stick. And we're the idiots.'

'I don't like that,' said Cooley.

'Who likes it?' Baker demanded. 'But there isn't a thing you can do about it. Do your work, take your pay, and that's all. Don't kid yourself we can ever get the bulge on them; we haven't got what it takes.'

Cooley thought hard about it, and he was one of the fifty-odd people who walked off the site with Galactic tools that day. The Galactics made no complaint. When daylight failed, they called in the first crew and sent another out under floating lights. The work went on, around the clock. The tools were stolen at a steady rate; the Galactics handed out more indifferently.

The site became level and smooth; the surface was glass-hard, almost too slick to walk on. The next thing the aliens did was to set up a tall pole on a tripod in the middle of the site. Most of the floating lights went out and drifted away. In the dusk, a network of fluorescent lines appeared on the glassy surface. It looked like the ground plan for a huge building. Some of the pale lines went a little askew because of minor irregularities in the surface, but the Galactics did not seem to mind. They called in part of the crew and made some adjustment in each man's stick. A narrow tab, something like the clip in an automatic, came out of the butt; a different one went in.

So equipped, the reduced crew was sent back onto the site and scattered along the diagram, one man every two hundred yards or so. They were instructed to walk backward along the lines, drawing their sticks after them.

There was some confusion. The tools now worked only on contact, and instead of flattening the surface down, they made it bulge up, like suddenly rising dough, to form a foot-high ridge. The ridge was pale in colour and felt porous and hard to the touch, like styrene foam.

A few men were called in and had still another set of control tabs put into their sticks. Wherever somebody had jumped, or twitched, and made a ridge where it didn't belong, these men wiped it out like wiping chalk with a wet sponge: the expanded material shrank again and became part of the dark surface.

Meanwhile, the rest of the crew, finishing the first set of lines, was walking along beside them, making the ridges twice as wide. They repeated this process until each ridge was nearly a yard across. Then they stepped up on top of the ridges and began again, making a second foot-high bulge on top of the first.

The building was going up. It was irregularly shaped, a little like an arrowhead, with an outer shell composed of many small compartments. The interior was left unpartitioned, a single area more than half a mile across.

When the shell was up ten feet, the aliens had connecting doorways cut between all the small chambers. A stick, looking no different from the others, was tossed into each chamber from the wall above. Where it landed, clear liquid immediately began to gush. The liquid rose, covered the stick, and kept on rising. It rose until it reached the level of the walls, and then stopped. A few minutes later, it was cold to the touch. In half an hour, it was frozen solid.

The control tabs were changed again, and a crew began walking across the frozen surface, forming another layer of the hard, dark, glassy substance. Afterwards, more doorways were cut in the outer shell, and the liquid drained off towards the river. The sticks that had been dropped into the chambers were recovered. Each had left a slight irregularity in the floor, which was smoothed out.

The second storey went up in the same way. Walking backward along the high walls, a good many people fell off. Others quit. The aliens hired more, and the construction went on.

Hardly anybody except a few high government officials got to see the inside of the alien spaceship; but the Galactics themselves became familiar sights in the towns and cities of the eastern seaboard. They walked the streets in inquisitive, faintly supercilious pairs, looking at everything, occasionally stopping to aim little fist-size machines which might or might not have been cameras.

Some of them fraternized with the populace, asking many earnest questions about local laws and customs. Some bought vast quantities of potatoes, playing cards, Cadillacs, junk jewellery, carpets, confetti, nylons and other goods, paying, as usual, with the happiness capsules. They ate local foods with interest and drank heroically without getting drunk, or even tipsy. Skin-tight clothes cut in imitation of the Galactics' bottle-green uniform began to appear on the market. There were Galactic dolls and Galactic spaceship toys.

Legislatures everywhere were relaxed and amiable. Wherever the Galactics had trouble, or sensed it coming, they smoothed the way with more of the happiness capsules. Prices were beginning to be marked not only in ' $ ' and 'c', but in 'Hc', for 'Hapcap'. Business was booming.

In the laboratories of the Bureau of Standards in Washington there was a concerted programme—one of many—to discover the secrets of the Galactic all-purpose tool. Specimens had been measured, x-rayed and cut apart. The material, whatever it was, seemed to have been formed in one piece. It was light, chemically inert and fairly strong. The hollow inside was irregularly curved, according to no discernible principle.

There were only two parts—the tool proper and the control tab which fitted into a slot in the handle. With the tab in, the tool functioned. It did work, while the dials of every test instrument calmly reported that no energy was being released. With the tab out, nothing happened at all.

The tabs for various functions could be distinguished by colour; otherwise, in shape and dimensions, they seemed identical.

The first—and last—breakthrough came when the tabs were examined by x-ray microscope. The substance, which had seemed amorphous, was found to have a crystalline structure, permanently stressed in patterns which differed consistently between tabs that produced different functions.

By an elaborate series of test heatings, compressions and deformations, Dr Crawford Reed succeeded in altering the stress pattern of a type 'A' tab to approximately that of a type 'C' tab.

When the tab was inserted in a tool, the laboratory went up in an explosion that demolished buildings within a radius of three city blocks.

The explosion was recorded by instruments in the giant spaceship. When he saw the record, the bored officer on duty smiled.

One of the aliens, who said his name was Pendrath go Pendrath, showed up frequently in the pleasant little town of Riverdale, New Jersey. He poked his nose into church bazaars, Little League baseball games, soda fountains, summer camps, chamber of commerce meetings. At first he gathered crowds wherever he went; then the natives, and even the tourists, got used to him.

Three nights after the rough shell of the building was finished, a young *Star-Ledger* reporter named Al Jenkins found him in the back of a bar, maudlin drunk.

Pendrath looked up as Jenkins slid into the booth next to him. 'Ah, my friend,' he said blurrily, 'how I regret your poor planet.'

'You don't like our planet?' said Jenkins.

'No, it is a nice little planet. Extremely picturesque. Pardon me.' Pendrath sipped from the glass he was holding. He blinked, and straightened up slightly.

'You must understand, that is Galactic progress,' he said. 'It cannot be helped. We all must go someday.'

Jenkins looked at him critically. 'You've been having quite a few of those, haven't you?' he said. 'I thought you people were immune to alcohol, or something.'

'No, it is the aps—as—aspirin,' said the alien. He produced a small bottle, and solemnly shook a tablet out into his palm. 'Your liquors gave me a headache, and so I took an apsirin—aspirin—and your aspirin is wonderful.' He looked lugubrious. 'To think, no more aspirin. No more church bazaar. No more baseball.'

'Why, what's going to happen to them?'

Pendrath spread his fingers and made an expressive fizzing noise with his mouth. 'Blooie,' he said.

Jenkins said incredulously, 'You are going to blow up the world?'

The alien nodded sadly. 'Soon our building will be finished. Then we will put in the big machines, and drill, drill.' He made twisting motions downwards with one hand. 'We will drill to the core. Then we will drop the transformer and close up the shaft. Then we will go away. Then your poor planet will go—' he made the fizzing noise again— 'Blooie.'

Jenkins' fists were clenched. 'But why? Why would you do a thing like that?'

'For dust,' Pendrath explained. 'Your little planet will all be dust. No big pieces left—nothing bigger than this.' He pinched his thumb and forefinger together, squinting, to show how tiny. 'We are making defences for the Galaxy. This sector is too open. We will make a little screen of dust here. If there is dust, a ship cannot go very fast. The dust slows it down. Some places, there is already dust. Other places, we will make it. It is the only way to protect ourselves from invasion.'

'Invasion by whom?'

Pendrath shrugged. 'Who can tell? We have to look ahead.'

Jenkins' hands began to shake. He took a dog-eared notebook out of his pocket, thumbing it open automatically; he looked at it and put it back. His hands didn't want to do anything but make fists. He said thickly, 'You lousy— and swung a left to Pendrath's beaky face.

The blow never landed. His fist slowed down and stopped; strain as hard as he would, he couldn't push it any farther.

'No, no,' said Pendrath, smiling sadly. 'No use. I regret very much.'

Jenkins' heart was thumping. 'Why us?' he burst out angrily. 'If you had to have dust, why couldn't you take one of the other planets? Jupiter, Venus—any of them— why pick the one we live on?'

Pendrath blinked at him. 'But on your other planets no one lives,' he said. 'Who, then, would do the work for us?'

He popped another tablet into his mouth. 'And besides,' he said, 'remember that this dust will make a blanket around your sun. It will make the planets very cold. You see, I have thought of all these things. And then suppose we went to some other sun, and did not come here at all. It would be just the same. You would make big spaceships, and we would have to come and finish you anyway. This way, it will be very quick—you will not feel a thing.'

Jenkins had lost his hat. He fumbled on the floor for it. 'We'll stop you', he said, red-faced over the tabletop. 'You'll be sorry you ever opened your mouth to me, mister. I'll spread this from here to Belfast.'

'You are going to tell?' the alien asked, in dull surprise.

'You bet your sweet life I'm going to tell!'

Pendrath nodded owlishly. 'It does not matter now. The work is nearly done. You cannot stop us, my poor friend.'

The story broke the following day, when the installation of the complex system of girders and braces in the interior of the building had already been finished. A hatch in the side of the ship was open, and under the aliens' direction, crews were carrying out a steady stream of machine parts to be assembled inside the building.

There were a thousand and one pieces of different sizes and shapes: gigantic torus sections, tubes, cylinders, globes; twisted pipes, jigsaw-puzzle pieces. The material was not metal, but the same light substance of which the tools were made.

Some of the tools were serving as grip-sticks: they clung like magnets to the machine parts, and to nothing else. Some, applied to massive pieces of equipment, made them extraordinarily slippery, so that it was easy to slide them across the site and into the building. Others were used in assembling: drawn along the join between two pieces, they made the two flow together into one.

The story did not reach the day shift at all. The second and third shifts turned up a little under strength; the aliens hired enough people from the crowd of curiosity-seekers to make up the difference.

At his regular press conference, the alien spokesman, Mr

Revash go Ren, said, 'Mr Jenkins' story is a malicious fabrication. The machines you mention will provide pleasant heating, air conditioning, Galactic standard gravitation, and other necessary services for the clerical workers in our offices. We are accustomed to have many conveniences of this kind, and that is why we cannot live or work in buildings suitable for you.'

Hersch of the *Times* demanded, 'Why does that take a half-mile area, when your office space is only a thin ring around the outside of the building?'

Revash smiled. 'Why do you take a whole cellar to heat your buildings?' he asked. 'One of your savages would say that a fire of sticks and a hole in the ceiling are sufficient.'

Hersch had no answer to that; nevertheless, belief in the story spread. By the end of the week, half a dozen newspapers were thumping the drum for a crusade. A Congressional investigating committee was appointed. More workers quit. When the labour supply slackened, the aliens doubled the pay, and got more applicants than there were jobs. Riots broke out on the Jersey side of the tubes. There were picket lines, fulminations from the pulpit, attempts at sabotage. The work went on just the same.

'The whole problem is psychological,' said Baker. 'We know what kind of people they are—it sticks out all over them— they're decadent. That's their weak point; that's where we've got to hit them. They've got the perfect machines, but they don't know how to use them. Not only that, they don't want to; it would soil their lily-white hands. So they come here, and they get us to do their dirty work, even though it means an extra risk.'

'That doesn't sound so decadent to me,' said Cooley argumentatively. It was past midnight, and they were still sitting in Baker's living room over a case of beer, hashing it all out. Cooley's face was flushed, and his voice a little loud. 'Take an archaeological expedition, say—I don't know, maybe to Mesopotamia or somewhere. Do they drag along a lot of pick and shovel men? They do not; they take the shovels, maybe, but they hire native labour on the spot. That isn't decadence, that's efficiency.'

'All right, but if we had to, we could get out there and pick up a shovel. They can't. It just wouldn't occur to them. They're overrefined, Ted; they've got to the point where the machines *have* to be perfect, or they couldn't stay alive. That's dangerous; that's where we've got to hit them.'

'I don't see it. Wars are won with weapons.'

'So what are we supposed to do: hit them with atom bombs that don't go off, or guns that don't shoot?'

Cooley put down his stein and reached for the tool that lay on the floor. It had rolled the last time he put it down. He said, 'Damn,' and reached farther. He picked it up, the same 'idiot stick' he had stolen from the Galactic site the first day. 'I'm betting on this,' he said. 'You know and I know they're working on it, day and night. I'm betting they'll crack it. *This* is a weapon, boy—a Galactic weapon. If we just get that—'

'Go ahead, wish for the moon,' said Baker bitterly. 'What you're talking about happens to be impossible. We can change the stress patterns in the control tabs, yes. We can even duplicate the formative conditions, probably, and get as many tabs as you want with the same pattern. But it's all empirical, Ted, just blind chance. We don't know *why* such and such a stress pattern makes the tool do a certain thing, and until we know that, all we can do is vary it at random.'

'So?'

'So there are millions of wrong patterns for every right one. There're the patterns that make things explode, like in Washington; there're the ones that boil the experimenter alive or freeze him solid, or bury him in a big lump of solid lead. There're the radioactive ones, the corrosive ones— and for every wrong guess, we lose at least one man.'

'Remote control?' said Cooley.

'First figure out what makes the tools operate when somebody's holding them, and stop when they let go.'

Cooley drank, frowning.

'And remember,' said Baker, 'there's just about one choice that would do us any good against the Galactics. One pattern, out of millions. No. It won't be technology that licks them; it'll be guts.'

He was right; but he was wrong.

Al Jenkins was in the *Star-Ledger* city room, gloomily reading a wire story about denunciations of the aliens issued by governors of eight states. 'What good is that?' he said, tossing it back onto the city editor's desk. 'Look at it.'

Through the window, they could see the top of the alien building shining in the distance. Tiny figures were crawling over the domed roof. The aliens had inflated a hemispherical membrane, and now the workers were going over it with the tools, forming a solid layer.

The dome was almost finished. Work on the interior of the building had stopped two days before.

'He knew what he was talking about,' said Jenkins. 'We couldn't stop them. We had three weeks to do it in, but we just couldn't get together that fast.'

Cigarette ash was spilling down the front of his shirt. He scrubbed at it absently, turned, and walked out of the office. The editor watched him go without saying anything.

One morning in July, two months after the aliens' landing, a ragged mob armed with Galactic tools appeared near the spaceship. Similar mobs had formed several times during the last few nights. When a native grew desperate, he lost what little intelligence he had.

The officer in charge, standing in the open doorway, looked them over disdainfully as they approached. There was no need for any defensive measures; they would try to club him with the tools, fail, and go away.

The native in the lead, a big, burly male, raised his tool like a pitchfork. The Galactic watched him with amusement. The next instant, he was dead, turned into bloody mush on the floor of the airlock.

The mob poured into the ship. Inside, the green-lit hallways were as dim and vast as a cathedral. Bored Galactics looked out of doorways. Their bland expressions changed to gapes of horror. Some ran; some hid. The tools cut them down.

The long corridors echoed to the rattle of running feet, to shouts of excitement and triumph, screams of dismay. The mob swept into every room; it was over in fifteen minutes.

The victors stopped, panting and sweaty, looking around them with the beginnings of wonder. The high-ceilinged rooms were hung with gleaming gold-and-green tapestries; the desks were carved crystal. Music breathed from somewhere, soothing and quiet.

A tray of food was steaming on a table. A transparent chart had been pulled out of a wall. Under each was a pulpy red smear, a puddle of disorganized tissue.

Baker and Cooley looked up and recognized each other. 'Guts,' said Baker wryly.

'Technology,' said Cooley. 'They underrated us; so did you.' He raised the tool he held, careful not to touch the butt. 'Ten thousand tries, I hear—and ten thousand dead men. All right, have it your way. I call that guts, too.' He lifted his head, staring off into the distance, trying to imagine the hundreds of research stations, hidden in remote areas, with their daily, ghastly toll of human life. 'Ten thousand,' he said.

Baker was shaking with reaction. 'We were lucky; it might have been a million . . .' He tried to laugh. 'Have to find a new name for this now—no more idiot stick.'

Cooley glanced at the floor. 'It depends,' he said grimly, 'which end of the stick the idiot's on.'

The Ark of James Carlyle

Cherry Wilder

One of the most enduring and popular themes in sf is the detailed and convincing depiction of an alien culture. Writers like Hal Clement, Larry Niven and Jack Vance have written some classic stories in this vein, and Australian author Cherry Wilder now joins their select company with a fine tale of an alien disaster, and the efforts of the human protagonist to save both himself and a group of natives.

Mrs Wilder is married and has two daughters. Her work has been widely published in literary reviews and includes some stories for men's magazines. She has recently turned to sf, having been a long-time fan since the days of Buck Rogers, and THE ARK OF JAMES CARLYLE is the first of several stories to have appeared in overseas magazines.

On the ninety-first day of his Met. duty Carlyle stepped out of the hut and gazed desperately at the cloudless sky. There were no quogs to meet him on the platform; the oily purple sea sucked gently at the wooden piles; his instruments had assured him there was a light westerly breeze. His delusion persisted and he had nothing to support it . . . not even the tangible evidence of an aching bunion. He did not dare call the station. How would he begin?

'Something tells me . . .'

He decided to walk round the island but he found an

ancient quog, the one he called the Chief, squatting at the foot of the ladder. He beckoned him on to the platform. The quogs were cryptorchids so for all he knew perhaps this was a Chieftainess; it was difficult to tell.

When he had first taken up his duty, before the boat brought him to the island, he had seen Mary Long, a young anthropologist who had tagged along with the landing party to the plateau, sexing a herd of quogs. She walked among them, picking the creatures up and solemnly examining their genital pouches. She was engrossed in her work; twenty or thirty quogs surrounded her and gently stripped off every stitch of her clothing before Carlyle or the other men could intervene. They sat round her and stared, their luminous eyes full of innocent curiosity.

Not a great deal of work had been done on quogs; they had been described as small land mammals, semi-erect bipeds, modified baboons. They were docile, certainly, and capable of performing many tasks; but they were also ugly, elusive and rank-smelling. Their odour had already ceased to bother Carlyle but he noticed that the quogs still kept upwind of *him*. He found himself describing them differently: they were like trolls, like squatting goblins, like little old men. At night he listened for one of their rare sounds, the qwok-qwok-qwok, hardly vocalized, that had given them their name.

The Chief, who was a big fellow, almost a metre tall, scrambled nimbly on to the platform.

'Where are the others?' asked Carlyle.

Every other day the platform had been lined with quogs who gave him berries, limpets, burrowing shrimps, in exchange for bacon cubes. He had tried them with everything he had: orange juice, vegetables, vitamins, but they liked the bacon best. Now the Chief tried to explain their absence. He could be heard only by cupping his long bluish hands before his tiny slit of a mouth to amplify the sound, the way Carlyle made owl-hoots as a boy.

'Mee-haw,' boomed the Chief faintly.

At first Carlyle did not understand. The mee-haw was a tree; in fact it was the only tree. The vegetation on AC14 was low, luxuriant and undistinguished except for the mee-haw trees, which reared up, with straight trunk and spreading crown of leafy branches, one hundred metres and more above the bushy islands in the still, purple sea. The timber, resembling balsa, was particularly easy to work. The platform on which Carlyle had his Met. hut was made entirely of the single mee-haw tree that had grown on the tiny island. The quogs had wept to see it fall down. Carlyle had had the uneasy notion that the mee-haw tree might be sacred to them.

Now the Chief pointed to the island; Carlyle was shaken again by his crazy premonition.

'Come on,' he said.

He climbed down from the platform and followed the Chief up the brush-covered slope. All the quogs on the island, about thirty of them forming one family group, were huddled together on the broad stump of the mee-haw tree.

'Why?' asked Carlyle. 'Why?'

The Chief cupped his hands and answered with a third quog word.

Carlyle strained to catch it.

'Aw-kee?'

The quogs on the stump waved their fingers: this was a way of laughing. To Carlyle's surprise they all began to vocalize, even the babies, pale blue and completely hairless, cupping their tiny hands. 'Aw-kee' was the nearest he could get to it.

'What's that?' asked Carlyle.

He already knew. He went into a mad pantomime, begging the quogs for confirmation, then he ran back to the Met. hut. He called the satellite without a glance at his instruments. He announced firmly:

'There's going to be a flood.'

The receiver crackled: What were his readings?

'The quogs told me,' said Carlyle.

The crackle became indignant. Readings, please. Carlyle turned hopelessly towards his instrument panel and his heart pounded. The barometer had dropped dramatically and was still falling. The wind had swung round to the south. The room became dark as he completed his report and huge drops of rain began a tattoo on the roof of the Met. hut.

He ran out on to the platform. The sky was a dome of blue-black cloud above a darkening sea; the waves flashed emerald and purple-black and broke in iridescent foam upon the shore. The word for it, Carlyle decided, was unearthly. Already drenched to the skin he cowered in the doorway of the hut. He was worried about the quogs; he guessed that their instinct to seek higher ground would keep them huddled on the mee-haw stump. The fragile shelters where they slept and did their weaving would be no protection against this rain. The picture of the quogs twisting their endless ropes from native flax lingered in his mind. He wished, idly, that the mee-haw tree had not been cut down.

Carlyle gave a cry: 'The tree!'

He peered out into the downpour, staring up at the dark centre of the island where the mighty mee-haw tree had stood, ready to shelter the quogs in its dense foliage. They made ropes . . . probably sent up a young male to loop slings over the branches, then the whole tribe went up.

There was a splashing and scrabbling at the foot of the platform. Carlyle knelt down and saw the Chief, already swimming awkwardly; the water had risen a metre in twenty minutes. The rain was a blinding cataract; a man who lay on his back would drown, thought Carlyle. He dragged the old quog aboard and bundled him into the hut. They sat gasping, the water pouring from the quog's grizzled hide, from Carlyle's coveralls.

'How far?' gasped Carlyle. 'How high does the water . . ?' He gestured with a horizontal hand, staring into the Chief's bulging dark eyes.

Carlyle was suddenly aware of an earlier moment. When the mee-haw tree came down . . . the day the quogs wept . . . he and Ensign Weiss noticed marks on its great trunk. A series of wavy bands, between three and four metres from the lowest branches . . . more than eighty metres from the ground. Carlyle understood, with another thump of fear . . . water marks. The water would rise until only the mee-haw tops rose like islands out of the purple sea. The only high ground on the entire planetoid was the plateau where his expedition had touched down briefly, far to the north. It had a large quog population . . . and no mee-haw trees.

The Chief touched Carlyle's knee gently with the tip of his prehensile tail.

'Sure,' said Carlyle. 'Sure. We have a real problem here, old buddy.'

He was calculating . . . One life-raft, inflatable, fully provisioned and powered, capacity six humans. All he had to do was launch the thing. And figure out some way of transporting thirty quogs to the plateau. The receiver gave his call signal but Carlyle paid no attention. He rushed out on to the platform again, into the deluge, and saw with alarm that the water was up to the cross supports. The scrap of beach and the lowest rank of undergrowth were already submerged. Sea and sky were joined in a blue-black curtain of moisture. Suddenly Carlyle gave a triumphant cry that brought the old quog scuttling to his side; he had realized that they were standing upon a raft.

He explained it to the Chief as he dug out the axe. The tribe must come aboard now, pronto; when the water rose he would knock out the supports of the platform and they would be launched. The wind and the current were driving towards the plateau . . . Maybe they could use the power pack of his own inflatable boat . . .

'Come on!' he shouted. 'We have to get them aboard!'

The Chief had been dancing and shivering at Carlyle's side, stretching out his arms to the island. He pointed through the rain and Carlyle saw that the quogs were coming.

It made sense, of course; the platform *was* a little higher than the top of the island. They came swarming through the bushes and flung themselves gamely into the water. Their awkward quog-paddle was very efficient; the first wave—pregnant females and mothers with babies on their backs—was already nosing towards the supports. The turbid water was alight with their bulbous eyes. Carlyle knelt down beside the Chief and began to heave the dripping creatures aboard. More than once Carlyle saw a big quog dive and drag up a half-drowned cub. The oldest animals took it pretty hard, they fought to stay on land; but the younger ones thrust them brutally into the water. All along the platform in the plunging rain the rest of the tribe were gently dancing and stamping, reaching out their arms in encouragement to those still in the water.

As the last of them were dragged aboard Carlyle herded them into the Met. hut and went over the side with the axe. The Chief and four husky off-siders watched him wallowing in water up to his neck and hammering with the back of the axe-head at one of the supports. The mee-haw piles had been embedded in heavy silt to a depth of two metres. Carlyle reckoned he could slide the tops of the piles out of the groove cut for them in the platform. But the first pile moved inward with a lurch the moment he hit it; he saw that the silt was swirling away in clouds as the water rose. He was treading water now, catching an occasional foothold on a rock. He moved under the platform, beat at the pile with the axehead, then heaved it outward with all his strength.

As the silt let go its hold the pile swung upwards in the water and the platform sagged down at one corner. Instantly two quogs were in the water grasping the mee-haw pile and using it to restore balance. Carlyle swam to the diagonal under the far corner of the hut and knocked it out like a loose tooth; two more quogs hove up out of the rain and balanced the platform. Carlyle knocked out the remaining leeward pile and felt the whole structure buckle and shift. He yelled to the quogs and scrambled back on to the platform. The decking heaved about crazily. The last pile on the seaward side gave way. Carlyle watched his two pairs of assistants climb expertly inboard and tapped the loose piles free of their grooves as they rode up on the surface of the flood. Leaning down he caught hold of one long pile as it clung to the side of the platform and shoved off from the island. The quogs on deck gathered to help him, bracing their leathery underbodies against the pole; the platform shuddered, then settled gently. The wind was rising and a strong current ran to the north. The mee-haw raft floated free upon the waste of waters.

Carlyle and his deck-hands carefully drew in their oar; he felt an extraordinary sense of well-being as they clustered around his knees. The rain had slackened but they still pressed forward into a wall of water. A gleam of violet penetrating the low ceiling of black cloud showed that the Star was shining. Carlyle glanced down at the Chief, who blinked solemnly through the rain. He remembered that he must answer the call signal and led the way into the Met. hut.

The quogs had packed themsleves in snugly under the big plastic dome. Carlyle couldn't think of any species who could carry off the situation better. Humans? Monkeys? Bedlam and filth. Okay, the quogs were a spooky lot, and the smell, *en masse*, was like camphorated garlic, but there were times when he appreciated their stillness, the way they organized themselves. He lifted aside a tiny blue paw, resting on the communicator, and called the satellite.

The signal was faint.

'Readings . . .'

He gave the readings.

'We observe dense cloud,' pipped the signal. 'Evaluate.'

Carlyle switched over to voice, although he didn't like talking to the computer. He made a report. The androgynous voice snapped:

'Evacuate. Use life-raft.'

Carlyle said, 'The emergency is way past that point. I have evacuated the native population.'

The quogs were vocalizing gently in the background . . . qwok-qwok-qwok . . . There was static, the voice signal was faint.

'Follow emergency procedures. No record . . . population. Save . . . self . . . data.'

Carlyle repeated stolidly. 'Evacuating with quogs.'

'Follow . . . procedures. No deviation . . . losing contact.'

Carlyle said coarsely, 'Screw yourself, tin-brain. Give me emergency voice contact.' He slammed the red button and Garrett answered.

'Jim . . . Jim? What the hell is going on down there?'

Carlyle gave his report all over again; the reply was broken and distant.

'We're losing signal.' Garrett was worried, 'What in blazes are you doing with those quogs?'

'Evacuating them. The island is submerged by now, I guess.'

'But *why*? This is no time . . . Tough luck . . . the quogs. No ethnological value . . . plenty more . . .'

'Hell!' said Carlyle. 'We cut down their tree!'

'Jim!' cried Garrett, with the static closing in. 'Take care . . . crazy raft . . . Can't allow . . . deviation emergency procedures!' The receiver went dead.

Carlyle felt a surge of panic as if his lifeline had snapped. His morale sagged at the thought of the satellite . . . warmth, filtered air, human company . . . He felt his conditioning slipping away. He was on the verge of apophobia, *Weltraumangst*, the fear that grew in interstellar space from contemplating vast distances. He remembered poor Ed Kravetts, a cadet in his year who tried to cover up a bad case of 'Yonders'. He staggered through his classes on the station red-eyed and queasy; a glance at one of the monitors made him sweat; the checking of an air-lock or a simple space walk left him shocked and pale. To see Kravetts struggling with a quantum equation was to apprehend the void: all the black distance that separated them from the tiny spinning globe of earth, a pin-point of light seen through the wrong end of a telescope.

Carlyle dragged himself back to his own world. 'Identify with the place you're in'—wasn't that Eva's way of saying it? Eva, E. M., Earth Mother, Commander Magnussen, come, beautiful Eva, aid me now. He sent his prayer off into deep space and doled out bacon cubes to all hands before striding out on deck. The rain had really eased off and the cloud was lifting. The mee-haw raft rushed on faster than before. With the current and a rising wind they were making maybe five knots. The Star was down; the brief blue night had settled on AC14.

The Chief leaned on his knuckle-pads beside Carlyle; they stared together over the wine-dark sea. Low waves came at the raft from the south-west, as the wind swung round. They were long, uncrested hillocks of water, that surged under the mee-haw logs and disappeared into the dusk, rolling in line across the surface of the endless sea.

'Those waves better keep low,' said Carlyle. 'Does the sea get rough?'

In his ninety-one days of Met. duty he had never seen

a choppy sea, never felt a drop of rain, never observed a significant drop in barometric pressure. He made wave-motions with his hands and the Chief replied with 'Aw-kee' and some new words. He thought of the sea rising up into roaring crests, high over the raft, huge rollers, hills and valleys where the pink foam boiled. He had to shut his eyes to shake off the nightmare picture of those waves, superimposed upon the harmless scene he was watching.

'I'd better get some sleep,' Carlyle muttered. He was wet and shaky, his morale still down. The whole project, the solitary Met. duty, was a test of his survival qualities and his potential as a colonist. Perhaps he had blown it with Garrett by evacuating the quogs . . . He stumbled back into the hut, found a way to his bunk, put on a fresh warm coverall from the thermopack. He didn't dare take any medication in case there was a sudden alert. Most of the quogs were sleeping; he caught the gleam of an eye here and there, the flicker of a blue hand. The Chief materialised at the foot of his bunk with two even more ancient creatures, so old that their skin was grey. They stared at Carlyle and clapped their long hands soundlessly. He felt an instant of revulsion . . . sleeping in a hut crammed with animals, for crissake. Then with a surge of weariness and a sense of strange well-being he fell asleep.

. . . He was wide awake in a dark room with a low ceiling. A range of scents and sounds assailed him: fresh air, wood-smoke, perfume, the waffling roar of a jet refuelling, insects, someone strumming idly on a moog. Earth. He was on Earth. Carlyle knew that he must be dreaming; he savoured his dream, taking in the outlines of the room. It was night; he was standing beside a window that opened on to a balcony. He glanced down at the thick, unpatterned carpet. A memory stirred. Had he been in this room before? Or was it simply the colour, a rippling mist-green, an earth colour. There was someone at the desk; Carlyle felt himself drift closer.

He peered at the dark figure . . . A caftan, a long fall of dark hair; he couldn't tell if it was a man or a woman. Yet something in the attitude of the head made him tremble, in his dream. Slowly Eva Magnussen turned until she saw him.

She blinked into the darkness of the room, switched off her cassette and removed the earpiece as he had seen her do a thousand times.

'Jim?' her voice was husky, hesitant. 'Jim Carlyle?'

'Eva?' In the dream his own voice was muffled.

'Where are you?' she asked. 'Is this some kind of experiment?'

'It's my dream,' he said. 'You know where I am.'

'Jim . . . I can *see* you.'

'I thought of you,' he said. 'I have a situation going here. My communications are gone. No word from upstairs. Seeing you helps a lot.'

'You're not alone,' she said. 'Who are they?'

'Quogs,' he said. 'They are great little guys. You might find a short report on them in the file on AC14. Not enough work done on quogs.'

'You say you are sleeping?'

'Sure. Eva, the sea is purple. Wine-dark sea . . .'

'Oh, Jim . . .'

'Don't!' he said. 'Eva . . . Don't cry. Think about what I said. I'm not one of your cadets any more. We could take a colonial posting.'

Then as she rose in her chair the dream tilted; he was looking down on the room. He saw the figure of Eva Magnussen, his instructress, Commander Magnussen, M.D., specialist in space psychology, rise up from her chair and run forward on the green carpet. He felt an instant of amazement and fear . . . it was like watching something else . . . real life . . . not a dream. He heard Eva cry out across the abyss of space and time:

'Jim . . . Jim Carlyle . . . I love you . . .'

Then the dream vanished in a swirl of colour and scent; he was back in the dark, in the flood, in the crowded Met. hut, with the quogs whistling in anxiety and the Chief tugging his arm.

'Okay!' said Carlyle. 'I see what's wrong.'

Rain was falling heavily again; the wind had become violent and ripped one of the panels out of the hut. The raft was bumping about in the water as the wind tore inside under the dome.

'I'll relax the panels,' said Carlyle to the Chief. 'I may need your team.'

The Chief summoned them up in the eerie violet light of dawn, while the rest of the passengers cowered away from the driving rain.

Carlyle went to work on the expanding ribs holding the panels. The hut began to fold down and the raft settled. Finally he grappled with the damaged panel, but he had the order wrong. He had been too busy providing shelter for the quogs—the torn panel should have been folded down first. He felt a thrill of warning; the eyes of the quogs glowed around him; he shot up a hand and turned sideways. The heavy strut holding one side of the panel broke with a rending crack and came down on his head. Carlyle's last conscious thought was, 'I am seeing stars . . .'

He was out, but not out cold for very long. He groped upwards towards consciousness through a fog of nausea and pain. Words whirled through the aching sunburst of his brain; he strove to move his legs, his hands, his fingers, to wrest open his leaden eyelids. He saw pictures . . . ragged scraps of film . . . the island, the satellite, a house in a green field . . . where? He felt himself, flying, moving, uplifted . . . lifted by a hundred strong, blue hands. He could see them so clearly through his closed eyelids. Whoever had blue hands . . . ? He remembered and laughed in his pain-fringed dream. 'Their hands were blue . . . and they went to sea . . . they went to sea in a sieve.'

Carlyle opened his eyes. He was on his bunk, the quogs all around him, their saucer eyes alight with concern.

'Concussion,' mumbled Carlyle. 'Got to take—medication.' He could not reach his head but the Chief guided his hand. There was a shallow cut on his scalp above the left ear and blood had soaked and matted his shaggy crop of hair, known in the service as the colonist's cut or the Buffalo Bill.

'Must take—antibiotic.'

Carlyle was heavily conditioned to protect himself against alien bacteria. He fought to stay conscious.

'Hogan . . .' he whispered to the Chief. 'Hogan the Medic. Up there. He can tell me what to take . . .'

He sank into a confused nightmare of purple microbes and the capsules in his medical pack.

Carlyle's head ached still and he began this comical dream. He was in a cabin on the satellite, lying just above the floor, floating. It was some guy's bedroom, with his locker, pin-ups, a green video cassette. He heard startled voices and saw two people sitting up in the bunk, clutching the sheet around them.

'Hi, Mary!' said Carlyle in his muffled dream voice. 'No clothes again!'

'Carlyle . . . what the hell!'

It was Dick Hogan, the Medic, naked too and for some reason frightened.

'Hogan!' cried Carlyle. 'You're just the guy I wanted to see.'

'Carlyle?' whispered Mary Long, the blonde anthropologist, 'Is it you, Jim?'

'Sure,' said Carlyle. 'I'm dreaming. I do a lot of dreaming down here. I have a concussion, Dick. Little cut on my scalp . . .'

The two lovers sat there petrified, unable to move. Carlyle laughed and could not make it out. He wasn't about to report them for fraternizing.

'Come on, now!' He laughed, weakly. 'What do I take, Dick? Not functioning too well . . . what antibiotic . . . the label . . .'

'UCF,' said Hogan automatically. 'You know that. Orange capsules.'

'Thanks . . .'

Then Mary Long pointed and began to scream.

'Quogs! I can see quogs!'

And the dream swirled away taking Carlyle with it.

After he got the Chief to feed him the orange capsules he slept long and heavily while his head mended. He woke at night, out on deck, with the raft still moving steadily in the grip of the current. They passed islands—no, not islands, but the tops of mee-haw trees, and on the raft the quogs danced, holding out their hands to the distance, to their brothers in the dripping branches. He woke in the hut and

saw a patch of indigo sky with the Star shining down.
Carlyle turned to the Chief; he was still lightheaded.

'Far and few . . .' said Carlyle. 'How does it go?' He
struggled drowsily on to one elbow.

> *Few and far, far and few,*
> *Are the lands where the Jumblies live,*
> *Their heads were green, and their hands were blue,*
> *And they went to sea in a sieve.*

Carlyle was laughing and the quogs waved their fingers.

In his sleep he heard someone calling his name; he woke
up and found the Chief, vocalizing through his hands.

'Cah-lah-ee!'

'Good try,' said Carlyle, flexing his limbs and feeling
stronger.

He pointed to the Chief, who slid across his nictitating
eyelids in a show of quog bashfulness.

'Tell me *your* name,' urged Carlyle.

The old quog boomed shyly: 'Sheef.'

Chief. The name Carlyle had given him, though he didn't
recall ever calling him that, unless in his delirium. He let
it go, puzzled. Either the quogs had no names or they were
like cats, who had special sounds they used to communicate
with humans.

Carlyle checked his instruments; the stormy conditions
were abating. A mee-haw off to port showed a fraction of
trunk. The flood waters were beginning to recede. His
chronometer told him he had been out of action for three
days. The Star hung low in a sky of aquamarine; he saw
the plateau dead ahead with the black cliffs rising up sheer.
The current was no more than a ripple and the mee-haw
raft moved sluggishly through the purple water.

He checked the plateau through his glasses, trying to
make out a possible landing-place that he remembered
where broken columns of black basalt had made an alien
giant's causeway. He saw a disturbance in the water, a line
of foam. Before he could register it properly he sensed the
anxiety of the quogs, growing into fear. Behind him they
huddled and whistled, crowding into the ragged heap of the
Met. hut. He stood on the raft, sandwiched between two

shock waves . . . the low wedge of foam moving towards them and the almost palpable fear given off by the quogs.

'What is it?' cried Carlyle.

The Chief, all of them, could give no answer, only this immense welling up of terror. Carlyle gazed at them blankly. A whale? A giant ray? The Great Horned Toad? He pushed through the crowd and took down a regulation magnum; then as an after-thought he reached down the new Fernlich, the automatic missile carbine. As he feathered its vents he heard the sound, a high vibrant scale of notes, swinging up and down on impossible frequencies. He might have heard it before, far out on the sea at night, so sweet and distant that it could be something he imagined. The quogs writhed in fear and pain, clasping their hands over their round ears, burrowing under the paraphernalia in the hut.

Carlyle rushed out into the waves of strange music. The ripple had divided into ten, a dozen pink clumps of foam, approaching swiftly on all sides. He could almost see them now . . . not too large, dark shapes swimming easily . . . like seals, maybe, or dolphins, slipping, weaving, gliding, just below the surface of the water. Carlyle squatted on the deck, fascinated. The music thrilled around him, his head sang, he felt dizzy. A young quog, crouched at the doorway of the hut, rolled over and died.

Carlyle sprang up, gasping. With an audible pop something reared up out of a patch of foam. A smooth pink bubble . . . At first he thought incredulously of a child's toy space-helmet, then he saw that it was a bubble of foam. The bubble burst and a sleek black head appeared. It did look like a seal but the coat was scaly, black crystalline scales, dark mother-of-pearl, breaking the bluish light into an alien spectrum. The creature was dancing on its tail, waving sleek webs like forepaws, only a few metres from the raft. Then, with a glissando of sound, infinitely sweet, like a peal of electronic bells, a single scaly tentacle whipped out from a curled position below the head and seized the body of the dead quog. The seal-lizard flipped its catch into the air and caught it playfully. There was a flash of teeth, a minor chord, and the quog's head was bitten off. A whistle of anguish rose from the burrowing, terrified quogs crammed inside the hut. Carlyle shouted at the top of his voice.

The creatures had never heard a human voice. There was an excited humming; a swish of dark bodies passing around and under the raft. A colony of pink bubbles grew to starboard, at a safe distance. The seal-lizards repeated what he recognized vaguely as the tone and pitch of his own voice. They boomed and cawed, bouncing about in the water. Carlyle accepted the invitation: he called again, telling them to clear off. The formation of bubbles began to move closer, tinkling, humming . . . testing . . . testing . . .

With a ringing head Carlyle realized what they were trying to find. The raft was drifting closer to the plateau; he grasped the oar, still lying on deck, and began to drive the clumsy craft along. He would never escape this way before the seal-lizards found *his* death frequency—the sound which would make this new creature with the harsh, loud voice fall down to be eaten. The seal-lizards moved alongside in formation. The noise was unbearable; Carlyle sang, groaned, shouted aloud. A tentacle, then another, flicked over the timbers of the raft, plucked at his boots, probed towards the quogs in the hut.

Carlyle dropped his oar and fired the magnum in the air. The seal-lizards hesitated, then pressed forward. A new wave of sound broke over the raft; he screamed and rolled upon the deck, pressing his hands over his ears. Through the mists of agonizing sound he saw the seal-lizards at the very edge of the boat. A row of neat, scaly black heads: narrow oval eyes, a structure of nasal beak and leathery appendages like whiskers . . . even so close they looked amazingly like seals. He could not see how they made their music. Their comical mouths opened upon murderous fangs. A tentacle gripped his wrist and pulled gently.

Roaring aloud to counteract their killing whine, Carlyle put one hand to the missile carbine and fired point-blank along the deck. A seal-lizard was blasted into mush. The missile that destroyed it passed on across the sea, then struck and exploded, sending up a column of water, fifty metres away.

There was a moment of utter silence, then the whole

band of seal-lizards dived like one creature. It could have been the shock-wave that did it, or the sound of the carbine, or simply the death of one of their number. Rising to his knees Carlyle saw them emerge far beyond the raft swimming in formation, fast and low . . . a ripple bearing away to the south-west. He caught only a few notes of their music across the dark waters.

The quogs crept out and surrounded him, helping him to stand. Everyone, Carlyle included, was partially deaf from the encounter. The quogs held their heads sideways and bounced on one leg, like a human bather with water in his ear. Carlyle shook hands with the Chief; it caught on. The whole party, dizzy with relief, shook hands promiscuously.

They were already within the shadow of the plateau: Carlyle and his crew, working the oar, struck a rock or a shoal, then another. They were over the flooded causeway where he had embarked for the island three months before. He levered the raft in towards a rock platform. The quogs had begun to stamp gently and hold out their hands to the plateau.

One moment there was no sign of life, only the glittering planes of the great stone mesa; the next, every plane and slope was alive with quogs. They spilled over the edge of the plateau in waves, until the black rock was blanketed with brown and grey and tawny fur. A strange noise, stranger even than the music of the seal-lizards, began to rise up from the multitude. They vocalized all together, by tens and hundreds, their weak voices blending into a vast muffled shout, that echoed out over the purple flood tide and reverberated from the chasms of the plateau.

'CAH-LAH-EE.'

As his own quogs pressed round him proudly, in silence, Carlyle recognized his own name. Then as the shout redoubled: 'CAH-LAH-EE,' he saw himself as a new creature, as the quogs perceived him: the clumsy, loud-voiced, white-handed giant of a new species. The dogged Cah-lah-ee, who made a marvellous craft from the looted remains of a mee-haw tree, who overcame the flood, did battle with seal-lizards and brought a whole tribe to safety.

The raft sidled into the platform and a nylon rope fell on

the deck. The quogs were so thick that Carlyle had not seen the landing party—Garrett, Hogan and Weiss. The sight of these men, his own kind, affected him powerfully. His sense of proportion was restored; he smiled and choked up, just as they all did. He felt as if he had returned from some other dimension, not a routine stint on AC14.

'Hey, there!' cried Garrett. 'Some welcome you got here, Lieutenant.'

'Am I glad to see you!' said Carlyle.

They heaved him ashore; the quogs were whisked off the raft by hundreds of willing hands.

Carlyle turned back to the Chief.

'See the raft is made fast,' he said.

The men of the landing party turned back and watched as the Chief and his off-siders tied up to a pillar of rock.

'Everything ship-shape!' said Dick Hogan.

'They know the ropes,' said Carlyle.

The party ascended through an aisle of quogs, still hooting his name; Carlyle acknowledged the applause as modestly as he could. He was looking ahead eagerly . . . Yes, there was the landing module on the plateau, among the bushes and the stony burrows of the upland quogs. He was going upstairs, back to the station. His limbs began to ache in anticipation of a steam bath and a bunk.

'How's the head?' asked Hogan.

'Oh, fine,' said Carlyle. 'It was just a simple concussion.'

Garrett turned to him.

'You get it, don't you, Jim? You understand what you've discovered.'

'I think so,' said Carlyle. 'I guess I knew all along. Or when they called out my name . . . Did you know it was my name?'

'We worked it out.' They laughed and looked at Carlyle expectantly, waiting for him to bell the cat.

'The quogs are able to transmit pictures,' said Carlyle. 'They are natural telesends.'

'The first in the Universe,' said Garrett.

'There's more to it than that, Max,' said Carlyle. 'Some kind of group intelligence . . .'

'They had us on the hop upstairs!' put in Weiss.

'What way?' asked Carlyle.

'Reports of hallucinations,' said Garrett. 'Weiss here saw you on the raft. Hogan . . .'

'I saw Hogan,' said Carlyle. 'Spoke to him. I thought it was a dream.'

He and Hogan exchanged glances, straight-faced; no one said a word about Mary Long. The quogs certainly had a trick of embarrassing that girl.

'Communication can extend over vast distances,' said Max Garrett.

He was smiling in an odd way; the men were still watching Carlyle closely. He couldn't read much in their faces, no pictures came to him; for a moment he wished they were quogs. Hogan dug him in the ribs.

'You got the prize, boy,' he said.

Garrett cleared his throat.

'We had word. Commander Eva Magnussen put in a report. She has also requested a P.I.C. with Lieutenant Carlyle.' A Personal Interplanetary Communication: something flashed from Earth to Armstrong Base to a chain of a hundred satellites. It was the spaceman's version of compassionate leave; marriages were contracted, births and deaths announced in this way. 'She has requested a colonial posting.'

Carlyle smiled foolishly and the men all shook him by the hand.

They were anxious to get him upstairs to sick bay; but Carlyle excused himself and turned aside. He bent down to the nearest quog.

'Where is my friend, the Chief?'

There was an immediate response in the scattered groups of quogs returning up the sides of the plateau. A strong impulse, stronger perhaps because of the numbers involved, directed him to a low cave some distance away. He strode over and found the Chief, with his wives and children, being regaled with berries and limpets and sweet-bark. He realized that he had been aware for some time that the Chief was in fact a male; he found no difficulty in sexing quogs at a glance. The Chief knew that he was leaving.

'I'll come back after a few days,' said Carlyle.

The pair of them stood in a clear space, looking out from the height of the plateau. The three giant causeways in the rock were explained, three great chutes that drained off the deluge of rain from the high ground. The purple sea spread out beneath them; the mee-haw trees marked the submerged islands. In a series of quick superimpositions Carlyle saw the great day when the flood receded altogether; when the Star approached its apogee and the islands became dry land again.

'Yes,' he said. 'I'll be back to see that.'

As he turned to rejoin the landing party Carlyle took in the scene: the three men beside their vehicle, tall visitors in regulation silversuits, and a fourth man, unkempt and hairy, in ragged coveralls, communing at a distance with the members of a new species. The men looked curiously towards Carlyle; their anxiety did not quite diminish as he came closer. The distance between Carlyle and the landing party could not be taken up in a few small steps. They saw tomorrow's man, who by some chance operation of goodwill, some accident of understanding, reached forward into new modes of being.

The Commuter

Phillip K. Dick

Phillip K. Dick has written a remarkable series of novels that explore
the nature of reality.—Not a subject to be taken lightly, yet he
succeeds in pursuing his obsession without appearing either glib or
pretentious.

His novels, *The Man In The High Castle, Ubik* and *The Three
Stigmata Of Palmer Eldritch,* offer some of the finest writing ever to
come out of the sf field. Their success has rather overshadowed
his skill as a short-story writer. The following tale is offered as a
reminder of this special talent—a somewhat chilling reminder.
THE COMMUTER is a Phillip K. Dick novel in miniature, a mysterious
confrontation between the real and the unreal.

The little fellow was tired. He pushed his way slowly
through the throng of people, across the lobby of the station,
to the ticket window. He waited his turn impatiently, fatigue
showing in his drooping shoulders, his sagging brown coat.

'Next,' Ed Jacobson, the ticket seller, rasped.

The little fellow tossed a five-dollar bill on the counter.
'Give me a new commute book. Used up the old one.' He
peered past Jacobson at the wall clock. 'Lord, is it really
that late?'

Jacobson accepted the five dollars. 'Okay, mister. One
commute book. Where to?'

'Macon Heights,' the little fellow stated.

'Macon Heights.' Jacobson consulted his board. 'Macon Heights. There isn't any such place.'

The little man's face hardened in suspicion. 'You trying to be funny?'

'Mister, there isn't any Macon Heights. I can't sell you a ticket unless there is such a place.'

'What do you mean? I live there!'

'I don't care. I've been selling tickets for six years and there is no such place.'

The little man's eyes popped with astonishment. 'But I have a home there. I go there every night. I—'

'Here.' Jacobson pushed him his chart board. 'You find it.'

The little man pulled the board over to one side. He studied it frantically, his fingers trembling as he went down the list of towns.

'Find it?' Jacobson demanded, resting his arms on the counter. 'It's not there, is it?'

The little man shook his head, dazed. 'I don't understand. It doesn't make sense. Something must be wrong. There certainly must be some—'

Suddenly he vanished. The board fell to the cement floor. The little fellow was gone—winked out of existence.

'Holy Caesar's Ghost,' Jacobson gasped. His mouth opened and closed. There was only the board lying on the cement floor.

The little man had ceased to exist.

'What then?' Bob Paine asked.

'I went around and picked up the board.'

'He was really gone?'

'He was gone, all right.' Jacobson mopped his forehead. 'I wish you had been around. Like a light he went out. Completely. No sound. No motion.'

Paine lit a cigarette, leaning back in his chair. 'Had you ever seen him before?'

'No.'

'What time of day was it?'

'Just about now. About five.' Jacobson moved towards the ticket window. 'Here comes a bunch of people.'

'Macon Heights.' Paine turned the pages of the State city guide. 'No listing in any of the books. If he reappears I want to talk to him. Get him inside the office.'

'Sure. I don't want to have nothing to do with him. It isn't natural.' Jacobson turned to the window. 'Yes, lady.'

'Two round trip tickets to Lewisburg.'

Paine stubbed his cigarette out and lit another. 'I keep feeling I've heard the name before.' He got up and wandered over to the wall map. 'But it isn't listed.'

'There is no listing because there is no such place,' Jacobson said. 'You think I could stand here daily, selling one ticket after another, and not know?' He turned back to his window. 'Yes, sir.'

'I'd like a commute book to Macon Heights,' the little fellow said, glancing nervously at the clock on the wall. 'And hurry it up.'

Jacobson closed his eyes. He hung on tight. When he opened his eyes again the little fellow was still there. Small wrinkled face. Thinning hair. Glasses. Tired, slumped coat.

Jacobson turned and moved across the office to Paine. 'He's back.' Jacobson swallowed, his face pale. 'It's him again.'

Paine's eyes flickered. 'Bring him right in.'

Jacobson nodded and returned to his window. 'Mister,' he said, 'could you please come inside?' He indicated the door. 'The Vice-President would like to see you for a moment.'

The little man's face darkened. 'What's up? The train's about to take off.' Grumbling under his breath, he pushed the door open and entered the office. 'This sort of thing has never happened before. It's certainly getting hard to purchase a commute book. If I miss the train I'm going to hold your company—'

'Sit down,' Paine said, indicating the chair across from his desk. 'You're the gentleman who wants a commute book to Macon Heights?'

'Is there something strange about that? What's the matter with all of you? Why can't you sell me a commute book like you always do?'

'Like—like we *always* do?'

The little man held himself in check with great effort.

'Last December my wife and I moved out to Macon Heights. I've been riding your train ten times a week, twice a day, for six months. Every month I buy a new commute book.'

Paine leaned towards him. 'Exactly which one of our trains do you take, Mr —'

'Critchet. Ernest Critchet. The B train. Don't you know your own schedules?'

'The B train?' Paine consulted a B train chart, running his pencil along it. No Macon Heights was listed. 'How long is the trip? How long does it take?'

'Exactly forty-nine minutes.' Critchet looked up at the wall clock. 'If I ever get on it.'

Paine calculated mentally. Forty-nine minutes. About thirty miles from the city. He got up and crossed to the big wall map.

'What's wrong?' Critchet asked with marked suspicion.

Paine drew a thirty-mile circle on the map. The circle crossed a number of towns, but none of them was Macon Heights. And on the B line there was nothing at all.

'What sort of place is Macon Heights?' Paine asked. 'How many people, would you say?'

'I don't know. Five thousand, maybe. I spend most of my time in the city. I'm a bookkeeper over at Bradshaw Insurance.'

'Is Macon Heights a fairly new place?'

'It's modern enough. We have a little two-bedroom house, a couple of years old.' Critchet stirred restlessly. 'How about my commute book?'

'I'm afraid,' Paine said slowly, 'I can't sell you a commute book.'

'What? Why not?'

'We don't have any service to Macon Heights.'

Critchet leaped up. 'What do you mean?'

'There's no such place. Look at the map yourself.'

Critchet gaped, his face working. Then he turned angrily to the wall map, glaring at it intently.

'This is a curious situation, Mr Critchet,' Paine murmured. 'It isn't on the map, and the State city directory doesn't list it. We have no schedule that includes it. There are no commute books made up for it. We don't—'

He broke off. Critchet had vanished. One moment he was there, studying the wall map. The next moment he was gone. Vanished. Puffed out.

'Jacobson!' Paine barked. 'He's gone!'

Jacobson's eyes grew large. Sweat stood out on his forehead. 'So he has,' he murmured.

Paine was deep in thought, gazing at the empty spot Ernest Critchet had occupied. 'Something's going on,' he muttered. 'Something damn strange.' Abruptly he grabbed his overcoat and headed for the door.

'Don't leave me alone!' Jacobson begged.

'If you need me I'll be at Laura's apartment. The number's some place in my desk.'

'This is no time for games with girls.'

Paine pushed open the door to the lobby. 'I doubt,' he said grimly, 'if this is a game.'

Paine climbed the stairs to Laura Nichols' apartment two at a time. He leaned on the buzzer until the door opened.

'Bob!' Laura blinked in surprise. 'To what do I owe this—'

Paine pushed past her, inside the apartment. 'Hope I'm not interrupting anything.'

'No, but—'

'Big doings. I'm going to need some help. Can I count on you?'

'On me?' Laura closed the door after him. Her attractively furnished apartment lay in half shadow. At the end of the deep green couch a single table lamp burned. The heavy drapes were closed. The phonograph was on low in the corner.

'Maybe I'm going crazy.' Paine threw himself down on the luxuriant green couch. 'That's what I want to find out.'

'How can I help?' Laura came languidly over, her arms folded, a cigarette between her lips. She shook her long hair back out of her eyes. 'Just what did you have in mind?'

Paine grinned at the girl appreciatively. 'You'll be surprised. I want you to go downtown tomorrow morning bright and early and—'

'Tomorrow morning! I have a job, remember? And the office starts a whole new string of reports this week.'

89

'The hell with that. Take the morning off. Go downtown to the main library. If you can't get the information there, go over to the county court house and start looking through the back tax records. Keep looking until you find it.'

'It? Find what?'

Paine lit a cigarette thoughtfully. 'Mention of a place called Macon Heights. I know I've heard the name before. Years ago. Got the picture? Go through the old atlases. Old newspapers in the reading room. Old magazines. Reports. City proposals. Propositions before the State legislature.'

Laura sat down slowly on the arm of the couch. 'Are you kidding?'

'No.'

'How far back?'

'Maybe ten years—if necessary.'

'Good Lord! I might have to—'

'Stay there until you find it.' Paine got up abruptly. 'I'll see you later.'

'You're leaving? You're not taking me out to dinner?'

'Sorry.' Paine moved towards the door. 'I'll be busy. Real busy.'

'Doing what?'

'Visiting Macon Heights.'

Outside the train endless fields stretched off, broken by an occasional farm building. Bleak telephone poles jutted up towards the evening sky.

Paine glanced at his watch. Not far, now. The train passed through a small town. A couple of gas stations, roadside stands, television store. It stopped at the station, brakes grinding. Lewisburg. A few commuters got off, men in overcoats with evening papers. The doors slammed and the train started up.

Paine settled back against his seat, deep in thought. Critchet had vanished while looking at the wall map. He had vanished the first time when Jacobson showed him the chart board—when he had been shown there was no such place as Macon Heights. Was there some sort of clue there? The whole thing was unreal, dreamlike.

Paine peered out. He was almost there—if there were

such a place. Outside the train the brown fields stretched off endlessly. Hills and level fields. Telephone poles. Cars racing alone the State highway, tiny black specks hurrying through the twilight.

But no sign of Macon Heights.

The train roared on its way. Paine consulted his watch. Fifty-one minutes had passed. And he had seen nothing. Nothing but fields.

He walked up the car and sat down beside the conductor, a white-haired old gentleman. 'Ever heard of a place called Macon Heights?' Paine asked.

'No, sir.'

Paine showed his identification. 'You're sure you never heard of any place by that name?'

'Positive, Mr Paine.'

'How long have you been on this run?'

'Eleven years, Mr Paine.'

Paine rode on until the next stop, Jacksonville. He got off and transferred to a B train heading back to the city. The sun had set. The sky was almost black. Dimly, he could make out the scenery out there beyond the window.

He tensed, holding his breath. One minute to go. Forty seconds. Was there anything? Level fields. Bleak telephone poles. A barren, wasted landscape between towns.

Between? The train rushed on, hurtling through the gloom. Paine gazed out fixedly. Was there something out there? Something beside the fields?

Above the fields a long mass of translucent smoke lay stretched out. A homogeneous mass, extending for almost a mile. What was it? Smoke from the engine? But the engine was diesel. From a truck along the highway? A brush fire? None of the fields looked burned.

Suddenly the train began to slow. Paine was instantly alert. The train was stopping, coming to a halt. The brakes screeched, the cars lurched from side to side, then silence.

Across the aisle a tall man in a light coat got to his feet, put his hat on, and moved rapidly towards the door. He leaped down from the train, onto the ground. Paine watched him, fascinated. The man walked rapidly away from the train across the dark fields. He moved with purpose, heading towards the bank of grey haze.

The man rose. He was walking a foot off the ground. He turned to the right. He rose again—now three feet off the ground. For a moment he walked parallel to the ground, still heading away from the train. Then he vanished into the bank of haze. He was gone.

Paine hurried up the aisle. But already the train had begun gathering speed. The ground moved past outside. Paine located the conductor, leaning against the wall of the car, a pudding-faced youth.

'Listen,' Paine grated. 'What was that stop!'

'Beg pardon, sir?'

'That stop! Where the hell were we?'

'We always stop there.' Slowly, the conductor reached into his coat and brought out a handful of schedules. He sorted through them and passed one to Paine. 'The B always stops at Macon Heights. Didn't you know that?'

'No!'

'It's on the schedule.' The youth raised his pulp magazine again. 'Always stops there. Always has. Always will.'

Paine tore the schedule open. It was true. Macon Heights was listed between Jackonsville and Lewisburg. Exactly thirty miles from the city.

The cloud of grey haze. The vast cloud, gaining form rapidly. As if something were coming into existence. As a matter of fact, something *was* coming into existence.

Macon Heights!

He caught Laura at her apartment the next morning. She was sitting at the coffee table in a pale pink sweater and dark slacks. Before her was a pile of notes, a pencil and eraser, and a malted milk.

'How did you make out?' Paine demanded.

'Fine. I got your information.'

'What's the story?'

'There was quite a bit of material.' She patted the sheaf of notes. 'I summed up the major parts for you.'

'Let's have the summation.'

'Seven years ago this August the county board of supervisors voted on three new suburban housing tracts to be set up outside the city. Macon Heights was one of them. There was a big debate. Most of the city merchants opposed the new tracts. Said they would draw too much retail business away from the city.'

'Go on.'

'There was a long fight. Finally two of the three tracts were approved. Waterville and Cedar Groves. But not Macon Heights.'

'I see,' Paine murmured, thoughtfully.

'Macon Heights was defeated. A compromise: two tracts instead of three. The two tracts were built up right away. You know. We passed through Waterville one afternoon. Nice little place.'

'But no Macon Heights.'

'No. Macon Heights was given up.'

Paine rubbed his jaw. 'That's the story, then.'

'That's the story. Do you realize I lost a whole half-day's pay because of this? You *have* to take me out, tonight. Maybe I should get another fellow. I'm beginning to think you're not such a good bet.'

Paine nodded absently. 'Seven years ago.' All at once a thought came to him. 'The vote! How close was the vote on Macon Heights?'

Laura consulted her notes. 'The project was defeated by a single vote.'

'A single vote. Seven years ago.' Paine moved out into the hall. 'Thanks, honey. Things are beginning to make sense. Lots of sense!'

He caught a cab out front. The cab raced him across the city, towards the train station. Outside, signs and streets flashed by. People and stores and cars.

His hunch had been correct. He *had* heard the name before. Seven years ago. A bitter county debate on a proposed suburban tract. Two towns approved; one defeated and forgotten.

But now the forgotten town was coming into existence—seven years later. The town and an undetermined slice of reality along with it. *Why?* Had something changed in the past? Had an alteration occurred in some past continuum?

That seemed like the explanation. The vote had been close. Macon Heights had *almost* been approved. Maybe certain parts of the past were unstable. Maybe that particular period, seven years ago, had been critical. Maybe it had never completely 'jelled'. An odd thought: the past changing, after it had already happened.

Suddenly Paine's eyes focussed. He sat up quickly. Across the street was a store sign, halfway along the block. Over a small, inconspicuous establishment. As the cab moved forward Paine peered to see:

BRADSHAW INSURANCE

(OR)

NOTARY PUBLIC

He pondered. Critchet's place of business. Did it also come and go? Had it always been there? Something about it made him uneasy.

'Hurry it up,' Paine ordered the driver. 'Let's get going.'

When the train slowed down at Macon Heights, Paine got quickly to his feet and made his way up the aisle to the door. The grinding wheels jerked to a halt and Paine leaped down onto the hot gravel siding. He looked around him.

In the afternoon sunlight, Macon Heights glittered and sparkled, its even rows of houses stretching out in all directions. In the centre of the town the marquee of a theatre rose up.

A theatre, even. Paine headed across the track towards the town. Beyond the train station was a parking lot. He stepped up onto the lot and crossed it, following a path past a filling station and onto a sidewalk.

He came out on the main street of the town. A double row of stores stretched out ahead of him. A hardware store. Two drug stores. A dime store. A modern department store.

Paine walked along, hands in his pockets, gazing around him at Macon Heights. An apartment building stuck up, tall and fat. A janitor was washing down the front steps. Everything looked new and modern. The houses, the stores, the pavement and sidewalks. The parking meters. A brown-uniformed cop was giving a car a ticket. Trees, growing at intervals. Neatly clipped and pruned.

He passed a big supermarket. Out in front was a bin of fruit, oranges and grapes. He picked a grape and bit into it.

The grape was real, all right. A big black concord grape, sweet and ripe. Yet twenty-four hours ago there had been nothing here but a barren field.

Paine entered one of the drug stores. He leafed through some magazines and then sat down at the counter. He ordered a cup of coffee from the red-cheeked little waitress.

'This is a nice town,' Paine said, as she brought the coffee.

'Yes, isn't it?'

Paine hesitated. 'How—how long have you been working here?'

'Three months.'

'Three months?' Paine studied the buxom little blonde. 'You live here in Macon Heights?'

'Oh, yes.'

'How long?'

'A couple of years, I guess.' She moved away to wait on a young soldier who had taken a stool down the counter.

Paine sat drinking his coffee and smoking, idly watching the people passing by outside. Ordinary people. Men and women, mostly women. Some had grocery bags and little wire carts. Automobiles drove slowly back and forth. A sleepy little suburban town. Modern, upper middle class. A quality town. No slums here. Small, attractive houses. Stores with sloping glass fronts and neon signs.

Some high school kids burst into the drugstore, laughing and bumping into each other. Two girls in bright sweaters sat down next to Paine and ordered lime drinks. They chatted gaily, bits of their conversation drifting to him.

He gazed at them, pondering moodily. They were real, all right. Lipstick and red fingernails. Sweaters and armloads of school books. Hundreds of high school kids, crowding eagerly into the drug store.

Paine rubbed his forehead wearily. It didn't seem possible. Maybe he was out of his mind. The town was *real*. Completely real. It must have always existed. A whole town couldn't rise up out of nothing; out of a cloud of grey haze. Five thousand people, houses and streets and stores.

Stores. Bradshaw Insurance.

Stabbing realization chilled him. Suddenly he understood. It was spreading. Beyond Macon Heights. Into the city. The city was changing, too. Bradshaw Insurance. Critchet's place of business.

Macon Heights couldn't exist without warping the city. They interlocked. The five thousand people came from the city. Their jobs. Their lives. The city was involved.

But how much? How much was the city changing?

Paine threw a quarter on the counter and hurried out of the drug store, towards the train station. He had to get back to the city. Laura, the change. Was she still there? Was his *own* life safe?

Fear gripped him. Laura, all his possessions, his plans, hopes and dreams. Suddenly Macon Heights was unimportant. His own world was in jeopardy. Only one thing mattered, now. He had to make sure of it; make sure his own life was still there. Untouched by the spreading circle of change that was lapping out from Macon Heights.

'Where to, buddy?' the cab driver asked, as Paine came rushing out of the train station.

Paine gave him the address of the apartment. The cab roared out into traffic. Paine settled back nervously. Outside the window the streets and office buildings flashed past. White collar workers were already beginning to get off work, swelling out onto the sidewalks to stand in clumps at each corner.

How much had changed? He concentrated on a row of buildings. The big department store. Had that always been there? The little boot-black shop next to it. He had never noticed that before.

NORRIS HOME FURNISHINGS. He didn't remember *that*. But how could he be sure? He felt confused. How could he tell?

The cab let him off in front of the apartment house. Paine stood for a moment, looking around him. Down at the end of the block the owner of the Italian delicatessen was out putting up the awning. Had he ever noticed a delicatessen there before?

He could not remember.

What had happened to the big meat market across the

street? There was nothing but neat little houses; older houses that looked like they'd been there plenty long. Had a meat market ever been there? The houses *looked* solid.

In the next block the striped pole of a barber shop glittered. Had there always been a barber shop there?

Maybe it had always been there. Maybe, and maybe not. Everything was shifting. New things were coming into existence, others going away. The past was altering, and memory was tied to the past. How could he trust his memory? How could he be sure?

Terror gripped him. Laura? His world . . .

Paine raced up the front steps and pushed open the door of the apartment house. He hurried up the carpeted stairs to the second floor. The door of the apartment was unlocked. He pushed it open and entered, his heart in his mouth, praying silently.

The living room was dark and silent. The shades were half pulled. He glanced around wildly. The light-blue couch, magazines on its arms. The low blonde-oak table. The television set. But the room was empty.

'Laura!' he gasped.

Laura hurried from the kitchen, eyes wide with alarm. 'Bob! What are you doing home? Is anything the matter?'

Paine relaxed, sagging with relief. 'Hello, honey.' He kissed her, holding her tight against him. She was warm and substantial; completely real. 'No, nothing's wrong. Everything's fine.'

'Are you sure?'

'I'm sure.' Paine took his coat off shakily and dropped it over the back of the couch. He wandered around the room, examining things, his confidence returning. His familiar blue couch, cigarette burns on its arms. His old ragged footstool. His desk where he did his work at night. His fishing rods leaning up against the wall behind the bookcase.

The big television set he had purchased only last month; that was safe, too.

Everything, all he owned, was untouched. Safe. Unharmed.

'Dinner won't be ready for half an hour,' Laura murmured anxiously, unfastening her apron. 'I didn't expect you home so early. I've just been sitting around all day. I did clean the stove. Some salesman left a sample of a new cleanser.'

'That's okay.' He examined a favourite Renoir print on the wall. 'Take your time. It's good to see all these things again. I—'

From the bedroom a crying sound came. Laura turned quickly. 'I guess we woke up Jimmy.'

'Jimmy?'

Laura laughed. 'Darling, don't you remember your own son?'

'Of course,' Paine murmured, annoyed. He followed Laura slowly into the bedroom. 'Just for a minute everything seemed strange.' He rubbed his forehead, frowning. 'Strange and unfamiliar. Sort of out of focus.'

They stood by the crib, gazing down at the baby. Jimmy glared back up at his mother and father.

'It must have been the sun,' Laura said. 'It's so terribly hot outside.'

'That must be it. I'm okay now.' Paine reached down and poked at the baby. He put his arm around his wife, hugging her to him. 'It must have been the sun,' he said. He looked down into her eyes and smiled.

The Oath

James Blish

The decade following the Second World War was a grim time for sf writers. The tensions of the Cold War and the threat of nuclear doom were preoccupations reflected constantly in the magazines of the time.

In a spate of futures depicting the world as it would exist after the 'inevitable' holocaust, most writers could express nothing but guilt and despair; their vision of the future seemed very bleak. Only a few kept their heads and achieved a quiet dignity in their work.

James Blish has been a giant among sf writers for more than twenty years. His stories display a style and grace blended with an intellectual passion uncommon to the genre. While he has always been an innovator, his orthodox works such as the time-and-space spanning epic, *Cities In Flight,* with its overwhelming climax of the death of a galaxy, exemplifies for many readers the special qualities of sf—qualities that cannot be found elsewhere. His short stories demonstrate not only his craftsmanship but his intelligent insight into, and compassion for, human nature.

THE OATH tells of an isolated incident in a post-catastrophe world. Underneath its deceptively quiet surface one may find much to think about, and characters not easy to forget.

Remembering conscientiously to use the hand brake as well as the foot, Dr Frank Tucci began to slow down towards the middle of the bridge, examining the toll booths ahead with a cold eye.

He despised everything about scouting by motor scooter, though he agreed, when forced to it, that a man on a scooter made the smallest possible target consistent with getting anywhere—and besides, it conserved petrol, of which there was very little left. Most of all he despised crossing bridges. It made him feel even more exposed than usual, and toll booths made natural ambushes.

These, however, were as deserted as they looked. The glass had been broken and the tills rifled. Without question the man who had taken the money had not lived long enough afterwards to discover that it was worthless. Still, the looting of money was unusual, for there had been little time for it. Most people outside target areas had died during the first two days; the thirty-eight-hour dose in the open had averaged 9100 roentgens.

Naturally the small town ahead would be thoroughly looted of food and other valuables, but that was different. There was a physician in the area—that was the man Dr Tucci had come all this way to see—and, as usual, people would have drifted in again to settle around him. People meant looting, necessarily. For one thing, they were accustomed to getting seventy per cent of their calcium from milk, and the only milk that was drinkable out here was canned stuff from before the Day. There might still be a cow or two alive outside the Vaults, but her milk would be lethal.

There would be no more dairy products of any kind for the lifetime of anyone now living, once the lootables were gone. There was too much strontium-90 in the soil. The Nutrition Board had worked out some way around the calcium supply problem, Tucci had heard, but he knew nothing about it; that wasn't his province.

His province was in the valley ahead, in the large reddish frame house where, all the reports assured him, he would find another doctor—or somebody who was passing for one. The house, he noted professionally, was fairly well situated. There was a broad creek running rapidly over a stone bed not far away, and the land was arable and in cultivation: truck crops for the most part, a good acre of them, enough to supply a small family by today's starvation standards. The family was there, that was evident: two children in the four-to-seven age bracket—hence survivors, both of them— were playing a stalking game in the rows of corn to which the other acre was planted.

Tucci wondered if the owner knew the Indian trick of planting pumpkins, beans, and a fish from the stream in the same hill with the corn. If he didn't, he wasn't getting more than half as much from the acre as he might.

The position was not optimum for defence. Though the centrally located house did offer clear shots all around, anyone could put it under siege almost indefinitely from the high ground which surrounded it. But presumably a doctor did not need to conduct a lonely defence against the rare roving band, since his neighbours would help him. A 'neighbour' in that sense would include anyone within a hundred miles who could pick up a weapon and get to the scene fast enough.

Even a mob might pause before it could come to that. Its first sight of the house would be from here, looking down into the valley; and on the roof of the house, over green paint much streaked by repeated anti-fallout hosings, was painted a large red cross.

That would hardly have protected the owner during the first six months after the Day, but that was more than a year ago. Things had settled somewhat since then. Initially a good deal of venom had expressed itself against doctors when the dying had discovered that they could not be saved. That was why, now, rumours of the existence of a physician could bring Dr Tucci two hundred bumpy miles on a rusty Lambretta whose side panels had fallen off, carrying a conspicuous five-gallon can of the liquid gold that was petrol on his luggage rack, sweating inside a bullet-proof suit in whose efficacy he thoroughly disbelieved.

He gunned the motor three times in neutral before putting the scooter back in gear and starting it slowly down the hill. The last thing he wanted was to seem to be sneaking up on anybody. Sure enough, as he clambered down from his perch onto the road in front of the house and lurched the scooter up onto its kickstand, he saw someone watching him from a ground-floor window.

He knew that he was an odd sight. Short dumpy men look particularly short and dumpy on motor scooters, and he doubted that his green crash-helmet and dark goggles made him look any less bizarre. But those, at least, he could take off. There was nothing he could do right now about the putatively bullet-proof coverall.

He was met at the door by a woman. She was a tall, muscular blonde wearing shorts and a halter, a cloth tying up her hair at the back. He approved of her on sight. She was rather pretty in her own heroic fashion, but more than that, she was obviously strong and active. That was what counted these days, although animal cunning was also very helpful.

'Good morning,' he said. He produced from his pocket the ritual gift of canned beans without which it was almost impossible to open negotiations with a stranger. 'My name is Frank Tucci, from up north. I'm looking for someone named Gottlieb, Nathan Gottlieb; I think—'

'Thank you, this is where he lives,' the woman said, with unusual graciousness. Obviously she was not afraid or suspicious. 'I'm Sigrid Gottlieb. You'll have to wait a while, I'm afraid. He's seeing another patient now, and there are several others waiting.'

'Patient?' Tucci said, without attempting to look surprised. He knew that he would overdo it. Just speaking slowly should be sufficient for an unsuspicious audience. 'But it's—of course everything's different now, but the Gottlieb I'm looking for is a poet.'

Another pause. He added, 'Er . . . was a poet.'

'Is a poet,' Sigrid said. 'Well, come in, please, Mr Tucci. He'll be astonished. At least, *I'm* astonished—hardly anybody knew his name, even Back Then.'

Score one, thanks to the Appalachian Vaults' monstrous library. Out of a personal crotchet, Tucci checked with the library each name that rumour brought him, and this time it had paid off. It never had before.

From here on out, it ought to be easy.

Nathan Gottlieb listened with such intensity that he reduced every other listener in Tucci's memory to little better than a catatonic. His regard made Tucci acutely aware of the several small lies upon which his story rested; and of the fact that Gottlieb was turning over and over in his hands the ritual can of beans Tucci had given Sigrid. In a while, perhaps Gottlieb would see that it had been made *after* the Day, and would draw the appropriate conclusions. Well, there was no help for it. Onward and upward.

Physically, Gottlieb was small and gaunt, nearly a foot

shorter than his wife, and rather swarthy. He looked as though, nude, you might be able to count all his bones. His somatotype suggested that he had not looked much plumper Back Then. But the body hardly mattered. What overwhelmed Tucci was the total, balanced alertness which informed its every muscle. Somehow, he kept talking.

'. . . Then when the word was brought in that there was not only a settlement here, but that a man named Nathan Gottlieb was some sort of key figure in it, it rang a bell. Sheer accident, since the name was common enough, and I'd never been much of a reader, either; but right away a line came to me and I couldn't get rid of it.'

'A line?'

'Yes. It goes: "And the duned gold clean drifted over the forelock of time." It had haunted me for years, and when I saw your name in the report, it came back, full force.'

'As a last line, it's a smasher,' Gottlieb said thoughtfully. 'Too bad the rest of the poem wasn't up to it. The trouble was, the minute I thought of it, I knew it was a last line, and I waited around for two years for a poem to come along to go with it. None ever did, so finally I constructed one synthetically, with the predictable bad results.'

'Nobody would ever know if you didn't tell them,' Tucci said with genuine warmth. He had, as a matter of fact, particularly admired that poem for the two whole days *since* he had first read it. 'In any event, I was sufficiently curious to don my parachute-silk underwear and come jolting down here to see if you were the same man as the one who wrote *The Coming-Forth*. I'm delighted to find that you are, but I'm overwhelmed to find you practising medicine as well! We're terribly short of physicians, and that happens to be my particular department. So, all in all, it's an incredible coincidence.'

'That's for true,' Gottlieb said, turning the can around in his hands. 'And there's still a part of it that I don't understand. Who is this "we" you mention?'

'Well. We just call it the Corporation now, since it's the last there is. Originally it was the Bryan Moving and Warehouse Corporation. If you lived in this area Back Then, you may remember our radio commercials on WASM-FM, for our

Appalachian Mountain Vaults. "Businessmen, what would happen to your records if some [unnamed] disaster struck? Put them in our mountain vaults, and die happy." That was the general pitch.'

'I remember. I didn't think you meant it.'

'We did. Oddly enough, a good many corporation executives took us at face value, too. When the Day came, of course, it was obvious that those papers were going to be no good to anybody. We threw them out and moved in ourselves, instead. We had thought that would be the most likely outcome and had been planning on it.'

Gottlieb nodded, and set the can on the floor between his feet, as though the question it had posed him was now answered. 'A sane procedure, that's for sure. Go on.'

'Well, since the Reds saturated Washington and the ten "hard" SAC sites out West, we appear to be the only such major survival project that came through. We've had better than a year to hear differently, and haven't heard a whisper. We know that there were several other industrial projects, but they were conducted in such secrecy that the enemy evidently concluded they were really military. We advertised ours on the radio and, like you, they didn't believe that we could be serious; or so we conclude.

'Now we're out and doing. We're trying to organize a— well, not a government exactly, since we don't want to make laws and we don't want to give orders—but at least the service functions of government, to help bring things into some kind of shape. Doing for people, in short, what they can't do for themselves, especially with things in their present shambles.'

'I see. And how do you profit?'

'Profit? In a great many ways, all intangible, but quite real. We attract specialists, which we need. This indebts the community to us and helps us manage it better. It's a large community now, about as big as New York and Pennsylvania combined, though it's shaped rather more like Texas. How many people are included I can't say; we may try to run a census in a year or so. Every specialist we recruit is, so to speak, an argument for reviving the institution of government.'

He paused, counted to ten, and added: 'I hope you are persuaded. Now that I've found you out, I'd be most reluctant to let you off the hook.'

Gottlieb said, 'I'm flattered, but I think you're making a mistake. I'm still only a poet, and as such, quite useless. I'm the world's worst medical man, even in these times.'

'Ah. Now that's something I've been burning to ask you. How *did* you get into this profession?'

'Deliberately. When Sigrid and I got alarmed by all those Berlin crises, and then the summit fiasco, and decided to start on a basement shelter out here, I had to start thinking of what I might be able to do if we did survive. There wasn't any way to make a living as a poet Back Then, either, but I'd always been able to turn a marginal dollar as a flack— you know, advertising copy, the trade papers, popular articles, ghosting speeches, all those dodges. But obviously there wasn't going to be anything doing in those lines in a primitive world.'

'So you chose medicine instead?' Tucci said. 'But why? Surely you had some training in it?'

'Some,' Gottlieb said. 'I was a medical laboratory technician for almost four years during the war—the Army's idea of what to do with a poet, I suppose. I did urinalyses, haemotology, blood chemistry, bacteriology, serology and so on; it involved some ward collecting too, so I got to see the patients, not just their body fluids. At first I did it all by the cookbook, but after a while I began to understand parts of it, and by God I seemed to have a feeling for it. I think most literary people might, if they'd just have been able to get rid of their notion that the humanities were superior to the sciences. You know, the pride of the professor of medieval Latin, really a desperately complicated language, is the fact that he couldn't "do" simple arithmetic. Hell, *anybody* can do arithmetic; my oldest daughter could "do" algebra at the age of nine, and I think she's a little retarded. Anyhow, that's why I chose medicine. Nowadays I understand why the real medicos had the intern system Back Then, though. There's nothing that turns you into a doctor like actually working at it, accumulating patient-hours and diagnostic experience.'

Tucci nodded abstractedly. 'What did you do for equipment, materia medica, and so on?'

'I don't have any equipment to speak of.   don't do even simple surgery; I have to be hyperconservative out of sheer ignorance—lancing a boil and installing a tube drain is as far in that line as I dare to go. And of course I've no electricity. I've been reading up on building a dam across my creek and winding a simple generator, but so far the proposition's been too much for me. I'm not at all handy, though I've been forced to try.

'As for supplies, that was easy—just a matter of knowing in advance what I hoped to do. I simply looted the local drug store the moment I came out of the hole, while everybody else who'd survived that long was busy loading up on canned goods and clothing and hardware. I was lucky that the whole dodge hadn't occurred to the pharmacist himself before the Day came, but it didn't. He hadn't even thought to dig himself a hole.

'I figured that anything I missed in the line of consumer goods would come my way later, if the doctor business paid off. And you'd be surprised how much of my medical knowledge comes from the package inserts the manufacturers used to include with the drugs. By believing a hundred per cent of the cautions and contra-indications, and maybe thirty per cent of the claims, I hardly ever poison a patient.'

'Hmmm,' Tucci said, suppressing a smile only by a heroic effort. 'How long will your supplies hold out?'

'Quite a while yet, I think. I'm being conservative there, too. In infectious cases, for instance, if I have a choice between an antibiotic and a synthetic—such as a sulpha drug—I use the antibiotic, since it has an expiration date and the sulpha drug doesn't. In another year I'm going to have to start doubling my antibiotic doses, but there's no use worrying about that—and I'll still have an ample stock of the synthetics.'

Tucci thought about it, conscientiously. It was a strange case, and he was not sure he liked it. Most of the few 'doctors' he had tracked down in the field were simple quacks, practising folk medicine or outright fakery to fill a gap left by the wholesale slaughter of specialists of all kinds, bar none—doctors, plumbers, farmers, you name it, it was almost extinct. Occasionally he had hit a survivor who had been a real physician Back Then; those had been great discoveries, and instantly recruited.

Gottlieb was neither one nor the other. He had no right to practise, by the old educational, lodge-brother or government standards. Yet obviously he was trying to do an honest job from a limited but real base of knowledge. The Vaults could use him, that was certain; but would they offer him the incentives they still reserved for the genuine, twenty-four-carat, pre-Day M.D.?

Tucci decided that they would have to. This was the first case of its kind, but it would not be the last. Sooner or later they would have to face up to it.

'I think we can solve at least some of your problems,' he said slowly. 'So far as shelf-life of antibiotics is concerned, we keep them in cold storage and have enough to last a good fifty years. We have electricity, and we can give you the use of a great deal of equipment, as you learn how to use it: for example, x-rays, fluoroscopes, ECGs, EEGs. I think we need you, Mr Gottlieb; and it's self-evident that you need us.'

Gottlieb shook his head, slowly, but not at all hesitantly. It took Tucci several seconds to register that that was what he was doing.

'No,' he said. 'You're very kind. But I'm afraid it doesn't attract me.'

The refusal was stunning, but Tucci was well accustomed to shocks. He drew a deep breath and came back fighting.

'For heaven's sake, why not? I don't like to be importunate, but you ought at least to think of what the other advantages might be. You could give up this marginal farming; we have a large enough community so we can leave that to experienced farmers. We use specialists in their specialities. You and your family could live in the Vaults, and breathe filtered air; that alone should run your children's life expectancy up by a decade or more. You know very well that the roentgen level in the open is still far above any trustable level, and if you came out of your hole in anything under three months—as I'm sure you did—you and your family have had your lifetime dose already. And, above all, you'd be able to practise medicine in a way that's quite impossible here, and help many more people than you're helping now.'

Gottlieb stood up. 'I don't doubt a word of that,' he said. 'The answer is still no. I could explain, but it would be faster in the long run if you first took a look at the kind of medicine I'm actually practising now. After that the explanations can be shorter, and probably more convincing.'

'Well . . . of course. It's your decision. I'll play it your way.'

'Good. I've still got three patients out there. I'm aware that you yourself are a bona-fide physician, Dr Tucci; you disguise it well, but not well enough. And you may not want me so badly when we're through.'

The first patient was a burly, bearded, twisted man with heavily calloused hands who might always have been a farmer; in any event, everybody in the field was some kind of farmer now. He stank mightily, and part of the stench seemed to Tucci to be alcohol. His troubles, which he explained surlily, were intimate.

'Before we go on, there's something we have to get clear, Mr Herwood,' Gottlieb told him, in what subsequently proved to be a set speech for new patients. 'I'm not a real doctor and I can't promise to help you. I know something about medicine and I'll do the best I can, as I see it. If it doesn't work, you don't pay me. Okay?'

'I don't give a damn,' the patient said. 'You do what you can, that's okay with me.'

'Good.' Gottlieb took a smear and rang a little hand bell on his desk. His fifteen-year-old daughter popped her head in through the swinging door that led to the kitchen, and Gottlieb handed her the slide.

'Check this for gram-positive diplococci,' he told her. She nodded and disappeared. Gottlieb filled in the time discussing payment with the patient. Herwood had, it turned out, a small case of anchovy fillets which he had liberated in the first days, when people were grabbing up anything, but nobody in his surviving family would eat them. Only tourists ate such stuff, not people.

The teenager pushed open the swinging door again. 'Positive,' she reported.

'Thanks, honey. Now, Mr Herwood, who's your contact?'

'Don't follow you.'

'Who'd you get this from?'

'I don't have to tell you that.'

'Of course you don't,' Gottlieb said. 'I don't have to treat you, either.'

Herwood squirmed in his straight-backed chair. He was obviously in considerable physical discomfort.

'You got no right to blackjack me,' he growled. 'I thought you was here to help people, not t' make trouble.'

'That's right. But I already told you. I'm not a real doctor. I never took the Hippocratic Oath and I'm not *bound* to help anybody. I make up my own mind about that. In this case, I want to see that woman, and if I don't get to see her, I don't treat you.'

'Well . . .' Herwood shifted again in the chair. 'All right, damn you. You got me over a barrel and you know it. I'll tell her to come in.'

'That's only a start,' Gottlieb said patiently. 'That leaves it up to her. Not good enough. I want to know her name, so if she doesn't show up for treatment here herself, I can do something about it.'

'You got not right.'

'I said so. But that's how it's going to be.'

The argument continued for several minutes more, but it was clear from the beginning that Gottlieb had won it . . . He gave the man an injection with matter-of-fact skill.

'That should start clearing up the trouble, but don't jump to conclusions when you begin to feel better. It'll be temporary. These things are stubborn. I'll need to see you three more times, at least. So don't forget to tell Gertie that I want to see her—and that I know who she is.'

Herwood left, muttering blackly. Gottlieb turned to his observer.

'I see a lot of that kind of thing, of course. I'm doing my best to stamp it out—which I might even be able to do in a population as small and isolated as this,' he said. 'I don't have any moral strictures on the subject, incidentally. The old codes are gone, and good riddance. In fact, without widespread promiscuity I can't see how we'll ever repopulate the world before we become extinct. But the diseases involved cost us an enormous sum in man-hours; and some of them have long latent periods that store up hell for the next generations. In *this* generation it's actually possible to wipe them out for good and all—and if it can be done, it should be done.'

'True,' Tucci said noncommitally. Thus far, he was baffled. Gottlieb had done nothing that he would not have done himself.

The next patient was also a man, shockingly plump, though as work-worn as his predecessor. Gottlieb greeted him with obvious affection. His symptoms made up an odd constellation, obviously meaningless to the patient himself; and after a while Tucci began to suspect that they meant very little to Gottlieb, either.

'How did that toe clear up?' Gottlieb was saying.

'All right, fine, Nat. It's just that I keep getting these boils and all, every time I hit a splinter, looks like. And lately I'm always thirsty, I can't seem to get enough water; and the more I drink the more it cuts into my sleep, so I'm tired all the time too. The same with food. People are talking—they say I eat like a pig, and it's true, and it shows. But I can't help it. A bad name to have, these days, and me with a family.'

'I know what you mean. But it's pretty indefinite now, Hal. We'll just have to wait and see what develops.' Gottlieb paused, and quite surreptitiously drew a deep, sad breath. 'Try to cut down a little on the intake; I'll give you *some* pills that will help you there, and some sleeping tablets. Don't hit the sleepy pills too hard, though.'

Payment was arranged. It was only nominal this time.

'Are you aware,' Tucci said when they were alone again, 'that you've just committed manslaughter—at the very least?'

'Sure I am,' Gottlieb said in a low voice. 'I told you you wouldn't like what you saw. The man's a new diabetic. There's nothing I can do for him, that's all.'

'Surely that's not so. I'm aware that you can't store insulin without any refrigeration, but surely there were some of the oral hypoglycaemic agents in the stock you found at the drug store—tolbutamide, carbutamide, chlorpropamide? If you don't recognize them by their old trade names, I can help you. In the meantime—well, at least you could have put the man on a rational diet.'

'I threw all those pills out,' Gottlieb said flatly. 'I don't treat diabetics. Period. You heard what I told Herwood: I never took the Hippocratic Oath, and I don't subscribe to it. In the present instance, we've having a hard enough time with all the new antisurvival mutations that have cropped up. I am not going to have any hand in preserving any of the old ones. If I ever hit a haemophiliac, the first thing I'll do is puncture him for a test—and forget to put a patch over the hole. Do you remember, Dr Tucci, that just before the Day there was a national society soliciting funds to look for a *cure* for haemophilia? When the Oath takes you that far, into saving lethal genes, either it's crazy or you are!'

'What would you have done with LaGuardia? Or Edison?' Tucci said evenly.

'Were they haemophiliacs?' Gottlieb said in astonishment.

'No. But they were diabetics. It's the same thing, in your universe.'

After a long time, Gottlieb said, almost to himself:

'I can't say. It isn't easy. Am I to save every lethal gene because I suspect that the man who carried it is a genius? That may have been worthwhile in the old days, when there were millions of diabetics. But now? The odds are all against it. I make harder decisions than that every day, Dr Tucci. Hal is no genius, but he's a friend of mine.'

'And so you've killed him.'

'Yes,' Gottlieb said stonily. 'He wasn't the first, and he won't be the last. There are not many people left in the world. We cannot tolerate lethal genes. The doctor who does may save one adult life—but he will kill hundreds of children. I won't do that. I never swore to preserve *every* life that was put in my hands, regardless of consequences. That's my curse . . . and my lever on the world.'

'In short, you have set yourself up to play God.'

'To *play* God?' Gottlieb said, 'Now you're talking non-sense. In this village, I *am* God . . . the only god that's left.'

The last patient was relatively commonplace. She had frequent, incapacitating headaches—and had earned them, for she had five children, two survivors and three new ones. While Gottlieb doled out aspirin to her (for which he charged a price so stiff—after all, there had been 15,670,944,200 aspirin tablets, approximately, in storage in the United States alone on the Day—that Tucci suspected it was intended to discourage a further visit), Tucci studied her fasciae and certain revealing tics, tremors, and failures of coordination which were more eloquent to him than anything she had said.

'There, that does it for today,' Gottlieb said. 'And with no more telephones, I'm almost never called out at night—never for anything trivial. I'll clean up and then we can talk further. You'll eat with us, of course. I have a canned Polish ham I've been saving for our first guest after the Day, and you've earned the right to be that guest.'

'I'd be honoured,' Tucci said. 'But first, one question. Have you a diagnosis for the last patient?'

'Oh, migraine, I suppose, though that's about as good as no diagnosis at all. Possibly menopausal—or maybe just copelessness. That's a disease I invented, but I see a lot of it. Why?'

'It's not copelessness. It's *glioblastoma multiforme*—a run-away malignant tumour of the brain. At the moment, that's only a provisional opinion, but I think exploration would confirm it. Aspirin won't last her long—and in the end, neither will morphine.'

'Well . . . I'm sorry. Annie's a warm and useful woman. But if you're right, that's that.'

'No. We have a treatment. We give the patient a boric acid injection—'

'Great God, 'Gottlieb said. 'The side effects must be fierce.'

'Yes, but if the patient is doomed anyhow? . . . After all, it's a little late in the day for gentleness.'

'Sorry. Go ahead. Why boric acid?'

'Boron won't ordinarily cross the blood-brain barrier,' Tucci explained. 'But it will concentrate in the tumour. Then we irradiate the whole brain with slow neutrons. The boron atoms split, emitting two quanta of gamma radiation per atom, and the tumour is destroyed. The fission fragments are nontoxic, and the neutrons don't harm the normal brain tissue. As for the secondary gammas, they can't get through more than a layer of tissue a single cell thick, so they never leave the tumour at all. It works very well—one of our inheritances from Back Then; a man named Lee Farr invented it.'

'Fantastic! If only poor Annie could have—' Gottlieb's mouth shut with the suddenness of a rabbit-trap, and his eyes began to narrow.

'Wait a minute,' he said. 'I'm being a little slow today. You said, "We *have* a treatment"—not "We *had*". What you mean me to understand is that you also have an atomic pile. That's the only possible source of slow neutrons.'

'Yes, we have one. It generates our electricity. It's clumsy and inefficient—but we've got it."

'All right,' Gottlieb said slowly. 'I'll go and change, and then we'll talk. But the purpose of my demonstration, Dr Tucci, is what I mean *you* to understand; and I wish you'd think about it a while, while I'm gone.'

The dinner was enormously pleasant; remarkably good even by the standards of the Vaults, and almost a unique experience in the field. Sigrid Gottlieb proved to be a witty table companion as well as an imaginative cook. Some of her shafts had barbs on them, for it was plain that she had overheard enough to divine Tucci's mission and had chosen to resent it. But these were not frequent enough or jagged enough to make Tucci believe that she was trying to make up her husband's mind for him. All well and good.

As for the children—the one prospect of the meal to which Tucci had not been looking forward, for as a bachelor he was categorically frightened of children—they were not even in evidence. They were fed in the kitchen by the eldest, the same girl who served as her father's laboratory technician.

There was no medical talk until dinner was over. Instead,

Gottlieb talked of poetry, with a curious mixture of intensity and wistfulness. This kept his guest a little on guard. Tucci knew more than most surviving Americans about the subject, he was sure, but far less than he had pretended to know.

Afterwards, however, Gottlieb got directly to the point. 'Any conclusions?' he said.

'A few,' Tucci said, refusing to be rushed. 'I'm still quite convinced that you'd be better off with us. I'm not terribly alarmed by your odd brand of medicine—and I don't know whether you were afraid I would be, or whether you meant me to be. In the Vaults, we sometimes have to short-circuit the Oath too, for similar reasons."

'Yes. I don't doubt that you do. The Oath was full of traps even Back Then,' Gottlieb said. 'But I hoped you'd see that there's more to my refusal to join you than that. To begin with Dr Tucci, *I don't like medicine;* so I don't care whether I could do it better in the Vaults, or not.'

'Oh? Well, then, you're quite right. I have somehow missed the point.'

'It's this. You say you are so well organized that you can use specialists as specialists, rather than requiring them to do their own subsistence farming, policing, and so on. But— could you use me *as a poet?* No, of course not. I'd have to practise medicine in the Vaults.

'But to what end? I really hate medicine. No, I shouldn't say that, but I'm certainly no fonder of it than I am of farming. I picked it as a profession because I knew it would be in demand after the Day—and that's all.

'In your Vaults I'd be an apprentice, to a trade I don't much like. After all, you're sure to have real M.D.s there, beginning with yourself. All of a sudden, I'd be nobody. And more than that, I'd lose control over policy—over the kind of medicine *I* think suitable for the world we live in now— which is the only aspect of my practice that does interest me. I don't want to save diabetics at your behest. I want to let them die, at mine. Call it playing God if you like, but nothing else makes sense to me now. Do you follow me?'

'I'm afraid I do. But go on anyhow.'

'There isn't much farther to go. I'm satisfied where I am— that's the essence of it. My patients may not be as well served by me as they think they are, but all the same they swear by me and come back for more. And I'm the only one of my kind in these parts. I don't have to farm my place to the last square inch because most of my fees are in kind—which is lucky, because I have a brown thumb. Sigrid is a little better with plants, but not much. I don't have to fortify it, or keep a twenty-four hour watch, because my patients wouldn't dare let anything happen to me. I don't need the medical facilities, the laboratories and equipment and so on that you're offering me, because I wouldn't know how to use them.

'So of course I'll keep on the way I've been going. What else could I do?'

'I'm sure,' Tucci said quietly, 'that you'd find plenty of time in the Vaults to practise poetry as well—and many people who value it. I doubt that you find either here.'

'What of it? Poetry has been a private art for a century, anyhow,' Gottlieb said bitterly. 'Certainly it's no art for a captive audience, which wants to pat the poet on the head because it thinks he's really valuable for something quite different, like writing advertising copy or practising medicine. I'm no longer interested in being tolerated. I wrote that off the day before the Day, and I'm not going back to it.'

'But surely if—'

'Listen to me, Dr Tucci,' Gottlieb said. 'If you are really running a sort of Institute for Advanced Study, and can promise me *all* my time to perfect myself as a poet, I'll go with you.'

'Obviously, I can't make such a promise.'

'Then I'll stay here. If I *have* to practise medicine, I may as well do so under conditions that I myself have laid down. Otherwise it would be too unrewarding for me to even tolerate. I wasn't really called to the vocation in the beginning, and there are times even now when it makes me quite sick. I can't help it; that's the way I am.'

'So we have nothing more to say to each other, it seems,' Tucci said. 'I'm truly sorry that it worked out this way. I had no idea that the question would even arise. But, in a way, I'm on your side. And besides, were you to come with us, you'd leave your own people without a doctor—and though many of them would doubtless follow you into our

115

community, there must be almost as many who wouldn't be able to do so.'

'That's true,' Gottlieb said, but he said it with a sort of convulsive shrug, as of a man who would dismiss the question and finds that it is not so easy as that. 'Thank you anyhow for the offer. I must say that I feel a little like a boy getting a diploma; all this fakery, and now . . . well; and it's run so late that you will have to spend the night with us. I don't want the Vaults to lose you on my account.'

'I'm grateful for all your thoughtfulness—yours, and your wife's as well.'

'Come back when you can,' Gottlieb said, 'and we'll talk poetry some more.'

'Thank you,' Tucci said inadequately. And that was all. He was guided up to bed, in the wake of a hurricane lamp.

Or was it all? In the insect-strident night, so full of reminders of how many birds had died after the Day, and how loaded with insensible latent death was the black air he breathed as he lay tense in the big cool bed, Tucci was visited by a whole procession of phantoms. Mostly they were images of himself. Some of them were dismissable as nightmares, surfacing during brief shallow naps from which he was awakened by convulsive starts that made his whole body leap against the sheets, as though his muscles were crazily trying to relax in a single bound the moment sleep freed them from the tensions of his cortex. He was used to that. It had been going on for years, and he had come to take it as a sign that though he was not yet deeply asleep, he would be shortly. In the meantime, the nightmares were fantastic and entertaining, not at all like the smothering, dread-loaded replays of the Day which woke him groaning and drenched with sweat many mornings just after dawn.

This time the starts did not presage deep sleep; instead, they left him wide awake and considering images of himself more disquieting than any he could remember having seen in dreams. One of the shallow nightmares was a fantasy of what might be going on in the Gottlieb's bedroom—evidently Sigrid had marked Tucci's celibate psyche more profoundly than he had realized—but from this he awoke suddenly to find himself staring at the invisible ceiling and straining to visualize, not the passages of love between the poet and his wife about which he had been dreaming, but what they might be saying about Dr Frank Tucci and his errand.

That errand hadn't looked hard to begin with. By all the rules of this kind of operation, Sigrid should now be bringing all possible feminine pressures to bear against Gottlieb's stand, and furthermore, she should be winning. After all, she would think first of her children, an argument of almost absolute potency compared with Gottlieb's abstract and selfish reasons for refusing to go to the Vaults. That was generally how it went.

But Gottlieb was not typical. He was, in fact, decidedly hard upon Tucci's image of himself. He was a quack, by his own admission, but he was not a charlatan—a distinction without a difference before the Day, but presently one of the highest importance, now that Tucci was forced to think about it. And in this cool darkness after the preliminary, complacent nightmares, Tucci was beginning to see himself with horror as a flipped coin. Not a quack, no. He was an authentic doctor with a pre-Day degree, nobody could take that away from him. But he *was* a charlatan, or at the very least a shill. When, after all, had Tucci last practised medicine? Not since the Day. Ever since, he had been scooting about the empty, menacingly quiet countryside on recruiting errands—practising trickery, not medicine.

Outside, a cloud rolled off the moon, and somewhere nearby a chorus of spring peepers began to sing: *Here we are, here we are, here we are* . . . They had been tadpoles in the mud when the hot water had come down toward the rivers in the spring floods; they might be bearing heavy radiation loads, but that was not something they were equipped to think about. They were celebrating only the eternal *now* in which they had become inch-long frogs, each with a St Andrew's cross upon its back . . . *Here we are, we made it* . . .

Here we are. We made it. Some are quacks, and nevertheless practise medicine as best they can. Some are flacks, for all their qualifications, and do nothing but shill . . . and burden the practitioners with hard decisions the Tuccis have become adroit at ducking. The Tuccis can always say that they were specialists before the Day—Tucci himself had been an eletrophysiologist, and most of the machines that he needed to continue down the road were still unavailable in the Vaults—but every doctor *begins* as a general practitioner. Was there any excuse, now, for shilling instead of practising?

The phantoms marched whitely across the ceiling. Their answer was *No*, and again, *No*.

In this world, in fact, Gottlieb was a doctor, and Dr Frank Tucci was not. That was the last nightmare of all.

He was ruminatively strapping his gear onto the baggage rack of the scooter, very early the next morning, when he heard the screen door bang and looked up to see Gottlieb coming down the front path towards him. There were, he saw for the first time, tall lilacs and lilies of the valley blooming all around the sides of the house. It was hard to believe that the world had ended, even here in Gottlieb's hollow. He straightened painfully in the bullet-proof suit and hoisted his bubble goggles.

'Nice of you', he said. 'But you really needn't have seen me off. Keeping doctor's hours, you need all the sleep you can store up.'

'Oh sure,' Gottlieb said abstractedly. He leaned on the sagging gate. 'But I wanted to talk to you. I had some trouble sleeping—I was thinking—I woke up this morning on the floor, and that hasn't happened to me since just before my final exams. If you've got a minute—'

'Of course. Certainly. But I'd like to get on the road before too long, to skip some of the heat of the day. This helmet absolutely fries my brains when the sun is high.'

'Sure, I only wanted to say—I've changed my mind.'

'Well. *That* was worth waiting for.' Tucci took the helmet off and dropped the goggles carefully into it. 'I hope you won't mind if I'm in a hurry, or rather, if *we're* in a hurry. We'll have trucks down here for you in about a week at the latest; it takes a while to get a convoy organized. We'll also send a bus, since I think you'll find that about half your patients will want to follow you, once you've explained the proposition to them.'

'That'll cost a lot of petrol,' Gottlieb said. He seemed embarrassed and disturbed.

Tucci waited a moment, and then said, very gently: 'If you don't mind, Mr Gottlieb, would you tell me why you reversed yourself? I'd about given up.'

'It's my own fault,' Gottlieb broke out, in a transport of anger. 'I must have given that speech about the Hippocratic Oath two thousand times in the last year or so. I never took the Oath, that's a fact, and I don't believe in it. But . . . you said I'd be able to treat more patients, and treat them better, if I went to work for you. That's been on my mind all night. And I can't get away from it. It began to look to me as though a man can't be just half a doctor, whether that's all he wants or not. And I did go into this doctor business by my own choice.'

He scuffed at the foot of the gate with one broganed toe, as though he might kick it if no one were watching him.

'So there I am. I have to go with you—and never mind that I'm giving up everything I've won so far—and a lot more that I hoped for. I may stop hating you five or ten years from now. But I could have spared myself, if I hadn't been so superior about Hippocrates all this time and just minded my own business.'

'The oath that you don't take,' Tucci agreed, resuming his goggles and helmet, 'is often more binding than the one you do.'

He stamped on the kick starter. Miraculously, the battered old Lambretta spat and began to snarl on the first try. Gottlieb stepped back, with a gesture of farewell. At the last moment, however, something else seemed to occur to him.

'Dr Tucci!' he shouted above the noise of the one-lung engine.

'Yes? Better make it loud, Mr Gottlieb—I'm almost deaf aboard this thing.'

'It's not "the forelock of time", you know,' Gottlieb said. He did not seem to be yelling, but Tucci could hear him quite plainly. 'The word in the poem is "forepaws".'

Tucci nodded gravely, glad that the helmet and goggles could be counted on to mask his expression, and put the scooter in gear. As he tooled off up the hill, his methodical mind began to chew slowly, gently, inexorably upon the question of who had been manipulating whom.

He knew that it would be a good many years before he had an answer.

Takeover Bid

John Baxter

John Baxter is a young Australian writer whose stories first appeared
in British and American magazines in the early Sixties. He has
published one novel, *The God Killers,* and edited two short story
collections of *Australian Science Fiction* which have become
pioneering works in the field. He left Australia for England in 1970,
and has since concentrated exclusively on writing for and about
the cinema. He has produced a number of excellent books on the
subject, of which the most recent has been a critical biography of
director Ken Russell.

Australia has always been a rather privileged nation. In TAKEOVER
BID Baxter thoughtfully projects some aspects of its way of life into
the not too distant future—with some intriguing results.

To set out on a journey at evening is an experience that has
always pleased me. There is a sense of stealing a march on
your fellows, of having broken the tyranny of the clock and
struck out on your own. So when it became evident on that
cold winter's afternoon that I would have to go to Crosswind
headquarters I bitched a little—it was expected—but
inwardly I rather looked forward to the rush trip. Even with
priority it wasn't possible to get a seat on any westbound jet
and I knew I would have to drive the three thousand odd
kilometres, but as I eased the car out of the office tube and

121

into the main traffic flow I felt more at ease than I had all week.

Lying back as the autopilot threaded me through the river of cars I had time to look around for the first time that day. There was a sunset over the city, one of those huge violet and orange affairs that one gets in Australia when the air is cold and clear. They're a good crowd-pleaser and the weather-control boys turn them on regularly, but I've never liked them. They have the look of scars and wounds, and their colours are livid rather than vivid. It's hardly the sort of thing one mentions in family therapy, but I've always looked on sunsets as a kind of omen, a forecast of trouble to come. In this case my instincts were right.

It took an hour to get out of the city proper and into the mountains, so night had fallen by the time I hit the main highway and set out to chase the sun. Behind me the city of Greater Sydney sprawled in a net of lights across the dark encroachment of the harbour. Along the foreshores, among the canyons of the city streets, out in the suburbs that covered the whole coastal plain, people were getting ready to eat, turning on their 3V sets, settling down for a quiet evening, while I scurried off into the interior on a task that would affect every one of them in some way or other. Seven million people in Sydney, another twenty-eight million in the rest of Australia, and unwittingly I held the fate of them all in my hands.

Now that I was locked on to the highway I began, as usual, to feel bored. Outside the dome the luminescent ribbon of roadway unwound at a steady three hundred kilometres per hour. A few cars flicked by going in the opposite direction and, looking back, I could see others following me at varying distances. Beyond the limits of the road there were probably houses, certainly farms, but if there were people anywhere around me I was unaware of them. The clear bubble of the car isolated me completely. There was not even any real contact with the road. The air cushion kept the car suspended just above the surface and the connection between the magnetized strip on which I was locked and the steering apparatus was electric and invisible.

Forced in on myself I became more acutely aware of my

sensations. Comfort: certainly; the car was custom built. Warmth; the heater was perfect. But hunger—this was one problem that the car would not solve for me. I poked around in the various recesses, but except for a few scraps of chocolate already turning white with age there seemed to be nothing in the car that was even remotely edible. I picked up the phone and punched the office number. Seconds later the pert face of the night receptionist floated on to the screen.

'Civil Aviation. Can I help you?' She looked closer. 'Oh, Mr Fraser.'

'Has Miss Freeman left yet?'

'I'm not sure. Wait, I'll try your office.'

There was a blip and the screen cleared to show Ilona Freeman's face. She smiled.

'Hi, Bill. What did you forget?'

'Food?'

'Try your case.'

I opened my satchel. Inside, along with the papers, were three thin plastic packs.

'Remind me to raise your salary,' I said.

'I'll remember that.'

'Anything come in since I left?'

'Only that he's continuing to improve. He hasn't woken yet—or he hadn't at seven anyway.'

'Right. See you Thursday.'

I cut off, took out one of the plastic packs and tore off the sealer strip. Steam and savoury odours puffed out. I folded the sides down and they locked into the shape of a shallow dish. Chicken Cacciatore with new potatoes and green peas. One of the others would hold lemon gelati; Ilona knew my tastes well enough. But I was puzzled by the third. I looked inside. Packed into the small space was the oddest assortment of fruits I had ever seen—or not seen; most of them were completely unknown to me. Long purple things like peapods, something that might have been a banana if it hadn't been pastel pink; berries in green, blue, white and magenta. The pack, like all the others, was marked EXPORT ONLY. Apparently the Assistant Director of Civil Aviation had made the unofficial V.I.P. list. Australia's export trade in food was its biggest money-spinner and the bureau guarded it jealously. It gave me an obscure satisfaction to know that the food I was despatching was to stay in the country rather than be sold to some well-to-do gourmand in Italy or France.

As I tucked into dinner the amusing side of the situation made me smile. Australia selling food to Europe? In the Fifties the idea of Australia exporting anything but the most basic raw materials—wool, wheat, steel—would have been ridiculous. Nobody had bargained for the immense expansion that would follow the opening up of Australia to Asian immigrants and the impetus this would give to the development of the inland desert. Up to 1970, settlement was in most cases confined to a narrow strip of coastline seldom more than a hundred and fifty kilometres wide. Now, in 1994, there were market gardens in the far west where once a farmer had been lucky to graze one sheep to the hectare, and they were well on the way to planting wheat where Lake Eyre had once turned a white mirror of dried salt to the sun.

The increased productivity had had its effect on the national character too. For decades Australia had lived on its muscles, trying to make up for its economic deficiencies by victories on other fronts. Australian sportsmen, artists and writers were world famous. It was fashionable in Europe and America to admire Australia, to fly in and spend a few weeks on air-conditioned safari into the desert, but like all fashions this was shallow. Beneath the veneer was a contempt. Australia had the status of a football scholar, a nation that had nothing but brute strength and native cunning to pit against the wealth and sophistication of its older fellows. So, when it suddenly fell heir to wealth, its first impulse was to strive with other countries for the goals that mattered: the cure for cancer, longevity, space. And so it had happened that in 1993 an Australian scientist had stumbled on the force field and, almost by accident, given mankind the stars.

Or at least so it had seemed at first. Out in the desert, somewhere north of Capricorn, a research station had been set up and the first cautious experiments made. A generator encapsulated itself in a force field that made an enclosure better, stronger, than the finest natural materials in existence. Such a bubble, stressed in a certain way, tended to disappear.

After a few experiments radio telescopes on the U.S. space station reported that there were odd objects receding from the earth at incredible speeds. More bubbles were sent out and tracked. Apparently such a field, being a perfect reflector, supplied nothing for the forces of space to hold on to. Like an orange seed squeezed between thumb and finger, it stored up the energy applied to it and then suddenly skidded out from between the two opposing forces at a speed that was dangerously close to that of light.

After three months they managed to find a way to make the acceleration gradual and to track and retrieve the force field bubbles. One was brought back. A rat was sent out and retrieved, then a chimpanzee. Then they sent a man. On 7 June 1994, Colonel Peter Chart, R.A.A.F., had set off along the track taken by other bubbles. And had returned. Or at least his body had. His mind seemed somehow to have been lost among the empty reaches of space. He had been taken from the bubble completely catatonic and had remained that way for three weeks. Then, on 2 July, he had quietly risen from his bed, killed a guard and run off into the desert. Nobody knew why, nobody knew how—but now they had found him and it was my responsibility as leader of the project to find out.

I would have worried about it all night, but the almost imperceptible hum of the motor lulled me into a doze. Occasionally I would wake when a car went by on the other lane, but by the time I had turned my head it was nothing but a glow disappearing in the distance behind me. Once—it must have been around 3 a.m., I suppose—I woke again and watched rather muzzily as a string of automatic ore-carriers roared past, their huge hoppers piled with chunks of rock torn from the mines of the Pilbara, farther north. The rust stains on those jagged nuggets were like dried blood—another omen, if I had cared to consider it such.

When I woke the sun was well up and my destination close. All around from horizon to horizon there was only desert. Sand, rocks and stunted spinifex. It was a desolate place, but that was why we had chosen it. A particular rock formation flashed past, reminding me to switch to manual control. A few minutes later I slowed down and turned off the highway where a sign saying MAXWELL DOWNS EXPERIMENTAL CATTLE BREEDING STATION pointed up a rough track. The surface was loose and as I switched the air cushion to maximum lift, a cloud of red dust rose in the air. Nobody could be unaware that I was coming.

I nosed along the track as fast as the surface allowed until it petered out at an old artesian well some fifteen kilometres from the highway. The mill turned desultorily in the hot breeze and a wheezing old pump brought up from the underground lakes a trickle of water as brackish and undrinkable as blood. There was no sound save the clanking of the pump and the splash of water. I waited. A few moments later the old concrete slab on which the pump-house had once rested tilted slowly and opened a dark cavern in the earth. I guided the car down the ramp and into the headquarters of Operation Crosswind.

All the Project's H.Q. was underground, though a few offices, my own included, had windows on to the desert, an executive amenity that we seldom used. At the bottom of the shaft I got out of the car and, as the garager trundled it off, looked up at the square of blue-white sky above. The heat was intense and enervating. My skin prickled and contracted under its dryness, and I was glad when the walkway carried me down into the air-conditioned part.

Col Talura was waiting for me at the other end. Col—for Colemara. His grandfather had fought with Nemarluk in the Kimberleys and smeared his body with the kidney fat of many white men. Col was a fully initiated member of the Arunta. I had seen his scars. He was also one of the first Aborigines to hold a Ph.D. and a B.Sc. Perhaps this contrast was the reason I had chosen him as my right-hand man. His combination of sophistication and allegiance to the old tribal ways made him a person worth studying. It interested me to see how he would react to this, his first crisis. However, there was not time for character analysis at the moment. We shook hands sketchily.

'Sorry I couldn't meet you,' he said. 'I just got back from the hospital this minute.'

'How is he?'

'Damned if I know. Physically he's in poor shape but no

danger. Mentally . . . well, the doctor can tell you better than I can. Want to go to the hospital?'

We stepped on to another walkway. Col took a folio of papers from under his arm.

'You'd better look through these,' he said. 'They're the search team's reports.'

I leafed through the papers: maps marked with search patterns and in one spot a triumphal cross marking where Chart had been found. It was a good thirty kilometres from the base, I noticed. Records of radio messages, various reports —and a few photographs. The first showed a plain littered with wind-smoothed rocks. 'Gibber country' the natives call it.

'This where they found him?' I asked.

Col nodded. 'Bad country,' he said. 'Almost impossible to search.'

I went through the other photographs. A shot of a car, abandoned. Only a service jeep; nothing but a power unit, a seat and a hemispherical dome. The dome was folded back. I looked at the next photograph. It was a shock.

'My God!'

Col didn't turn. He knew what I was looking at.

'A mess, isn't he? Third degree burns, exposure, thirst— nasty.'

'He's naked.'

'That's how we found him. It's not unusual. People lost in the desert often get delirious and throw off their clothes. I don't know how he survived in his condition. It's been as hot as this for weeks.'

The walkway ended at the door of the hospital. The doctor was waiting there to meet us.

'How is he?' I asked.

'A mess. But he should pull through.'

'Can I see him?'

'If you like. But he can't talk. We've got him in a skin tank.'

We walked down a corridor and he led us into the room where Chart was. The whole chamber was bathed in blue luminescence. On the walls, ripples of light flowed endlessly in the blueness. The room contained only the tank, a long coffin-like plastic bath connected to quietly humming machinery. In it a man floated. This was neither the Peter Chart I had known six months ago nor the seared animal of the photograph, but another composite half-formed creature. The skin over his whole body was soft and pink like that of a child. Every line and wrinkle had been smoothed out. Above the mask the man's eyes were closed in sleep.

I turned to the doctor. There was no real need to whisper, but I had the feeling that to talk loudly in here would somehow disturb the delicate balance in which Chart was held.

'Are you taking brain readings?' I asked.

He moved to a small machine connected to the side of the tank near Chart's head. A wire connected it to two electrodes taped to his forehead. The doctor cranked the recorder on the side and a slip of paper slid up from the interior of the machine. He handed it to me.

'This is the complete record since he came in.'

I examined the graph on the sheet. Something about it was odd but I wasn't sure what. Then I realized. There was an unnatural evenness about the pattern. Catatonics have an especially complicated brain pattern. Physically they are motionless but subconsciously their brains remain active, endlessly considering the problem that has forced them to shut down their bodies in protest. Yet Chart's mind was just as inactive as his body. There was nothing on the graph but the mumble of a brain carrying on natural functions. Only in one place was there a variation. The graph suddenly leaped almost off the scale and for a centimetre or so moved crazily about before settling down again. This must have been the period immediately before Chart's sudden flight. I didn't mention it until we were outside in the corridor again.

Then I said, 'How did it happen?'

The doctor scratched his ear nervously.

'It's my fault,' he said, 'though I must say I think anybody would have done the same thing in the circumstances. After he'd been in a coma for a few days and all the usual tests had been made, we left him under minimum security: a nurse to see to the feeding and such, and a guard just in case something happened. On the night he escaped the girl went out as usual about 2 a.m. to refill the nutrient bottle. Chart hadn't changed at all during the day. As you can see from the graph he was completely unconscious right up to then. Yet suddenly he leapt out of coma into instant life, strangled the guard with his bare hands, sneaked out of the hospital and stole a car. Medically, it's impossible—but he did it.'

'Is there any possible explanation that might cover the situation?' Col asked. 'It doesn't matter how far-fetched it is, just so long as it fits.'

The doctor looked more confused.

'I wish it was that easy. As far as I can see, we've tried everything that might logically have caused this particular situation, and none of them fit. Human beings aren't as complex as you might think. Of course, you sometimes get bizarre symptoms for fairly simple diseases, but as a rule the cause and effect are fairly easy to link up. But this . . . I mean, the symptoms and the possible causes aren't even of the same order!'

I chewed this over.

'So what it amounts to,' I said, 'is that Chart is suffering from some unknown mental aberration presumably caused by his experiences on the flight.'

'Well, no', he said uneasily. 'That's the odd thing. No matter how basic the trauma is, we could have detected it. We tested Chart for all expected troubles. The isolation, the silence, the recirculated air—none of them could possibly have affected him. His mind was incapable of reacting to any of them in this particular way. If you like, he was immune to neurosis. There *are* things he could have reacted to, of course, but none of them occurred during the flight. We've got a complete brain-wave record of the whole period. *Nothing* happened to him in the bubble.'

'If it's not mental, then how about physical? Some new virus . . .'

'No, that's impossible too. The field would keep out everything that might conceivably have affected him. He was completely insulated. Anyway, the infection effects would have registered in the brain pattern.'

So it wasn't physical and it wasn't mental—or at least not physical or mental in the sense that we were used to.

We were at a dead end. There was only one thing to do—
test. We began next day.

It isn't hard to set up a force field. It needs a few thousand
kilowatts of power and something to perch your projector on,
otherwise you find a quantity of floor included in the field.
Once the field is formed it's impervious to anything from
gamma rays to a punch from a human fist. Nothing hitting
the field can penetrate it, not even sub-atomic particles.
This is what makes it particularly good for space flight.
The radiation hazard ceases to exist. For tests, we had set
up the usual projector complex, a framework rather like
an old-fashioned automobile chassis, on top of a shaft. In
the centre, directly over the shaft, was the projector, in
front of it the pilot's seat and console, and behind the
air-recirculating equipment. The only new feature was a
two-way TV link, the cable of which ran down the support
shaft. Ordinarily the shaft was retracted by the pilot before
launching, allowing the field to complete itself, but in this
case we needed some type of observing mechanism. The
seal was tight. Except for the link the test pilot was just as
Chart had been.

After the field had been turned on and the link tested
there was nothing to do but wait. For the first few days
I spent most of my time in the control bay watching the
image of Tevis, the test pilot, on the monitor screen, but
soon the strain began to tell and I forced myself away from
the project. Col Talura felt the same way, and so we spent
a few days on the surface hunting small game and generally
puttering about in the desert. On one of these trips, hunting
farther south than I had ever been before, I was surprised
to see the brown surface of the Nullabor give way without
warning to an area of dead black that stretched as far as
I could see. It was a huge and static shadow mantling the
brown earth, a great inkblot on creation. Col saw my
surprise.

'Woomera,' he explained, pointing to the south.

I looked through the binoculars and saw the distant glint
of metal. Another Common Europe rocket, no doubt, on
its way to Station I or perhaps farther out.

'What's all this, then?' I asked, indicating the blackness.

Col's face betrayed his resentment.

'Security,' he explained. 'They cleared the whole area for eighty kilometres around and sprayed it with a metallic solution. It gives Woomera a sort of radar mirror, a neutral surface that shows up anything that moves on it. Their scopes can pick up anything that walks out on to that area. And there's no cover. They ground up the rocks and cleared every bit of vegetation.'

'Well, it's their land,' I said, swinging the 'copter around to avoid the area.

Col's reaction was unexpected. 'Why? We were here first, weren't we?'

Whether he meant Australians in general or his own people in particular I didn't know, though I suspected the latter.

'There's the treaty . . .'

Col consigned the treaty and the men who had made it to eternal damnation in a few Arunta phrases and I let the matter drop, making, however, a mental note to keep an eye on Col's oversensitive nationalism. In our business it didn't pay to be careless of politics.

The whole question of Woomera came to a head some days later. Early in the morning Col stormed into my office and dropped a pea-sized object on to the desk. I squinted at it, a tiny pearl of intertwined wires around a central red crystal—a bugging device.

'Where was this planted?' I asked.

'It wasn't, luckily. We'd just finished a fresh wall sealer job in the main lounge when one of the boys hit the wrong button and knocked off a patch. This was in the wet plastic.'

'Why did the main lounge need a new plas job?'

Col scowled. 'I'm way ahead of you. The old wall was discoloured by fumes; the fumes came from a coffee machine that was slightly miswired; a man named Bronski did the wiring . . .'

'And he went A.W.O.L. some weeks ago. These boys are experts.'

I looked at the tiny bug again. Naturally there were no markings but the thing reeked of E.L.D.O. We had, I thought, effectively prevented the Russians and the Chinese from penetrating Crosswind, but there was something particularly irksome about being spied on by supposed allies.

Col voiced my conclusion. 'Woomera?' he asked.

I was about to say 'Where else?' when the desk plate lit up.

'A Colonel Thompson to see you.'

'Thompson?'

'From Woomera.'

Col and I exchanged glances.

'Tell him to wait,' I said, 'and give me the latest Woomera staff list.'

The plate cleared and a string of names began to move across it.

EUROPEAN LAUNCHER DEVELOPMENT ORGANIZATION

Head: General Sir Gordon Glenwright
Deputy: General Sir Stuart Millar

Thompson's name appeared halfway through the first twenty names:

2/ic Security: Colonel Sanchez Thompson

'A minor V.I.P.,' Col said. 'What does he want?'

'There's one way to find out.' I told the secretary to let him in.

It cannot be said too often that appearances are deceptive. This is especially true in intelligence work. The public image of the spy is a very complete and detailed one, so much so that one is almost obliged to pattern real spies along the complete opposite of the popular idea. Sanchez Thompson seemed almost to go too far. He was so obviously not a spy that he could hardly have been anything else. He stuttered. He bit his fingernails. He dressed without style or taste. I had never thought that the mass-produced British army officer's uniform could look badly cut, but on him it seemed almost scarecrowish. However, his eyes missed nothing, and when he had something important to say he never stuttered. I wasted no time with amenities. Almost before he had sat down I pushed the bug across the desk towards him.

'Yours, I think.'

He picked it up unsmilingly and held it as I had earlier between thumb and forefinger.

'A beautiful piece of work,' he said.

'And very useful.'

'They fill in the gaps—the sort of thing we can't get in . . . other ways.'

'Meaning spies?' Col snapped. I was surprised at his tone. Apparently his emotions ran closer to the surface than I had guessed.

Thompson pursed his lips and glanced at me. I said nothing. He looked back to Col.

'Meaning spies,' he agreed.

Col's palm slammed down on the desk-top.

'Well, you damned little peeping tom. What business is it of yours what we do here? Why don't you keep your nose out of our business and get back where you came from. We don't want you.'

Thompson wilted under the tirade. He was a diplomat. Verbal slanging wasn't in his line.

'We have an agreement . . .' he said weakly.

'An agreement thirty-five years old! An agreement that you've abused ever since you got it. Just like the Americans up north. You're nothing but . . .'

I held up my hand. 'Col . . .'

'Interfering little . . .'

'*Col!*'

He lapsed into sullen silence.

'You're probably interested in the tests we're running, Colonel,' I said. 'Would you care to see the set-up?'

Col seemed hardly to believe his ears. We left him sitting in the office, motionless. I suppose he thought I was selling him and the whole project down the river, but the pattern wasn't hard to see. There was little about Crosswind that E.L.D.O. didn't know. Thompson's casual visit proved that. I wondered what errand he had come on.

'I suppose you have something to tell me,' I said as we moved towards the test area.

He reached into his pocket and handed me a sheet of paper. I glanced through it. It was a legal opinion signed by one of the most eminent international jurists; even I knew his name, though the law was a closed book to me. Briefly it suggested that, should the situation ever come to a head, it seemed likely that E.L.D.O. could take over Crosswind under its agreement with the Australian government, as any experimental work in connection with spaceflight in this country should be done under E.L.D.O. auspices.

'Experimental work,' I said. 'But what if we can make this thing work? You would be shut out then, wouldn't you?'

'Indeed we would, Mr Fraser—if it worked.'

So it seemed that, unless I was very lucky, I would be working for Common Europe before very long, taking my orders from Paris. And Washington, of course. Col had been right there. The difference in greed between the Europeans and the Americans was tiny. Both had approached the situation in the same way back in the Fifties. With E.L.D.O. —the European consortium set up in 1960 to try and break the American domination of space research—it had been, 'Let us use your outback for test firings and we'll give you prestige.' With the U.S., it had been, 'Give us an area to build a military base and we'll give you protection.' In the troubled days of the mid-century, Australia had desperately wanted prestige and protection, but more, it had wanted the feeling of 'belonging,' of being a 'power'. The politicians had handed out land by the thousands of hectares to the Americans at North West Cape and given the Europeans almost complete control of Woomera. A few decades later they saw their mistake, but it was too late to back out then.

I passed Thompson through the guard, and we walked together towards the huge globe that filled the bay. Caught and thrown back by the perfect reflective power of the field, our images, bent and elongated, looked back at us like wry caricatures.

'It's a fascinating thing,' Thompson said. 'I look forward to working on it.'

I ignored the remark and walked over to where a group of technicians were clustered around the TV monitor. Tevis, the test pilot, was talking, reeling off a string of figures to one of the controllers. He looked drawn but healthy. There was no sign of any ill effects, nor of the symptoms Chart had exhibited. I checked my watch. He had been in the field seven hours longer than Chart.

'How is he?' I asked the doctor.

'Seems perfectly well. The brain-wave pattern is normal.'

I thought about it for a moment. Then I said, 'Right—turn it off.'

There was a descending whine as the generators cut out. The field shimmered and then faded slowly into invisibility. From the top of the shaft Tevis looked down, blinking in the bright light of the bay.

There was nothing else to be done at the test site so we caught the walkway that led back to the office. On the way I asked the inevitable question.

'How much time do we have?'

Thompson shrugged. 'It's not up to me, Mr Fraser. If I could take your acceptance back with me . . .'

'No chance. I'll have to take this up with my superiors in Sydney and Canberra.'

'There won't be any need,' Thompson said. 'We've already arranged that. You should get confirmation in a few hours.'

My first impulse was to hit him and wipe that self-satisfied look from his face, but the urge passed. There was nothing to be gained from violence.

'Well,' I said, 'it seems you've thought of everything. What are your orders . . . sir.'

The E.L.D.O. man looked embarrassed for the second time that day.

'You're taking the wrong attitude, Mr Fraser. There's nothing personal in this. We've both been in this game for a long time. It's a business, nothing more. Can we afford to have feelings?'

I wasn't in the mood for a discussion of ethics, or for that matter any sort of discussion.

'What about tomorrow?' I said.

'If you like,' Thompson said. 'And I hope you can look at things a little clearer then.'

When I got back to the office Col was still there. My surprise must have been obvious because he smiled.

'I gather you expected me to be gone,' he said.

I sat down heavily. 'Well, you must admit it was a fair assumption.'

'You don't give me credit for much intelligence, do you? Would *you* have run away?'

'No, but . . .' I stopped.

Col jumped on my words.

'But you're not an Abo? I thought that was it!'

Coming so close on the conversation with Thompson his remark took me off guard. I tried to retrieve the situation.

'Next you'll tell me I'm prejudiced. You know me better than that, Col.'

'Aren't you prejudiced, Bill?'

'Don't be absurd.'

'It's not as ridiculous as you think,' Col said. 'Why did you pick me for this job? Not because of my qualifications —there were plenty of white men with the same degrees. Not because I needed it—there's no shortage of work these days. No—you chose me because I'm black—an Aboriginal —an Abo. You give it away every time you look at me.'

Abruptly I turned my chair to face the window and, for some reason that even now I find hard to fathom, hit the button to clear it for the first time in years. The afternoon sunlight streamed in off the desert, blindingly clear. But it was not only the sun that made my face burn.

'Why bring all this up now?' I said.

'It has to be discussed some time.'

I thought about it for a moment. Then I said, 'I don't deny the fact that you weren't white influenced me, but it wasn't a matter of prejudice.'

'Don't fool yourself, Bill. It was. You were being charitable. Pity is just as much prejudice as hate, you know. You're always talking about the old days when Australia was a country to be patronized. Don't you see you're patronizing me?'

Just then, I wanted nothing more than to have that conversation end as quickly as possible.

'Well, you won't have to put up with it much longer,' I said. 'Crosswind is finished. Tomorrow E.L.D.O. moves in.'

Col was surprisingly calm.

'I gathered that,' he said.

'It had to come. We were lucky to get away with it this long.'

'*Did* it have to come?' Col said. 'Or do you mean you're glad it came?'

I heard the door close, but I didn't turn around. I was still there, looking out over the desert, when night began to close in.

For the next few hours I went through the motions of cleaning up the office. The whole thing had seemed very easy when Thompson and I had discussed it—just a simple matter of transferring power from one person to another.

But Col had disturbed me. Part of his outburst had been sheer bad temper, no doubt, but that still left a considerable residue of fact. He was right about a number of things. My hiring him for the job had been partly influenced by the fact that he was an Aboriginal. At the time I had rationalized it as an interest in his particular attitude to the work, but it was becoming clear that there was more to it than that. I was seeing my motives become more and more obvious as the evasions covering them were drained away. It was less than edifying.

As for giving up Crosswind, I had to admit that the takeover by E.L.D.O. had seemed to lift a weight from my shoulders. For the past two years I had worked hard on the project, and worked well too, I thought. There had been little time to think about the imponderables such as loyalty. Did I care about the project? Or was it just the interest in a job to be done? I decided to sleep on it. No doubt I would have woken in the morning with the whole thing carefully rationalized in my mind and the depths of character Col had revealed all covered up again, but things were destined to be different.

About 3 a.m. I woke to the supremely irritating screech of the bonephone I always wore when on call. The tiny alarm wedged against my mastoid bone jabbed me awake in a second. I ripped the thing off and groped for the communicator switch. It was Col.

'Chart's gone again,' he said. 'Out into the desert.'

'Gone? I thought he was still in the tank.'

'He was, but he broke out and rigged up a booby trap with the fluid and some of the wiring. When the guards came in they got a shock that knocked them unconscious.'

'How long has he been gone?'

'Two hours maybe.'

Still half asleep I struggled into my clothes and stumbled along the corridors to the main garage. All the doors of the big hangar were open and the damp chill of the desert night made the air freezing. Breathing it was like inhaling icy water. Streams of vapour puffed from the nostrils and every conversation was marked by the white fog. Col had already organized search parties and the bay was full of the sound of motors as the two-man cars revved up and climbed the ramps into the starless night. I could see their searchlights patching the desert all around. I watched as Col sent out the last parties.

'Want to go?' he asked.

I shook my head. With my meagre knowledge of the desert there was little I could do.

'Well, one of the crews is short a man,' Col said. 'I was thinking . . .'

'You go,' I said. 'I wouldn't be much use to you.'

A minute later the last ship slid up the ramp and left me alone in the hangar.

Someone had spread an ordnance map on the floor. I walked over and looked down at it. It was incomprehensible to me, but that was probably my drowsiness. I wondered where Chart was; where a man could go in the desert. What could he hope to find among the rocks and sand? There were no towns, no oases, no wells. Most of the map mirrored this aridity. It was brown, plain and unrelieved—except, I noticed, for a web of thin black lines that covered it like the work of an industrious spider. Out of curiosity I checked the key—odd to think that if the map had faced the other way I wouldn't have bothered—and saw that they were magnetic field lines graphed during the last I.G.Y. by a team of trivia-minded Belgians. The lines wandered in delicate curves over the desert, almost always singly but sometimes running parallel and occasionally congregating into huge knots marking areas of particular magnetic density.

There were two knots like that in our vicinity. On one of them somebody had scrawled an X in blue pencil. It came to me I had seen this map before. The X marked the spot where Chart had been found the first time.

And if that knot of lines coincided with the place he had run to the first time . . .

Outside it was still dark, but a false dawn lighted the east with a pale glow. Luckily there were still cars available. I climbed into one and set out to the west, my shadow racing before me like a long finger.

It took me less than half an hour to reach the place I had marked on the map; the second knot of magnetic lines, almost identical with the one on which Chart had been found last time. The sun was well up by the time I killed the power and settled quietly on to the top of a low hill that seemed almost a marker. I got out. There was no movement, no sound, and for the first time it occurred to me to wonder if my hunch was wrong. The fear was short-lived. Walking to the top of the rise I looked down its far side to see a single car standing abandoned. I looked out beyond it to the plain. About 500 metres away a figure was moving slowly and deliberately in the slanting dawn light. I could see his shadow, gaunt and elongated as was mine, rippling on the rocks. I set out after him.

It took only a few minutes to reach Chart. He was not walking away from me or from the car. He seemed not to be aware of where he was going. Rather his path followed the lines of force I had seen on the map. For a while he walked slowly in a straight line. Then he stopped, turned, walked back, then turned again. I drew close, but he took no notice of me. Soon I was beside him, but still he said nothing, merely walking purposefully towards the rising sun. He was naked from the tank, his skin unnaturally pink and shining. All the lines were smoothed out. He was wet, new-born, a creature with whom I had no common ground. I looked into his eyes and saw that they had ceased to have any life. They were lenses, objects for seeing. Any life in Peter Chart had retreated deep inside him into the dim red centres of his being. His life was governed by his need and his hunger.

Hunger. This was the thing we had never even considered. All our calculations had been based on an overdose, an encroachment of some kind, either of some new germ or an unknown stimulus. In a way, we had outsmarted ourselves —we had never looked for the thing that was not there, the omission that should have been obvious. The force field was proof against radiation. In fact, that was one of its big advantages. It reflected every kind of radiation—light, heat, gamma, even types not yet discovered. A man inside a force field was cut off from all this. For the first time in his life, for the first time in the life of his entire species, he was insulated.

Since the first cell formed in the ocean man has had a flood of atomic particles flowing through him every second of his existence. Suddenly, for one man, it stops. How could we know what effect it had? Chart had collapsed completely, reduced from an intelligent man to a mindless addict of a drug he didn't recognize by a need he never knew he had. He came back to earth with only one thought in his mind—to find the thing his journey had deprived him of. The place where radiation, caught in the earth's gravitational field, spouted up again into space provided the greatest concentration near where he landed, so he went there. Nothing could be allowed to stand in his way. He had only one thought—to feed.

'I don't see how the test failed then,' Col said. 'Tevis was perfectly all right when we took him out.'

I had wondered about that too, until I remembered the TV link. 'There was some leakage along the metal stand, of course, but the TV camera must have given him enough direct radiation to live on. But we'd better keep him under observation.'

Col and I faced each other over the desk. We were both thinking the same thing.

'Can we lick it?' Col asked.

'I don't see how.'

'Are you going to try?'

I thought about it for a moment, then I reached for the phone.

'Get me Woomera. Colonel Thompson.'

A few seconds later Thompson's face came on to the screen. He wasn't trying to hide his self-satisfaction.

'Mr Fraser! As a matter of fact I was just leaving to come over.'

'Don't bother,' I said. 'I'm rejecting the orders you gave yesterday. All my guards have been ordered to shoot on sight anybody approaching the perimeter. Good morning.'

I cut the connection, though not too quickly to miss the very satisfying expression of complete amazement on Thompson's face.

Col's expression was almost as dazed.

'Can we pull it off?' he asked.

'We can try. It'll take them a few hours to find out that I'm not joking and a bit longer to see whether I'm insane or not. After that they'll have to go through channels and I think I can guarantee that will take a long time.'

Outside, the sun was up. For the first time since I had come to the desert, I realized that here was the real Australia. The sand, the rock, the sun—this was the country to which I owed my loyalty, just as it was to Col Talura's ideas that I owed my allegiance, not to the old myths on which I had been brought up. There was no unpleasantness in the country or the ideas that I had not put there. Given time, I thought it would not be hard to learn a devotion to both. The least I could do was to try.

Comes Now the Power

Roger Zelazny

Telepathy as a theme in sf has been utilized in every possible way, from paranoid pursuit tales to touching stories of talented children and visitors from Outside.

Roger Zelazny has achieved an enviable reputation with a succession of award-winning novels such as *Lord of Light* and *Creatures of Light and Darkness*. He is also a skilled writer of short fiction, who constantly surprises with his remarkable ability to create a different style for every story.

Zelazny has written here a gently moving tale of a lonely telepath who discovers one day that he is no longer alone. His search for the girl he knows only in his mind, and the subsequent denouement —all depicted with consummate artistry in the space of a few thousand words—show the author at the peak of his power.

It was into the second year now, and it was maddening.

Everything which had worked before failed this time.

Each day he tried to break it, and it resisted his every effort.

He snarled at his students, drove recklessly, blooded his knuckles against many walls. Nights, he lay awake cursing.

But there was no one to whom he could turn for help. His problem would have been non-existent to a psychiatrist, who doubtless would have attempted to treat him for something else.

So he went away that summer, spent a month at a resort: nothing. He experimented with several hallucinogenic drugs: again, nothing. He tried free-associating into a tape recorder, but all he got when he played it back was a headache.

To whom does the holder of a blocked power turn, within a society of normal people?

. . . To another of his own kind, if he can locate one.

Milt Rand had known four other persons like himself: his cousin Gary, now deceased; Walker Jackson, a Negro preacher who had retired to somewhere down South; Tatya Stefanovich, a dancer, presently somewhere behind the Iron Curtain; and Curtis Legge, who, unfortunately, was suffering a schizoid reaction, paranoid type, in a State institution for the criminally insane. Others he had brushed against in the night, but had never met and could not locate now.

There had been blockages before, but Milt had always worked his way through them inside of a month. This time was different and special, though. Upsets, discomforts, disturbances, can dam up a talent, block a power. An event which seals it off completely for over a year, however, is more than a mere disturbance, discomfort, or upset.

The divorce had beaten hell out of him.

It is bad enough to know that somewhere someone is hating you; but to have known the very form of that hatred and to have proven ineffectual against it, to have known it as the hater held it for you, to have lived with it and felt it growing around you, this is more than distasteful circumstance. Whether you are offender or offended, when you are hated and you live within the circle of that hate, it takes a thing from you: it tears a piece of spirit from your soul, or, if you prefer, a way of thinking from your mind; it cuts and does not cauterize.

Milt Rand dragged his bleeding psyche around the country and returned home.

He would sit and watch the woods from his glassed-in back porch, drink beer, watch the fireflies in the shadows, the rabbits, the dark birds, an occasional fox, sometimes a bat.

He had been fireflies once, and rabbits, birds, occasionally a fox, sometimes a bat.

The wildness was one of the reasons he had moved beyond suburbia, adding an extra half hour to his commuting time.

Now there was a glassed-in back porch between him and these things he had once been part of. Now he was alone.

Walking the streets, addressing his classes at the Institute, sitting in a restaurant, a theatre, a bar, he was vacant where once he'd been filled.

There are no books which tell a man how to bring back the power he has lost.

He tries everything he can think of, while he is waiting. Walking the hot pavements of a summer noon, crossing against the lights because traffic is slow, watching kids in swimsuits play around a gurgling hydrant, filthy water sluicing the gutter about their feet, as mothers and older sisters in halters, wrinkled shirts, bermudas and sunburnt skins watch them, occasionally, while talking to one another in entranceways to buildings or the shade of a storefront awning, Milt moves across town, heading nowhere in particular, growing claustrophobic if he stops for long, his eyebrows full of perspiration, sunglasses streaked with it, shirt sticking to his sides and coming loose, sticking and coming loose as he walks.

Amid the afternoon, there comes a time when he has to rest the two fresh-baked bricks at the ends of his legs. He finds a treelawn bench flanked by high maples, eases himself down into it and sits there thinking of nothing in particular for perhaps twenty-five minutes.

Hello.

Something within him laughs or weeps.

Yes, hello, I am here! Don't go away! Stay! Please!

You are—like me . . .

Yes, I am. You can see it in me because you are what you are. But you must read here and send here, too. I'm frozen. I—Hello? Where are you?

Once more, he is alone.

He tries to broadcast. He fills his mind with the thoughts and tries to push them outside his skull.

Please come back! I need you. You can help me. I am desperate. I hurt. Where are you?

Again, nothing.

He wants to scream. He wants to search every room in every building on the block.

Instead, he sits there.

At 9.30 that evening they meet again, inside his mind.

Hello?

Stay! Stay, for God's sake! Don't go away this time! Please don't! Listen, I need you! You can help me.

How? What is the matter?

I'm like you. Or was, once. I could reach out with my mind and be other places, other things, other people. I can't do it now, though. I have a blockage. The power will not come. I know it is there. I can feel it. But I can't use . . . Hello?

Yes, I am still here. I can feel myself going away, though. I will be back. I . . .

Milt waits until midnight. She does not come back. It is a feminine mind which has touched his own. Vague, weak, but definitely feminine, and wearing the power. She does not come back that night, though. He paces up and down the block, wondering which window, which door . . .

He eats at an all-night café, returns to his bench, waits, paces again, goes back to the café for cigarettes, begins chain-smoking, goes back to the bench.

Dawn occurs, day arrives, night is gone. He is alone, as birds explore the silence, traffic begins to swell, dogs wander the lawns.

Then, weakly, the contact:

I am here. I can stay longer this time, I think. How can I help you? Tell me.

All right. Do this thing: Think of the feeling, the feeling of the out-go, out-reach, out-know that you have now. Fill your mind with that feeling and send it to me, as hard as you can.

It comes upon him then as once it was: the knowledge of the power. It is earth and water, fire and air to him. He stands upon it, he swims in it, he warms himself by it, he moves through it.

It is returning! Don't stop now!

I'm sorry. I must. I'm getting dizzy . . .

Where are you?

Hospital . . .

He looks up the street to the hospital on the corner, at the far end, to his left.

What ward? He frames the thought but knows she is already gone, even as he does it.

Doped-up or feverish, he decides, and probably out for a while now.

He takes a taxi back to where he had parked, drives home, showers and shaves, makes breakfast, cannot eat.

He drinks orange juice and coffee and stretches out on the bed.

Five hours later he awakens, looks at his watch, curses.

All the way back into town, he tries to recall the power. It is there like a tree, rooted in his being, branching behind his eyes, all bud, blossom, sap and colour, but no leaves, no fruit. He can feel it swaying within him, pulsing, breathing; from the tips of his toes to the roots of his hair he feels it. But it does not bend to his will, it does not branch within his consciousness, furl there its leaves, spread the aromas of life.

He parks in the hospital lot, enters the lobby, avoids the front desk, finds a chair beside a table filled with magazines.

Two hours later he meets her.

He is hiding behind a copy of *Holiday* and looking for her.

I am here.

Again, then! Quickly! The power! Help me to rouse it!

She does this thing.

Within his mind, she conjures the power. There is a movement, a pause, a movement, a pause. Reflectively, as though suddenly remembering an intricate dance step, it stirs within him, the power.

As in a surfacing bathyscaphe, there is a rush of distortions, then a clear, moist view without.

She is a child who has helped him.

A mind-twisted, fevered child, dying . . .

He reads it all when he turns the power upon her.

Her name is Dorothy and she is delirious. The power came upon her at the height of her illness, perhaps because of it.

Has she helped a man come alive again, or dreamed that she helped him? she wonders.

She is thirteen years old and her parents sit beside her bed. In the mind of her mother a word rolls over and over, senselessly, blocking all other thoughts, though it cannot keep away the feelings:

Methotrexate, methotrexate, methotrexate, meth . . .

In Dorothy's thirteen-year-old breastbone there are needles of pain. The fevers swirl within her, and she is all but gone to him.

She is dying of leukaemia. The final stages are already arrived. He can taste the blood in her mouth.

Helpless within his power, he projects:

You have given me the end of your life and your final strength. I did not know this. I would not have asked it of you if I had.

Thank you, she says, *for the pictures inside you.*

Pictures?

Places, things I saw . . .

There is not much inside me worth showing. You could have been elsewhere, seeing better.

I am going again . . .

Wait!

He calls upon the power that lives within him now, fused with his will and his senses, his thoughts, memories, feelings. In one great blaze of life, he shows her Milt Rand.

Here is everything I have, all I have ever been that might please. Here is swarming through a foggy night, blinking on and off. Here is lying beneath a bush as the rains of summer fall about you, drip from the leaves upon your fox-soft fur. Here is the moon-dance of the deer, the dream drift of the trout beneath the dark swell, blood cold as the waters about you.

Here is Tatya dancing and Walker preaching; here is my cousin Gary, as he whittles, contriving a ball within a box, all out of one piece of wood. This is my New York and my Paris. This, my favourite meal, drink, cigar, restaurant, park, road to drive on late at night; this is where I dug tunnels, built a lean-to, went swimming; this, my first kiss; these are the tears of loss; this is exile and alone, and recovery, awe, joy; these, my grandmother's daffodils; this, her coffin, daffodils about it; these are the colours of the music I love, and this is my dog who lived long and was good. See all the things that heat the spirit, cool within the mind, are encased in memory and one's self. I give them to you, who have no time to know them.

He sees himself standing on the far hills of her mind. She laughs aloud then, and in her room somewhere high away a hand is laid upon her and her wrist is taken between fingers and thumb as she rushes towards him suddenly grown large. His great black wings sweep forward to fold her wordless spasm of life, then are empty.

Milt Rand stiffens within his power, puts aside a copy of *Holiday* and stands, to leave the hospital, full and empty, empty, full, like himself, now, behind.

Such is the power of the power.

Litterbug

Tony Morphett

Science fiction writers have always been fascinated with the possible outcome of man's first contact with an alien species. While a vast number of stories have used an alien invasion as a setting for this theme, a few rather more sober and thought-provoking encounters have been imagined as taking place beyond the Earth, either on a newly discovered planet or in the neutral area of deep space. But has anyone approached it from this angle? Thought-provoking, yes—but *sober*? The jolly shade of Henry Kuttner would approve of Rafferty and his fascinating invention.

Tony Morphett is one of Australia's best-known television dramatists. He has devised and produced a number of award-winning shows for the Australian Broadcasting Commission, and has also written major novels and short stories. LITTERBUG is his singular contribution to the sf field, although he admits to having 'dozens of ideas for further stories' if the pressure of television work ever allows him time.

Rafferty stood pretty tall, was built like a fullback and had a reputation for gentleness except on certain specific occasions. This was one of those occasions. He had got home, thumbed the lock on his front door, and from a habit dating back to less civilized periods in his life, he had gone inside without turning the light on.

And had known that in the dark house he wasn't alone.

It could have been smell, it could have been sound, it could have been that other thing which was just *the feel*, and which had saved his life on occasion. But he knew they

151

were there, and he moved fast; he moved silent from the front door. They must have heard the lock, so the area of the lock was somewhere not to be.

'That you, Joe?'

A voice from the laboratory. It must have been his not turning on the light. A man coming through his own front door turns the light on. Therefore the voice thought that the noise had been made by another of the intruders. Rafferty smiled. The intruders were fortunate that they didn't see that smile. It was not at all a nice smile.

Now he knew there were two of them, otherwise the one who had spoken would not have pinned the noise source to one name. Now, at the laboratory door, he could see one of them, partly silhouetted by a torch held in the left hand while the right hand moved across the face of a control panel.

Rafferty had a reputation for gentleness, but under some circumstances he had no social graces whatsoever, and when he saw someone else's hand on his laboratory pet, Emily Post went out the window and Rafferty turned from an engineer into a hunting primate. A very fast-moving hunting primate.

It is not true that the man didn't know what hit him. He said later that he *did* know what had hit him. He said it was the roof. It was actually the edge of Rafferty's hand. Rafferty had tackled him; they had gone down together; Rafferty's right hand had moved twice. Once up, once down. Then *the feel* had taken over, and Rafferty had rolled away just fast enough for the second man's blackjack to strike his shoulder, not the base of his skull. Every man got one chance with Rafferty, and that had been Joe's. Still lying on the floor, he scooped the man's feet from under him, then realized he had caught himself a pro. The man struck at him again on the way down. Rafferty blocked with his left forearm, had to block again as the man's bladed left hand came into action, and then felt an increased respect as his opponent flicked away the blackjack and struck for Rafferty's solar plexus with a right forearm-hand-extended-finger assembly as straight and solid as a quarter-staff. What Rafferty thought had saved him was his own right hook which laid his opponent out at the same time as Rafferty started to concentrate on unknotting his stomach. At least, he thought, he'd be on his feet before they were conscious.

And then the light went on. For an engineer, he had made one assumption too many.

There had been three of them.

It was infuriating. He could have taken the third one, gun and all, if there'd been anything in his belly except a black gaping pain which would not let him stand. The slight, grey-haired man with glasses didn't look as if he knew one end of his 44 magnum from the other. Which worried Rafferty more than if he'd looked like a killer who wouldn't let it go off by accident.

'Mr Rafferty, I must ask you to abstain from further violence. I realize that, as a citizen, you have a perfect right to be irritated at this intrusion on your privacy. But please do not be violent.'

Rafferty swallowed so hard it straightened out most of the knots. 'That is the craziest speech I've ever heard a burglar make.'

'Unfortunately,' the little grey man with the big gun continued, 'we felt it necessary to have a little more information before we approached you more . . .' he cleared his throat, 'ah, formally.'

'We haven't,' said Rafferty, 'even been introduced.'

'Since, however, you returned as you did . . . somewhat prematurely, Mr Rafferty . . .'

'Next time I come through my own door, I'll knock.'

'I think we had better come into the open. I'd like you to accompany us if you would.'

Rafferty's deep breath straightened out the rest of the knots. 'Look, you're holding the gun, and that makes me very polite. But may I put it this way? You break into my house, you tamper with expensive lab equipment, one of your men turns my solar plexus into a disaster area, and *then* you ask ever so politely for me to accompany you. Who the hell are you? And, apart from the gun, why should I go anywhere?'

'We all work for the government. My department . . .

well, it doesn't really *have* a name. These two gentlemen,'
he nodded to his two now-conscious companions, 'work for
a rather better-known bureau. Perhaps you could . . . ?'

The two men produced leather cases. Flipped them open.
Rafferty looked at the metal shields. He must, he decided,
be in better fighting trim than he had thought. 'All right,
I'll come along.'

The little man handed the gun to the operative called
Joe. 'I'll have to telephone. There are two people who'll
want to meet you.'

Rafferty lowered himself into the chair. The office was
comfortable, but there was nothing soft about it. The little
grey man sat at the desk. He had introduced himself as
Watson. The other two men in the room he knew from
reputation, technical journals and television: Professor
Clemens, a Nobel prize-winner in physics, and Dr Simpson
Navarre, one of the government's chief scientific advisers.
Watson looked up from a slim file on his desk. 'Now, Mr
Rafferty, what we wish to talk to you about is your, ah,
matter transmitter.'

'I don't have one. I make garbage disposal units.'

Professor Clemens leaned forward. 'Mr Rafferty, let's
save a bit of time. You *call* them garbage disposal units.
Now, as I understand it, a conventional garbage disposal
unit is like a mincing machine. You put matter in one end
and it comes out the other end ground up fine enough to
be washed away.'

'Do you know,' said Rafferty, 'I don't believe I've ever
discussed garbage with a Nobel prize-winner before?'

'That'll be enough, Rafferty! You're in trouble enough
without impudence!' Watson sounded angry. Rafferty
diagnosed a chronic case of lack of sense of humour.

Rafferty stood up. 'Good evening.'

'You'll . . .'

Navarre turned on the grey government man. 'Be quiet,
Watson!' Navarre went on more quietly. 'We wish to talk
to Mr Rafferty about garbage.'

Clemens joined in the smile. 'Garbage *disposal*. In a
conventional unit you put matter in the form of, say,

orange peel in one end, and you get matter in the form of slush out the other. In your unit, Mr Rafferty, you put matter in one end, and *nothing* comes out the other end. In fact, there would appear to *be* no other end.'

'Well, that seems to me to be an advantage,' Rafferty said. 'It saves water, prevents clogging . . .'

'Mr Rafferty,' Navarre broke in, 'please don't play the hillbilly. You know exactly what we mean. *Where does the garbage go?*'

Rafferty smiled. 'I don't know.'

'You don't know?' Clemens was out of his chair. 'You must know! You built it. You manufacture it. You must know where it goes!'

'Does it work?' Rafferty said.

'Yes,' Clemens said tightly, 'it works.'

'Is it a good garbage disposal unit?'

'Yes. It is a good garbage disposal unit. Which is like opening a bottle on a metal edge in a Polaris sub., and calling the submarine a good bottle opener.'

'I asked is it a good garbage disposal unit?'

'All right, I agree it's a good garbage disposal unit.'

'And I,' Rafferty said, 'am an engineer. It works.'

Watson leaned forward. 'Mr Rafferty, I think you should be informed of a few things. For a start, if we want to, we can lock you up and throw away the key.'

'You're the one who threatened me before.' Rafferty sounded quiet and unamused.

'You have endangered the security of this country and the security of the Free World by applying for a patent on a device which has immense military potential. When your patent application was rejected because you couldn't explain the principle, you went ahead anyway, manufactured your device, and now you're selling it to anyone with the money to pay for it. That means anyone in a number of embassies which even *you* ought to be able to name. In short, Mr Rafferty, you are a traitor.'

Rafferty's chair was empty and Rafferty was leaning across the government man's desk. Rafferty took Watson by the shoulders and squeezed in a way which Rafferty thought was gentle. 'Mr Watson,' he crooned, 'you are no longer holding a gun. Unless you are, never say that again. Understand?' He let go. He walked back to his chair. Watson tried to get his shoulders back into place.

Navarre cloaked his smile. 'I can understand your resentment, Mr Rafferty, but what Mr Watson meant was that you might have shown your device to the government first. We *are* interested in new ideas . . .'

'I did.'

Navarre put his head in his hands like a man who had heard it before. 'Go on.'

'I tried it on the army, navy and air force and a set of very well-qualified young men told me my maths wasn't as good as it might be, and anyway the effect was theoretically impossible.'

'But didn't you show them a working model?'

'Have you ever tried to demonstrate a perpetual motion machine to a government physicist? Or a mermaid to a government marine biologist? Or telekinesis to a government psychologist? The majority of scientists want to ask only those questions they can answer. The fact that they could throw my maths was enough. The fact that I didn't have even a bachelor's degree didn't help much.'

'You don't have a degree?' Watson's spectacles were twin barrels. 'You mean you were lying to us when you called yourself an engineer?'

Clemens smiled. 'I shouldn't worry too much about degrees, Mr Watson. Thomas Alva Edison didn't have one either, and it was probably the saving of him.'

Rafferty looked across at Clemens. He decided he could possibly warm to this man.

Navarre, the government adviser, was still looking unhappy. Rafferty guessed that other people in the army, navy and air force would be looking even more unhappy the next day. Navarre spoke. 'So we've done it again. We'll just have to see what we can salvage. Presumably, Mr Rafferty, you weren't trying to make a garbage disposal unit when you started?'

'No. I was trying to do what the burglar over there suggested,' he said, nodding at Watson. 'I was trying to push matter from one place to another without actually carrying it. A man paddling a log and a man riding a rocket, they're not different in *kind*; you're only talking about an improvement in technique. I was looking for a difference in *kind*.'

'I've got scientists who say it's impossible,' Watson said.

Rafferty didn't look very nice when his eyes narrowed. 'Mr Watson, in my lab I've got a unit just big enough for a man your size. Would you like to try it out and then talk about possibilities and impossibilities?'

'So you started out to make a matter transmitter,' Navarre said. 'How did it turn into a garbage disposal unit?'

'Money. As you can probably read in that file there, my factory's for repetition engineering, and this thing's just a hobby of mine. The firm makes enough so it can be a high-priced hobby, and there have been economic by-products in the past, but still, so far it's been a hobby. Well, I ran into a dead-end. The transmitter—the matter transmitter—works fine. It's, uh, the *receiver* end that still has some bugs to iron out.'

'What bugs?' Clemens said.

'One very simple one. It doesn't work. The transmitter's fine. You put something in, you throw the power, it goes away. It doesn't disintegrate, burn, atomize, or get washed down a drain. It just goes away. Now it ought to be going into the receiver. But it doesn't. It goes somewhere else.'

'Where?'

'I don't know. It must be going somewhere. I used to watch the newspapers. I used to have this nightmare that an explorer was going to some back and say that he'd found the Lost Valley of the Incas and it was filled to the brim with orange peel and beer cans and coffee grounds. Now I think the stuff's not ending up on this planet at all. The odds are it's in deep space somewhere. It's going somewhere in space-time, anyway. I'm conventional enough not to believe that all that matter's just being destroyed. So I had a matter transmitter but no matter receiver. I needed development money, a lot of it, so I went to the government. Whose representatives, Dr Navarre, told me very politely that I had shot my lid.' Rafferty lit a cigarette. 'Now that didn't alter the fact I still needed money for development, and the thing it worked best at was getting rid of things. Which to me said garbage disposal. So I put in about a dozen fail-safe devices to stop tampering idiots from losing arms, and I got it on the market this week, and the orders look very nice indeed. No status-home is going to be without one.'

'The government will recompense you, but we've got to get every single one back.' Watson winced at Navarre's use of the word 'recompense,' but nodded.

Rafferty smiled. 'I wish you luck then. They're already distributed coast-to-coast, and our sales are running into thousands.'

It wasn't until a week later that the garbage started coming back.

Rafferty always ate breakfast in his laboratory, because that was the place in the house the best morning sun got to. It was also the place in the house where he felt most comfortable.

He finished eating, put a toast crust and two egg shells into the rind of a grapefruit, and threw the lot into the maw of his big experimental Watson-sized disposal unit. He switched the power on and turned away to pour himself some coffee.

Sproiiing!

Rafferty looked back. His unit had never said *sproiiing* before. He was in time to see the grapefruit rind, the two egg shells and the toast crust come flying through the opening. Something else followed them.

On the domestic models there were spring-loaded doors and an automatic shut-off if they were opened. Rafferty's lab model ran to power rather than to refinements like doors and idiot-proofing.

Rafferty went to the machine. The power was still on. The grey vortex in the transmission area was as it should have been. Rafferty had a peach left over from his breakfast. He put it on the conveyor belt. The conveyor belt bore the peach into the grey vortex, where it disappeared. Rafferty waited.

Squelch!

Rafferty straightened up, wiping peach out of his eyes.

Rafferty was a gentle man and would never have laid hands on his own invention, and besides there wasn't an axe in the laboratory. He left the machine for the moment, and looked at what had come out the first time. He seemed to remember seeing something fly out that he hadn't thrown in.

He picked it up. It resembled a cat and it resembled a four-legged bunch of broccoli, and it wasn't either. It was dead, and among the things it *didn't* resemble was a bunch of violets. Rafferty got a towel and a carving knife. The towel he tied round his mouth and nose. His past included being a slaughterman and skin-diving for a marine biologist, so he didn't think anyone would mind if he had a first, semi-professional cut.

He had made three cuts and decided it wasn't cat or broccoli, fish or steer, when the phone rang.

'Rafferty.'

'Jim here, from the factory. Two of the units on the test bench. Garbage is coming *back* through them.'

'Other stuff as well? Stuff that doesn't look like . . . well, normal sorts of garbage?'

'Well, I don't know, what some people throw out, others'd live on for a week. I mean, what's *normal* garbage?'

'But you're just getting back what you're putting in?'

'Yeah.'

'How fast?'

'Some oozes back; some flies back.'

'Any pattern?'

'Not yet.'

'I'll keep in touch.'

He hung up. Looked at the broccoli cat again. No pattern. At least he'd have something to throw at the first biologist who told him that a broccoli cat was theoretically impossible and that his DNA spelling grades were on the other side of illiterate.

Then he took an apple, and tossed it into the grey vortex. Then instantly switched off the power. And waited. Nothing. So when he switched off, the stuff couldn't get back. Logical, except that it was illogical for it to come back at all.

He sat on the stool at his drawing board, and he cracked his scarred knuckles for a while and stared at the wall like

159

he was going to take it apart. Then he swung on the stool, and leaned back, and took a piece of paper tape in his right hand. Put one twist into it, and held the two ends between finger and thumb, making a Moebius strip. He knew that the pad of his finger and the pad of his thumb were touching different parts of the same side of the strip. That they were both thirty centimetres and one millimetre apart. He threw the tape away. Somewhere . . .

Where?

He looked out the laboratory window. Then he whistled as he went to the lab unit, turned it on, then went to the bookshelves on the wall and selected a volume. Then watched as the grey vortex of the unit slowly enveloped the book of maps of the night sky as seen from earth.

The phone rang.

'Rafferty?'

'Yes. That's Watson, is it?'

'We want to see you, Rafferty. There's been a complication.'

'You mean the garbage is coming back through *your* test units too?'

'Not on the phone, Rafferty, not on the phone. You'll be picked up in five minutes.'

'I've things to do at the factory.'

'Five minutes, Rafferty.'

Rafferty hung up, and then phoned his factory, and made a priority order for delivery to him that afternoon.

The biologist looked up from his examination of the broccoli cat. He smiled. 'It's an extremely convincing fake, gentlemen.'

'Fake?' Navarre's hands were tightening.

'Well, of course, nothing like this exists.'

'Thank you, Professor.' After the man had gone, Navarre used the telephone. 'Send me a *real* biologist. If the ancestors of that one had been as adaptable as he is, he would now be a sea squirt which knew that free oxygen was a poison and that mobility and limbs were something an adult grew out of.' He sat down.

Rafferty grinned at him. 'Any other . . . fakes coming back through the units?'

'We're sifting the material as fast as we can. It appears that there's some vegetable material that's . . . well, unknown, but that . . . thing of yours is the first . . . is it an animal?'

'Roughly speaking, yes. Can you find out for me what it breathes and eats?'

Watson cleared his throat. 'Now your theory, Rafferty, is that you've somehow . . . punched—I think was your word—punched a hole in space-time, and the other end of the hole is on some planet circling another star.'

'Yes, I think so.'

'But even if we accept the principle of punching holes in space-time,' Clemens said, 'the odds against finding the other ends of those holes on another planet in another solar system . . . well, the odds are, if you'll pardon the expression, astronomical.'

'I shan't pardon the expression,' Rafferty said, 'but odds like that have come off before. And if you don't believe they've come off this time, then tell me where on this planet the broccoli cat comes from.'

'But why should the thing come back through the machine at all?' Watson couldn't bring himself to call it a broccoli cat.

'You ever live in a slum, Mr Watson? I guess not.' Rafferty had his grin tucked down at the corners. 'Well, you throw garbage onto someone else's back landing, they'll throw it back, uh? And some people, they get mad, they'll throw a dead cat with it.' Rafferty's hands were palms up, and more pious than his eyes. 'It's terrible what some people'll do when they get mad.'

Navarre had a grin of his own. 'Well, I've had the problem of First Contact on my hands for three years now, and I never thought it'd be garbage over the fence.'

'And that, Dr Navarre, is because you've never lived in a slum either. But where you can put a dead cat, you can put other things. And I thought even a cat thrower's not going to throw back something that looks important. So that's why I sent him the star maps.'

'What star maps?' Navarre was quiet, cold.

'You know the sort of book. Amateur astronomers use them. They show the night sky, northern and southern

skies as they are at the various months of the year. I sent it
through my lab unit this morning. Nearest thing I could
give them to an address.'

The way Watson looked, Rafferty should have had a
snakebite kit on him. 'You're under arrest, Rafferty. Last
week I called you a traitor. Today you proved it. Gave
them our address, did you? Do you expect them to pay you?'

'Pay me, Watson?'

'When they invade.'

'No one's going to be invading, Mr Watson. They can't
be closer than four light-years. They're probably further.'

'They can get a dead cat here. They can get an army
here in the same way.'

'But, Watson,' and Rafferty smiled, 'how do you know
the cat was dead when it left there?'

'What do you mean?'

'Maybe it was alive, and got killed on the trip through.'

'But who'd throw a live animal into a thing like that?
Why, it'd be . . .'

'Please don't say *inhuman*, Watson. I don't think I could
bear it.' Navarre turned to Rafferty. 'You mean you don't
think someone could go through there alive?'

'I don't know. Until I knew there was something at the
other end, I wasn't very keen about trying it. Couldn't see
myself making a laughing exit into hard vacuum and
absolute zero. Or into the centre of a sun. But now? Well,
the odds are better. But I still say that there's tourism and
tourism.'

Watson was putting down his phone. 'The General will
be here in one moment.'

'General?'

'Rafferty's action has made this a military matter.'

The General heard them through and then refilled his
corncob pipe. 'Should have been in on this at the jump.
But it's not irretrievable. One thing, we've got no problem
delivering the bombs.'

'The bombs!' Rafferty stood up.

'Of course. Now they know where we are, we'll have to
exterminate them. You say a grapefruit rind came back
through your unit. Could just as easily have been a grenade.

Or an H-bomb. We have to hit them first. Before they hit us.'

'But they've shown no signs . . .'

'Can you assure me they won't?'

'I don't know them!'

'Neither do I, Mr Rafferty, neither do I.' He turned to Watson. 'I'll be recommending a simultaneous, all-out attack. Enough to take an earth-size planet apart.'

Professor Clemens leaned forward. 'General, I must protest! This is our first chance to contact what might be an intelligent alien species, and . . .'

'You're not a military man, Professor. You wouldn't understand.'

Rafferty was sitting again, and looking relaxed. Which was a danger sign. 'General, I'm not a military man either, but I guess it'd take a lot of power to smash an earth-size planet.'

'An immense amount,' Clemens said before the general could answer.

'And we know these units provide a two-way tunnel,' Rafferty continued. 'Now, Watson, how many units have you got back so far?'

'Fifteen hundred, give or take twenty. As at close of business yesterday.'

'Leaves about four thousand still in the field. Now supposing you used about a thousand in your attack . . .'

'I'm afraid that's classified . . .'

'Just supposing. Now these four thousand you haven't got back yet: if any were open, that is, switched on, during the attack, it'd be just like pumping high-pressure steam into a sieve. You would literally be getting your own back. You were talking about assurances, General. Can you assure me they'd all be closed? Even if you made it an order? Can you assure me that among four thousand human beings there wouldn't be some who'd forget to turn off, or who wouldn't hear the radio and TV announcements, or some who wouldn't see it as a way to buck authority, or some who'd just think it would be a good ideal to blow this planet at the same time? I think until you get all the sets back, General, and I'll make damn sure you don't, I think until then we'd better try talking to them. So I'd like to see my laboratory unit. I left it on. I just wonder whether the postman's been there.'

'But you're under arrest,' Watson said.

'Watson,' said Navarre, 'he's released into my custody. And if you want to find out if I have the authority, I suggest you check higher up. Now, Mr Rafferty, we'll go check that letter box.'

The sheets were probably synthetic, but they had the feel of an extremely thin leather. The markings on them were obviously writing, but which way it ran was by no means obvious. Rafferty revised his original thought. Was it so obvious that it was writing? At least they had shut Watson up for a while. He seemed hypnotized by the pale grey sheets with their black markings.

Clemens looked at Navarre. 'Black on grey? Implies brighter light on their world?'

Navarre shrugged. 'Could be. I wouldn't be in a hurry to assume anything. They may not see in the same range we do. Do we know that it's writing? Do we even know whether the information is in the black marks or in what we'd call the background?'

Watson came out of his trance. 'But you notice one thing. You sent them star maps. They've sent back something which could easily be the equivalent of the *Daily News*. Hardly, Mr Rafferty, a fair exchange.'

Rafferty shrugged. 'You're all educated men. Which of you has a book of star charts in your home?' Only Navarre nodded. 'One in three. And you three are scarcely representative of humanity in general. My guess is that he's sent through what he figures is a similar artifact as a sign of good faith. I think we can expect some more.' The four of them looked at the machine. Nothing happened.

Nothing happened for another three-quarters of an hour. Then the grey vortex at the back of the machine changed. Clemens was watching at the time, and he called the others over. They gathered, and watched as the sheets emerged from the vortex and piled in the transmission area of the machine. Rafferty switched off, reached in and got them, and then switched on again. He spread the sheets on the bench. They were star maps.

Rafferty looked at Watson. 'Looks like someone with common sense got to their soldiers and bureaucrats, Mr Watson. It seems they've sent us their address.' He turned to Navarre. 'How much astronomy do your computers know, Dr Navarre?'

'Enough.' Navarre grinned. 'I'll get the boys working on it. By the way, you can stay here if you like. I don't think we'll lock you up just yet.'

Rafferty smiled, and stretched. 'Guess I could use a little lab time, anyway. Might even be able to get the bugs out of it. Seems the transmitter's a mite overpowered.'

'There'll be a guard round your house,' Navarre said. 'They won't bother you. Some of our technical people will be over later. We might have to move you out of the house altogether in the next week or so, but we can leave that until later.'

They left Rafferty alone with his machine. As soon as they were gone, he rang his factory. 'That set-up I asked for this morning: send it over.'

Then he fed some picture magazines into the unit, and was busy at his bench until the arrival of some crates from the factory.

He opened them, and from the contents quickly assembled a disposal unit. From the last box he took the Ni-Cad batteries he had ordered. If you couldn't expect the same power supply in different countries on your own planet, to be optimistic about standard power on someone else's wasn't optimism, it was idiocy. When he finished, he had a self-powered unit big enough to send a book or a cat, but not big enough for a sabre-toothed tiger. And the whole thing was small enough to put through the feed jaw of his big laboratory unit.

And it was too heavy to lift. Rafferty's prodigies of Anglo-Saxon four-letter expression should by rights have produced the smell of ozone. Then he stopped talking, and smiled. Outside his house, he approached one of his guards.

'Can you help me with something?'

The guard raised a hand to one of his colleagues to cover for him. 'Sure. What?'

'Just something I want to lift.'

The guard followed him inside. Together they man-handled the small unit into the lab machine. They watched, Rafferty with satisfaction, the guard with awe, as it disappeared into the grey vortex.

'Never seen the inside of one of those things before. Kinda pretty, isn't it?'

'It works,' Rafferty said. Then he smiled the gentle smile. 'Which means I think it's kinda pretty.'

'Where's it go?'

'I'll tell you when I find out,' Rafferty said.

'Vega,' Navarre said. 'A planet orbiting round Vega.'

'Vega,' Rafferty repeated. 'How far's that?'

'Twenty-six and a half light years.'

'A long way.' It was a very rare thing for Rafferty to feel small. And even when he did feel small, Rafferty never said so. 'It makes me feel small,' Rafferty said.

'It's a long way to throw a dead cat.'

Rafferty joined in the smile. 'Broccoli cat. Do we know what it breathes and eats yet?'

'Breathes an oxygen-nitrogen mixture. Slightly richer in oxygen, they think. Food? The planet's got a carbon-hydrogen cycle, but they suggest you don't try eating his brother if you find him. Apparently there's a metal distribution on the planet that . . .'

And he stopped, because at that moment the window opened in the air.

Watson hurriedly backed behind the laboratory's central bench.

Clemens walked closer to it like a man mesmerized.

Navarre stared.

Rafferty smiled the smile that Watson had grown to know and loathe.

It was a grey, shimmering window in the air, big enough for a book, too small for a sabre-toothed tiger. And out of it things started to flow. Sheets of what they thought was writing, small objects which could have been cups, toys, anything at all, and finally what looked like a magazine. The flow stopped, the window irised in on itself, and vanished. Rafferty picked up the thing that looked like a magazine. Every page was devoted to a single picture. What was pictured was a . . . creature. Humanoid enough if you didn't define the term too closely, residual feathery scales, and nothing else. Rafferty turned from the magazine to one of the other sheets, where there was a picture of a similar creature, except that this one was wearing what could have been called clothes. Rafferty grinned and turned to Watson, handing him the magazine. 'I think you should have this for your files. It's the first known example of the interstellar delivery of a . . . . girlie magazine.'

Watson looked at three of the pictures, snapped the magazine shut and then in a way which Rafferty found disconcerting, blushed. 'It appears,' Watson said, 'that at the other end we have a Vegan version of Mr Rafferty.'

Navarre's voice was cold. 'At the other end of *what*, Rafferty?'

'How do you mean?'

'These things didn't come out of *your* machine, Rafferty. What was that we saw in the air?'

'Oh, that? I sent 'em through a small unit.'

'You what!' Watson came round the bench to Navarre. There were tears in his eyes. 'Please, Dr Navarre, you must let me have him. Just a simple firing squad, nothing elaborate, nothing elaborate, just a simple, simple, simple . . .' He wandered away into a corner.

'Why did you do it, Rafferty?' Navarre was beginning to sound old.

'He'd been polite enough to send his address. Figured I'd send him something so he could get in touch when he wanted, instead of having to wait for me to open the tunnel.'

'Rafferty, you're going to come with us.'

'Sure, but can I send him a copy of *Playboy* first?'

'If you must.'

Two days later they came to him in his cell. It looked like a comfortably furnished hotel room, but as far as Rafferty was concerned, anything he couldn't get out of was a cell.

Navarre opened the conversation. 'Rafferty, you're coming back home.'

'I'm quite comfortable here, thanks.'

'Nevertheless, you're coming home.'

Rafferty detected a hardening of Navarre's attitude. It was an effect he had had the opportunity of studying in many other people he had come into contact with. 'Why?'

'Because it appears you're the only man who has more than a mechanic's knowledge of these things. On your feet.'

Rafferty shrugged. Navarre had disappointed him. The only point on which Rafferty's knowledge of his device was wider than that of his highly prized mechanics was that Rafferty knew that by guess and by the seat of his faded levis and by fiddling and by *the feel*, he had made the thing work. He had tried to explain to Navarre that this didn't mean theoretical knowledge. He had told Navarre that Edison hadn't known what electricity was. Navarre still wouldn't believe that Rafferty was simply what he said he was: an engineer.

So Rafferty shrugged, and followed Navarre out of his comfortable cell.

Now his home itself was a cell, but Rafferty found he didn't mind much. He was getting to know his Vegan neighbour, and the anthropologists who came round to exchange artefacts with the Vegans were good company.

The next three months were busy. Although the air was right and the temperatures and gravities matched closely enough to be tolerable, small animals sent through the machines died quickly of sicknesses from which they had no immunities. So far, neither side was willing to send through an ambassador, only to have him die of a xeno-analogue to a cold in the nose or a splinter under the nail. Fortunately, something in the matter-shift prevented an exchange of atmospheres, but after the first experimental animal died, they took to freezing and sealing off the carcasses.

In his time, Rafferty had made many strange friendships, and now he was getting on passably well with the Vegan whose home contained the other end of the tunnel created by the lab unit. Rafferty called the Vegan Kelly because he couldn't manage the mixture of clicks, groans and diphthongs that the Vegan had put on to tape on the tape recorder they had sent him. In the three months he and Kelly had established a kind of basic picture and written form of communication, and then used it to send messages back and forth after hours, like two rather unskilled radio hams.

So he half suspected he knew what Navarre was talking about when the government scientific adviser arrived, almost choking on his anger.

'Rafferty! What have you done to us now?'

'What do you mean?'

'We've got reports of three more windows. That means the Vegans have got three more machines. Did you make them and send them through this?'

'I'm a lot of things, Dr Navarre,' Rafferty said with some dignity, 'but I am not a goddamn altruist! And as long as you're impounding everything that comes through, there's no way of their paying. So of course I didn't send them any.'

'Well, they've got them. How?'

'I admit I sent them the plans,' said Rafferty. 'Much more sensible than sending them the units, anyway. They pay me a royalty, and I collect when trade gets easier.' He lit a cigarette. 'Did you know Kelly tried to tell me he'd never heard of compound interest? I just pointed out that since he had worked out how to use the unit I'd sent him, he belonged to a technological civilization, and that I couldn't conceive of technology without compound interest. Then he broke down and admitted he was a trader himself.'

'How in the . . . how did you express the concept of compound interest in sign language?'

'I'm just a simple engineer, but the day I can't explain compound interest to a Vegan is the day I go out of business.'

Suddenly, Navarre began to sob. This embarrassed Rafferty, who hated having men cry in public. Navarre looked up, and out of his tear-stained face shone what they used to call a look of indescribable horror. 'Watson was right,' Navarre muttered. 'Poor Watson, he was right. They should have used a firing squad.'

Rafferty wanted to change the subject. 'Whatever happened to Watson?'

'Transfer. He's doing accounts in the naval dockyards now. Poor fellow. He was right all along.' With an effort, Navarre steadied his voice. 'So they've got the plans now and they're manufacturing.'

'Well, of course.'

'Of course. Of course.' Navarre tottered out. Rafferty wondered whether there was any room left in the accounts branch of the naval dockyard.

The next day, Navarre was back. 'Can I have a drink?'

Rafferty got him a drink.

Navarre took it in one. 'The Soviet Union is calling it a gross imperialist provocation. The French have mobilized and are on the point of declaring war on every other member of the United Nations. The British are calling it an attack on the Monarchy, and the Chinese are rattling rockets and talking about running-dog revisionist stooges of fascist Wall Street imperialism.' He reached out his glass and Rafferty filled it again. Navarre emptied it without seeming to notice. 'Something like vegetable peel falling out of the air in Lenin's tomb. Dead Vegan cats in the Louvre. The Royal Coach covered with something which I hope is indescribable. The Majority Leader was talking in the House when a grey shimmering window opened in front of him and he was hit in the face with the Vegan equivalent of a pail of wash water. And the Chinese say that their Great Helmsman was on his fifteenth lap of the Yangtze when he was sunk and nearly drowned by a barrage of strangely shaped softdrink bottles. Apparently he was only saved by remembering his own thoughts.'

Rafferty poured him another drink, and then poured one for himself. 'I knew I'd forgotten to tell you something yesterday.'

'What was that?'

'I forgot to tell you Kelly was selling them as garbage disposal units.'

Six months later, Navarre was looking a lot better. The Earth-Vegan trade treaty had been signed, and wholesale garbage disposal was a thing of the past. Rafferty was doing well. Kelly, as head of Vegan Export, was also doing well.

Then one day Rafferty got a phone call from the office. It was his business manager. 'Mr Rafferty, Vegan Export has just made an announcement about its new transmission unit.'

'Oh?'

'They're taking advantage of a clause in the trade treaty to sell them on the Earth market,' the manager continued.

'*Oh?*'

'And they're undercutting us seven and half percent.'

'Seven and a . . . thanks.'

Rafferty drove around looking for a vacant lot. When he got back to his laboratory, he turned on his unit, and sent through a message for Kelly to come to the end of the tunnel.

When the acknowledgment came that Kelly was there, Rafferty shaped up like a pitcher and let fly.

At speed, the very dead cat hurtled into the grey vortex.

Rapidly, Rafferty switched off.

Slowly, Rafferty smiled.

As a grey, shimmering window appeared in the air, and a bucket of Vegan wash water swept his bench clear.

Rafferty still smiled. After all, it wasn't every day that a man could trade with a nice, quiet, sensible friend like Kelly.

Late

A. Bertram Chandler

Captain Chandler has been writing sf for more than a quarter of a century—and sailing the world in everything from tramp steamers to troop transports for a similar period. He is currently captain of an Australian coastal freighter.

He is best known for his novels and short stories woven around a character called Grimes, a sort of futuristic Hornblower. These tales, together with his 'Rim Worlds' series, form a continuous and consistent 'future history' of his own devising, an achievement he shares with only a handful of other sf writers.

Occasionally he puts aside his personal world of tomorrow and writes something quite different from what we have come to expect. His recent novel, *The Bitter Pill*, was such a venture. So is the following story.

Readers may discover a subtle quality in LATE that reminds them of the sea, of the feeling of isolation that cuts them off from the rest of the world, and the vast distances and the loneliness of the solitary sailor. This is hardly surprising when one considers how familiar the author is with this environment, and how well he portrays the feelings of his protagonist.

He was a big man, this Jelks—big, with a ruddy complexion, china blue eyes, and thinning blond hair. He was a slow man—slow, but thorough and . . . slow. In the days of his not too far distant youth he had been told, often, by parents and teachers driven to and beyond the point of exasperation, that he would be late for his own funeral. On these frequent occasions he had smiled his slow, amiable smile and, the rebuke seemingly having failed to register, had plodded stolidly ahead with whatever had been the work in hand. In spite of his slowness—and because of his thoroughness—

173

he had won scholarship after scholarship, had, whilst still in his early thirties, become the sort of scientist and mathematician ignored by the popular press but still possessing a solid reputation among his academic peers.

'Jelks', old Professor Hartley had said, 'will be the ideal man for the job. He's slow—I grant you that. He'll be late for his own funeral. But he's thorough. He'll be hanging up there for weeks—observing, monitoring, making out reports, cooped up in a tiny tin coffin. Some men it'd drive nuts. It'd drive me nuts. Not Jelks. He'll monitor, and he'll observe; he'll make out and transmit his reports—and they'll be good, useful reports.'

'I can take it, then, that you recommend him,' said the Air Vice-Marshal. 'Of course, there's the security angle.'

'That's up to you people,' said the Professor.

The security angle was, of course, checked with far greater thoroughness than had been Jelk's scientific qualifications for the job. But no pink stain upon his political purity was found. He had never, so far as could be discovered, ever talked to a Communist. He had never read one single copy of the *Daily Worker*. Politically, his mind resembled that hard vacuum into which he was soon to be transported. There was no risk whatsoever that the knowledge he would win would ever find its way to the wrong side of the Iron Curtain.

He was commissioned, then, after a series of somewhat unpleasant medical tests. He purchased a uniform with the two and a half rings of a Squadron Leader on the sleeves and with an Observer's half wing on the breast. In the mess of the Station to which he had been posted he was just that— an observer, watching, with quiet wonderment, the fast young men with their split-second reaction times who, with the careless ease of the young man in the song, flung their sleek jets and rockets about the sky. He met the crew who were to put the satellite up in its orbit, the technicians who were to build and assemble his extraterrestrial laboratory for him around the nucleus of the third stage of the big step rocket. He was given the opportunity to learn something about rocket piloting himself.

'He'll never make a pilot,' said the Flight Lieutenant.

'He's slow. He's so slow that he'll be late for his own funeral.'

'Not to worry,' said the Wing Commander, 'He'll be taken out to the satellite, he'll be brought back. After all—boffins are wingless birds . . .'

With others of the team, Jelks was flown to Woomera. He stood with Air Marshals and Air Commodores and watched the big, three-stage rocket lift on its glaring column of fire, dwindle to a vapour trail in the cloudless sky. He watched the blips on the screens, saw that the first and second steps were falling as predicted, that the third step had established itself in its orbit. He watched the second rocket blast off—the one with equipment and technicians aboard, the one whose third step would bring back the crew of the first rocket. He did not, some weeks later, witness the blasting off of the third rocket (she was using the first and second stages of the first one) because he was in it.

He took the acceleration well, did Jelks, and was unaffected by free fall. When the time came, he put on his spacesuit as unconcernedly as if he had been dressing at his usual time in the morning in the bedroom of his Cambridge lodgings. He checked the various zippers and other fastenings with far less concern than a man heeding an admonitory notice in a public convenience. But even Jelks could not be unaffected by the spectacle visible outside the outer door of the airlock—the vast globe of Earth, green and brown and blue and silver; the space station, hanging seemingly motionless, with its spidery antennae and scanners, its solar mirrors, the big, inflated plastic sphere that had been the living and sleeping quarters for the assembly crew.

The speaker built into Jelk's helmet sputtered into life. 'Doctor Jelks! Can you hear me? There's a lifeline rigged to the satellite.'

'I've found it, thanks.'

'Well, good luck, Doctor. See you in a week's time.'

'Thanks, Brown. Don't forget to bring some newspapers.'

Jelks pulled himself, hand over hand, to the airlock door of the space station. His clumsy, gloved hands manipulated the opening mechanism. He stood inside the tiny compartment waiting for the green light to glow. It came on, and he opened the inner door and drifted into his laboratory.

Warren was there—another Squadron Leader—fully dressed except for his helmet. He helped Jelks to remove his, then said, 'Here you are, Doctor. All ready for you. All tested and working.'

'I'll take your word for it,' said Jelks. He had come to know Warren, had recognized in him a thoroughness almost equal to his own.

'Exactly the same as the mock-up,'' said Warren.

'So I see.'

'The transmitter's sealed, of course,' Warren went on.

'Not to be used except in an emergency,' said Jelks. 'They told me. There's only one emergency I can think of. Did you ever work out the chances of being struck by a meteor?'

'No,' said Warren. 'But at times that plastic tent of ours out there seemed far too flimsy.'

'Live in it for a hundred years,' said Jelks, 'and you *might* be hit by one large enough to do real damage. Well—all the best.' His following words carried quotation marks fore and aft. 'Happy landings.'

'Be good,' said Warren.

'And careful,' said Jelks. He grinned. 'Slow *and* careful. I know what they say about me. I just want to keep things that way.'

He helped the other Squadron Leader on with his helmet, checked the fastenings of Warren's suit as meticulously as he had done those of his own. He drifted with him to the inner airlock door, watched the indicator lights until Warren was clear of the satellite and on his way to the waiting rocket. Jelks went, then, to one of the ports, watched the spaceship, now free of the lifeline, emit a brief, vivid jet of flame and slowly drop away from his field of vision. He took off the rest of his suit then, stowed it carefully in the locker designed for this purpose. For the next few hours he busied himself checking every smallest detail of the life-sustaining apparatus of his spatial laboratory. After he had done this he prepared for his first tests, his first experiments. He was a happy man— weeks of highly interesting work lay ahead of him and there was no urgency. Neither lack of gravity nor absence of company bothered him.

At the end of a week the rocket made its rendezvous with

the space station. Brown—the Flight Lieutenant who was captain of the little spaceship—came across himself on the lifeline, brought with him the promised newspapers. He took with him recordings made by the instruments, also Jelk's first report. He said. 'I don't think that the news has leaked out yet. When our friends on the other side of the Curtain *do* find out, there's going to be a mass liquidation of astronomers.'

'Anything in these?' asked Jelks, patting the bundle of newspapers.

'There's Jane of course—but she hasn't been the same girl since the purity drive set in . . . Overdressed in every instalment. Talking of purity drives—some crank reckons that the End of the World is at hand.'

'Then it's high time that we pushed ahead with the Interplanetary Project,' said Jelks.

'What do you think you're out here for?' asked the Flight Lieutenant.

After the spaceship had gone, Jelks settled down with his newspapers. There was even less haste than there had been before—it would be all of six weeks before the next rendezvous. He read the news items with an attitude of godlike detachment. He did the crossword puzzles. The listed radio programmes reminded him that not once had he used the receiver that was part of the station's equipment. He resolved that from now on he would, at least, keep up with the news. He read the accounts of the meetings at which the self-styled Prophet John had spoken, marvelled that in this day and age, the age of atomic power and space travel, anybody should subscribe to this mystical claptrap. Then he went back to work.

It was two days before the rocket was due that Jelks was making a series of observations of Earth from the station. He was over the night hemisphere, sliding swiftly in his South-North orbit while the great, shadowed globe turned slowly beneath him. The sky was clear above South America and Jelks could see the city lights—Buenos Aires, Rio, Santiago. He was surprised when the darkness swept suddenly over the tiny, glimmering sparks that were the homes of men, thought at first that the fault lay in his instruments. It was over North America that he saw the golden glow and the thousand-mile-long lightnings. His vehicle carried him over the Pole and south over the sunlit hemisphere. But neither land nor sea could be distinguished —all Earth was obscured by an impenetrable layer of dense black cloud.

It must be, thought Jelks, some meteorological phenomenon. He was a physicist, and a good one, and he knew of no weapon that could have produced such an effect. On the other hand—and he felt the beginnings of cold, sickening fear—he was also a meteorologist of sorts, and he knew of no meteorological explanation for what he was seeing. Slowly, unhurriedly (he refused to hurry), he switched on the receiver. Slowly, unhurriedly, he tried waveband after waveband. The set was dead. Slowly, unhurriedly, Jelks took photographs of the black ball over which he swung in his orbit, jotted down in his log what he had seen—the obscuration of the city lights, the golden glow and the dreadful lightnings. Again he returned to the radio and this time, but all too briefly, caught what seemed to be a broadcast of some great choir, somewhere. It was the merest echo, and in spite of all his care and skill he was unable to bring the controls of the set back to the right setting.

He was tired then—a tiredness that came, he knew, more from strain than from overwork. I can do nothing, he thought. He put his cameras on automatic control, then strapped himself into his bunk. He slept—a deep sleep untroubled by dream or nightmare.

When he awoke, he went straight to the most convenient port, looked down to the world. He was over the sunlit hemisphere again and Europe was below him. The black overcast was gone. Over Russia there was smoke—it was, he thought, a forest fire, covering thousands of square miles. He turned his telescope first on London. London still stood— there were no craters, no fires. Paris, Berlin, Rome, Moscow —all were, seemingly, untouched. After a while he was able to see the cities of the Southern Hemisphere, and he saw nothing to arouse his apprehension. But there was a bush fire in Australia and, within his field of view some time later, another forest fire in Canada.

The radio was still dead.

His chronometers told him that it lacked minutes of his rendezvous with the rocket from Woomera. His chronometers told him that the rocket from Woomera should now be alongside the space station—but space was empty. His chronometers told him that the rocket from Woomera was all of two hours overdue.

'I was hoping that Brown would be able to tell me something,' he muttered to himself as he broke the seals on the transmitter. He hesitated before switching on. Was this an emergency? He decided to give Brown another hour, and filled in the time by vainly hunting up and down the wavebands of his receiver.

He switched on the set, waited for it to warm up. His fingers reached out for the key. 'James calling Rosie Bell,' he sent in the prearranged code, on the agreed wavelength. 'James calling Rosie Bell. I am worried.' He sent again, 'James calling Rosie Bell.' Again he sent, 'James calling Rosie Bell. James calling . . . James calling . . .'

He broke out the emergency brandy bottle. Moving slowly and methodically, never forgetting to allow for the conditions of free fall, he managed to take a drink without wasting a drop of the fluid. Suddenly he felt lost and lonely, and Earth very dear and very far away. Somehow, for no reason, he remembered the thing that had always been said about him—that he would be late for his own funeral. Unless I get back to Earth, he thought, I shan't have one.

He put on his spacesuit, went outside. He studied the exterior of the station. The wings were still there—it had been worth nobody's while to remove them. The solar mirrors, the various antennae and the telescope tubes were removable. The rocket motor was, he knew, still workable, and there was fuel. It would not be an impossible task to convert the station into what it had originally been—a replica of the rocket whose rendezvous was now hours overdue.

Jelks worked slowly and carefully. He stripped the rocket of all aerodynamically undesirable excrescences. He then reduced weight by the jettison of equipment and fittings from the interior. The records he kept, also the Geiger counter. Then, strapped to his desk in the strangely bare and spacious cabin of the station, he worked out his flight plan. Then, satisfied that nothing had been left unnecessarily to chance, he secured himself in the pilot's seat and fired the braking blast. The huddle of dumped instruments and machinery dropped away from the station. Jelks allowed himself briefly to wonder whether it would ever be picked up and used again.

Then the station had to be turned—a simple enough task using the built-in, manually operated flywheel. Jelks sat at the controls—waiting. He allowed himself one experimental wiggle of the control surfaces, but no more. He did not allow his eyes to stray from the air-speed indicator, ever alert for the first warning quiver of the needle.

His reaction times were slow—but then, even at his initial supersonic speed, he had to come down a long way. Through the first high cirrus he swept, and the temperature inside the ship rose to an uncomfortable level. He hoped that the refrigerating unit would prove equal to the strain. Out of sunlight into darkness he swept—and saw the lights of cities and of vast fires beneath him. Out of darkness into sunlight he screamed—and there was the sea, and ships, and the European coastline. Down, he spiralled, down, down. He felt the wrenching shock as his first ribbon parachute took hold and then was wrenched from the fuselage.

A less slow man would have fought the controls, would have striven grimly for mastery of the machine in which he rode. Not Jelks. He knew his limitations; he knew, too, the excellence of the design of the ship. He knew that she would, almost, land herself without damage. His main anxiety was that the landing should take place on a site of his own selection.

Gently, carefully, he eased the ship down, determined not to repeat the mistake that had lost him one of his parachutes. Gently, carefully, he brought her round in a wide arc, round again in a smaller one. England was beneath him—cities and towns and green fields. London was beneath him, then the seaside towns of the south coast and the blue-green waters of the Channel. Ships he saw in the narrow sea, but there were no aircraft in the air. He thought it strange that no investigatory jet or rockets had been sent up to intercept and challenge.

Lower he spiralled, lower. He could see traffic on the roads now. He could not be sure—the speed at which he was still travelling made accurate observation impossible—but the cars, the coaches, and the trucks seemed to be stationary. At one crossroads he glimpsed an untidy huddle of machines, saw the black scar of fire on grass verge and hedgerows.

At last he was over the station to which he had first been posted. The long runway was clear. Remembering his radio, he called the tower. There was no reply. He looked down to the windsock and saw that his line of approach could not be bettered. He lowered his undercarriage, released the last of his braking parachutes. The concrete was sweeping beneath him with terrifying speed. One wheel of the undercarriage touched, bounced, touched again. The ship heeled over, the tip of his port delta wing dug into the concrete. Landing strip and administration buildings wheeled before him, around him. Something struck the back of his head and he took no further interest in the details of the landing.

His first waking thought was to wonder who would have to pay for all the damage that he had done. 'One space station, complete,' he muttered. 'That'll make a nasty hole in a month's pay . . .' He realized, slowly, that he was hanging upside down in his securing straps. Before releasing himself he worked things out in his methodical manner, snapped open the catches so that he was able to ease himself gently down onto his shoulders. A clumsy, slow-motion somersault brought him to a sitting posture.

The airlock doors were hopelessly jammed, but it didn't matter, the cabin was so wrenched and battered that it was easy for him to force his way out at the minor cost of a slightly lacerated hand and a badly torn trouser knee. The unaccustomed gravity made him feel heavy and tired; for all of five minutes he stood beside the wreckage of the rocket waiting for somebody to come out to him. Somewhere a dog —one of the Station's Alsatians?—was barking hysterically.

Slowly, he walked toward the Mess. If there were anybody

in Administration, he thought, they'd have seen me come in. They couldn't have missed it. He noticed that the Alsatian he had heard barking was trailing him, keeping well back. He wished that he had a weapon of some kind—there was something mad about the appearance of the brute.

All doors in the Station were open. Jelks went first to the bar—hungry, uncharacteristically, for company. The bar was deserted. There were four pint tankards standing on the counter, each perhaps two-thirds full. The beer was stale and flat, and had dead flies in it. In another glass—a martini?—a wasp was drowned. Jelks went behind the bar, found a glass, poured himself a stiff whisky. After it he felt better. He picked up a newspaper on one of the tables, looked at the date. It was a Sunday paper. It was the day that he had seen the golden glow and the supernal lightnings, the day of the impenetrable black overcast.

Jelks stood there and shouted. 'Anybody at home? Is anybody at home?' Only the barking of the half-mad Alsatian outside answered him. 'Is anybody here?' bellowed Jelks.

Jelks went into the pantry adjoining the dining room, found a stale loaf of bread and some butter that wasn't quite rancid. He opened a tin of sardines, made a filling yet unsatisfying meal. He watched the flies that came to feast on the crumbs on his plate almost with affection. Dogs, he thought, and flies. And I heard a bird singing . . . It can't be radioactive dust . . . There shouldn't be any need to get the Geiger counter from the ship. It's probably smashed, anyhow.

He stiffened abruptly as he heard a new sound—then relaxed. It was the sound of bells, it was the church clock in the village, two miles distant, striking the hour. In the still air the sound carried well; yet, somehow, was tenuous, could have been some ghostly carillon pealing in the almost airless depths of a lunar crater.

'I will go to the village,' said Jelks—to the flies, to the barking dog outside, to nobody in particular. He picked up the remains of the loaf, took it with him. 'Here!' he said to the dog. The Alsatian stopped barking, looked at Jelks suspiciously. The man threw the bread down gently, watched the dog as it sniffed the food and then began to eat ravenously. He waited until it had finished eating, then said, 'Come on, boy.' The dog followed him, close to heel, but only as far as the gates.

So Jelks had to walk alone to the village. After the first half mile he regretted that he had never learned to drive—he could have had his pick of the Station cars, of the abandoned vehicles along the road. The sun was high in the cloudless sky and he was perspiring inside his coveralls. His feet were tender in the thin, canvas shoes that had been his footwear in the space station. Yet, in spite of his discomfort, he was able to watch, to observe, to see the animals in the fields, the birds in the sky and in the hedgerows. He was able to *feel*— able to sense the impalpable something that Chesterton had called so aptly 'the smell of Sunday morning.' But it was not a Sunday.

He was footsore and weary when he reached the village. On the window ledge of the first cottage a fat, tortoiseshell cat regarded him gravely. Jelks put out his hand to touch the animal, to stroke it. It responded to his advances with feline courtesy but without much enthusiasm. Jelks left the cat to its own devices, knocked on the cottage door. There was no reply. He opened the door, went inside. A smell of burning still lingered in the kitchen—the fire was out, but the Sunday joint was a mess of charred, acrid stinking meat. On the oven the saucepans in which the vegetables had been boiling were dry and their contents ruined. On the kitchen table was a half-finished cup of tea—in which floated the inevitable drowned, bedraggled flies.

It must have been a disaster of some kind, thought Jelks. I shall find them in the church . . . He left the cottage, walked slowly along the street to the tall, gray spire. His mind conjured up images of what he would find there—huddled corpses, victims of some fearful weapon produced by the biochemists. He walked more slowly than was justified by his sore feet.

The church was empty. The sunlight struck the stained glass of the windows, a patina of rainbow colouring on altar and altar cloth, reflected by dull gleaming metal. But there was damage. In places the stone flooring of the aisle had been ripped up, the underlying earth scattered untidily and carelessly. The man (the last man, the only man) stared uncomprehendingly at this—he thought—vandalism, then walked slowly out through the side door to the graveyard.

There, in the warm sunlight, he gazed at the overset headstones, the heaped and scattered earth, the odd, terrifying craters. He began to laugh—quietly at first, then with mounting hysteria. Abruptly he stopped and stood there, scarcely breathing, straining his ears to try to catch some faint echo of the trumpet that once (and once only) had sounded, the trumpet that he would never hear.

Mother Hitton's Littul Kittons

Cordwainer Smith

'Cordwainer Smith' was the pseudonym for Dr Paul Linebarger, a political scientist who was also the godson of Sun Yat-Sen and author of the definitive textbook on psychological warfare. He did not start writing sf until rather late in life, and his identity was kept a closely guarded secret until his untimely death in the late Sixties.

Dr Linebarger was a man with a lifetime of oriental studies behind him when he began to write sf, and a deep understanding of the need to rework our myths for each new generation. Towards the end of his life he spent some time in Australia, lecturing in political science at the Australian National University. He had a unique and abiding vision of Australia and her peoples which was expressed in his fiction; a collection of his 'Old Norstrilia' stories will appear in the U.S. this year. The following story brilliantly blends fragments of his visionary 'future history' with a fairy tale most small children know by heart . . . but which you may hardly recognize in this remarkable transformation.

> Poor communications deter theft;
> good communications promote theft;
> perfect communications stop theft.
> *Van Braam*

1

The moon spun. The woman watched. Twenty-one facets had been polished at the moon's equator. Her function was to arm it. She was Mother Hitton, the Weapons Mistress of Old North Australia.

She was a ruddy-faced, cheerful blonde of indeterminate age. Her eyes were blue, her bosom heavy, her arms strong. She looked like a mother, but the only child she had ever had died many generations ago. Now she acted as mother to a planet, not to a person; the Norstrilians slept well because they knew she was watching. The weapons slept their long, sick sleep.

185

This night she glanced for the two-hundredth time at the warning bank. The bank was quiet. No danger lights shone. Yet she felt an enemy out somewhere in the universe—an enemy waiting to strike at her and her world, to snatch at the immeasurable wealth of the Norstrilians—and she snorted with impatience. Come along, little man, she thought. Come along, little man, and die. Don't keep me waiting.

She smiled when she recognized the absurdity of her own thought.

She waited for him.

And he did not know it.

He, the robber, was relaxed enough. He was Benjacomin Bozart, and was highly trained in the arts of relaxation.

No one at Sunvale, here on Ttiollé, could suspect that he was a Senior Warden of the Guild of Thieves, reared under the light of the starry-violet star. No one could smell the odour of Viola Siderea upon him. 'Viola Siderea', the Lady Ru had said, 'was once the most beautiful of worlds and it is now the most rotten. Its people were once models for mankind, and now they are thieves, liars and killers. You can smell their souls in the open day.' The Lady Ru had died a long time ago. She was much respected, but she was wrong. The robber did not smell to others at all. He knew it. He was no more 'wrong' than a shark approaching a school of cod. Life's nature is to live, and he had been nurtured to live as he had to live—by seeking prey.

How else could he live? Viola Siderea had gone bankrupt a long time ago, when the photonic sails had disappeared from space and the planoforming ships began to whisper their way between the stars. His ancestors had been left to die on an off-trail planet. They refused to die. Their ecology shifted and they became predators upon man, adapted by time and genetics to their deadly tasks. And he, the robber, was champion of all his people—the best of their best.

He was Benjacomin Bozart.

He had sworn to rob Old North Australia or to die in the attempt, and he had no intention of dying.

The beach at Sunvale was warm and lovely. Ttiollé was

a free and casual transit planet. His weapons were luck and himself: he planned to play both well.

The Norstrilians could kill.

So could he.

At this moment, in this place, he was a happy tourist at a lovely beach. Elsewhere, elsewhen, he could become a ferret among conies, a hawk among doves.

Benjacomin Bozart, Thief and Warden. He did not know that someone was waiting for him. Someone who did not know his name was prepared to waken death, just for him. He was still serene.

Mother Hitton was not serene. She sensed him dimly but could not yet spot him.

One of her weapons snored. She turned it over.

A thousand stars away, Benjacomin Bozart smiled as he walked toward the beach.

2

Benjacomin felt like a tourist. His tanned face was tranquil. His proud, hooded eyes were calm. His handsome mouth, even without its charming smile, kept a suggestion of pleasantness at its corners. He looked attractive without seeming odd in the least. He looked much younger than he actually was. He walked with springy, happy steps along the beach of Sunvale.

The waves rolled in, white-crested, like the breakers of Mother Earth. The Sunvale people were proud of the way their world resembled Manhome itself. Few of them had even seen Manhome, but they had all heard a bit of history and most of them had a passing anxiety when they thought of the ancient government still wielding political power across the depth of space. They did not like the old Instrumentality of Earth, but they respected and feared it. The waves might remind them of the pretty side of Earth; they did not want to remember the not-so-pretty side.

This man was like the pretty side of old Earth. They could not sense the power within him. The Sunvale people smiled absently at him as he walked past them along the shoreline.

The atmosphere was quiet and everything around him

serene. He turned his face to the sun. He closed his eyes. He let the warm sunlight beat through his eyelids, illuminating him with its comfort and its reassuring touch.

Benjacomin dreamed of the greatest theft that any man had ever planned. He dreamed of stealing a huge load of the wealth from the richest world that mankind had ever built. He thought of what would happen when he would finally bring riches back to the planet of Viola Siderea where he had been reared. Benjacomin turned his face away from the sun and languidly looked over the other people on the beach.

There were no Norstrilians in sight yet. They were easy enough to recognize. Big people with red complexions; superb athletes and yet, in their own way, innocent, young, and very tough. He had trained for this theft for two hundred years, his life prolonged for the purpose by the Guild of Thieves on Viola Siderea. He himself embodied the dreams of his own planet, a poor planet once a crossroads of commerce, now sunken to being a minor outpost for spoliation and pilferage.

He saw a Norstrilian woman come out from the hotel and go down to the beach. He waited, and he looked, and he dreamed. He had a question to ask and no adult Australian would answer it.

'Funny,' thought he, 'that I call them 'Australians' even now. That's the old, old Earth name for them—rich, brave, tough people. Fighting children standing on half the world . . . and now they are the tyrants of all mankind. They hold the wealth. They have the santaclara, and other people live or die depending upon the commerce they have with the Norstrilians. But I won't. And my people won't. We're men who are wolves to man.'

Benjacomin waited gracefully. Tanned by the light of many suns, he looked forty though he was two hundred. He dressed casually, by the standards of a vacationer. He might have been an intercultural salesman, a senior gambler, an assistant starport manager. He might even have been a detective working along the commerce lanes. He wasn't. He was a thief. And he was so good a thief that people turned to him and put their property in his hands because he was reassuring, calm, grey-eyes, blonde-haired. Benjacomin waited. The woman glanced at him, a quick glance full of open suspicion.

What she saw must have calmed her. She went on past. She called back over the dune, 'Come on, Johnny, we can swim out here.' A little boy, who looked eight or ten years old, came over the dune top, running toward his mother.

Benjacomin tensed like a cobra. His eyes became sharp, his eyelids narrowed.

This was the prey. Not too young, not too old. If the victim had been too young he wouldn't know the answer; if the victim were too old it was no use taking him on. Norstrilians were famed in combat; adults were mentally and physically too strong to warrant attack.

Benjacomin knew that every thief who had approached the planet of the Norstrilians—who had tried to raid the dream world of Old North Australia—had gotten out of contact with his people and had died. There was no word of any of them.

And yet he knew that hundreds of thousands of Norstrilians must know *the* secret. They now and then made jokes about it. He had heard these jokes when he was a young man, and now he was more than an old man without once coming near the answer. Life was expensive. He was well into his third lifetime and the lifetimes had been purchased honestly by his people. Good thieves all of them, paying out hard-stolen money to obtain the medicine to let their greatest thief remain living. Benjacomin didn't like violence. But when violence prepared the way to the greatest theft of all time, he was willing to use it.

The woman looked at him again. The mask of evil which had flashed across his face faded into benignity; he calmed. She caught him in that moment of relaxation. She liked him.

She smiled and, with that awkward hesitation so characteristic of the Norstrilians, she said, 'Could you mind my boy a bit while I go in the water? I think we've seen each other here at the hotel.'

'I don't mind,' said he. 'I'd be glad to. Come here, son.'

Johnny walked across the sunlight dunes to his own death. He came within reach of his mother's enemy.

But the mother had already turned.

The trained hand of Benjacomin Bozart reached out. He seized the child by the shoulder. He turned the boy toward him, forcing him down. Before the child could cry out, Benjacomin had the needle into him with the truth drug.

All Johnny reacted to was pain, and then a hammerblow inside his own skull as the powerful drug took force.

Benjacomin looked out over the water. The mother was swimming. She seemed to be looking back at them. She was obviously unworried. To her, the child seemed to be looking at something the stranger was showing him in a relaxed, easy way.

'Now, sonny,' said Benjacomin, 'tell me, what's the outside defence?'

The boy didn't answer.

'What is the outer defence, sonny? What is the outer defence?' repeated Benjacomin. The boy still didn't answer.

Something close to horror ran over the skin of Benjacomin Bozart as he realized that he had gambled his safety on this planet, gambled the plans themselves for a chance to break the secret of the Norstrilians.

He had been stopped by simple, easy devices. The child had already been conditioned against attack. Any attempt to force knowledge out of the child brought on a conditioned reflex of total muteness. The boy was literally unable to talk.

Sunlight gleaming on her wet hair, the mother turned around and called back, 'Are you all right, Johnny?'

Benjacomin waved to her instead. 'I'm showing him my pictures, ma'am. He likes 'em. Take your time.' The mother hesitated and then turned back to the water and swam slowly away.

Johnny, taken by the drug, sat lightly, like an invalid, on Benjacomin's lap.

Benjacomin said, 'Johnny, you're going to die now and you will hurt terribly if you don't tell me what I want to know.' The boy struggled weakly against his grasp. Benjacomin repeated. 'I'm going to hurt you if you don't tell me what I want to know. What are the outer defences? What are the outer defences?'

The child struggled and Benjacomin realized that the boy was putting up a fight to comply with the orders, not a fight to get away. He let the child slip through his hands and the boy put out a finger and began writing on the wet sand. The letters stood out.

A man's shadow loomed behind them.

Benjacomin, alert, ready to spin, kill or run, slipped to the ground beside the child and said, 'That's a jolly puzzle. That is a good one. Show me some more.' He smiled up at the passing adult. The man was a stranger. The stranger gave him a very curious glance which became casual when he saw the pleasant face of Benjacomin, so tenderly and so agreeably playing with the child.

The fingers were still making the letters in the sand.

There stood the riddle in letters: MOTHER HITTON'S LITTUL KITTONS.

The woman was coming back from the sea, the mother with questions. Benjacomin stroked the sleeve of his coat and brought out his second needle, a shallow poison which it would take days or weeks of laboratory work to detect. He thrust it directly into the boy's brain, slipping the needle up behind the skin at the edge of the hairline. The hair shadowed the tiny prick. The incredibly hard needle slipped under the edge of the skull. The child was dead.

Murder was accomplished. Benjacomin casually erased the secret from the sand. The woman came nearer. He called to her, his voice full of pleasant concern, 'Ma'am, you'd better come here, I think your son has fainted from the heat.'

He gave the mother the body of her son. Her face changed to alarm. She looked frightened and alert. She didn't know how to meet this.

For a dreadful moment she looked into his eyes.

Two hundred years of training took effect . . . She saw nothing. The murderer did not shine with murder. The hawk was hidden beneath the dove. The heart was masked by the trained face.

Benjacomin relaxed in professional assurance. He had been prepared to kill her too, although he was not sure that he could kill an adult, female Norstrilian. Very helpfully said he, 'You stay here with him. I'll run to the hotel and get help. I'll hurry.'

He turned and ran. A beach attendant saw him and ran

toward him. 'The child's sick,' he shouted. He came to the mother in time to see blunt, puzzled tragedy on her face and with it, something more than tragedy: doubt.

'He's not sick,' said she. 'He's dead.'

'He can't be.' Benjacomin looked attentive. He felt attentive. He forced the sympathy to pour out of his posture, out of all the little muscles of his face. 'He can't be. I was talking to him just a minute ago. We were doing little puzzles in the sand.'

The mother spoke with a hollow, broken voice that sounded as though it would never find the right chords for human speech again, but would go on forever with the ill-attuned flats of unexpected grief. 'He's dead,' she said. 'You saw him die and I guess I saw him die, too. I can't tell what's happened. The child was full of santaclara. He had a thousand years to live but now he's dead. What's your name?'

Benjacomin said, 'Eldon. Eldon the salesman, ma'am. I live here lots of times.'

3

Mother Hitton's littul kittons. Mother Hitton's littul kittons.

The silly phrase ran in his mind. Who was Mother Hitton? Who was she the mother of? What were *kittons?* Were they a misspelling for 'kittens?' Little cats? Or were they something else?

Had he killed a fool to get a fool's answer?

How many more days did he have to stay there with the doubtful, staggered woman? How many days did he have to watch and wait? He wanted to get back to Viola Siderea; to take the secret, bad as it was, for his people to study. Who was Mother Hitton?

He forced himself out of his room and went downstairs.

The pleasant monotony of a big hotel was such that the other guests looked interestedly at him. He was the man who had watched while the child died on the beach.

Some lobby-living scandalmongers that stayed there had made up fantastic stories that he had killed the child. Others attacked the stories, saying they knew perfectly well who

Eldon was. He was Eldon the salesman. It was ridiculous.

People hadn't changed much, even though the ships with the Go-Captains sitting at their hearts whispered between the stars, even though people shuffled between worlds—when they had the money to pay their passage back and forth—like leaves falling in soft, playful winds. Benjacomin faced a tragic dilemma. He knew very well that any attempt to decode the answer would run directly into the protective devices set up by the Norstrilians.

Old North Australia was immensely wealthy. It was known the length and breadth of all the stars that they had hired mercenaries, defensive spies, hidden agents and alerting devices.

Even Manhome—Mother Earth herself, whom no money could buy—was bribed by the drug of life. An ounce of the santaclara drug, reduced, crystallized and called 'stroon', could give forty to sixty years of life. Stroon entered the rest of the Earth by grams and kilograms, but it was refined back on North Australia by the tonne. With treasure like this, the Norstrilians owned an unimaginable world whose resources overreached all conceivable limits of money. They could buy anything. They could pay with other peoples' lives.

For hundreds of years they had given secret funds to buying foreigners' services to safeguard their own security.

Benjacomin stood there in the lobby: *Mother Hitton's littul kittons*.

He had all the wisdom and wealth of a thousand worlds stuck in his mind but he didn't dare ask anywhere as to what it meant.

Suddenly he brightened.

He looked like a man who had thought of a good game to play, a pleasant diversion to be welcomed, a companion to be remembered, a new food to be tasted. He had had a very happy thought.

There was one source that wouldn't talk. The library. He could at least check the obvious, simple things, and find out what there was already in the realm of public knowledge concerning the secret he had taken from the dying boy.

His own safety had not been wasted; Johnny's life had

not been thrown away—if he could find any one of the four words as a key. *Mother* or *Hitton* or *Littul,* in its special meaning, or *Kitton.* He might yet break through to the loot of Norstrilia.

He swung jubilantly, turning on the ball of his right foot. He moved lightly and pleasantly toward the billiard room, beyond which lay the library. He went in.

This was a very expensive hotel and very old-fashioned. It even had books made out of paper, with genuine bindings. Benjacomin crossed the room. He saw that they had the *Galactic Encyclopaedia* in two hundred volumes. He took down the volume headed 'Hi-Hi'. He opened it from the rear, looking for the name 'Hitton' and there it was. 'Hitton, Benjamin—pioneer of old North Australia. Said to be originator of part of the defence system. Lived A.D. 10719–17213.' That was all. Benjacomin moved among the books. The word 'kittons' in that peculiar spelling did not occur anywhere, neither in the encyclopaedia nor in any other list maintained by the library. He walked out and upstairs, back to his room.

'Littul' had not appeared at all. It was probably the boy's own childish mistake.

He took a chance. The mother, half blind with bewilderment and worry, sat in a stiff-backed chair on the edge of the porch. The other women talked to her. They knew her husband was coming. Benjacomin went up to her and tired to pay his respects. She didn't see him.

'I'm leaving now, ma'am. I'm going on to the next planet, but I'll be back in two or three subjective weeks. And if you need me for urgent questions, I'll leave my addresses with the police here.'

Benjacomin left the weeping mother.

Benjacomin left the quiet hotel. He obtained a priority passage.

The easy-going Sunvale Police made no resistance to his demand for a sudden departure visa. After all, he had an identity, he had his own funds, and it was not the custom of Sunvale to contradict its guests. Benjacomin went on the ship and as he moved towards the cabin in which he could rest for a few hours, a man stepped up beside him. A youngish man, hair parted in the middle, short of stature, grey of eyes.

This man was the local agent of the Norstrilian secret police.

Benjacomin, trained thief that he was, did not recognize the policeman. It never occurred to him that the library itself had been attuned and that the word 'kittons' in the peculiar Norstrilian spelling was itself an alert. Looking for that spelling had set off a minor alarm. He had touched the trip-wire.

The stranger nodded. Benjacomin nodded back. 'I'm a travelling man, waiting over between assignments. I haven't been doing very well. How are you making out?'

'Doesn't matter to me. I don't earn money; I'm a technician. Liverant is the name.'

Benjacomin sized him up. The man was a technician all right. They shook hands perfunctorily. Liverant said, 'I'll join you in the bar a little later. I think I'll rest a bit first.'

They both lay down then and said very little while the momentary flash of planoform went through the ship. The flash passed. From books and lessons they knew that the ship was leaping forward in two dimensions while, somehow or other, the fury of space itself was fed into the computers—and that these in turn were managed by the Go-Captain who controlled the ship.

They knew these things but they could not feel them. All they felt was the sting of a slight pain.

The sedative was in the air itself, sprayed in the ventilating system. They both expected to become a little drunk.

The thief Benjacomin Bozart was trained to resist intoxication and bewilderment. Any sign whatever that a telepath had tried to read his mind would have been met with fierce animal resistance, implanted in his unconscious during early years of training. Bozart was not trained against deception by a technician; it never occurred to the Thieves' Guild back on Viola Siderea that it would be necessary for their own people to resist deceivers. Liverant had already been in touch with Norstrilia—Norstrilia whose money reached across the stars, Norstrilia who had alerted a hundred thousand worlds against the mere thought of trespass.

Liverant began to chatter. 'I wish I could go further than

195

this trip. I wish that I could go to Olympia. You can buy anything in Olympia.'

'I've heard of it,' said Bozart. 'It's sort of a funny trading planet with not much chance for businessmen, isn't it?'

Liverant laughed and his laughter was merry and genuine. 'Trading? They don't trade. They swap. They take all the stolen loot of a thousand worlds and sell it over again and they change and they paint it and they mark it. That's their business there. The people are blind. It's a strange world, and all you have to do is to go in there and you can have anything you want. Man,' said Liverant, 'what I could do in a year in that place! Everybody is blind except me and a couple of tourists. And there's all the wealth that everybody thought he's mislaid, half the wrecked ships, the forgotten colonies (they've all been cleaned out), and bang! it all goes to Olympia.'

Olympia wasn't really that good and Liverant didn't know why it was his business to guide the killer there. All he knew was that he had a duty and the duty was to direct the trespasser.

Many years before either man was born the code word had been planted in directories, in books, in packing cases and invoices: *Kittons* misspelled. This was the cover name for the outer moon of Norstrilian defence. The use of the cover name brought a raging alert ready into action, with systemic nerves as hot and quick as incandescent tungsten wire.

By the time that they were ready to go to the bar and have refreshments, Benjacomin had half forgotten that it was his new acquaintance who had suggested Olympia rather than another place. He had to go to Viola Siderea to get the credits to make the flight to take the wealth, to win the world of Olympia.

4

At home on his native planet Bozart was a subject of a gentle but very sincere celebration.

The Elders of the Guild of Thieves welcomed him. They congratulated him. 'Who else could have done what you've done, boy? You've made the opening move in a brand new game of chess. There has never been a gambit like this before. We have a name; we have an animal. We'll try it right here.' The Thieves' Council turned to their own encyclopaedia. They turned through the name 'Hitton' and then found the reference 'kitton'. None of them knew that a false lead had been planted there—by an agent in their world.

The agent, in his turn, had been seduced years before, debauched in the middle of his career, forced into temporary honesty, blackmailed and sent home. In all the years that he had waited for a dreaded countersign—a countersign which he himself never knew to be an extension of Norstrilian intelligence—he never dreamed that he could pay his debt to the outside world so simply. All they had done was to send him one page to add to the encyclopaedia. He added it and then went home, weak with exhaustion. The years of fear and waiting were almost too much for the thief. He drank heavily for fear that he might otherwise kill himself. Meanwhile, the pages remained in order, including the new one, slightly altered for his colleagues. The encyclopaedia indicated the change like any normal revision, though the whole entry was new and falsified:

Beneath this passage one revision ready. Dated 24th year of second issue.
The reported 'Kittons' of Norstrilia are nothing more than the use of organic means to induce the disease in Earth-mutated sheep which produces a virus in its turn, refinable as the santaclara drug. The term 'Kittons' enjoyed a temporary vogue as a reference term both to the disease and to the destructibility of the disease in the event of external attack. This is believed to have been connected with the career of Benjamin Hitton, one of the original pioneers of Norstrilia.

The Council of Thieves read it and the Chairman of the Council said 'I've got your papers ready. You can go try them now. Where do you want to go? Through Neuhamburg?'

'No,' said Benjacomin. 'I thought I'd try Olympia.'

'Olympia's all right,' said the Chairman. 'Go easy. There's

only one chance in a thousand you'll fail. But if you do, we might have to pay for it.'

He smiled wryly and handed Benjacomin a blank mortgage against all the labour and all the property of Viola Siderea.

The Chairman laughed with a sort of snort. 'It'd be pretty rough on us if you had to borrow enough on the trading planet to force us to become honest—and then lost out anyhow.'

'No fear,' said Benjacomin. 'I can cover that.'

There are some worlds where all dreams die, but square-clouded Olympia is not one of them. The eyes of men and women are bright on Olympia, for they see nothing.

'Brightness was the colour of pain,' said Nachtigall, 'when we could see. If thine eye offend thee, pluck thyself out, for the fault lies not in the eye but in the soul.'

Such talk was common in Olympia, where the settlers went blind a long time ago and now think themselves superior to sighted people. Radar wires tickle their living brains; they can perceive radiation as well as can an animal-type man with little aquariums hung in the middle of his face. Their pictures are sharp, and they demand sharpness. Their buildings soar at impossible angles. Their blind children sing songs as the tailored climate proceeds according to the numbers, geometrical as a kaleidoscope.

There went the man, Bozart himself. Among the blind his dreams soared, and he paid money for information which no living person had ever seen.

Sharp-clouded and aqua-skied, Olympia swam past him like another man's dream. He did not mean to tarry there, because he had a rendezvous with death in the sticky, sparky space around Norstrilia.

Once in Olympia, Benjacomin went about his arrangements for the attack on Old North Australia. On his second day on the planet he had been very lucky. He met a man named Lavender and he was sure he had heard the name before. Not a member of his own Guild of Thieves, but a daring rascal with a bad reputation among the stars.

It was no wonder that he had found Lavender. His pillow had told him Lavender's story fifteen times during his sleep in the past week. And, whenever he dreamed, he dreamed dreams which had been planted in his mind by the Norstrilian counter-intelligence. They had beaten him in getting to Olympia first and they were prepared to let him have only that which he deserved. The Norstrilian Police were not cruel, but they were out to defend their world. And they were also out to avenge the murder of a child.

The last interview which Benjacomin had with Lavender in striking a bargain before Lavender agreed was a dramatic one.

Lavender refused to move forward.

'I'm not going to jump off anywhere. I'm not going to raid anything. I'm not going to steal anything. I've been rough, of course I have. But I don't get myself killed and that's what you're bloody well asking for.'

'Think of what we'll have. The wealth. I tell you, there's more money here than anything else anybody's ever tried.'

Lavender laughed. 'You think I haven't heard that before? You're a crook and I'm a crook. I don't go anything that's speculation. I want my hard cash down. I'm a fighting man and you're a thief and I'm not going to ask you what you're up to . . . but I want my money first.'

'I haven't got it,' said Benjacomin.

Lavender stood up.

'Then you shouldn't have talked to me. Because it's going to cost you money to keep me quiet whether you hire me or not.'

The bargaining process started.

Lavender looked ugly indeed. He was a soft, ordinary man who had gone to a lot of trouble to become evil. Sin is a lot of work. The sheer effort it requires often shows in the human face.

Bozart stared him down, smiling easily, not even contemptuously.

'Cover me while I get something from my pocket,' said Bozart.

Lavender did not even acknowledge the comment. He did not show a weapon. His left thumb moved slowly across the outer edge of his hand. Benjacomin recognized the sign, but did not flinch.

'See,' he said. 'A planetary credit.'

Lavender laughed. 'I've heard that, too.'

'Take it,' said Bozart.

The adventurer took the laminated card. His eyes widened. 'It's real,' he breathed. 'It is real.' He looked up, incalculably more friendly. 'I never even saw one of these before. What are your terms?'

Meanwhile the bright, vivid Olympians walked back and forth past them, their clothing all white and black in dramatic contrast. Unbelievable geometric designs shone on their cloaks and their hats. The two bargainers ignored the natives. They concentrated on their own negotiations.

Benjacomin felt fairly safe. He placed a pledge of one year's service of the entire planet of Viola Siderea in exchange for the full and unqualified services of Captain Lavender, once of the Imperial Marines Internal Space Patrol. He handed over the mortgage. The year's guarantee was written in. Even on Olympia there were accounting machines which relayed the bargain back to Earth itself, making the mortgage a valid and binding commitment against the whole planet of thieves.

'This,' thought Lavender, 'was the first step of revenge.' After the killer had disappeared his people would have to pay with sheer honesty. Lavender looked at Benjacomin with a clinical sort of concern.

Benjacomin mistook his look for friendliness and Benjacomin smiled his slow, charming, easy smile. Momentarily happy, he reached out his right hand to give Lavender a brotherly solemnification of the bargain. The men shook hands, and Bozart never knew with what he shook hands.

5

'Grey lay the land, oh. Grey grass from sky to sky. Not near the weir, dear. Not a mountain, low or high—only hills and grey grey. Watch the dappled, dimpled twinkles blooming on the star bar.

'That is Norstrilia.

'All the muddy gubbery is gone—all the work and the waiting and the pain.

'Beige-brown sheep lie on blue-grey grass while the clouds rush past, low overhead, like iron pipes ceilinging the world.

'Take your pick of sick sheep, man, it's the sick that pays. Sneeze me a planet, man, or cough me up a spot of immortality. If it's barmy there, where the noddies and the trolls like you live, it's too right here.

'That's the book, boy.

'If you haven't seen Norstrilia, you haven't seen it. If you did see it, you wouldn't believe it.

'Charts call it Old North Australia.'

Here in the heart of the world was the farm which guarded the world. This was the Hitton place.

Towers surrounded it and wires hung between the towers, some of them drooping crazily and some gleaming with the sheen not shown by any other metal made by men from Earth. Within the towers there was open land. And within the open land there were twelve thousand hectares of concrete. Radar reached down to within millimetre smoothness of the surface of the concrete and the other radar threw patterns back and forth, down through molecular thinness. The farm went on. In its centre there was a group of buildings. That was where Katherine Hitton worked on the task which her family had accepted for the defence of her world.

No germ came in, no germ went out. All the food came in by space transmitter. Within this, there lived animals. The animals depended on her alone. Were she to die suddenly, by mischance or as a result of an attack by one of the animals, the authorities of her world had complete facsimiles of herself with which to train new animal tenders under hypnosis.

This was a place where the grey wind leapt forward released from the hills, where it raced across the grey concrete, where it blew past the radar towers. The polished, faceted, captive moon always hung due overhead. The wind hit the buildings, themselves grey, with the impact of a blow, before it raced over the open concrete beyond and whistled away into the hills.

Outside the buildings, the valley had not needed much camouflage. It looked like the rest of Norstrilia. The concrete itself was tinted very slightly to give the impression of poor, starved, natural soil. This was the farm, and this the woman. Together they were the outer defence of the richest world mankind had ever built.

Katherine Hitton looked out the window and thought to herself, 'Forty-two days before I go to market and it's a welcome day that I get there and hear the jig of a music.

> 'Oh, to walk on market day,
> And see my people proud and gay!'

She breathed deeply of the air. She loved the grey hills —though in her youth she had seen many other worlds. And then she turned back into the building to the animals and the duties which awaited her. She was the only Mother Hitton and these were her littul kittons.

She moved among them. She and her father had bred them from Earth mink, from the fiercest, smallest, craziest little minks that had ever been shipped out from Manhome. Out of these minks they had made their lives to keep away other predators who might bother the sheep, on whom the stroon grew. But these minks were born mad.

Generations of them had been bred psychotic to the bone. They lived only to die and they died so that they could stay alive. These were the kittons of Norstrilia. Animals in whom fear, rage, hunger and sex were utterly intermixed; who could eat themselves or each other; who could eat their young, or people, or anything organic; animals who screamed with murder-lust when they felt love; animals born to loathe themselves with a fierce and livid hate and who survived only because their waking moments were spent on couches, strapped tight, claw by claw, so that they could not hurt each other or themselves. Mother Hitton let them waken only a few moments in each lifetime. They bred and killed. She wakened them only two at a time.

All that afternoon she moved from cage to cage. The sleeping animals slept well. The nourishment ran into their bloodstreams; they lived sometimes for years without awaking. She bred them when the males were only partly awakened and the females aroused only enough to accept her veterinary treatments. She herself had to pluck the young away from their mothers as the sleeping mothers begot them. Then she nourished the young through a few happy weeks of kittonhood, until their adult natures began to take, their eyes ran red with madness and heat and their emotions sounded in the sharp, hideous, little cries they uttered through the building; and the twisting of their neat, furry faces, the rolling of their crazy, bright eyes and the tightening of their sharp, sharp claws.

She woke none of them this time. Instead, she tightened them in their straps. She removed the nutrients. She gave them delayed stimulus medicine which would, when they were awakened, bring them suddenly full waking with no lulled stupor first.

Finally, she gave herself a heavy sedative, leaned back in a chair and waited for the call which would come.

When the shock came and the call came through, she would have to do what she had done thousands of times before.

She would ring an intolerable noise through the whole laboratory.

Hundreds of the mutated minks would awaken. In awakening, they would plunge into life with hunger, with hate with rage and with sex; plunge against their straps; strive to kill each other, their young, themselves, her. They would fight everything and everywhere, and do everything they could to keep going.

She knew this.

In the middle of the room there was a tuner. The tuner was a direct, empathic relay, capable of picking up the simpler range of telepathic communications. Into this tuner went the concentrated emotions of Mother Hitton's littul kittons.

The rage, the hate, the hunger, the sex were all carried far beyond the limits of the tolerable, and then all were thereupon amplified. And then the waveband on which this telepathic control went out was amplified, right there beyond the studio, on the high towers that swept the mountain ridge, up and beyond the valley in which the laboratory lay. And Mother Hitton's moon, spinning geometrically, bounced the relay into a hollow englobement.

From the faceted moon, it went to the satellites—sixteen of them, apparently part of the weather control system.

These blanketed not only space, but nearby subspace. The Norstrilians had thought of everything.

The short shocks of an alert came from Mother Hitton's transmitter bank.

A call came. Her thumb went numb.

The noise shrieked.

The minks wakened.

Immediately the room was full of chattering, scraping, hissing, growling and howling.

Under the sound of the animal voices, there was the other sound: a scratchy, snapping sound like hail falling on a frozen lake. It was the individual claws of hundreds of minks trying to tear their way through metal panels.

Mother Hitton heard a gurgle. One of the minks had succeeded in tearing its paw loose and had obviously started to work on its own throat. She recognized the tearing of fur, the ripping of veins.

She listened for the cessation of that individual voice, but she couldn't be sure. The others were making too much noise. One mink less.

Where she sat, she was partly shielded from the telepathic relay, but not altogether. She herself, old as she was, felt queer wild dreams go through her. She thrilled with hate as the thought of beings suffering out beyond her—suffering terribly, since they were not masked by the built-in defences of the Norstrilian communications system.

She felt the wild throb of long-forgotten lust.

She hungered for things she had not known she remembered. She went through the spasms of fear that the hundreds of animals expressed.

Underneath this, her sane mind kept asking, 'How much longer can I take it? How much longer must I take it? Lord God, be good to your people here on this world! Be good to poor old me.'

The green light went on.

She pressed a button on the other side of her chair. The gas hissed in. As she passed into unconsciousness, she knew that her kittons passed into instant unconsciousness too.

She would waken before they did and then her duties would begin: checking the living ones, taking out the one that had clawed out its own throat, taking out those who had died of heart attacks, re-arranging them, dressing their wounds, treating them alive and asleep—asleep and happy—breeding, living in their sleep—until the next call should come to waken them for the defence of the treasures which blessed and cursed her native world.

6

Everything had gone exactly right. Lavender had found an illegal planoform ship. This was no inconsequential accomplishment, since planoform ships were very strictly licensed and obtaining an illegal one was a chore on which a planet full of crooks could easily have worked a lifetime.

Lavender had been lavished with money—Benjacomin's money.

The honest wealth of the thieves' planet had gone in and had paid the falsifications and great debts, imaginary transactions that were fed to the computers for ships and cargoes and passengers that would be almost untraceably commingled in the commerce of ten thousand worlds.

'Let him pay for it,' said Lavender, to one of his confederates, an apparent criminal who was also a Norstrilian agent. 'This is paying good money for bad. You better spend a lot of it.'

Just before Benjacomin took off Lavender sent on an additional message.

He sent it directly through the Go-Captain, who usually did not carry messages. The Go-Captain was a relay commander of the Norstrilian fleet, but he had been carefully ordered not to look like it.

The message concerned the planoform licence—another twenty-odd tablets of stroon which could mortgage Viola Siderea for hundreds upon hundreds of years. The Captain said: 'I don't have to send that through. The answer is yes.'

Benjacomin came into the control room. This was contrary to regulations, but he had hired the ship to violate regulations.

The Captain looked at him sharply. 'You're a passenger, get out.'

Benjacomin said: 'You have my little yacht on board. I am the only man here outside of your people.'

'Get out. There's a fine if you're caught here.'

'It does not matter,' Benjacomin said. 'I'll pay it.'

'You will, will you?' said the Captain. 'You would not be paying twenty tablets of stroon. That's ridiculous. Nobody could get that much stroon.'

Benjacomin laughed, thinking of the thousands of tablets he would soon have. All he had to do was to leave the planoform ship behind, strike once, go past the kittons and come back.

His power and his wealth came from the fact that he knew he could now reach it. The mortgage of twenty tablets of stroon against this planet was a low price to pay if it would pay off at thousands to one. The Captain replied: 'It's not worth it, it just is not worth risking twenty tablets tor your being here. But I can tell you how to get inside the Norstrilian communications net if that is worth twenty-seven tablets.'

Benjacomin went tense.

For a moment he thought he might die. All this work, all this training – the dead boy on the beach, the gamble with the credit, and now this unsuspected antagonist!

He decided to face it out. 'What do you know?' said Benjacomin.

'Nothing,' said the Captain.

'You said "Norstrilia".'

'That I did,' said the Captain.

'If you said Norstrilia, you must have guessed it. Who told you?'

'Where else would a man go if you look for infinite riches? If you get away with it. Twenty tablets is nothing to a man like you.'

'It's two hundred years' worth of work from three hundred thousand people,' said Benjacomin grimly.

'When you get away with it, you will have more than twenty tablets, and so will your people.'

And Benjacomin thought of the thousands and thousands of tablets. 'Yes, that I know.'

'If you don't get away with it, you've got the card.'

'That's right. All right. Get me inside the net. I'll pay the twenty-seven tablets.'

'Give me the card.'

Benjacomin refused. He was a trained thief, and he was alert to thievery. Then he thought again. This was the crisis of his life. He had to gamble a little on somebody.

He had to wager the card. 'I'll mark it and then I'll give it back to you.' Such was his excitement that Benjacomin did not notice that the card went into a duplicator, that the transaction was recorded, that the message went back to Olympic Centre, that the loss and the mortgage against the planet of Viola Siderea should be credited to certain commercial agencies on Earth for three hundred years to come.

Benjacomin got the card back. He felt like an honest thief.

If he did die, the card would be lost and his people would not have to pay. If he won, he could pay that little bit out of his own pocket.

Benjacomin sat down. The Go-Captain signalled to his pinlighters. The ship lurched.

For half a subjective hour they moved, the Captain wearing a helmet of space upon his head, sensing and grasping and guessing his way, stepping to stepping stone, right back to his home. He had to fumble the passage, or else Benjacomin might guess that he was in the hands of double agents.

But the Captain was well trained. Just as well trained as Benjacomin.

Agents and thieves, they rode together.

They planoformed inside the communications net. Benjacomin shook hands with them. 'You are allowed to materialize as soon as I call.'

'Good luck, sir,' said the Captain.

'Good luck to me,' said Benjacomin.

He climbed into his space yacht. For less than a second in real space, the grey expanse of Norstrilia loomed up. The ship which looked like a simple warehouse disappeared into planoform, and the yacht was on its own.

The yacht dropped.

As it dropped, Benjacomin had a hideous moment of confusion and terror.

He never knew the woman down below but she sensed him plainly as he received the wrath of the much-amplified kittons. His conscious mind quivered under the blow. With a prolongation of subjective experience which made one or two seconds seem like months of hurt drunken bewilderment, Benjacomin Bozart swept beneath the tide of his own personality. The moon relay threw minkish minds against him. The synapses of his brain re-formed to conjure up might-have-beens, terrible things that never happened to any man. Then his knowing mind whited out in an overload of stress.

His subcortical personality lived on a little longer.

His body fought for several minutes. Mad with lust and hunger, the body arched in the pilot's seat, the mouth bit deep into his own arm. Driven by lust, the left hand tore at his face, ripping out his left eyeball. He screeched with animal lust as he tried to devour himself . . . not entirely without success.

The overwhelming telepathic message of Mother Hitton's Littul Kittons ground into his brain.

The mutated minks were fully awake.

The relay satellites had poisoned all the space round him with the craziness to which the minks were bred.

Bozart's body did not live long. After a few minutes, the arteries were open, the head slumped forward and the yacht was dropping helplessly toward the warehouses which it had meant to raid. Norstrilian police picked it up.

The police themselves were ill. All of them were ill. All of them were white-faced. Some of them had vomited. They had gone through the edge of the mink defence. They had passed through the telepathic band at its thinnest and weakest point. This was enough to hurt them badly.

They did not want to know.

They wanted to forget.

One of the younger policemen looked at the body and said, 'What on earth could do that to a man?'

'He picked the wrong job,' said the police captain.

The young policeman said: 'What's the wrong job?'

'The wrong job is trying to rob us, boy. We are defended, and we don't want to know how.'

The young policeman, humiliated and on the verge of anger, looked almost as if he would defy his superior, while keeping his eyes away from the body of Benjacomin Bozart.

The older man said: 'It's all right. He did not take long to die and this is the man who killed the boy Johnny, not very long ago.'

'Oh, him? So soon?'

'We brought him.' The old police officer nodded. 'We let him find his death. That's how we live. Tough, isn't it?'

The ventilators whispered softly, gently. The animals slept again. A jet of air poured down on Mother Hitton. The telepathic relay was still on. She could feel herself, the sheds, the faceted moon, the little satellites. Of the robber there was no sign.

She stumbled to her feet. Her raiment was moist with perspiration. She needed a shower and fresh clothes . . .

Back at Manhome, the Commercial Credit Circuit called shrilly for human attention. A junior subchief of the Instrumentality walked over to the machine and held out his hand.

The machine dropped a card neatly into his fingers.

He looked at the card.

'Debit Viola Siderea—credit Earth Contingency—sub-credit Norstrilian account—four hundred million man megayears.'

Though all alone, he whistled to himself in the empty room. 'We'll all be dead, stroon or no stroon, before they finish paying that!' He went off to tell his friends the odd news.

The machine, not getting its card back, made another one.

A Song Before Sunset

David Grigg

There is a line in Chekhov's *Three Sisters* where Toozenback says,
'Fancy being able to play so exquisitely, and yet having nobody,
nobody at all to appreciate it !' This fragment of dialogue was the
seed for the following story.

The catastrophe theme has been a vital part of sf since its beginnings. It represents a deep and universal desire to stop all this
nonsense and start afresh. Often the transition period between the
prevailing state and a world more idyllic is presented as rather
grim; British writers, from Wells to Wyndham, have inexplicably
made it their own. (Perhaps it has something to do with their climate.)

Now David Grigg, a young Melbourne author and playwright,
portrays a moving interlude in just such a transition.

It took him three weeks to find the sledgehammer.

He was hunting rats among the broken concrete and
rusted metal of an ancient supermarket. The sun was
beginning to descend over the jagged horizons of the city,
casting shadows like giant gravestones onto the nearer
buildings. An edge of blackness had begun to creep across the
rubble that was all that remained of the store.

He picked his way carefully from one piece of concrete to
another, skirting the twisted metal, looking for a hole or a
cover that might make a suitable nest for a brood of rats,

here and there using his stick to turn over a loose chunk in the vain hope of finding a can of food undiscovered after years of looting.

At his waist hung three large rats, their heads squashed and bloody from his stick. Rats were still fat enough and slow enough these days to be caught by surprise with a blow on the head, which was fortunate, for his eye and his skill with the slingshot he carried were not as they had once been.

He rested a while, sniffing at the cold wind. There would be a frost tonight, and his bones knew fear of the cold. He was getting old.

He was sixty-five, and the years had starved him. The flesh of his youth had loosened and sagged, leaving his frame thinly draped and his eyes starting from his bony head like some curious troll.

He was sixty-five, and his hair, grey many years ago, now raised a white halo about his leather-coloured face. That he had survived so long was a wonder to him, for his earlier years had not prepared him for this present world. But somehow he had learned to fight and kill and run and all else that had been necessary in the long years since the city had died.

The days now, however, were not so foul and desperate as they had once been. Now it was seldom that he feared he would starve to death. But in the bad days, like many others, he had eaten human flesh.

His name was Parnell, and he had gone on living.

The sun was sinking fast, and he turned about to go back before the dark could overtake him. It was as he turned that he caught the dull shine of metal in the corner of his eye. He peered more closely, put out his hand and heaved a sledgehammer up from the rubble. He swung its mass experimentally, weighed it in his hands, and felt its movement. After a moment he was forced to put it down again, as his arms began to tremble with unaccustomed strain. But no matter: given enough time, he knew this was the tool to realise the hope he had been hugging to himself for three weeks. He tied the hammer awkwardly to his belt and began to hurry home, fleeing the shadow of the city.

It was almost dark when he reached his home, a weather-stained stone house hedged around with the tangled jungle of an overgrown garden. Inside, he carefully lit each of the smoky candles in the living room, calling up a cancerous light that spread relentlessly into the corners. His door was locked and barred, and at last he sat in peace before the wood-wormed piano in the main room. He sighed a little as his fingers tapped at the yellowed and splitting keys, and felt an accustomed sorrow as the fractured notes ascended. This piano had perhaps been a good learner's instrument in its day, but time had not been kind to it. Even if he had not feared attracting the attention of the dwellers in the dark outside, the effort of playing was more agony than pleasure.

Music had once been his life. Now his greatest aim was only to quiet the rumbling of his belly. Then he remembered, his eyes drifted to the hammer he had found in the rubble that day, and his hope came alive again, as it had weeks ago.

But there was no time to daydream, no time for hoping. There was time before he slept only to clean and skin the rats he had caught. Tomorrow he was to go trading with the Tumbledown Woman.

The Tumbledown Woman and her mate lived in the midst of a hundred decrepit trams in an old depot. Why they chose to live there was a question none who traded with her had ever managed to solve. Here she stayed, and here she traded. Her store counter was a solitary tram left on the rails a few metres outside the depot, its paint peeling away but still bearing pathetic advertisements of a lost age. While the outside of the tram offered far-away holidays and better deodorants, the Tumbledown Woman inside traded garbage as the luxuries of a world which had died. Inside, arrayed along the wooden seats or hung from the ceiling were tin cans with makeshift hand-grips, greasy home-made candles, racks of suspect vegetables grown no one knew where, rows of dead rats, cats, rabbits and the occasional dog, plastic spoons, bottles, coats of ratskin and all sorts of items salvaged from the debris of oft-looted shops.

The Tumbledown Woman was old, and she was black, and she was ugly, and she cackled when she saw Parnell approaching slowly in the chill morning. She had survived better than many men through the crisis, by being more ruthless and more cruel than they had ever managed to be to her in the years before. She rubbed her hands together with a dry, dry sound, and greeted Parnell with a faded leer.

'Two rats, Tumbledown Woman, fresh killed yesterday,' he opened without hesitation.

'I give you something good for them, Mr Piano Player,' she sneered.

'Then that will be the first time ever. What?'

'A genuine diamond ring, twenty-four carat gold, see!' And she held the flashing gem to the sun.

Parnell didn't bother to smile at her taunt. 'Give me food, and be done with your mocking.'

She sneered again, and offered him a cabbage and two carrots. Nodding, he handed her the skinned corpses, lodged the food in his bag, and turned to go. But he was carrying the sledgehammer at his side, and she stopped him with a yell.

'Hey, piano player man, that hammer! I give you good fur coat for it! Genuine rabbit!'

He turned and saw that she was not mocking him this time. 'When I've finished with it, maybe. Then we'll see.' His reply seemed to make her pleased, for she grinned and yelled again: 'Hey, piano man, you hear the news about Ol' Man Edmonds? Them Vandalmen come an' kill him, burn down that book place Ol' Man Edmonds live in!'

Parnell gasped in shock. 'The Library? They burnt the Library down?'

'That's right!'

'My God!' He stood, silent and bewildered for a long minute as the Tumbledown Woman grinned at him. Then, unable to speak further in his anger, he clamped his hands together in bitter frustration and walked off.

The sledgehammer was an awkward thing to carry. Slipped into his belt with the metal head at his waist, the wooden handle beat at his legs as he walked. If he carried it in his arms, his muscles protested after no more than a few minutes, and he was forced to rest. He was getting old, and he knew it. The slide to death was beginning to steepen and he was not, he thought, very far from its end.

In slow, weary stages he walked the distance into the heart of the corpse that was the city: long ago its pulse had stopped. He walked past the rusty hulks of cars and along the dust-filled tram-tracks, through streets of shattered buildings standing in rows like jagged reefs. Long ago the lungs of the city had expired their last breath; the tall chimneys were fallen, casting scattered bricks across the road before him.

He came at last to the centre and faced again the strongly barred and sealed doors of the old City Hall, half buried in the rubble of its long-crumbled entranceway. Even if he had been able to break open the bars of the door, he would have needed to clear away the rubble to allow the doors to open. Such was beyond him.

But at the side of the building, the skeleton of a truck lay crazily against the wall, mounted on the pavement and nuzzled face to face with a tree that now made a leafy wilderness of the cab.

Parnell climbed onto the truck and carefully ascended until he perched with little comfort on a branch of the tree, close to a barred window. Three weeks ago he had cleaned away the grime on the glass to see the dusty corridors inside. On the far wall of the corridor was a direction sign, faded and yellowed, but still bearing the words: CONCERT HALL.

Once again, looking at that dim sign, he was filled to overflowing with memories of concerts he had given. His hands followed a memory of their own on the keys, the music spiralled and, after, the almost invisible audience in the darkened hall applauded again and again . . .

His memories vanished as he swung the sledgehammer from his shoulder, jarring it into the bars of the window. Dust showered and cement crumbled. The task looked easier than he had at first thought, which was fortunate, for the one stroke had weakened him terribly. He swung again, and the bars moved and bent. Somehow, he found the strength for another swing, and the bars buckled and came loose and smashed through the glass into the corridor beyond.

Triumph came to him in a cloud of weakness, leaving him gasping and his arms weak and trembling. He sat for a long moment on the branch, gaining strength and hope to venture within.

At last he swung his legs over the edge and dropped onto the corridor floor. Glass crackled. He reached into his bag and brought out a small candle and some precious matches. The box of usable matches had cost him ten ratskins at the Tumbledown Woman's tram two weeks ago. He lit the candle and yellow light flooded into the dusty corridor.

He walked along it, making footprints in the virgin dust. A memory floated back to him of telecasts of moon explorers, placing footprint after footprint in age-old lunar dust, and he smiled a grim smile.

Eventually he came to a set of double doors, barred and padlocked. Here he was forced to rest again before he could smash the lock with his hammer, and step into the space-like blackness beyond.

After his eyes had adjusted to the light of the candle, dimmed by the open space, he saw row upon row of once plush seats. Somewhere a rat scurried, and above he could hear the soft rustle and squeaks of what might be a brood of bats on the high ceiling.

The aisle stretched before him, sloping slightly downwards. Parnell walked forward slowly, kicking up dust. In the dark immensity of the hall, his candle was just a spark, illuminating only a tight circle around him and filtering through puffs of dust stirred by his passage.

On the stage, metal gleamed back images of the candle-flame from scattered corners. Around him were the music stands and music sheets of a full orchestra, filmed with years of dust. Here was a half-opened instrument case, and in it the still-shining brass of a french horn, abandoned by some long-gone performer in forgotten haste. And shrouded in white, topped by a tarnished candelabra, stood the grand piano.

Parnell's heart began a heavier, more rapid beat as he brushed dust from the sheet covering the piano. With an anxious hand he lit the candelabra with his own meagre candle, and lifted it high as the light swelled across the stage. He could see other instruments now, long lost by their players: here a violin, there an oboe, cast aside by a time that had made their possession unimportant.

Placing the light on the floor, he carefully eased the sheet from the piano. Yellow light danced on the black surface of polished wood and sparkled in the brass.

For a long, long time his aged hands could do no more than caress the instrument with a growing affection. Finally, he sat on the piano stool, realizing perhaps for the first time how tired he was. The key, he saw with relief, was still in the lock. No doubt he could have forced it, but it would have broken his heart to have damaged that perfect form.

Turning the key in the lock, he lifted the cover and ran his hand softly over the white and black of the piano keys. He sat back, and with a self-conciously wry gesture, flipped his ragged coat away from his seat and turned to face the hall.

A full house tonight, Mr Parnell. All of London queues to hear you. The radio stations are paying fortunes to broadcast your concert. The audience is quiet, expectant. Can you hear them breathe, out there? Not a cough, not a sneeze, not a mutter as they wait, hushed, to hear the first notes drop from your fingertips. The music trembles in your hands, waiting to begin—now!

Discords shattered the empty hall, and the bats, disturbed, flew in a twittering crowd above the deserted, rotting seats. Parnell let out his breath in a painful sigh.

The instrument would have to be painstakingly retuned, note by note. His goal had yet to be reached. But now, at last, he could reach out and *touch* it. Now, one by one, he began to realize the difficulties that remained. He felt his hunger and saw the candles burning fast. He could probably find pitch-pipes in the hall, but he would need some kind of tool to tighten the strings of the piano. And he would have to support himself somehow while he spent his time in here and was unable to hunt or forage. He would have to go back to the Tumbledown Woman, and see what she would offer him in trade for the sledgehammer. It was no fur coat he would be getting, he knew.

Outside again, he opened his bag and took out the food he had brought with him. He sat on the truck eating pieces of roasted rat and raw cabbage, pondering whether there was some way he could net and kill some of the brood of bats within the hall. No doubt they would make curious eating, but perhaps their leathery wings might have a use . . . ? But all these schemes were impractical, and he dismissed them.

In the distance, over the broken buildings, a thin trail of black smoke was rising leisurely towards the sky. The day had become bright and cloudless, and the smoke was a smear against the blue. Puzzled, Parnell wondered what was burning. The trail was too contained to be a forest fire. Unless some building had spontaneously ignited, after all these years, it had to be the work of men. Unable to arrive at any more satisfactory a conclusion, he turned away, thrusting the question from his mind.

After bundling away the remnants of the food, he loosely replaced the bars of the window to make his entry less obvious to any passing wanderer. Heaving up the sledge-hammer, he began the long walk away from his heart's desire.

The Tumbledown Woman had turned sour in the late afternoon, like a fat black toad basking in the last rays of the sun. She sat on the running-board of the tram; greeted Parnell with little enthusiasm. Her withered husband now sat atop the tram and glared menacingly at the horizon, an ancient shotgun beneath his arm, ignoring his wife and Parnell equally.

Parnell sat and bickered with the woman for nearly an hour. She would still offer him the fur coat, but he wanted an adjustable spanner, candles, matches and food in exchange for the sledgehammer, and these were expensive items. In the end, Parnell gave in and accepted her final offer, which was everything he wanted except the food.

The Tumbledown Woman hung the sledgehammer in a prominent position within the tram and gave him the items he wanted. She turned and looked at him with a bitter eye. 'You crazy, piano player man, you know that?'

Parnell, leaning wearily in the doorway of the tram, cradling his candles, was moved to agree with her. 'I suppose you're right.'

'Sure I'm right!' she answered, nodding her head vigorously. 'You a crazy coot.'

'Must be crazy to come and trade with you,' he said, but the woman just glared at him. Then he remembered: 'There was a lot of smoke in the south this morning. Do you know what it was?'

The Tumbledown Woman grinned and winked at him. 'Sure I know. Didn' I tell you this morning about them

Vandalmen? Them Vandalmen coming all over this town now. Last week burn down Ol' Man Edmonds and his books. Now it's that picture place. Sure crazy, them Vandalmen.' And she pottered around the tram, arranging and rearranging her goods.

Parnell's heart sank a little more. 'The Art Gallery?'

'Yeah, that's what I hear. Limpin' Jack, he been south this morning, he told me. Them Vandalmen don't like them books or them pictures, no way.'

Parnell's anger warmed within him, only to turn into bitter frustration for the lack of an object. Most of the things he treasured had been destroyed during the crisis. Now those that were left were going the same way, in senseless destruction.

'What do they do it for?' he protested, sitting down in an empty seat to stop himself shaking. 'What point is there in what they do?'

'Who cares?' said the woman. 'Can't eat them books, can't keep warm in them pictures. Them Vandalmen crazy to burn them, sure, but who cares?'

'All right,' said Parnell, 'all right.' The answers he felt within him would mean nothing to the Tumbledown Woman. All he could do was smother his loss and sorrow, hide it away. He clenched his jaws and wearily picked up his trades, placed them in his bag and stepped out of the tram. The Tumbledown Woman watched him go with a tired disgust. Her husband sat above, glaring, glaring, at the darkening horizon, his gun beneath his arm.

Parnell spent the morning of the next day hunting rats again in the rows of time-shattered houses that still stood in uniform lines to the west of the city. After a few hours of vain search he was lucky and found a rabbit warren riddling the soft earth in an overgrown and enclosed back yard. He caught two surprised rabbits before the others ran for safety. He spent the rest of the morning cleaning and roasting the rabbits and salting their skins.

In the afternoon he was again within the dark hall, beginning the long task of tuning each string of the piano to a perfect pitch. Had he been a professional tuner, he would have been able to proceed with greater speed, but he was forced to go at a frustrating creep, making trial-and-error decisions as he listened to each string, hearing it in relation to the others he had tuned, listening to the pitch-pipes, then tightening the string again with his rusty spanner.

He measured time by the rate at which the smoky candles burned, and left again before darkness fell.

Days passed in this way, until he could hardly trust his hearing and had to leave off for hours at a time before he could resume. Every time he emerged from the hall to eat or to let his eyes and ears repair, there was smoke somewhere on the horizon.

There came a day when he was finished; when he had tested the piano with scales and simple exercises and was sure the tuning was perfect. He knew then that he was afraid to begin, afraid to sit down and play a real piece of music on the piano. His hands still remembered his favourite pieces but there was a hollow fear in his heart that he would fumble and distort the music in some way. He had kept his hands strong and his fingers limber by fighting the aged monster of a piano in his house for all these years, but he could not tell whether or not he still retained his skill. It had been a long time.

Parnell made his way outside the hall and sat, despondent and trembling, on the rusty, overgrown truck. It was early afternoon and, for the first time in days, there was no smoke to be seen in the sky. He ate the last of the rabbit and realized he would have to go hunting the following day. He laughed at himself for an old fool, gulped water from his bottle, lit his candle and hurried back inside the hall, trailed by clouds of dust.

On the stage he had cleared the music stands to one side, leaving the grand piano alone and uncluttered. Now he dusted the polished surface one more time, buffed the brass lettering, raised the lid, lit the candelabra, and sat before the keyboard.

The bats twittered tumultuous applause. He bowed his head slightly towards the moth-eaten velvet of the empty seats, and began to play.

He began with a Beethoven Piano Sonata, Opus 109. It flowed; it swelled; it poured from the strings of that mag-

nificent piano as his hands moved and fell, remembering
what his brain was unsure of. And he knew, listening, that
he had not lost his skill, that somehow it had been kept
somewhere safe within him, sleeping through the years of
torment. He wove a web of music, cast motion and light
and harmony into the darkness, wrapped himself within its
sound, and played on. And as he played, he wept.

The piece ended; he began another. And another. Beethoven, Mozart and Chopin were resurrected. The music
expanded through the hours, a torrent of joy, of sorrow,
and of yearning. He was blind and insensate and deaf to all
but his music, insulated from the outside world by the castle
of sound he was building around himself.

At last Parnell stopped, his hands throbbing and aching,
and raised his eyes above the level of the piano.

Standing before him was a Vandal. A sneer was on his
face, and in his arms he cradled the sledgehammer Parnell
had traded to the Tumbledown Woman. There was blood
on its head.

The Vandal stood and regarded him contemptuously, all
the time stroking, stroking, the shaft of the hammer he
carried. He was dressed in roughly cured leather and rusted
metal. Around his neck he wore a dozen metal necklaces
and chains that dangled on his bare and hairy chest—
crosses and swastikas, peace symbols and fishes—clinking
gently against each other. He was dirty, his hair was greasy
and awry, and on his forehead was burned a V-shaped scar.
He smelt.

Parnell was unable to speak. Fear had made stone of him
and his heart flopped around inside him like a grounded fish.

The Vandal uttered a hoarse giggle, enjoying the shock
on Parnell's face. 'Hey, old man, you play real pretty! Tell
me now, Music Man, how well do you sing?'

Parnell's voice was a rustle in his throat: 'I can't.'

The Vandal shook his head in mock sorrow. 'That's too
bad, Mister Music Man. But I tell you, you're gonna sing
real good when I'm finished with you. Real good and loud.'
He shifted the sledgehammer to bring out a long knife. It
cast fiery gleams about the stage as its edge caught the
candlelight.

Parnell felt as though he was about to be sick but, insanely, his old anger grew in him even in the face of his fear. 'Why?' he asked, his voice trembling, 'why do you want to kill me? What harm am I doing you?'

The eyes of the Vandal narrowed in concentration and fierce humour. 'Why? Why not?' And the knife flashed yellow at Parnell's eyes.

'All that you do . . . destroying all the beautiful things, the books, the pictures . . .' Parnell was becoming excited in spite of his fear: 'Those things are all we have left of our heritage, our culture; of civilization, of Man's greatness, don't you see? You're no more than barbarians, killing and burning . . .' He stopped as the Vandal waved the knife towards him, his face losing its mirth.

'Listen, pretty music man, you're pretty with your music and pretty with your words, but you talk a lot of shit. You know what your pretty culture gave us? Gave us dirt and fighting and eating each other, man. You're nice and old, pretty man; you were old when the murdering and the hunger started. Me and mine, we were just kids then. You know how it was for us? We had to run and hide so as not to be food for grown-ups; we had to eat dirt and scum to live, man. That's what your pretty heritage was for us, pretty man, so don't bullshit me about how great Man was, cause he ain't.'

The Vandal was leaning over Parnell, breathing his foul breath hard into the old man's face. Parnell grew silent as the Vandal drew back and glared. 'And you sitting here in the dark playing that nice music—all you wish is that it was back the way it was! Well, me and mine are making sure that it ain't never back that way again. Now you tell me, man, what good did that music, that culture, ever do, hey?'

Parnell's thoughts were tumbling. At last he said simply: 'It gave people pleasure, that's all.'

The Vandal regained his sneer. 'Okay, Mister Music Man, killing you is gonna give me lots of pleasure. But first, man, it's gonna give me real kicks to smash up this pretty music thing in front of you just so you can enjoy it too. How about that?' And, turning, the Vandal hefted the sledgehammer and raised it high above the strings of the grand piano.

Something snapped within Parnell.

He leapt up and grasped at the Vandal's arms. Surprised, he let the hammer drop. Parnell clawed at his face. The Vandal swung out a hairy fist, catching Parnell a jarring blow on the jaw and almost striking him to the ground, but Parnell's hands were about the Vandal's throat. Parnell's hands were the only part of him that was not weak and trembling—hands made iron-firm by decades of exercise on the keyboard—and his thumbs were digging into the Vandal's windpipe. The youth began to choke, and tried vainly to tear Parnell's hands away, but the gnarled fingers were locked in a murderous grip; they tightened with hysterical energy. For a seemingly endless moment the two hung together in a bizarre embrace. Then the Vandal crumpled to the stage, with Parnell on top of him, throttling the life from him.

The Vandal was dead.

Parnell let out a choking cry and retched violently over the edge of the stage. He crouched on his knees for some time, transformed by reaction and horror into a mindless animal.

Eventually he turned around and stared with strange emotion at the body of the Vandal. Outside the hall, very faintly, he could hear the yells and shouts of the rest of the pack of new barbarians as they burned and looted. Inside, there was only the quiet of death and the soft twittering of the bats.

He crawled towards the piano where the sledgehammer lay. He stood, using the hammer as a prop for his trembling legs, then took it into his arms.

With one anguished swing, he brought the sledgehammer crashing down into the piano strings.

The shock jarred his whole body. The strings snapped with violent twangs and wood splintered, filling the air with jagged sound. The candelabra, toppling, plunged to the floor and went out, spilling darkness throughout the hall.

The silence seemed to last for a long time.

Sundance

Robert Silverberg

Robert Silverberg has probably written more sf than anyone alive. It is rare that such a prolific writer can produce work of such a consistently high standard. His novels and short stories have collected an enviable number of awards, and he continues to go from strength to strength, each new story more ambitious than the last.

Readers and critics who are continually bemoaning the imminent death of the short story should take heart that the genre is alive and well in the dozens of original sf anthologies and magazines appearing annually, and the story that follows is a powerful example of what contemporary sf is all about.

In SUNDANCE Silverberg has taken the classic theme of an encounter with aliens and worked it into a grim metaphor of genocide. The story is a trap; once you are inside it becomes impossible to escape. Step in . . .

Today you liquidated about 50 000 Eaters in Sector A, and now you are spending an uneasy night. You and Herndon flew east at dawn, with the green-gold sunrise at your backs, and sprayed the neural pellets over a thousand hectares along the Forked River. You flew on into the prairie beyond the river, where the Eaters have already been wiped out, and had lunch sprawled on that thick, soft carpet of grass where the first settlement is expected to rise. Herndon picked some juiceflowers, and you enjoyed half an hour of mild hallucinations. Then, as you headed towards

225

the 'copter to begin an afternoon of further pellet-spraying, he said suddenly, 'Tom, how would you feel about this if it turned out that the Eaters weren't just animal pests? That they were *people*, say, with a language and rites and a history and all?'

You thought of how it had been for your own people.

'They aren't,' you said.

'Suppose they were. Suppose the Eaters—'

'They aren't. Drop it.'

Herndon has this streak of cruelty in him that leads him to ask such questions. He goes for the vulnerabilities; it amuses him. All night now his casual remark has echoed in your mind. Suppose the Eaters . . . Suppose the Eaters . . . Suppose . . . Suppose . . .

You sleep for a while, and dream, and in your dreams you swim through rivers of blood.

Foolishness. A feverish fantasy. You know how important it is to exterminate the Easters fast, before the settlers get here. They're just animals, and not even harmless animals at that; ecology-wreckers is what they are, devourers of oxygen-liberating plants, and they have to go. A few have been saved for zoological study. The rest must be destroyed. Ritual extirpation of undesirable beings—the old, old story. But let's not complicate our job with moral qualms, you tell yourself. Let's not dream of rivers of blood.

The Eaters don't even *have* blood, none that could flow in rivers, anyway. What they have is, well, a kind of lymph that permeates every tissue and transmits nourishment along the interfaces. Waste products go out the same way, osmotically. In terms of process, it's structurally analogous to your own kind of circulatory system, except there's no network of blood vessels hooked to a master pump. The life-stuff just oozes through their bodies, as though they were amoebas or sponges or some other low-phylum form. Yet they're definitely high-phylum in nervous system, digestive set-up, limb-and-organ template, etc. Odd, you think. The thing about aliens is that they're alien, you tell yourself—not for the first time.

The beauty of their biology for you and your companions is that it lets you exterminate them so neatly.

You fly over the grazing grounds and drop the neural pellets. The Eaters find and ingest them. Within an hour the poison has reached all sectors of the body. Life ceases; a rapid breakdown of cellular matter follows, the Eater literally falling apart molecule by molecule the instant that nutrition is cut off; the lymph-like stuff works like acid; a universal lysis occurs; flesh and even the bones, which are cartilaginous, dissolve. In two hours, a puddle on the ground. In four, nothing at all left. Considering how many millions of Eaters you've scheduled for extermination here, it's sweet of the bodies to be self-disposing. Otherwise what a charnel-house this world would become!

Suppose the Eaters . . .

Damn Herndon. You almost feel like getting a memory-editing in the morning. Scrape his stupid speculations out of your head. If you dared. If you dared.

In the morning he does not dare. Memory-editing frightens him; he will try to shake free of his new-found guilt without it. The Eaters, he explains to himself, are mindless herbivores, the unfortunate victims of human expansionism, but not really deserving of passionate defence. Their extermination is not tragic; it's just too bad. If Earthmen are to have this world, the Eaters must relinquish it. There's a difference, he tells himself, between the elimination of the plains Indians from the American prairie in the nineteenth century and the destruction of the bison on that same prairie. One feels a little wistful about the slaughter of the thundering herds; one regrets the butchering of millions of the noble brown woolly beasts, yes. But one feels outrage, not mere wistful regret, at what was done to the Sioux. There's a difference. Reserve your passions for the proper cause.

He walks from his bubble at the edge of the camp towards the centre of things. The flagstone path is moist and glistening. The morning fog has not yet lifted, and every tree is bowed, the long, notched leaves heavy with droplets of water. He pauses, crouching, to observe a spider-analogue spinning its asymmetrical web. As he watches, a small amphibian, delicately shaded turquoise, glides as inconspicuously as possible over the mossy ground. Not inconspicuously enough; he gently lifts the little creature and puts it on the back of his hand. The gills flutter in anguish, and the amphibian's sides quiver. Slowly, cunningly, its colour changes until it matches the coppery tone of the hand. The camouflage is excellent. He lowers his hand and the amphibian scurries into a puddle. He walks on.

He is forty years old, shorter than most of the other members of the expedition, with wide shoulders, a heavy chest, dark glossy hair, a blunt, spreading nose. He is a biologist. This is his third career, for he has failed as an anthropologist and as a developer of real estate. His name is Tom Two Ribbons. He has been married twice but has had no children. His great-grandfather died of alcoholism; his grandfather was addicted to hallucinogens; his father had compulsively visited cheap memory-editing parlours. Tom Two Ribbons is conscious that he is failing a family tradition, but he has not yet found his own mode of self-destruction.

In the main building he discovers Herndon, Julia, Ellen, Schwartz, Chang, Michaelson and Nichols. They are eating breakfast; the others are already at work. Ellen rises and comes to him and kisses him. Her short soft yellow hair tickles his cheeks. 'I love you,' she whispers. She has spent the night in Michaelson's bubble. 'I love you,' he tells her, and draws a quick vertical line of affection between her small pale breasts. He winks at Michaelson, who nods, touches the tops of two fingers to his lips, and blows them a kiss. We are all good friends here, Tom Two Ribbons thinks.

'Who drops pellets today?' he asks.

'Mike and Chang,' says Julia. 'Sector C.'

Schwartz says, 'Eleven more days and we ought to have the whole peninsula clear. Then we can move inland.'

'If our pellet supply holds up,' Chang points out.

Herndon says, 'Did you sleep well, Tom?'

'No,' says Tom. He sits down and taps out his breakfast requisition. In the west, the fog is beginning to burn off the mountains. Something throbs in the back of his neck. He has been on this world nine weeks now, and in that time it has undergone its only change of season, shading from dry weather to foggy. The mists will remain for many months. Before the plains parch again, the Eaters will be gone and the settlers will begin to arrive. His food slides down the chute and he seizes it. Ellen sits beside him. She is a little more than half his age; this is her first voyage; she is their keeper of records, but she is also skilled at editing. 'You look troubled,' Ellen tells him. 'Can I help you?'

'No. Thank you.'

'I hate it when you get gloomy.'

'It's a racial trait,' says Tom Two Ribbons.

'I doubt that very much.'

'The truth is that maybe my personality reconstruct is wearing thin. The trauma level was so close to the surface. I'm just a walking veneer, you know.'

Ellen laughs prettily. She wears only a sprayon half-wrap. Her skin looks damp; she and Michaelson have had a swim at dawn. Tom Two Ribbons is thinking of asking her to marry him, when this job is over. He has not been married since the collapse of the real estate business. The therapist suggested divorce as part of the reconstruct. He sometimes wonders where Terry has gone and with whom she lives now. Ellen says, 'You seem pretty stable to me, Tom.'

'Thank you,' he says. She is young. She does not know.

'If it's just a passing gloom I can edit it out in one quick snip.'

'Thank you,' he says. 'No.'

'I forgot. You don't like editing.'

'My father—'

'Yes?'

'In fifty years he pared himself down to a thread,' Tom Two Ribbons says. 'He had his ancestors edited away, his whole heritage, his religion, his wife, his sons, finally his name. Then he sat and smiled all day. Thank you, no editing.'

'Where are you working today?' Ellen asks.

'In the compound, running tests.'

'Want company? I'm off all morning.'

'Thank you, no,' he says, too quickly. She looks hurt. He tries to remedy his unintended cruelty by touching her arm lightly and saying. 'Maybe this afternoon, all right? I need to commune a while. Yes?'

'Yes,' she says, and smiles, and shapes a kiss with her lips. After breakfast he goes to the compound. It covers a thousand hectares east of the base; they have bordered it with neural-field projectors at intervals of eighty metres, and this is a sufficient fence to keep the captive population of two hundred Eaters from straying. When all the others have been exterminated, this study group will remain. At the south-west corner of the compound stands a lab bubble from which the experiments are run: metabolic, psychological, physiological, ecological. A stream crosses the compound diagonally. There is a low ridge of grassy hills at its eastern edge. Five distinct copses of tightly clustered knifeblade trees are separated by patches of dense savanna. Sheltered beneath the grass are the oxygen-plants, almost completely hidden except for the photosynthetic spikes that jut to heights of three or four metres at regular intervals, and for the lemon-coloured respiratory bodies, chest high, that make the grassland sweet and dizzying with exhaled gases. Through the fields move the Eaters in a straggling herd, nibbling delicately at the respiratory bodies.

Tom Two Ribbons spies the herd beside the stream and goes towards it. He stumbles over an oxygen-plant hidden in the grass but deftly recovers his balance and, seizing the puckered orifice of the respiratory body, inhales deeply. His despair lifts. He approaches the Eaters. They are spherical, bulky, slow-moving creatures, covered by masses of coarse orange fur. Saucer-like eyes protrude above narrow rubbery lips. Their legs are thin and scaly, like a chicken's, and their arms are short and held close to their bodies. They regard him with bland lack of curiosity. 'Good morning, brothers!' is the way he greets them this time, and he wonders why.

I noticed something strange today. Perhaps I simply sniffed too much oxygen in the fields; maybe I was succumbing to a suggestion Herndon planted; or possibly it's the family masochism cropping out. But while I was observing the Eaters in the compound, it seemed to me, for the first time, that they were behaving intelligently, that they were functioning in a ritualized way.

I followed them around for three hours. During that time

they uncovered half a dozen outcroppings of oxygen-plants. In each case they went through a stylized pattern of action before starting to munch. They:

Formed a straggly circle around the plants.

Looked towards the sun.

Looked towards their neighbours on left and right around the circle.

Made fuzzy neighing sounds *only* after having done the foregoing.

Looked towards the sun again.

Moved in and ate.

If this wasn't a prayer of thanksgiving, a saying of grace, then what was it? And if they're advanced enough spiritually to say grace, are we not therefore committing genocide here? Do chimpanzees say grace? Christ, we wouldn't even wipe out chimps the way we're cleaning out the Eaters! Of course, chimps don't interfere with human crops, and some kind of coexistence would be possible, whereas Eaters and human agriculturalists simply can't function on the same planet. Nevertheless, there's a moral issue here. The liquidation effort is predicated on the assumption that the intelligence level of the Eaters is about on a par with that of oysters, or, at best, sheep. Our consciences stay clear because our poison is quick and painless and because the Eaters thoughtfully dissolve upon dying, sparing us the mess of incinerating millions of corpses. But if they pray—

I won't say anything to the others just yet. I want more evidence, hard, objective. Films, tapes, record cubes. Then we'll see. What if I show that we're exterminating intelligent beings? My family knows a little about genocide, after all, having been on the receiving end just a few centuries back. I doubt that I could halt what's going on here. But at the very least I could withdraw from the operation. Head back to Earth and stir up public outcries.

I hope I'm imagining this.

I'm not imagining a thing. They gather in circles; they look to the sun; they neigh and pray. They're only balls of jelly on chicken-legs, but they give thanks for their food. Those big round eyes now seem to stare accusingly at me.

Our tame herd here knows what's going on: that we have descended from the stars to eradicate their kind, and that they alone will be spared. They have no way of fighting back or even of communicating their displeasure, but they *know*. And hate us. Jesus, we have killed two million of them since we got here, and in a metaphorical way I'm stained with blood, and what will I do, what can I do?

I must move very carefully, or I'll end up drugged and edited.

I can't let myself seem like a crank, a quack, an agitator. I can't stand up and *denounce!* I have to find allies. Herndon, first. He surely is on to the truth; he's the one who nudged *me* to it, that day we dropped pellets. And I thought he was merely being vicious in his usual way!

I'll talk to him tonight.

He says, 'I've been thinking about that suggestion you made. About the Eaters. Perhaps we haven't made sufficiently close psychological studies. I mean, if they really *are* intelligent—'

Herndon blinks. He is a tall man with glossy dark hair, a heavy beard, sharp cheekbones. 'Who says they are, Tom?'

'You did. On the far side of the Forked River, you said—'

'It was just a speculative hypothesis. To make conversation.'

'No, I think it was more than that. You really believed it.'

Herndon looks troubled. 'Tom, I don't know what you're trying to start, but don't start if. If I for a moment believed we were killing intelligent creatures, I'd run for an editor so fast I'd start an implosion wave.'

'Why did you ask me that thing, then?' Tom Two Ribbons says.

'Idle chatter.'

'Amusing yourself by kindling guilts in somebody else? You're a bastard, Herndon. I mean it.'

'Well, look, Tom, if I had any idea that you'd get so worked up about a hypothetical suggestion—' Herndon shakes his head. 'The Eaters aren't intelligent beings. Obviously. Otherwise we wouldn't be under orders to liquidate them.'

'Obviously,' says Tom Two Ribbons.

Ellen said, 'No, I don't know what Tom's up to. But I'm pretty sure he needs a rest. It's only a year and a half since his personality reconstruct, and he had a pretty bad breakdown back then.'

Michaelson consulted a chart. 'He's refused three times in a row to make his pellet-dropping run. Claiming he can't take time away from his research. Hell, we can fill in for him, but it's the idea that he's ducking chores that bothers me.'

'What kind of research is he doing?' Nichols wanted to know.

'Not biological,' said Julia. 'He's with the Eaters in the compound all the time, but I don't see him making any tests on them. He just watches them.'

'And talks to them,' Chang observed.

'And talks, yes,' Julia said.

'Who knows?'

Everyone looked at Ellen. 'You're closest to him,' Michaelson said. 'Can't you bring him out of it?'

'I've got to know what he's in, first,' Ellen said. 'He isn't saying a thing.'

You know that you must be very careful, for they outnumber you, and their concern for your mental welfare can be deadly. Already they realize you are disturbed, and Ellen has begun to probe for the source of the disturbance. Last night you lay in her arms and she questioned you, obliquely, skilfully, and you knew what she is trying to find out. When the moons appeared she suggested that you and she stroll in the compound, among the sleeping Eaters. You declined, but she sees that you have become involved with the creatures.

You have done probing of your own—subtly, you hope. And you are aware that you can do nothing to save the Eaters. An irrevocable commitment has been made. It is 1876 all over again; these are the bison, these are the Sioux, and they must be destroyed, for the railway is on its way. If you speak out here, your friends will calm you and pacify you and edit you, for they do not see what you see. If you return to Earth to agitate, you will be mocked and recommended for another reconstruct. You can do nothing. You can do nothing.

You cannot save, but perhaps you can record.

Go out into the prairie. Live with the Eaters; make yourself their friend; learn their ways. Set it down, a full account of their culture, so that at least that much will not be lost. You know the techniques of field anthropology. As was done for your people in the old days, do now for the Eaters.

He finds Michaelson. 'Can you spare me for a few weeks?' he asks.

'Spare you, Tom? What do you mean?'

'I've got some field studies to do. I'd like to leave the base and work with Eaters in the wild.'

'What's wrong with the ones in the compound?'

'It's the last chance with wild ones, Mike. I've got to go.'

'Alone, or with Ellen?'

'Alone.'

Michaelson nods slowly. 'All right, Tom. Whatever you want. Go. I won't hold you here.'

I dance in the prairie under the green-gold sun. About me the Eaters gather. I am stripped; sweat makes my skin glisten; my heart pounds. I talk to them with my feet, and they understand.

They understand.

They have a language of soft sounds. They have a god. They know love and awe and rapture. They have rites. They have names. They have a history. Of all this I am convinced.

I dance on thick grass.

How can I reach them? With my feet, with my hands, with my grunts, with my sweat. They gather by the hundreds, by the thousands, and I dance. I must not stop. They cluster about me and make their sounds. I am a conduit for strange forces. My great-grandfather should see me now! Sitting on his porch in Wyoming, the firewater in his hand, his brain rotting—see me now, old one! See the dance of Tom Two Ribbons! I talk to these strange ones with my feet under a sun that is the wrong colour. I dance. I dance.

'Listen to me,' I say. 'I am your friend; I alone, the only one you can trust. Trust me, talk to me, teach me. Let me preserve your ways, for soon the destruction will come.'

I dance, and the sun climbs, and the Eaters murmur.

There is the chief. I dance towards him, back, towards; I bow; I point to the sun; I imagine the being that lives in that ball of flame; I imitate the sounds of these people; I kneel; I rise; I dance. Tom Two Ribbons dances for you.

I summon skills my ancestors forgot. I feel the power flowing in me. As they danced in the days of the bison, I dance now, beyond the Forked River.

I dance, and now the Eaters dance too. Slowly, uncertainly, they move towards me; they shift their weight; lift leg and leg; sway about. 'Yes, like that!' I cry. 'Dance!'

We dance together as the sun reaches noon height.

Now their eyes are no longer accusing. I see warmth and kinship. I am their brother, their redskinned tribesman, he who dances with them. No longer do they seem clumsy to me. There is a strange ponderous grace in their movements. They dance. They dance. They caper about me. Closer, closer, closer!

We move in holy frenzy.

They sing, now, a blurred hymn of joy. They throw forth their arms, unclench their little claws. In unison they shift weight, left foot forward, right, left, right. Dance, brothers, dance, dance, dance! They press against me. Their flesh quivers; their smell is a sweet one. They gently thrust me across the field, to a part of the meadow where the grass is deep and untrampled. Still dancing, we seek for the oxygen-plants, and find clumps of them beneath the grass, and they make their prayer and seize them with their awkward arms, separating the respiratory bodies from the photosynthetic spikes. The plants, in anguish, release floods of oxygen. My mind reels. I laugh and sing. The Eaters are nibbling the lemon-coloured perforated globes, nibbling the stalks as well. They thrust their plants at me. It is a religious ceremony, I see. Take from us; eat with us; join with us; this is the body; this is the blood; take, eat, join. I bend forward and put a lemon-coloured globe to my lips. I do not bite; I nibble, as they do, my teeth slicing away the skin of the globe. Juice spurts into my mouth, while oxygen drenches my nostrils. The Eaters sing hosannas. I should be in full paint for this, paint of my forefathers, feathers too, meeting their religion in the regalia of what should have been mine. Take, eat, join. The juice of the oxygen-plant flows in my veins. I embrace my brothers. I sing, and as my voice leaves my lips it becomes an arch that glistens like new steel, and I pitch my song lower, and the arch turns to tarnished silver. The Eaters crowd close. The scent of their bodies is fiery red to me. Their soft cries are puffs of steam. The sun is very warm; its rays are tiny jagged pings of puckered sound, close to the top of my range of hearing—plink! plink! plink! The thick grass hums to me, deep and rich, and the wind hurls points of flame along the prairie. I devour another oxygen-plant, and then a third. My brothers laugh and shout. They tell me of their gods: the god of warmth, the god of food, the god of pleasure, the god of death, the god of holiness, the god of wrongness, and the others. They recite for me the names of their kings, and I hear their voices as splashes of green mould on the clean sheet of the sky. They instruct me in their holy rites. I must remember this, I tell myself, for when it is gone it will never come again. I continue to dance. They continue to dance. The colour of the hills becomes rough and coarse, like abrasive gas. Take, eat, join. Dance. They are so gentle!

I hear the drone of the 'copter, suddenly.

It hovers far overhead. I am unable to see who flies in it. 'No,' I scream. 'Not here! Not these people! Listen to me! This is Tom Two Ribbons! Can't you hear me? I'm doing a field study here! You have no right—!'

My voice makes spirals of blue moss edged with red sparks. They drift upwards and are scattered by the breeze.

I yell, I shout, I bellow. I dance and shake my fists. From the wings of the 'copter the jointed arms of the pellet-distributors unfold. The gleaming spigots extend and whirl. The neural pellets rain down into the meadow, each tracing a blazing track that lingers in the sky. The sound of the 'copter becomes a furry carpet stretching to the horizon, and my shrill voice is lost in it.

The Eaters drift away from me, seeking the pellets, scratching at the roots of the grass to find them. Still dancing, I leap into their midst, striking the pellets from their hands, hurling them into the stream, crushing them to powder. The Eaters growl black needles at me. They turn away and search for more pellets. The 'copter turns and flies off, leaving a trail of dense oily sound. My brothers are gobbling the pellets eagerly.

There is no way to prevent it.

Joy consumes them and they topple and lie still. Occasionally a limb twitches; then even this stops. They begin to dissolve. Thousands of them melt on the prairie, sinking into shapelessness, losing their spherical forms, flattening, ebbing into the ground. The bonds of the molecules will no longer hold. It is the twilight of protoplasm. They perish. They vanish. For hours I walk the prairie. Now I inhale oxygen; now I eat a lemon-coloured globe. Sunset begins with the ringing of leaden chimes. Black clouds make brazen trumpet calls in the east and the deepening wind is a swirl of coaly bristles. Silence comes. Night falls. I dance. I am alone.

The 'copter comes again, and they find you, and you do not resist as they gather you in. You are beyond bitterness. Quietly you explain what you have done and what you have learned, and why it is wrong to exterminate these people. You describe the plant you have eaten and the way it affects your senses, and as you talk of the blessed synesthesia, the texture of the wind and the sound of the clouds and the timbre of the sunlight. They nod and smile and tell you not to worry, that everything will be all right soon, and they touch something cold to your forearm, so cold that it is a whirl and a buzz and the deintoxicant sinks into your vein and soon the ecstasy drains away, leaving only the exhaustion and the grief.

He says, 'We never learn a thing, do we? We export all our horrors to the stars. Wipe out the Armenians, wipe out the Jews, wipe out the Tasmanians, wipe out the Indians, wipe out everyone who's in the way, and then come out here and do the same damned murderous thing. You weren't

237

with me out there. You didn't dance with them. You didn't see what a rich, complex culture the Eaters have. Let me tell you about their tribal structure. It's dense: seven levels of matrimonial relationships, to begin with, and an exogamy factor that requires—'

Softly Ellen says, 'Tom, darling, nobody's going to harm the Eaters.'

'And the religion,' he goes on. 'Nine gods, each one an aspect of *the* god. Holiness and wrongness both worshipped. They have hymns, prayers, a theology. And we, the emissaries of the god of wrongness—'

'We're not exterminating them,' Michaelson says. 'Won't you understand that, Tom? This is all a fantasy of yours. You've been under the influence of drugs, but now we're clearing you out. You'll be clean in a little while. You'll have perspective again.'

'A fantasy?' he says bitterly. 'A drug dream? I stood out in the prairie and saw you drop pellets. And I watched them die and melt away. I didn't dream that.'

'How can we convince you?' Chang asks earnestly. 'What will make you believe? Shall we fly over the Eater country with you and show you how many millions there are?'

'But how many millions have been destroyed?' he demands.

They insist that he is wrong. Ellen tells him again that no one has ever desired to harm the Eaters. 'This is a scientific expedition, Tom. We're here to *study* them. It's a violation of all we stand for to injure intelligent life-forms.'

'You admit that they're intelligent?'

'Of course. That's never been in doubt.'

'Then why drop the pellets?' he asks. 'Why slaughter them?'

'None of that has happened, Tom,' Ellen says. She takes his hand between her cool palms. 'Believe us. Believe us.'

He says bitterly, 'If you want me to believe you, why don't you do the job properly? Get out the editing machine and go to work on me. You can't simply *talk* me into rejecting the evidence of my own eyes.'

'You were under drugs all the time,' Michaelson says.

'I've never taken drugs! Except for what I ate in the

meadow, when I danced—and that came after I had watched
the massacre going on for weeks and weeks. Are you saying
that it's a retroactive delusion?'

'No, Tom,' Schwartz says. 'You've had this delusion all
along. It's part of your therapy, your reconstruct. You
came here programmed with it.'

'Impossible,' he says.

Ellen kisses his fevered forehead. 'It was done to reconcile
you to mankind, you see. You had this terrible resentment
of the displacement of your people in the nineteenth century.
You were unable to forgive the industrial society for scatter-
ing the Sioux, and you were terribly full of hate. Your
therapist thought that if you could be made to participate
in an imaginary modern extermination, if you could come
to see it as a necessary operation, you'd be purged of your
resentment and able to take your place in society as—'

He thrusts her away. 'Don't talk idiocy! If you knew the
first thing about reconstruct therapy, you'd realize that no
reputable therapist could be so shallow. There are no one-
to-one correlations in reconstructs. No, don't touch me.
Keep away. Keep away.'

He will not let them persuade him that this is merely a
drug-born dream. It is no fantasy, he tells himself, and it is
no therapy. He rises. He goes out. They do not follow him.
He takes a 'copter and seeks his brothers.

Again I dance. The sun is much hotter today. The Eaters
are more numerous. Today I wear paint; today I wear
feathers. My body shines with my sweat. They dance with
me, and they have a frenzy in them that I have never seen
before. We pound the trampled meadow with our feet. We
clutch for the sun with our hands. We sing, we shout, we
cry. We will dance until we fall.

This is no fantasy. These people are real, and they are
intelligent, and they are doomed. This I know.

We dance. Despite the doom, we dance.

My great-grandfather comes and dances with us. He too
is real. His nose is like a hawk's, not blunt like mine, and he
wears the big headdress, and his muscles are like cords
under his brown skin. He sings, he shouts, he cries.

239

Others of my family join us.

We eat the oxygen-plants together. We embrace the Eaters. We know, all of us, what it is to be hunted.

The clouds make music and the wind takes on texture and the sun's warmth has colour.

We dance. We dance. Our limbs know no weariness.

The sun grows and fills the whole sky, and I see no Eaters now, only my own people, my father's fathers across the centuries, thousands of gleaming skins, thousands of hawks' noses, and we eat the plants, and we find sharp sticks and thrust them into our flesh, and the sweet blood flows and dries in the blaze of the sun, and we dance, and we dance, and some of us fall from weariness, and we dance, and the prairie is a sea of bobbing headdresses, an ocean of feathers, and we dance, and my heart makes thunder, and my knees become water, and the sun's fire engulfs me, and I dance, and I fall, and I dance, and I fall, and I fall, and I fall.

Again they find you and bring you back. They give you the cool snout on your arm to take the oxygen-plant drug from your veins, and then they give you something else so you will rest. You rest and you are very calm. Ellen kisses you and you stroke her soft skin, and then the others come in and they talk to you, saying soothing things, but you do not listen, for you are searching for realities. It is not an easy search. It is like falling through many trapdoors, looking for the one room whose floor is not hinged. Everything that has happened on this planet is your therapy, you tell yourself, designed to reconcile an embittered aborigine to the white man's conquest; nothing is really being exterminated here. You reject that and fall through and realize that this must be the therapy of your friends; they carry the weight of accumulated centuries of guilts and have come here to shed that load, and you are here to ease them of their burden, to draw their sins into yourself and give them forgiveness. Again you fall through, and see that the Eaters are mere animals who threaten the ecology and must be removed; the culture you imagined for them is your hallucination, kindled out of old churnings. You try to withdraw your objections to this necessary extermination, but you fall through again and discover that there is no extermination except in your mind, which is troubled and disordered by your obsession with the crime against your ancestors, and you sit up, for you wish to apologize to these friends of yours, these innocent scientists whom you have called murderers. And you fall through.

The Oh in Jose

Brian Aldiss

Future generations of literary historians may come to regard Brian Aldiss as science fiction's first man of letters. A leading novelist and short story writer in the genre for more than a decade, he has done more than any of his contemporaries to remove the artificial barriers that have kept sf apart from the mainstream of literature. His fiction has appeared in mass-circulation magazines such as *Nova*, *Punch* and *Queen*, as well as the leading sf magazines. He has written 'straight' novels like *The Hand-Reared Boy*, which have become best-sellers, and most recently *Billion-Year Spree*, the definitive history of science fiction. With such a wide-ranging talent, it seems that only Aldiss could have written THE OH IN JOSE —a charming meditation on the art of storytelling.

They had seen no human habitation for two days when they came unexpectedly on a mountain village. Here their servant arranged that an old woman should guide them over the mountains and back to civilization.

After spending an uncomfortable night in the village, they were off early next morning, the five of them: the old woman on foot, the servant on a mule leading a pack mule, and the three men on horses. Of the men, one was by some years the oldest, a spare man with a trim white beard and somewhat over-meticulous gestures. The two younger men were of contrasting type; one of them, the *bon viveur*, was a thick-set man in his forties, with a plump face and an intelligent glance not entirely marred by a snub nose. His humorous manner acted as a foil for the more serious ways of the youngest man, who was a philatelist of some repute, although only among other philatelists.

Each of the men was pleased with the excellent company afforded by his two fellows. They had established among themselves a combination of seriousness and gaiety, of reserve and intimacy, which is rare and which more than compensated for the ardours of their long and difficult journey. Where the road would allow it, they spent much of each morning, before the sun was too hot, conversing as they rode; and these conversations were often protracted after dusk, while the servant prepared and they ate their supper.

But now, as the old woman led them higher into the hills, and as the scene became more desolate, the elder fell silent. The *bon viveur* was delivering a long mock-heroic about why people told stories of what their dentists did, but finally he too lapsed into silence. All that morning, they rode in a quiet broken only by the echoes of the horses' movements among the canyons they traversed, or by an occasional word from the servant to his mules.

The *bon viveur* secretly resented this silence that he felt radiated from the elder and rebuked him inwardly for not thrusting off a fit of old man's melancholy. His feeling was that they were three intelligent men whose inward resources should be proof against transitory outside influences. So when they stopped at midday to take the cold meat, wine, and coffee that the servant set before them, the *bon viveur* said to the philatelist in a provoking tone, 'Our old guide woman is more silent and dismal even than we are. We've not had a word out of her, or out of us.'

'She has more right to be taciturn than we have,' the philatelist said with a laugh. 'Think what awaits us over the mountains: hot baths, music, elevators to whisk us to choice restaurants, libraries, conversation and the company of fair women! What awaits her? Only that dreadful village again, and work till her life's end.' Addressing himself to the old woman in her own tongue, he called, 'Hey, my charming madam, you only left your home at dawn today! Are you pining already for some vagabond of a husband?'

The old woman had come barefoot from the village with seemingly no provision for the three- or four-day journey but a loaf tucked under her shawl. She sat now away from them, awaiting the order to move on again, and did not look up or answer when the philatelist spoke.

'You'll have to find something else to distract yourself with,' the elder said, not approving this baiting of an old woman.

As they got up to go, and were mounting their horses, the servant came over and told the *bon viveur* and the philatelist, rather shamefacedly, that he had heard in the village that the old woman was once a great beauty who had suffered a great love and a great betrayal.

The *bon viveur* laughed and nudged his friend in the ribs. 'All these old crones claim to have been great beauties,' he said. 'We shall indeed have to find something else to distract ourselves with.'

Although the elder smarted a little at this remark, which he felt to be directed against him, he said nothing, and they rode on; but as it happened it was only a half hour later that they found something to distract them back into their old companionable humour.

They worked their way through a defile, the end of which was marked by one wretched tree clinging to the rock face, and were suddenly on a plateau. To one side lay mountain peaks, ribbed with snow and half-hidden under fuming cloud, while to the other lay an immense panorama of the land they had so painfully traversed, all the way to the distant sea, now hidden in the hazes of noon. With a common instinct, the three men turned aside from the way the woman led and directed their mounts towards the precipice.

For a long while they stood drinking in this view of the distant world of grass and shade and fertility, so different from the place in which they now stood. At last the elder said, 'Well, I still say there is nothing more melancholy than a mountain, but it was worth the journey just to look down at this spectacle. Sometime, I would like to have you gentlemen's opinions on why a view from a height has such power to move the spirit.'

'Come and look at this!' exclaimed the philatelist. Something in his voice made the others turn immediately to see what he had found.

Perched a few feet away from them, on the very lip of the plateau, so that its outer edge hung into space, was a giant rock. It was grey in colour, and most of its surface had been worn smooth by the elements. But what drew the attention of the men was a human addition to the rock. Someone had carved here in its centre, and in large letters, the name JOSE.

'Well, that's a disappointment, I must say,' the *bon viveur* remarked humorously. 'Just when I was thinking we were the first people ever to set foot in this remote spot.'

'I wonder who Jose was, and why he carved his name here of all places,' the elder said. 'And when. And a dozen other questions connected with the mysterious Jose.'

'Perhaps he carved this as his memorial and then jumped over the edge,' suggested the *bon viveur*. 'I can think of few more dramatic spots in which to commit suicide, if one were so inclined.'

'I've an idea,' said the philatelist. 'Here we have a little mystery at our very feet. Let's each tell a story about this Jose. Obviously, it is beyond our power to arrive at the truth about him, so let's each arrive at a fiction about him.'

'Good idea,' said the *bon viveur*, 'though I have run out of bright ideas. The oldest among us must tell his Jose story first.'

'Seconded,' agreed the philatelist and, turning to the elder man, asked him to think of a story.

The elder stroked his beard a little and protested that he was being given the hardest task in beginning; but he was a resourceful old man and, setting one foot on the carved rock, he stared into space and began his story.

'I am not at all sure,' he said, 'that this name was not written here by supernatural means, for this plainly is a supernatural place. If I have doubts, it is because Jose is hardly a supernatural name. Of all names it is the most earthy; all round the world, you can find peasants called Jose or Joe or Joze or some close local equivalent. Of all names, it is the most impersonal, the name of a force rather than a man. You know, in the first human tribe, all the males were probably called Jose.

'Consider the letters that form the name. Look at this three-fingered E! It reminds one, doesn't it, of a crude agricultural implement, a rake that every peasant uses to rake the detritus of each season wearily from his land. And the J! Isn't that another implement, the first, the curving sickle that must cut down the weeds and the choking grass from the land? What about this awkward S he has made in the rock, of all the letters the most difficult to cut? Is it not the slow meandering path taken by his beast, along the shores of a lake, or winding over a mountain track? And look at the O in JOSE! What a symbol you have there, my friends—a symbol of the earth itself, which Jose will inherit, and of fertility, which is as much the concern of the Joses of our world as it is of the earthworm. You see what Jose means; it is a natural force like the rock on which it is written.

'But this particular inscription has something individual about it, I fancy. You notice how the J is bitten deep, but the other letters are formed more shallowly. The E is too small. It all goes to show that this Jose lacked assurance. You may wonder why, and I will tell you.

'This Jose was a quiet boy, not particularly clever, not particularly dull, not particularly brave, not particularly anything. But one day when he was going on the way to his father's house, he was stopped in the lane by four bigger boys. Jose did not know these boys, and we can imagine that directly he saw them he could tell from their looks that there was trouble coming. Perhaps he tried to run from them, but they caught him and made him stand before them.

' "What is your name?" they demanded.

' "Jose."

' "Okay, Jose—explain yourself."

'He tried to evade the question, indeed he tried to evade them, but always they grabbed him by the collar and said, "Explain yourself."

' "I was born in the village," he said pathetically at last.

' "Why were you born, boy? Explain yourself."

'No answer he could give seemed to satisfy them. Moreover, the answers were not satisfactory even to Jose himself.

When finally he escaped, their question worried him even more than his fresh bruises. Explain himself? He was totally unable to do so! Now it would be foolish of me to claim, even as an omniscient storyteller with the power of life and death over my character, that Jose never forgot that searching demand to explain himself. But let us say that it would come back to him at odd and sometimes inconvenient moments in his life, to puzzle and worry him: when he was making merry with his friends, when he was flirting with a village girl, or perhaps when one of them jilted him; or when he was in church, or ill, or taking a holiday, or swimming in the river, or lying lazily in his marriage bed, or cradling his firstborn, or sweating in the noonday field, or even squatting in the flimsy W.C. at the bottom of his patch of land. What I mean to say is, that at various moments throughout Jose's life, the good ones or the bad, he would suddenly feel that a big question hung over him, that there was something about him that needed explaining, something that he was quite unable to explain.

'He kept this thing secret, even from his wife whom he loved. He told himself it was not important, and you two gentlemen may like to judge if he was correct in so thinking. But not to let my story grow too long, for I grant you that stories about simple peasants can become very long indeed, Jose's wife died one day. He was full of grief, so much so that he persuaded his old mother to look after his son for a week while he himself saddled up the donkey and rode off into the hills to be alone with his melancholy. It's not my job to tell you why people have such an instinct, for to me hills are melancholy places in their own right, and more likely to induce than cure gloom. Still, for the purpose of my story, we have to have Jose riding into the hills—these hills, you know. The assumption will stand since it is not contrary to human nature.

'In the hills, Jose let the mule—no, we said donkey, didn't we?—he let the animal go where it would while he thought about his life and the meaning of life. But when it came to the meaning of life, he could no more explain himself than when he was a lad being bullied in the lane. In the depths of his brooding, he sat where we stand now, and he carved his name in this rock. And we three are not privileged to know whether Jose had the wit to see that his name was his explanation, and that he himself was self-explanatory.'

This story was much appreciated by the *bon viveur* and the philatelist.

'I shall make a poor showing after that fine and philosophical story unless I have a drop of wine first,' said the *bon viveur*. He motioned to the servant, who now stood respectfully behind them, holding the horses. The old guide woman remained beyond the group, dissociating herself from them. When the servant came forward with a bag of wine and the *bon viveur* had slaked his throat, he said apologetically. 'Well, here is my story of Jose, though I'm afraid I'm going to have to move this hulking boulder over to another site for the purposes of the narrative.'

'It is the privilege of fiction to move mountains,' observed the philatelist, and with that encouragement, the *bon viveur* began his tale.

'With a certain amount of diligence, it was possible to grow very good vines in Jose's field. His field lay at the foot of a mountain next to a lake, so that it was sheltered and it was not too arduous to get water to moisten the roots of the vines.

'Jose was cross-eyed. He had other and more serious troubles also. The field was small, and would barely support him and his pigs and his donkey. Then there were the changes of government, and the changes of forms of government; and although each form of government proclaimed itself more interested in Jose's welfare than the last, each one seemed to require Jose to work harder than the last.

'There was also the rock. The rock was shaped like an elephant's foot and had fallen away from the mountain in some forgotten time, perhaps even before there were men to forget, or indeed elephants to have feet. The rock occupied a lot of Jose's land where he might more profitably have grown vines. But he never resented it. On his twenty-first birthday he carved his name on it, and every day of his working life he rested his back against it.

'For all his troubles, Jose married a good girl from the nearby town and was happy with her. She possessed the sound sense to love him for his crossed eye and to smell sweet even when she sweated from labouring in the field with him. He planted his vines closer to the mountain and worked harder than before, in order to support her and the government.

'A son was born to Jose. Jose rejoiced, and planted his vines closer to the lake. A second son was born, and the vines were planted closer to the big rock. In due season, the next year to be precise, a third son was born. After the rejoicing was done, Jose planted his vines closer together. And he worked a little harder, and got a little drunk when he thought he worked too hard.

'The years came and went as fast as governments, and the sons grew up tall and scraggy because there was not over-much to eat. The eldest son drifted into town and became full of the theories of the current régime. He came back to see his father wearing a steel-grey suit and said: "Father, you are a reactionary and obtuse old fool of a goat, if you will pardon my saying so. If you let the government buy your land for a reasonable pittance, you could go on working on it and they would come with dynamite and blast that elephant's foot out of the way, so that you could grow many more vines than you do—increase production, as we call it in the city." He even got a man to photograph the rock with a foreign-made camera, but Jose was not to be moved.

'The government fell, and the first son was shot for his ideas. The second son joined the army. One day, he came back to see his father dressed in a captain's uniform and said, 'So, Dad, you antiquated old numbskull, I see you are still toiling your life out round the elephant's foot! Did you never learn what graft was when you were young? The army are going to build a new road a couple of kilometres from here. Give me the word and I'll send them the rock to build the road with, and they can haul it away with bulldozers.' He even got a sergeant to survey and photograph the rock, but Jose was no more to be moved than his rock.

'There was a revolution, and the second son was shot for the good of the country. The youngest son grew up very crafty, perhaps because he had starved the most, and went into banking. He saw what little effect his brothers' words had had on his father, and addressed the old man thus, "My dear and hard-working old paternal pot, my informed friends in the city tell me there is every reason to suspect that there may be a great well of oil under the elephant's foot. You could be rich beyond the dreams of avarice and buy mother two new frocks if that were so. Why do you not look? If you and mother broke down a barrow-load of rock each day and flung it into the lake, at the end of two years or maybe less or maybe more, you would have the land clear. I can get you a barrow wholesale if you agree." He even induced a fellow banker to take a colour photograph of the rock, but Jose was not to be moved.

'The next day, the president of the country absconded with all the gold from the bank, and the government fell. But Jose's wife sent the three photographs of the rock that looked so like an elephant's foot to a big magazine, whereupon it became a great tourist attraction at twenty-five cents a time, and Jose never had to grow vines any more.'

The elder and the philatelist greatly enjoyed this story, the latter especially since he was by profession a banker and appreciated the dig his friend had had at him.

'So I must now tell my Jose story,' he said, 'which I certainly shall not enjoy as much as yours. To ensure that it has at least some merit I will borrow elements from both your tales, the peasant and the rock. But if you don't mind we will leave such trivial items as bankers and revolutions out of it and look at the whole matter in its proper perspective.'

So saying, he embarked upon his story.

'Imagine a sheet of ice, miles and miles wide, covering much of the world. At its most extensive, it reached only half way up the mountain. Then it grew grey, and crumpled and melted and disappeared. In its place, a lake formed, lying at the foot of the mountain.

'Slowly the weather grew warmer. It became hot by day, though the nights remained cool. Several times, the mountain split and its flanks fell into the lake. Things grew on these piles of stones, and along the new ground exposed by the lake as it shrank. In spring, the whole shelf was covered with yellow flowers.

'Distantly, a river broke through on a new course and poured its waters into the lake, whereupon the lake stopped shrinking. Things swam in the lake; some of them climbed out of the lake. Some of those that climbed out died in the field, but others gained new qualities and flourished.

'One of the animals was ungainly and slow. In the palm of its skull lay a pool of mud through which trickled the waters of its new discovery called thought. It sank into the rock. Of its thought there remained no trace, but the pattern of its bones lay in the quiet strata, making a pattern more pleasing than in life.

'Another animal was full of a vast and automatic fury. Its cry when it hunted cut like a knife and struck the rocks with the force of a hammer. One day, a slab of the mountainside fell upon it, and the slab resembled the head of a serpent.

'Another creature was patient. It tilled the soil between the mountain and the lake and planted vines in the soil and tended them year by year. When it was young, it carved its name JOSE on the rock shaped like a serpent head, and spent the rest of its life in the field, working everywhere round the rock. One day it staggered into the shade of the rock and never rose again.

'Another being learned to extract the energy it required direct from the soil. It bloomed and ferreted and crackled, and again part of the mountain fell, making an avalanche that splashed into the lake for half a day. The thing slowly annihilated the rubble from the mountain, until it disintegrated from ripeness.

'Now a being of splendour arose that could extract its necessary energy from the whole universe, and so needed to pay no attention to mountain, field, or lake. Because it was sufficient to itself, it destroyed all other life and sat through an eternity sketching elaborate patterns of light in its being, until it was itself translated into light.

'The last thing was a thing of infinite love and infinite might. It grieved for the destruction that had been and determined to create a new system of life based only remotely on the old. It looked about at the silent mountain and lake; finally it built an entire new universe, shaping it out of the

'O' in JOSE that was carved in the serpent head rock.

'On planets in the new universe, mountains and lakes began to appear. They worked out their own enormous processes in solitude, for the being of love and might had built them a universe safe from life.'

The *bon viveur* and the elder both declared themselves impressed by this story, and the latter added, 'You take a more bleak and long view of humanity than I dare do at my time of life. You don't really find life as meaningless as all that, do you?'

The philatelist spread his hands. 'Yes, sometimes I do—in a place like this, for instance. We are only passing through, and our mood will change. But look at the wretched old guide woman, for instance. What has life to offer her? And look at the region in which she lives, at this profound and aloof grandeur all about us. Is not its meaning greater and more enduring than man's?'

The elder shuddered. 'My friend, I prefer to believe that this mountain has no meaning at all until it is translated through man's understanding.'

As he spoke, the servant touched him respectfully on the arm. 'Excuse me, sir, but I think we really ought to be moving on, because we don't want to be still up here in this exposed place when night falls.'

'You are absolutely right, my friend. You are a practical man. All our endeavours should be devoted towards getting away from this lifeless tomb. Whoever Jose was, he has no interest for any of us now. Tell the old woman to lead on.'

They mounted their horses and turned away from the rock with its brief inscription. They followed the servant across the drab and stony soil. The old woman led them on never once casting her eye back at the spot where, as a young and passionate woman, she had blazed the name of her faithless lover.

The Man Who Came Early

Poul Anderson

Long before sf became popular and fashionable, Mark Twain wrote a novel, *A Connecticut Yankee at the Court of King Arthur*, in which his protagonist gets a beastly knock on the head and is hurled backward in time, where he subsequently introduces all sorts of modern innovations into Arthurian society. The idea persisted and was taken up from time to time and developed by several generations of sf writers. Poul Anderson tells his tale from the viewpoint of the people of the past, among whom the modern-day protagonist suddenly appears. The cultural setting that Anderson chooses seems harsh by our standards but this only serves to enhance his point. Drawing upon his deep knowledge of history in this memorable story, Anderson succeeds in bringing to life the landscape and characters of a past age.

Yes, when a man grows old he has heard so much that is strange there's little more can surprise him. They say the king in Miklagard has a beast of gold before his high seat, which stands up and roars. I have it from Eilif Eiriksson, who served in the guard down there, and he is a steady fellow when not drunk. He has also seen the Greek fire used; it burns on water.

So, priest, I am not unwilling to believe what you say about the White Christ. I have been in England and France myself, and seen how the folk prosper. He must be a very powerful god, to ward so many realms . . . and did you say that everyone who is baptized will be given a white robe? I would like to have one. They mildew, of course, in this cursed wet Iceland weather, but a small sacrifice to the house-elves should . . . No sacrifices? Come now! I'll give up horseflesh if I must, my teeth not being what they were, but every sensible man knows how much trouble the elves make if they're not fed.

. . . Well, let's have another cup and talk about it. How do you like the beer? It's my own brew, you know. The cups I got in England, many years back. I was a young man then . . . times goes, time goes. Afterwards I came back and inherited this, my father's steading, and have not left it since. Well enough to go in viking as a youth, but grown older you see where the real wealth lies: here, in the land and the cattle.

Stoke up the fires, Hjalti. It's growing cold. Sometimes I think the winters are colder than when I was a boy. Thorbrand of the Salmondale says so, but he believes the gods are angry because so many are turning from them. You'll have trouble winning Thorbrand over, priest. A stubborn man. Myself I am open-minded, and willing to listen at least.

. . . Now then. There is one point on which I must correct you. The end of the world is not coming in two years. This I know.

And if you ask me how I know, that's a very long tale, and in some ways a terrible one. Glad I am to be old, and safely in the earth before that great tomorrow comes. It will be an eldritch time before the frost giants march . . . oh, very well, before the angel blows his battle horn. One reason I hearken to your preaching is that I know the White Christ will conquer Thor. I know Iceland is going to be Christian erelong, and it seems best to range myself on the winning side.

No, I've had no visions. This is a happening of five years ago, which my own household and neighbours can swear to. They mostly did not believe what the stranger told; I do, more or less, if only because I don't think a liar could wreak so much harm. I loved my daughter, priest, and after it was over I made a good marriage for her. She did not naysay it, but now she sits out on the ness-farm with her husband and never a word to me; and I hear he is ill pleased with her silence and moodiness, and spends his nights with an Irish concubine. For this I cannot blame him, but it grieves me.

Well, I've drunk enough to tell the whole truth now, and whether you believe it or not makes no odds to me. Here . . . you girls! . . . fill these cups again, for I'll have a dry throat before I finish the telling.

It begins, then, on a day in early summer, five years ago. At that time, my wife Ragnhild and I had only two unwed children still living with us: our youngest son Helgi, of seventeen winters, and our daughter Thorgunna, of eighteen. The girl, being fair, had already had suitors. But she refused them, and I am not a man who would compel his daughter. As for Helgi, he was ever a lively one, good with his hands but a breakneck youth. He is now serving in the guard of King Olaf of Norway. Besides these, of course, we had about ten housefolk—two Irish thralls, two girls to help with the women's work, and half a dozen hired carles. This is not a small steading.

You have not seen how my land lies. About two miles to the west is the bay; the thorps at Reykjavik are about five miles south. The land rises towards the Long Jökull, so that my acres are hilly; but it's good hayland, and there is often driftwood on the beach. I've built a shed down there for it, as well as a boathouse.

There had been a storm the night before, so Helgi and I were going down to look for drift. You, coming from Norway, do not know how precious wood is to us Icelanders, who have only a few scrubby trees and must bring all our timber from abroad. Back there men have often been burned in their houses by their foes, but we count that the worst of deeds, though it's not unknown.

I was on good terms with my neighbours, so we took only hand weapons. I my axe, Helgi a sword, and the two carles we had with us bore spears. It was a day washed clean by the night's fury, and the sun fell bright on long wet grass. I saw my garth lying rich around its courtyard, sleek cows and sheep, smoke rising from the roof hole of the hall, and knew I'd not done so ill in my lifetime. My son Helgi's hair

fluttered in the low west wind as we left the steading behind
a ridge and neared the water. Strange how well I remember
all which happened that day; somehow it was a sharper
day than most.

When we came down to the strand, the sea was beating
heavy, white and grey out to the world's edge. A few gulls
flew screaming above us, frightened off a cod washed up
onto the shore. I saw there was a litter of no few sticks,
even a baulk of timber . . . from some ship carrying it that
broke up during the night, I suppose. That was a useful
find, though, as a careful man, I would later sacrifice to be
sure the owner's ghost wouldn't plague me.

We had fallen to and were dragging the baulk towards
the shed when Helgi cried out. I ran for my axe as I looked
the way he pointed. We had no feuds then, but there are
always outlaws.

This one seemed harmless, though. Indeed, as he stumbled
nearer across the black sand I thought him quite unarmed
and wondered what had happened. He was a big man and
strangely clad—he wore coat and breeches and shoes like
anyone else, but they were of peculiar cut and he bound
his trousers with leggings rather than thongs. Nor had I
ever seen a helmet like his: it was almost square, and came
down to cover his neck, but it had no nose guard; it was
held in place by a leather strap. And this you may not
believe, but it was *not metal yet had been cast in one piece!*

He broke into a staggering run as he neared, and flapped
his arms and croaked something. The tongue was none I
had ever heard, and I have heard many; it was like dogs
barking. I saw that he was clean-shaven and his black hair
cropped short, and thought he might be French. Otherwise
he was a young man, and good-looking, with blue eyes and
regular features. From his skin I judged that he spent much
time indoors, yet he had a fine manly build.

'Could he have been shipwrecked?' asked Helgi.

'His clothes are dry and unstained,' I said; 'nor has he
been wandering long, for there's no stubble on his chin. Yet
I've heard of no strangers guesting hereabouts.'

We lowered our weapons, and he came up to us and
stood gasping. I saw that his coat and the shirt behind

were fastened with bonelike buttons rather than laces, and were of heavy weave. About his neck he had fastened a strip of cloth tucked into his coat. These garments were all in brownish hues. His shoes were of a sort new to me, very well cobbled. Here and there on his coat were bits of brass, and he had three broken stripes on each sleeve; also a black band with white letters, the same letters being on his helmet. Those were not runes, but Roman letters—thus: MP. He wore a broad belt, with a small clublike thing of metal in a sheath at the hip and also a real club.

'I think he must be a warlock,' muttered my carle, Sigurd. 'Why else all those tokens?'

'They may only be ornament, or to ward against witch-craft,' I soothed him. Then, to the stranger. 'I hight Ospak Ulfsson of Hillstead. What is your errand?'

He stood with his chest heaving and a wildness in his eyes. He must have run a long way. Then he moaned and sat down and covered his face.

'If he's sick, best we get him to the house,' said Helgi. His eyes gleamed—we see so few new faces here.

'No . . . no . . . ' The stranger looked up. 'Let me rest a moment—'

He spoke the Norse tongue readily enough, though with a thick accent not easy to follow and with many foreign words I did not understand.

The other carle, Grim, hefted his spear. 'Have vikings landed?' he asked.

'When did vikings ever come to Iceland?' I snorted. 'It's the other way around.'

The newcomer shook his head, as if it had been struck. He got shakily to his feet. 'What happened?' he said. 'What happened to the city?'

'What city?' I asked reasonably.

'Reykjavik!' he groaned. 'Where is it?'

'Five miles south, the way you came—unless you mean the bay itself,' I said.

'No! There was only a beach, and a few wretched huts, and—'

'Best not let Hjalmar Broadnose hear you call his thorp that,' I counselled.

'But there was a city!' he cried. Wildness lay in his eyes. 'I was crossing the street, it was a storm, and there was a crash and then I stood on the beach and the city was gone!

'He's mad,' said Sigurd, backing away. 'Be careful . . . if he starts to foam at the mouth, it means he's going berserk.'

'Who are you?' babbled the stranger. 'What are you doing in those clothes? Why the spears?'

'Somehow,' said Helgi, 'he does not sound crazed—only frightened and bewildered. Something evil has happened to him.'

'I'm not staying near a man under a curse!' yelped Sigurd, and started to run away.

'Come back!' I bawled. 'Stand where you are or I'll cleave your louse-bitten head!'

That stopped him, for he had no kin who would avenge him; but he would not come closer. Meanwhile the stranger had calmed down to the point where he could at least talk evenly.

'Was it the *aitchbomb*?' he asked. 'Has the war started?'

He used that word often, *aitchbomb*, so I know it now, though unsure of what it means. It seems to be a kind of Greek fire. As for the war, I knew not which war he meant, and told him so.

'There was a great thunderstorm last night,' I added. 'And you say you were out in one too. Perhaps Thor's hammer knocked you from your place to here.'

'But where is here?' he replied. His voice was more dulled than otherwise, now that the first terror had lifted.

'I told you. This is Hillstead, which is on Iceland.'

'But that's where I was!' he mumbled. 'Reykjavik . . . what happened? Did the *aitchbomb* destroy everything while I was unconscious?'

'Nothing has been destroyed,' I said.

'Perhaps he means the fire at Olafsvik last month,' said Helgi.

'No, no, no!' He buried his face in his hands. After a while he looked up and said, 'See here. I am Sergeant Gerald Roberts of the United States Army base on Iceland. I was in Reykjavik and got struck by lightning or something. Suddenly I was standing on the beach, and got frightened and ran. That's all. Now, can you tell me how to get back to the base?'

Those were more or less his words, priest. Of course, we did not grasp half it, and made him repeat it several times and explain the words. Even then we did not understand, except that he was from some country called the United States of America, which he said lies beyond Greenland to the west, and that he and some others were on Iceland to help our folk against their enemies. Now this I did not consider a lie—more a mistake or imagining. Grim would have cut him down for thinking us stupid enough to swallow that tale, but I could see that he meant it.

Trying to explain it to us cooled him off. 'Look here,' he said, in too reasonable a tone for a feverish man, 'perhaps we can get at the truth from your side. Has there been no war you know of? Nothing which—well, look here. My country's men first came to Iceland to guard it against the Germans . . . now it is the Russians, but then it was the Germans. When was that?'

Helgi shook his head. 'That never happened that I know of,'. he said. 'Who are these Russians?' He found out later that Gardariki was meant. 'Unless,' he said, 'the old warlocks—'

'He means the Irish monks,' I explained. 'There were a few living here when the Norsemen came, but they were driven out. That was, hm, somewhat over a hundred years ago. Did your folk ever help the monks?'

'I never heard of them!' he said. His breath sobbed in his throat. 'You . . . didn't you Icelanders come from Norway?'

'Yes, about a hundred years ago,' I answered patiently. 'After King Herald Fairhair took all the Norse lands and—'

'*A hundred years ago!*' he whispered. I saw whiteness creep up under his skin. 'What year is this?'

We gaped at him. 'Well, it's the second year after the great salmon catch,' I tried.

'What year after Christ, I mean?' It was a hoarse prayer.

'Oh, so you are a Christian? Hm, let me think . . . I talked with a bishop in England once—we were holding him for ransom—and he said . . . let me see . . . I think he said this Christ man lived a thousand years ago, or maybe a little less.'

'A thousand—' He shook his head; and then something went out of him, he stood with glassy eyes—yes, I have seen glass, I told you I am a travelled man—he stood thus, and when we led him towards the garth he went like a small child.

You can see for yourself, priest, that my wife Ragnhild is still good to look upon even in eld, and Thorgunna took after her. She was—is—tall and slim, with a dragon's hoard of golden hair. She being a maiden then, it flowed loose over her shoulders. She had great blue eyes and a small heart-shaped face and very red lips. Withal she was a merry one, and kind-hearted, so that all men loved her. Sverri Snorrason went in viking when she refused and was slain, but no one had the wit to see that she was unlucky.

We led this Gerald Samsson—when I asked, he said his father was named Sam—we led him home, leaving Sigurd and Grim to finish gathering the driftwood. There are some who would not have a Christian in their house, for fear of witchcraft, but I am a broad-minded man and Helgi, of course, was wild for anything new. Our guest stumbled like a blind man over the fields, but seemed to wake up as we entered the yard. His eyes went around the buildings that enclosed it, from the stables and sheds to the smokehouse, the brewery, the kitchen, the bathhouse, the god-shrine, and thence to the hall. And Thorgunna was standing in the doorway.

Their gazes locked for a moment, and I saw her colour but thought little of it then. Our shoes rang on the flagging as we crossed the yard and kicked the dogs aside. My two thralls paused in cleaning out the stables to gawk, until I got them back to work with the remark that a man good for naught else was always a pleasing sacrifice. That's one useful practice you Christians lack; I've never made a human offering myself, but you know not how helpful is the fact that I could do so.

We entered the hall and I told the folk Gerald's name and how we had found him. Ragnhild set her maids hopping, to stoke up the fire in the middle trench and fetch beer, while I led Gerald to the high seat and sat down by him. Thorgunna brought us the filled horns.

Gerald tasted the brew and made a face. I felt somewhat offended, for my beer is reckoned good, and asked him if there was aught wrong. He laughed with a harsh note and said no, but he was used to beer that foamed and was not sour.

'And where might they make such?' I wondered testily.

'Everywhere. Iceland, too—no . . .' He stared emptily before him. 'Let's say . . . in Vinland.'

'Where is Vinland?' I asked.

'The country to the west whence I came. I thought you knew . . . wait a bit.' He shook his head. 'Maybe I can find out—have you heard of a man named Leif Eiriksson?'

'No,' I said. Since then it has struck me that this was one proof of his tale, for Leif Eiriksson is now a well-known chief; and I also take more seriously those tales of land seen by Bjarni Herjulfsson.

'His father, maybe—Eirik the Red?' asked Gerald.

'Oh yes,' I said. 'If you mean the Norseman who came hither because of a manslaughter, and left Iceland in turn for the same reason, and has now settled with other folk in Greenland.'

'Then this is . . . a little before Leif's voyage,' he muttered. 'The late tenth century.'

'See here,' demanded Helgi, 'we've been patient with you, but this is no time for riddles. We save those for feasts and drinking bouts. Can you not say plainly whence you come and how you got here?'

Gerald covered his face, shaking.

'Let the man alone, Helgi,' said Thorgunna. 'Can you not see he's troubled?'

He raised his head and gave her the look of a hurt dog that someone has patted. It was dim in the hall, enough light coming in by the loft windows so no candles were lit, but not enough to see well by. Nevertheless, I marked a reddening in both their faces.

Gerald drew a long breath and fumbled about; his clothes were made with pockets. He brought out a small parchment box and from it took a little white stick that he put in his mouth. Then he took out another box, and a wooden stick from it which burst into flame when scratched. With the fire he kindled the stick in his mouth, and sucked in the smoke.

We all stared. 'Is that a Christian rite?' asked Helgi.

'No . . . not just so.' A wry, disappointed smile twisted his lips. 'I'd have thought you'd be more surprised, even terrified.'

'It's something new,' I admitted, 'but we're a sober folk on Iceland. Those fire sticks could be useful. Did you come to trade in them?'

'Hardly.' He sighed. The smoke he breathed in seemed to steady him, which was odd, because the smoke in the hall had made him cough and water at the eyes. 'The truth is . . . something you will not believe. I can scarce believe it myself.'

We waited. Thorgunna stood leaning forward, her lips parted.

'That lightning bolt—'Gerald nodded wearily. 'I was out in the storm, and somehow the lightning must have struck me in just the right way, a way that happens only once in many thousands of times. It threw me back into the past.'

Those were his words, priest. I did not understand, and told him so.

'It's hard to see,' he agreed. 'God give that I'm only dreaming. But if this is a dream, I must endure till I wake up . . . well, look. I was born one thousand, nine hundred and thirty-two years after Christ, in a land to the west which you have not yet found. In the twenty-third year of my life, I was in Iceland as part of my country's army. The lightning struck me, and now . . . now it is less than one thousand years after Christ, and yet I am here—almost a thousand years before I was born, I am here!'

We sat very still. I signed myself with the Hammer and took a long pull from my horn. One of the maids whimpered, and Ragnhild whispered so fiercely I could hear. 'Be still. The poor fellow's out of his head. There's no harm in him.'

I agreed with her, though less sure of the last part of it. The gods can speak through a madman, and the gods are not always to be trusted. Or he could turn berserker, or he could be under a heavy curse that would also touch us.

He sat staring before him, and I caught a few fleas and cracked them while I thought about it. Gerald noticed and asked with some horror if we had many fleas here.

'Why, of course,' said Thorgunna. 'Have you none?'

'No.' He smiled crookedly. 'Not yet.'

'Ah,' she sighed, 'you *must* be sick.'

She was a level-headed girl. I saw her thought, and so did Ragnhild and Helgi. Clearly, a man so sick that he had no fleas could be expected to rave. There was still some worry about whether we might catch the illness, but I deemed it unlikely; his trouble was all in the head, perhaps from a blow he had taken. In any case, the matter was come down to earth now, something we could deal with.

As a godi, a chief who holds sacrifices, it behoved me not to turn a stranger out. Moreover, if he could fetch in many of those little fire-kindling sticks, a profitable trade might be built up. So I said Gerald should go to bed. He protested, but we manhandled him into the shut-bed and there he lay tired and was soon asleep. Thorgunna said she would take care of him.

The next day I decided to sacrifice a horse, both because of the timber we had found and to take away any curse there might be on Gerald. Furthermore, the beast I had picked was old and useless, and we were short of fresh meat. Gerald had spent the day lounging moodily around the garth, but when I came into supper I found him and my daughter laughing.

'You seem to be on the road to health,' I said.

'Oh yes. It . . . could be worse for me.' He sat down at my side as the carles set up the trestle table and the maids brought in the food. 'I was ever much taken with the age of the vikings, and I have some skills.'

'Well,' I said, 'if you've no home, we can keep you here for a while.'

'I can work,' he said eagerly. 'I'll be worth my pay.'

Now I knew he was from a far land, because what chief would work on any land but his own, and for hire at that? Yet he had the easy manner of the highborn, and had clearly eaten well all his life. I overlooked that he had made no gifts; after all, he was shipwrecked.

'Maybe you can get passage back to your United States,' said Helgi. 'We could hire a ship. I'm fain to see that realm.'

'No,' said Gerald bleakly.' There is no such place. Not yet.'

'So you still hold to that idea you came from tomorrow?' grunted Sigurd. 'Crazy notion. Pass the pork.'

'I do,' said Gerald. There was a calm on him now. 'And I can prove it.'

'I don't see how you speak our tongue, if you come from so far away,' I said. I could not call a man a liar to his face, unless we were swapping brags in a friendly way, but . . .

'They speak otherwise in my land and time,' he replied, 'but it happens that in Iceland the tongue changed little since the old days, and I learned it when I came there.'

'If you are a Christian,' I said, 'you must bear with us while we sacrifice tonight.'

'I've naught against that,' he said. 'I fear I never was a very good Christian. I'd like to watch. How is it done?'

I told him how I would smite the horse with a hammer before the god, and cut his throat, and sprinkle the blood about with willow twigs; thereafter we would butcher the carcass and feast. He said hastily:

'There's my chance to prove what I am. I have a weapon that will kill the horse with . . . with a flash of lightning.'

'What is it?' I wondered. We all crowded around while he took the metal club out of his sheath and showed it to us. I had my doubts; it looked well enough for hitting a man, perhaps, but had no edge, though a wondrously skilful smith had forged it. 'Well, we can try,' I said.

He showed us what else he had in his pockets. There were some coins of remarkable roundness and sharpness, a small key, a stick with lead in it for writing, a flat purse holding many bits of marked paper; when he told us solemnly that some of this paper was money, even Thorgunna had to laugh. Best of all was a knife whose blade folded into the handle. When he saw me admiring that, he gave it to me, which was well done for a shipwrecked man. I said I would give him clothes and a good axe, as well as lodging for as long as needful.

No, I don't have the knife now. You shall hear why. It's a pity, for it was a good knife, though rather small.

'What were you ere the war arrow went out in your land?' asked Helgi. 'A merchant?'

'No,' said Gerald. 'I was an . . . *engineer* . . . that is, I was learning how to be one. That's a man who builds things, bridges and roads and tools . . . more than just an artisan. So I think my knowledge could be of great value here.' I saw a fever in his eyes. 'Yes, give me time and I'll be a king!'

'We have no king in Iceland,' I grunted. 'Our forefathers came hither to get away from kings. Now we meet at the Things to try suits and pass new laws, but each man must got his own redress as best he can.'

'But suppose the man in the wrong won't yield?' he asked.

'Then there can be a fine feud,' said Helgi, and went on to relate with sparkling eyes some of the killings there had lately been. Gerald looked unhappy and fingered his *gun*. That is what he called his fire-spitting club.

'Your clothing is rich,' said Thorgunna softly. 'Your folk must own broad acres at home.'

'No,' he said, 'our . . . our king gives every man in the army clothes like these. As for my family, we owned no land, we rented our home in a building where many other families also dwelt.'

I am not purse-proud, but it seemed to me he had not been honest, a landless man sharing my high seat like a chief. Thorgunna covered my huffiness by saying, 'You will gain a farm later.'

After dark we went out to the shrine. The carles had built a fire before it, and as I opened the door the wooden Odin appeared to leap forth. Gerald muttered to my daughter that it was a clumsy bit of carving, and since my father had made it I was still more angry with him. Some folks have no understanding of the fine arts.

Nevertheless, I let him help me lead the horse forth to the altar stone. I took the blood-bowl in my hands and said he could now slay the beast if he would. He drew his *gun*, put the end behind the horse's ear, and squeezed. There was a crack, and the beast quivered and dropped

with a hole blown through its skull, wasting the brains—
a clumsy weapon. I caught a whiff of smell, sharp and
bitter like that around a volcano. We all jumped, one of the
women screamed, and Gerald looked proud. I gathered my
wits and finished the rest of the sacrifice as usual. Gerald
did not like having blood sprinkled over him, but then, of
course, he was a Christian. Nor would he take more than
a little of the soup and flesh.

Afterwards Helgi questioned him about the *gun*, and he
said it could kill a man at bowshot distance but there was
no witchcraft in it, only use of some tricks we did not know
as yet. Having heard of the Greek fire, I believed him.
A *gun* could be useful in a fight, as indeed I was to learn,
but it did not seem very practical—iron costing what it
does, and months of forging needed for each one.

I worried more about the man himself.

And the next morning I found him telling Thorgunna
a great deal of foolishness about his home, buildings tall as
mountains and wagons that flew or went without horses.
He said there were eight or nine thousand thousands of folk
in his city, a burgh called New Jorvik or the like. I enjoy
a good brag as well as the next man, but this was too much
and I told him gruffly to come along and help me get in
some strayed cattle.

After a day scrambling around the hills I knew well enough
that Gerald could scarce tell a cow's prow from her stern.
We almost had the strays once, but he ran stupidly across
their path and turned them so the work was all to do again.
I asked him with strained courtesy if he could milk, shear,
wield scythe or flail, and he said no, he had never lived
on a farm.

'That's a pity,' I remarked, 'for everyone on Iceland
does, unless he be outlawed.'

He flushed at my tone. 'I can do enough else,' he answered.
Give me some tools and I'll show you metalwork well done.'

That brightened me, for truth to tell, none of our household was a very gifted smith. 'That's an honourable trade,'
I said, 'and you can be of great help. I have a broken sword
and several bent spearheads to be mended, and it were no

bad idea to shoe all the horses.' His admission· that he did not know how to put on a shoe was not very dampening to me then.

We had returned home as we talked, and Thorgunna came angrily forward. 'That's no way to treat a guest, father!' she said. 'Making him work like a carle, indeed!'

Gerald smiled. 'I'll be glad to work,' he said. 'I need a . . . a stake . . . something to start me afresh. Also, I want to repay a little of your kindness.'

That made me mild towards him, and I said it was not his fault they had different customs in the United States. On the morrow he could begin work in the smithy, and I would pay him, yet he would be treated as an equal, since craftsmen are valued. This earned him black looks from the housefolk.

That evening he entertained us well with stories of his home; true or not, they made good listening. However, he had no real polish, being unable to compose even two lines of verse. They must be a raw and backward lot in the United States. He said his task in the army had been to keep order among the troops. Helgi said this was unheard-of, and he must be a brave man who would offend so many men, but Gerald said folk obeyed him out of fear of the king. When he added that the term of a levy in the United States was two years, and that men could be called to war even in harvest time, I said he was well out of a country with so ruthless and powerful a king.

'No,' he answered wistfully, 'we are a free folk, who say what we please.'

'But it seems you may not do as you please,' said Helgi.

'Well,' he said, 'we may not murder a man just because he offends us.'

'Not even if he has slain your own kin?' asked Helgi.

'No. It is for the . . . the king to take vengeance on behalf of us all.'

I chuckled. 'Your yarns are good,' I said, 'but there you've hit a snag. How could the king even keep track of all the murders, let alone avenge them? Why, the man wouldn't even have time to beget an heir!'

He could say no more for all the laughter that followed.

The next day Gerald went to the smithy, with a thrall to pump the bellows for him. I was gone that day and night, down to Reykjavik to dicker with Hjalmar Broadnose about some sheep. I invited him back for an overnight stay, and we rode into the garth with his son Ketill, a red-haired sulky youth of twenty winters who had been refused by Thorgunna.

I found Gerald sitting gloomily on a bench in the hall. He wore the clothes I had given him, his own having been spoiled by ash and sparks—what had he awaited, the fool? He was talking in a low voice with my daughter.

'Well,' I said as I entered, 'how went it?'

My man Grim snickered. 'He has ruined two spearheads, but we put out the fire he started ere the whole smithy burned.'

'How's this?' I cried. 'I thought you said you were a smith.'

Gerald stood up, defiantly. 'I worked with other tools, and better ones, at home,' he replied. 'You do it differently here.'

It seemed he had built up the fire too hot; his hammer had struck everywhere but the place it should; he had wrecked the temper of the steel through not knowing when to quench it. Smithcraft takes years to learn, of course, but he should have admitted he was not even an apprentice.

'Well,' I snapped, 'what can you do, then, to earn your bread?' It irked me to be made a fool of before Hjalmar and Ketill, whom I had told about the stranger.

'Odin alone knows,' said Grim. 'I took him with me to ride after your goats, and never have I seen a worse horseman. I asked him if he could even spin or weave, and he said no.'

'That was no question to ask a man!' flared Thorgunna. 'He should have slain you for it!'

'He should indeed,' laughed Grim. 'But let me carry on the tale. I thought we would also repair your bridge over the foss. Well, he can just barely handle a saw, but he nearly took his own foot off with the adze.'

'We don't use those tools, I tell you!' Gerald doubled his fists and looked close to tears.

I motioned my guests to sit down. 'I don't suppose you can butcher a hog or smoke it either,' I said.

'No.' I could scarce hear him.

'Well, then, man . . . what *can* you do?'

'I—' He could get no words out.

'You were a warrior,' said Thorgunna.

'Yes—that I was!' he said, his face kindling.

'Small use in Iceland when you have no other skills,' I grumbled, 'but perhaps, if you can get passage to the eastlands, some king will take you in his guard.' Myself I doubted it, for a guardsman needs manners that will do credit to his master; but I had not the heart to say so.

Ketill Hjalmarsson had plainly not liked the way Thorgunna stood close to Gerald and spoke for him. Now he sneered and said: 'I might even doubt your skill in fighting.'

'That I have been trained for,' said Gerald grimly.

'Will you wrestle with me then?' asked Ketill.

'Gladly!' spat Gerald.

Priest, what is a man to think? As I grow older, I find life to be less and less the good-and-evil, black-and-white thing you say it is; we are all of us some hue of grey. This useless fellow, this spiritless lout who could even be asked if he did women's work and not lift axe, went out in the yard with Ketill Hjalmarsson and threw him three times running. There was some trick he had of grabbing the clothes as Ketill charged . . . I called a stop when the youth was nearing murderous rage, praised them both, and filled the beer-horns. But Ketill brooded sullenly on the bench all evening.

Gerald said something about making a *gun* like his own. It would have to be bigger, a *cannon* he called it, and could sink ships and scatter armies. He would need the help of smiths, and also various stuffs. Charcoal was easy, and sulphur could be found in the volcano country, I suppose, but what is this saltpetre?

Also, being suspicious by now, I questioned him closely as to how he would make such a thing. Did he know just how to mix the powder? No, he admitted. What size would the *gun* have to be? When he told me—at least as long as a man—I laughed and asked him how a piece that size could be cast or bored, even if we could scrape together that much iron. This he did not know either.

'You haven't the tools to make the tools to make the tools,' he said. I don't know what he meant by that. 'God help me, I can't run through a thousand years of history all by myself.'

He took out the last of his little smoke sticks and lit it. Helgi had tried a puff earlier and gotten sick, though he remained a friend of Gerald's. Now my son proposed to take a boat in the morning and go up to Ice Fjord, where I had some money outstanding I wanted to collect. Hjalmar and Ketill said they would come along for the trip, and Thorgunna pleaded so hard that I let her come along too.

'An ill thing,' muttered Sigurd. 'All men know the landtrolls like not a woman aboard a ship. It's unlucky.'

'How did your father ever bring women to this island?' I grinned.

Now I wish I had listened to him. He was not a clever man, but he often knew whereof he spoke.

At this time I owned a half share in a ship that went to Norway, bartering wadmal for timber. It was a profitable business until she ran afoul of vikings during the disorders while Olaf Tryggvason was overthrowing Jarl Haakon there. Some men will do anything to make a living—thieves, cut-throats, they ought to be hanged, the worthless robbers pouncing on honest merchantmen. Had they any courage or honesty they would go to Ireland, which is full of plunder.

Well, anyhow, the ship was abroad, but we had three boats and took one of these. Besides myself, Thorgunna and Helgi, Hjalmar and Ketill went along, with Grim and Gerald. I saw how the stranger winced at the cold water as we launched her, and afterwards took off his shoes and stockings to let his feet dry. He had been surprised to learn we had a bath house—did he think us savages?—but still, he was dainty as a woman and soon moved upwind of our feet.

There was a favouring breeze, so we raised mast and sail. Gerald tried to help, but of course did not know one line from another and got them tangled. Grim snarled at him and Ketill laughed nastily. But erelong we were under way, and he came and sat by me where I had the steering oar.

He had plainly lain long awake thinking, and now he

ventured timidly: 'In my land they have . . . will have a rig and rudder which are better than this. With them, you can criss-cross against the wind.'

'Ah, so now our skilled sailor must give us redes!' sneered Ketill.

'Be still,' said Thorgunna sharply. 'Let Gerald speak.'

He gave her a sly look of thanks, and I was not unwilling to listen. 'This is something which could easily be made,' he said. 'I've used such boats myself, and know them well. First, then, the sail should not be square and hung from a yardarm, but three-cornered, with the third corner lashed to a yard swivelling from the mast. Then, your steering oar is in the wrong place—there should be a rudder in the middle of the stern, guided by a bar.' He was eager now, tracing the plan with his fingernail on Thorgunna's cloak. 'With these two things, and a deep keel—going down to about the height of a man for a boat this size—a ship can move across the path of the wind . . . so. And another sail can be hung between the mast and the prow.'

Well, priest, I must say the idea had its merits, and were it not for fear of bad luck—for everything of his was unlucky —I might even now play with it. But there are clear drawbacks, which I pointed out to him in a reasonable way.

'First and worst,' I said, 'this rudder and deep keel would make it all but impossible to beach the ship or sail up a shallow river. Perhaps they have many harbours where you hail from, but here a craft must take what landings she can find, and must be speedily launched if there should be an attack. Second, this mast of yours would be hard to unstep when the wind dropped and oars came out. Third, the sail is the wrong shape to stretch as an awning when one must sleep at sea.'

'The ship could lie out, and you could go to land in a small boat,' he said. 'Also, you could build cabins aboard for shelter.'

'The cabins would get in the way of the oars,' I said, 'unless the ship were hopelessly broad-beamed or unless the oarsmen sat below a deck like the galley slaves of Miklagard; and free men would not endure rowing in such foulness.'

'Must you have oars?' he asked like a very child.

Laughter barked along the hull. Even the gulls hovering to starboard, where the shore rose darkly, mewed their scorn. 'Do they also have tame winds in the place whence you came?' snorted Hjalmar. 'What happens if you're becalmed—for days, maybe, with provisions running out—'

'You could build a ship big enough to carry many weeks' provisions,' said Gerald.

'If you have the wealth of a king, you could,' said Helgi. 'And such a king's ship, lying helpless on a flat sea, would be swarmed by every viking from here to Jomsborg. As for leaving the ship out on the water while you make camp, what would you have for shelter, or for defence if you should be trapped there?'

Gerald slumped. Thorgunna said to him gently: 'Some folks have no heart to try anything new. I think it's a grand idea.'

He smiled at her, a weary smile, and plucked up the will to say something about a means for finding north even in cloudy weather—he said there were stones which always pointed north when hung by a string. I told him kindly that I would be most interested if he could find me some of this stone; or if he knew where it was to be had, I could ask a trader to fetch me a piece. But this he did not know, and fell silent. Ketill opened his mouth, but got such an edged look from Thorgunna that he shut it again; his looks declared plainly enough what a liar he thought Gerald to be.

The wind turned contrary after a while, so we lowered the mast and took to the oars. Gerald was strong and willing, though clumsy; however, his hands were so soft that erelong they bled. I offered to let him rest, but he kept doggedly at the work.

Watching him sway back and forth, under the dreary creak of the tholes, the shaft red and wet where he gripped it, I thought much about him. He had done everything wrong which a man could do—thus I imagined then, not knowing the future—and I did not like the way Thorgunna's eyes strayed to him and rested there. He was no man for my daughter, landless and penniless and helpless. Yet I could not keep from liking him. Whether his tale was true or only a madness, I felt he was honest about it; and surely there was something strange about the way he had come. I noticed the cuts on his chin from my razor; he had said he was not used to our kind of shaving and would grow a beard. He had tried hard. I wondered how well I would have done, landing alone in this witch country of his dreams, with a gap of forever between me and my home.

Perhaps that same misery was what had turned Thorgunna's heart. Women are a kittle breed, priest, and you who leave them alone belike understand them as well as I who have slept with half a hundred in six different lands. I do not think they even understand themselves. Birth and life and death, those are the great mysteries, which none will ever fathom, and a woman is closer to them than a man.

The ill wind stiffened, the sea grew iron-grey and choppy under low, leaden clouds, and our headway was poor. At sunset we could row no more, but must pull in to a small unpeopled bay and make camp as well as could be on the strand.

We had brought firewood along, and tinder. Gerald, though staggering with weariness, made himself useful, his little sticks kindling the blaze more easily than flint and steel. Thorgunna set herself to cook our supper. We were not warded by the boat from a lean, whining wind; her cloak fluttered like wings and her hair blew wild above the streaming flames. It was the time of light nights, the sky a dim dusky blue, the sea a wrinkled metal sheet and the land like something risen out of dream-mists. We men huddled in our cloaks, holding numbed hands to the fire and saying little.

I felt some cheer was needed, and ordered a cask of my best and strongest ale broached. An evil Norn made me do that, but no man escapes his weird. Our bellies seemed all the emptier now when our noses drank in the sputter of a spitted joint, and the ale went swiftly to our heads. I remember declaiming the death song of Ragnar Hairybreeks for no other reason than I felt like declaiming it.

Thorgunna came to stand over Gerald where he slumped. I saw how her fingers brushed his hair, ever so lightly, and Ketill Hjalmarsson did too. 'Have they no verses in your land?' she asked.

'Not like yours,' he said, looking up. Neither of them looked away again. 'We sing rather than chant. I wish I had my *guitar* here—that's a kind of harp.'

'Ah, an Irish bard!' said Hjalmar Broadnose.

I remember strangely well how Gerald smiled, and what he said in his own tongue, though I know not the meaning: '*Only on me mither's side, begorra.*' I suppose it was magic.

'Well, sing for us,' asked Thorgunna.

'Let me think,' he said. 'I shall have to put it in Norse words for you.' After a little while, staring up at her through the windy night, he began a song. It had a tune I liked, thus:

> *From this valley they tell me you're leaving,*
> *I shall miss your bright eyes and sweet smile.*
> *You will carry the sunshine with you,*
> *That has brightened my life all the while . . .*

I don't remember the rest, except that it was not quite decent.

When he had finished, Hjalmar and Grim went over to see if the meat was done. I saw a glimmering of tears in my daughter's eyes. 'That was a lovely thing,' she said.

Ketill sat upright. The flames splashed his face with wild, running hues. There was a rawness in his tone: 'Yes, we've found what this fellow can do: sit about and make pretty songs for the girls. Keep him for that, Ospak.'

Thorgunna whitened, and Helgi clapped hand to sword. I saw how Gerald's face darkened, and his voice was thick: 'That was no way to talk. Take it back.'

Ketill stood up. 'No,' he said, 'I'll ask no pardon of an idler living off honest yeomen.'

He was raging, but he had sense enough to shift the insult from my family to Gerald alone. Otherwise he and his father would have had the four of us to deal with. As it was, Gerald stood up too, fists knotted at his sides, and said, 'Will you step away from here and settle this?'

'Gladly!' Ketill turned and walked a few yards down the beach, taking his shield from the boat. Gerald followed. Thorgunna stood with stricken face, then picked up his axe and ran after him.

'Are you going weaponless?' she shrieked.

Gerald stopped, looking dazed. 'I don't want that,' he mumbled. 'Fists—'

Ketill puffed himself up and drew sword. 'No doubt you're used to fighting like thralls in your land,' he said. 'So if you'll crave my pardon, I'll let this matter rest.'

Gerald stood with drooped shoulders. He stared at Thorgunna as if he were blind, as if asking her what to do. She handed him the axe.

'So you want me to kill him?' he whispered.

'Yes,' she answered.

Then I knew she loved him, for otherwise why should she have cared if he disgraced himself?

Helgi brought him his helmet. He put it on, took the axe, and went forward.

'Ill is this,' said Hjalmar to me. 'Do you stand by the stranger, Ospak?'

'No,' I said. 'He's no kin or oath-brother of mine. This is not my quarrel.'

'That's good,' said Hjalmar. 'I'd not like to fight with you, my friend. You were ever a good neighbour.'

We went forth together and staked out the ground. Thorgunna told me to lend Gerald my sword, so he could use a shield too, but the man looked oddly at me and said he would rather have the axe. They squared away before each other, he and Ketill, and began fighting.

This was no holmgang, with rules and a fixed order of blows and first blood meaning victory. There was death between those two. Ketill rushed in with the sword whistling in his hand. Gerald sprang back, wielding the axe awkwardly. It bounced off Ketill's shield. The youth grinned and cut at Gerald's legs. I saw blood well forth and stain the ripped breeches.

It was murder from the beginning. Gerald had never used an axe before. Once he even struck with the flat of it. He would have been hewed down at once had Ketill's sword not been blunted on his helmet and had he not been quick on his feet. As it was, he was soon lurching with a dozen wounds.

'Stop the fight!' Thorgunna cried aloud and ran forth. Helgi caught her arms and forced her back, where she struggled and kicked till Grim must help. I saw grief on my son's face but a malicious grin on the carle's.

Gerald turned to look. Ketill's blade came down and slashed his left hand. He dropped the axe. Ketill snarled and readied to finish him. Gerald drew his *gun*. It made a flash and a barking noise. Ketill fell, twitched for a moment, and was quiet. His lower jaw was blown off and the back of his head gone.

There came a long stillness, where only the wind and the sea had voice.

Then Hjalmar trod forth, his face working but a cold steadiness over him. He knelt and closed his son's eyes, as token that the right of vengeance was his. Rising, he said, 'That was an evil deed. For that you shall be outlawed.'

'It wasn't magic,' said Gerald in a numb tone. 'It was like a . . . a bow. I had no choice. I didn't want to fight with more than my fists.'

I trod between them and said the Thing must decide this matter, but that I hoped Hjalmar would take weregild for Ketill.

'But I killed him to save my own life!' protested Gerald.

'Nevertheless, weregild must be paid, if Ketill's kin will take it,' I explained. 'Because of the weapon, I think it will be doubled, but that is for the Thing to judge.'

Hjalmar had many other sons, and it was not as if Gerald belonged to a family at odds with his own, so I felt he would agree. However, he laughed coldly and asked where a man lacking wealth would find the silver.

Thorgunna stepped up with a wintry calm and said we would pay it. I opened my mouth, but when I saw her eyes I nodded. 'Yes, we will,' I said, 'in order to keep the peace.'

'Then you make this quarrel your own?' asked Hjalmar.

'No,' I answered. 'This man is no blood of my own. But if I choose to make him a gift of money to use as he wishes, what of it?'

Hjalmar smiled. There was sorrow crinkled around his eyes, but he looked on me with old comradeship.

'Erelong this man may be your son-in-law,' he said. 'I know the signs, Ospak. Then indeed he will be of your folk. Even helping him now in his need will range you on his side.'

'And so?' asked Helgi, most softly.

'And so, while I value your friendship, I have sons who will take the death of their brother ill. They'll want revenge on Gerald Samsson, if only for the sake of their good names, and thus our two houses will be sundered and one manslaying will lead to another. It has happened often enough erenow.' Hjalmar sighed. 'I myself wish peace with you, Ospak, but if you take this killer's side it must be otherwise.'

I thought for a moment, thought of Helgi lying with his skull cloven, of my other sons on their garths drawn to battle because of a man they had never seen, I thought of having to wear byrnies every time we went down for driftwood and never knowing when we went to bed whether we would wake to find the house ringed in by spearmen.

'Yes,' I said, 'you are right, Hjalmar. I withdraw my offer. Let this be a matter between you and him alone.'

We gripped hands on it.

Thorgunna gave a small cry and fled into Gerald's arms. He held her close. 'What does this mean?' he asked slowly.

'I cannot keep you any longer,' I said, 'but belike some crofter will give you a roof. Hjalmar is a law-abiding man and will not harm you until the Thing has outlawed you. That will not be before midsummer. Perhaps you can get passage out of Iceland ere then.'

'A useless one like me?' he replied bitterly.

Thorgunna whirled free and blazed that I was a coward and a perjurer and all else evil. I let her have it out, then laid my hands on her shoulders.

'It is for the house,' I said. 'The house and the blood, which are holy. Men die and women weep, but while the kindered live our names are remembered. Can you ask a score of men to die for your own hankerings?'

Long did she stand, and to this day I know not what her answer would have been. It was Gerald who spoke.

'No,' he said. 'I suppose you have right, Ospak . . . the right of your time, which is not mine.' He took my hand, and Helgi's. His lips brushed Thorgunna's cheek. Then he turned and walked out into the darkness.

I heard, later, that he went to earth with Thorvald Hallsson, the crofter of Humpback Fell, and did not tell his host what had happened. He must have hoped to go unnoticed until he could arrange passage to the eastlands somehow. But of course word spread. I remember his brag that in the United States men had means to talk from one end of the land to another. So he must have looked down on us, sitting on our lonely garths, and not know how fast word could get around. Thorvald's son, Hrolf, went to Brand Sealskin-boots to talk about some matter, and of course mentioned the stranger, and soon all the western island had the tale.

Now if Gerald had known he must give notice of a man-slaying at the first garth he found, he would have been safe at least till the Thing met, for Hjalmar and his sons are sober men who would not kill a man still under the protection of the law. But as it was, his keeping the matter secret made him a murderer and therefore at once an outlaw. Hjalmar and his kin rode up to Humpback Fell and haled him forth. He shot his way past them with the *gun* and fled into the hills. They followed him, having several hurts and one more death to avenge. I wonder if Gerald thought the strangeness of his weapon would unnerve us. He may not have known that every man dies when his time comes, neither sooner nor later, so that fear of death is useless.

At the end, when they had him trapped, his weapon gave out on him. Then he took up a dead man's sword and defended himself so valiantly that Ulf Hjalmarsson has limped ever since. It was well done, as even his foes admitted; they are an eldritch race in the United States, but they do not lack manhood.

When he was slain, his body was brought back. For fear of the ghost, he having perhaps been a warlock, it was burned, and all he had owned was laid in the fire with him. That was where I lost the knife he had given me. The barrow stands out on the moor, north of here, and folk shun it, though the ghost has not walked. Now, with so much else happening, he is slowly being forgotten.

And that is the tale, priest, as I saw it and heard it. Most men think Gerald Samsson was crazy, but I myself believed he did come from out of time, and that his doom was that no man may ripen a field before harvest season. Yet I look into the future, a thousand years hence, when they fly through the air and ride in horseless wagons and smash whole cities with one blow. I think of this Iceland then, and of the young United States men there to help defend us in a year when the end of the world hovers close. Perhaps some of them, walking about on the heaths, will see that barrow and wonder what ancient warrior lies buried there, and they may even wish they had lived long ago in his time when men were free.

Call Him Lord

Gordon R. Dickson

For almost a quarter of a century, Gordon Dickson has been quietly
writing some of the finest sf in the field, yet it is only in recent years
that people have begun to sit up and take notice. The gentle strain
of lyricism that runs through the enormous body of his work can
be linked to the folk traditions of the American people. CALL HIM
LORD is a quietly moving tale of a far future when man has
expanded his empire into the universe, leaving Earth to become
a quaint arcadian delight, preserved and protected as one enormous
parkland . . . and as a proving ground for those who would rule
their small portion of the galaxy.

There are many characteristics desirable in an Emperor that can be done without
if necessary. But there is one that any true ruler absolutely must possess.

> He called and commanded me
> —Therefore, I knew him;
> But later on, failed me; and
> —Therefore, I slew him!
>
> *Song of the Shield Bearer*

The sun could not fail in rising over the Kentucky hills, nor
could Kyle Arnam in waking. There would be eleven hours
and forty minutes of daylight. Kyle rose, dressed, and went
out to saddle the grey gelding and the white stallion. He
rode the stallion until the first fury was out of the arched
and snowy neck; and then led both horses around to tether
them outside the kitchen door. Then he went in to breakfast.

The message that had come a week before was beside his
plate of bacon and eggs. Teena, his wife, was standing at the
breadboard with her back to him. He sat down and began
eating, rereading the letter as he ate.

'. . . The Prince will be travelling incognito under one of his family titles, as Count Sirii North; and should not be addressed as "Majesty". *You will call him "Lord"* . . .'

'Why does it have to be you?' Teena asked.

He looked up and saw how she stood with her back to him.

'Teena—' he said, sadly.

'Why?'

'My ancestors were bodyguards to his—back in the wars of conquest against the aliens. I've told you that,' he said. 'My forefathers saved the lives of his, many times when there was no warning—a Rak spaceship would suddenly appear out of nowhere to lock on, even to flagship. And even an Emperor found himself fighting for his life, hand to hand.'

'The aliens are all dead now, and the Emperor's got a hundred other worlds! Why can't his son take his Grand Tour on them? Why does he have to come here to Earth—and you?'

'There's only one Earth.'

'And only one you, I suppose?'

He sighed internally and gave up. He had been raised by his father and his uncle after his mother died, and in an argument with Teena he always felt helpless. He got up from the table and went to her, putting his hands on her and gently trying to turn her about. But she resisted.

He sighed inside himself again and turned away to the weapons cabinet. He took out a loaded slug pistol, fitted it into the stubby holster it matched, and clipped the holster to his belt at the left of the buckle, where the hang of his leather jacket would hide it. Then he selected a dark-handled knife with a six-inch blade and bent over to slip it into the sheath inside his boot top. He dropped the cuff of his trouser leg back over the boot top and stood up.

'He's got no right to be here,' said Teena fiercely to the breadboard. 'Tourists are supposed to be kept to the museum areas and the tourist lodges.'

'He's not a tourist. You know that,' answered Kyle, patiently. 'He's the Emperor's oldest son and his great-grandmother was from Earth. His wife will be, too. Every fourth generation the Imperial line has to marry back into Earth stock. That's the law—still.' He put on his leather jacket, sealing it closed only at the bottom to hide the slug-gun holster, half turned to the door—then paused.

'Teena?' he asked.

She did not answer.

'Teena!' he repeated. He stepped to her, put his hands on her shoulders and tried to turn her to face him. Again, she resisted, but this time he was having none of it.

He was not a big man, being of middle height, round-faced, with sloping and unremarkable-looking, if thick, shoulders. But his strength was not ordinary. He could bring the white stallion to its knees with one fist wound in its mane—and no other man had ever been able to do that. He turned her easily to look at him.

'Now, listen to me—' he began. But, before he could finish, all the stiffness went out of her and she clung to him, trembling.

'He'll get you into trouble—I know he will!' she choked, muffledly into his chest. 'Kyle, don't go! There's no law making you go!'

He stroked the soft hair of her head, his throat stiff and dry. There was nothing he could say to her. What she was asking was impossible. Ever since the sun had first risen on men and women together, wives had clung to their husbands at times like this, begging for what could not be. And always the men had held them, as Kyle was holding her now—as if understanding could somehow be pressed from one body into the other—and saying nothing, because there was nothing that could be said.

So, Kyle held her for a few moments longer, and then reached behind him to unlock her intertwined fingers at his back, and loosen her arms around him. Then, he went. Looking back through the kitchen window as he rode off on the stallion, leading the grey horse, he saw her standing just where he had left her. Not even crying, but standing with her arms hanging down, her head down, not moving.

He rode away through the forest of the Kentucky hillside. It took him more than two hours to reach the lodge. As he rode down the valleyside towards it, he saw a tall, bearded man, wearing the robes they wore on some of the Younger

Worlds, standing at the gateway to the interior courtyard of the rustic, wooded lodge.

When he got close, he saw that the beard was greying and the man was biting his lips. Above a straight, thin nose, the eyes were bloodshot and circled beneath as if from worry or lack of sleep.

'He's in the courtyard,' said the grey-bearded man as Kyle rode up. 'I'm Montlaven, his tutor. He's ready to go.' The darkened eyes looked almost pleadingly up at Kyle.

'Stand clear of the stallion's head,' said Kyle. 'And take me in to him.'

'Not that horse, for him—' said Montlaven, looking distrustfully at the stallion, as he backed away.

'No,' said Kyle. 'He'll ride the gelding.'

'He'll want the white.'

'He can't ride the white,' said Kyle. 'Even if I let him, he couldn't ride this stallion. I'm the only one who can ride him. Take me in.'

The tutor turned and led the way into the grassy court-yard, surrounding a swimming pool and looked down upon, on three sides, by the windows of the lodge. In a lounging chair by the pool sat a tall young man in his late teens, with a mane of blond hair, a pair of stuffed saddlebags on the grass beside him. He stood up as Kyle and the tutor came towards him.

'Majesty,' said the tutor, as they stopped, 'this is Kyle Arnam, your bodyguard for the three days here.'

'Good morning, Bodyguard . . . Kyle, I mean.' The Prince smiled mischievously. 'Light, then. And I'll mount.'

'You ride the gelding, Lord,' said Kyle.

The Prince stared at him, tilted back his handsome head, and laughed.

'I can ride, man!' he said. 'I ride well.'

'Not this horse, Lord,' said Kyle, dispassionately. 'No one rides this horse but me.'

The eyes flashed wide, the laugh faded—then returned.

'What can I do?' The wide shoulders shrugged. 'I give in—always I give in. Well, almost always.' He grinned up at Kyle, his lips thinned, but frank. 'All right.'

He turned to the gelding—and with a sudden leap was in

the saddle. The gelding snorted and plunged at the shock; then steadied as the young man's long fingers tightened expertly on the reins and the fingers of the other hand patted a grey neck. The Prince raised his eyebrows, looking over at Kyle, but Kyle sat stolidly.

'I take it you're armed, good Kyle?' the Prince said slyly. 'You'll protect me against the natives if they run wild?'

'Your life is in my hands, Lord,' said Kyle. He unsealed the leather jacket at the bottom and let if fall open to show the slug pistol in its holster for a moment. Then he resealed the jacket again at the bottom.

'Will—' The tutor put his hand on the young man's knee. 'Don't be reckless, boy. This is Earth and the people here don't have rank and custom like we do. Think before you—"

'Oh, cut it out, Monty!' snapped the Prince. 'I'll be just as incognito, just as humble, as archaic and independent as the rest of them. You think I've no memory! Anyway, it's only for three days or so until my Imperial father joins me. Now, let me go!'

He jerked away, turned to lean forward in the saddle, and abruptly put the gelding into a bolt for the gate. He disappeared through it, and Kyle drew hard on the stallion's reins as the big white horse danced and tried to follow.

'Give me his saddlebags,' said Kyle.

The tutor bent and passed them up. Kyle made them fast on top of his own, across the stallion's withers. Looking down, he saw there were tears in the bearded man's eyes.

'He's a fine boy. You'll see. You'll know he is!" Montlaven's face, upturned, was mutely pleading.

'I know he comes from a fine family,' said Kyle, slowly. 'I'll do my best for him.' And he rode off out of the gateway after the gelding.

When he came out of the gate, the Prince was nowhere in sight. But it was simple enough for Kyle to follow, by dinted brown earth and crushed grass, the marks of the gelding's path. This brought him at last through some pines to a grassy open slope where the Prince sat looking skywards through a single-lens box.

When Kyle came up, the Prince lowered the instrument and without a word, passed it over. Kyle put it to his eye and looked skywards. There was the whir of the tracking unit and one of Earth's three orbiting power stations swam into the field of vision of the lens.

'Give it back,' said the Prince.

'I couldn't get a look at it earlier,' went on the young man as Kyle handed the lens to him. 'And I wanted to. It's a rather expensive present, you know—it and the other two like it—from our Imperial treasury. Just to keep your planet from drifting into another ice age. And what do we get for it?'

'Earth, Lord,' answered Kyle. 'As it was before men went out to the stars.'

'Oh, the museum areas could be maintained with one station and a half-million caretakers,' said the Prince. 'It's the other two stations and you billion or so free-loaders I'm talking about. I'll have to look into it when I'm Emperor. Shall we ride?'

'If you wish, Lord.' Kyle picked up the reins of the stallion and the two horses with their riders moved off across the slope.

'. . . And one more thing,' said the Prince, as they entered the farther belt of pine trees. 'I don't want you to be misled—I'm really very fond of old Monty, back there. It's just that I wasn't really planning to come here at all—*Look at me, Bodyguard!*'

Kyle turned to see the blue eyes that ran in the Imperial family blazing at him. Then, unexpectedly, they softened. The Prince laughed.

'You don't scare easily, do you, Bodyguard . . . Kyle, I mean?' he said. 'I think I like you after all. But look at me when I talk.'

'Yes, Lord.'

'That's my good Kyle. Now, I was explaining to you that I'd never actually planned to come here on my Grand Tour at all. I didn't see any point in visiting this dusty old museum world of yours with people still trying to live like they lived in the Dark Ages. But—my Imperial father talked me into it.'

'Your father, Lord?' asked Kyle.

'Yes, he bribed me, you might say,' said the Prince thoughtfully. 'He was supposed to meet me here for these three days. Now, he's messaged there's been a slight delay —but that doesn't matter. The point is, he belongs to the school of old men who still think your Earth is something precious and vital. Now, I happen to like and admire my father, Lyle. You approve of that?'

'Yes, Lord.'

'I thought you would. Yes, he's the one man in the human race I look up to. And to please him, I'm making this Earth trip. And to please him—only to please *him*, Kyle—I'm going to be an easy Prince for you to conduct around to your natural wonders and watering spots and whatever. Now, you understand me—and how this trip is going to go. Don't you?' He stared at Kyle.

'I understand,' said Kyle.

'That's fine,' said the Prince, smiling once more. 'So now you can start telling me all about these trees and birds and animals so that I can memorize their names and please my father when he shows up. What are those little birds I've been seeing under the trees—brown on top and whitish underneath? Like that one—there!'

'That's a Veery, Lord,' said Kyle. 'A bird of the deep woods and silent places. Listen—' He reached out a hand to the gelding's bridle and brought both horses to a halt. In the sudden silence, off to their right they could hear a silver bird-voice, rising and falling, in a descending series of crescendos and diminuendos, that softened at last into silence. For a moment after the song was ended the Prince sat staring at Kyle, then seemed to shake himself back to life.

'Interesting,' he said. He lifted the reins Kyle had let go and the horses moved forward again. 'Tell me more.'

For more than three hours, as the sun rose towards noon, they rode through the wooded hills, with Kyle identifying bird and animal, insect, tree and rock. And for three hours the Prince listened—his attention flashing and momentary, but intense. But when the sun was overhead that intensity flagged.

'That's enough,' he said. 'Aren't we going to stop for lunch? Kyle, aren't there any towns around here?'

'Yes, Lord,' said Kyle. 'We've passed several.'

'Several?' The Prince stared at him. 'Why haven't we come into one before now? Where are you taking me?'

'Nowhere, Lord,' said Kyle. 'You lead the way, I only follow.'

'I?' said the Prince. For the first time he seemed to become aware that he had been keeping the gelding's head always in advance of the stallion. 'Of course. But now it's time to eat.'

'Yes, Lord,' said Kyle. 'This way.'

He turned the stallion's head down the slope of the hill they were crossing and the Prince turned the gelding after him.

'And now listen,' said the Prince, as he caught up. 'Tell me I've got it all right.' And to Kyle's astonishment, he began to repeat, almost word for word, everything that Kyle had said. 'Is it all there? Everything you told me?'

'Perfectly, Lord,' said Kyle. The Prince looked slyly at him. 'Could you do that, Kyle?'

'Yes,' said Kyle. 'But these are things I've known all my life.'

'You see?' The Prince smiled. 'That's the difference between us, good Kyle. You spend your life learning something—I spend a few hours and I know as much about it as you do.'

'Not as much, Lord,' said Kyle, slowly.

The Prince blinked at him, then jerked his hand dismissingly, and half-angrily, as if he were throwing something aside.

'What little else there is probably doesn't count,' he said.

They rode down the slope and through a winding valley and came out at a small village. As they rode clear of the surrounding trees a sound of music came to their ears.

'What's that?' The Prince stood up in his stirrups. 'Why there's dancing going on, over there.'

'A beer garden, Lord. And it's Saturday—a holiday here.'

'Good. We'll go there to eat.'

They rode around to the beer garden and found tables back away from the dance floor. A pretty, young waitress came and they ordered, the Prince smiling sunnily at her until she smiled back—then hurried off as if in mild confusion. The Prince ate hungrily when the food came and drank a stein and a half of brown beer, while Kyle ate more lightly and drank coffee.

'That's better,' said the Prince, sitting back at last. 'I had an appetite . . . Look there, Kyle! Look, there are five, six, . . .

seven drifter platforms parked over there. Then you don't all ride horses?'

'No,' said Kyle. 'It's as each man wishes.'

'But if you have drifter platforms, why not other civilized things?'

'Some things fit, some don't, Lord,' answered Kyle. The Prince laughed.

'You mean you try to make civilization fit this old-fashioned life of yours, here?' he said. 'Isn't that the wrong way around—' He broke off. 'What's that they're playing now? I like that. I'll bet I could do that dance.' He stood up. 'In fact, I think I will.'

He paused, looking down at Kyle.

'Aren't you going to warn me against it?' he asked.

'No, Lord,' said Kyle. 'What you do is your own affair.'

The young man turned away abruptly. The waitress who had served them was passing, only a few tables away. The Prince went after her and caught up with her by the dance floor railing. Kyle could see the girl protesting—but the Prince hung over her, looking down from his tall height, smiling. Shortly, she had taken off her apron and was out on the dance floor with him, showing him the steps of the dance. It was a polka.

The Prince learned with fantastic quickness. Soon, he was swinging the waitress around with the rest of the dancers, his foot stamping on the turns, his white teeth gleaming. Finally the number ended and the members of the band put down their instruments and began to leave the stand.

The Prince, with the girl trying to hold him back, walked over to the band leader. Kyle got up quickly from his table and started toward the floor.

The band leader was shaking his head. He turned abruptly and slowly walked away. The Prince started after him, but the girl took hold of his arm, saying something urgent to him.

He brushed her aside and she stumbled a little. A waiter among the tables on the far side of the dance floor, not much older than the Prince and nearly as tall, put down his tray and vaulted the railing onto the polished hardwood. He came up behind the Prince and took hold of his arm, swinging him around.

'. . . Can't do that here,' Kyle heard him say, as Kyle came up. The Prince struck out like a panther—like a trained boxer—with three quick lefts in succession into the face of the waiter, the Prince's shoulder bobbing, the weight of his body in behind each blow.

The waiter went down. Kyle, reaching the Prince, herded him away through a side gap in the railing. The young man's face was white with rage. People were swarming onto the dance floor.

'Who was that? What's his name?' demanded the Prince, between his teeth. 'He put his hand on me! Did you see that? *He put his hand on me!*'

'You knocked him out,' said Kyle. 'What more do you want?'

'He manhandled me—*me!*' snapped the Prince. 'I want to find out who he is!' He caught hold of the bar to which the horses were tied, refusing to be pushed farther. 'He'll learn to lay hands on a future Emperor!'

'No one will tell you his name,' said Kyle. And the cold note in his voice finally seemed to reach through to the Prince and sober him. He stared at Kyle.

'Including you?' he demanded at last.

'Including me, Lord,' said Kyle.

The Prince stared a moment longer, then swung away. He turned, jerked loose the reins of the gelding and swung into the saddle. He rode off. Kyle mounted and followed.

They rode in silence into the forest. After a while, the Prince spoke without turning his head.

'And you call yourself a bodyguard,' he said, finally.

'Your life is in my hands, Lord,' said Kyle. The Prince turned a grim face to look at him.

'Only my life?' said the Prince. 'As long as they don't kill me, they can do what they want? Is that what you mean?'

Kyle met his gaze steadily.

'Pretty much so, Lord,' he said.

The Prince spoke with an ugly note in his voice.

'I don't think I like you, after all, Kyle,' he said. 'I don't think I like you at all.'

'I'm not here with you to be liked, Lord,' said Kyle.

'Perhaps not,' said the Prince, thickly. 'But I know *your* name!'

They rode on in continued silence for perhaps another half hour. But then gradually the angry hunch went out of the young man's shoulders and the tightness out of his jaw. After a while he began to sing to himself, a song in a language Kyle did not know; and as he sang, his cheerfulness seemed to return. Shortly, he spoke to Kyle, as if there had never been anything but pleasant moments between them.

Mammoth Cave was close and the Prince asked to visit it. They went there and spent some time going through the cave. After that they rode their horses up along the left bank of the Green River. The Prince seemed to have forgotten all about the incident at the beer garden and be out to charm everyone they met. As the sun was at last westering toward the dinner hour, they came finally to a small hamlet back from the river, with a roadside inn mirrored in an artificial lake beside it, and guarded by oak and pine trees behind.

'This looks good,' said the Prince. 'We'll stay overnight here, Kyle.'

'If you wish, Lord,' said Kyle.

They halted, and Kyle took the horses around to the stable, then entered the inn to find the Prince already in the small bar off the dining room, drinking beer and charming the waitress. This waitress was younger than the one at the beer garden had been; a little girl with soft, loose hair and round brown eyes that showed their delight in the attention of the tall, good-looking, young man.

'Yes,' said the Prince to Kyle, looking out of corners of the Imperial blue eyes at him, after the waitress had gone to get Kyle his coffee. 'This is the very place.'

'The very place?' said Kyle.

'For me to get to know the people better—what did you think, good Kyle?' said the Prince and laughed at him. 'I'll observe the people here and you can explain them—won't that be good?'

Kyle gazed at him, thoughtfully.

'I'll tell you whatever I can, Lord,' he said.

They drank—the Prince his beer, and Kyle his coffee—and went in a little later to the dining room for dinner. The Prince, as he had promised at the bar, was full of questions about what he saw—and what he did not see.

'. . . But why go on living in the past, all of you here?' he asked Kyle. 'A museum world is one thing. But a museum people—' he broke off to smile and speak to the little, soft-haired waitress, who had somehow been diverted from the bar to wait upon their dining room table.

'Not a museum people, Lord,' said Kyle. 'A living people. The only way to keep a race and a culture preserved is to keep it alive. So we go on in our own way, here on Earth, as a living example for the Younger Worlds to check themselves against.'

'Fascinating . . .' murmured the Prince; but his eyes had wandered off to follow the waitress, who was glowing and looking back at him from across the now-busy dining room.

'Not fascinating. Necessary, Lord,' said Kyle. But he did not believe the younger man had heard him.

After dinner, they moved back to the bar. And the Prince, after questioning Kyle a little longer, moved up to continue his researches among the other people standing at the bar. Kyle watched for a little while. Then, feeling it was safe to do so, slipped out to have another look at the horses and to ask the innkeeper to arrange a saddle lunch put up for them the next day.

When he returned, the Prince was not to be seen.

Kyle sat down at a table to wait; but the Prince did not return. A cold, hard knot of uneasiness began to grow below Kyle's breastbone. A sudden pang of alarm sent him swiftly back out to check the horses. But they were cropping peacefully in their stalls. The stallion whickered, low-voiced, as Kyle looked in on him, and turned his white head to look back at Kyle.

'Easy, boy,' said Kyle and returned to the inn to find the innkeeper.

But the innkeeper had no idea where the Prince might have gone.

'. . . If the horses aren't taken, he's not far,' the innkeeper said. 'There's no trouble he can get into around here. Maybe he went for a walk in the woods. I'll leave word for the night staff to keep an eye out for him when he comes in. Where'll you be?'

'In the bar until it closes—then, my room,' said Kyle.

He went back to the bar to wait, and took a booth near an open window. Time went by and gradually the number of other customers began to dwindle. Above the ranked bottles, the bar clock showed nearly midnight. Suddenly, through the window, Kyle heard a distant scream of equine fury from the stables.

He got up and went out quickly. In the darkness outside, he ran to the stables and burst in. There in the feeble illumination of the stable's night lighting, he saw the Prince, pale faced, clumsily saddling the gelding in the centre aisle between the stalls. The door to the stallion's stall was open. The Prince looked away as Kyle came in.

Kyle took three swift steps to the open door and looked in. The stallion was still tied, but his ears were back, his eyes rolling, and a saddle lay tumbled and dropped on the stable floor beside him.

'Saddle up,' said the Prince thickly from the aisle. 'We're leaving.' Kyle turned to look at him.

'We've got rooms at the inn here,' he said.

'Never mind. We're riding. I need to clear my head.' The young man got the gelding's cinch tight, dropped the stirrups and swung heavily up into the saddle. Without waiting for Kyle, he rode out of the stable into the night.

'So, boy . . .' said Kyle soothingly to the stallion. Hastily he untied the big white horse, saddled him, and set out after the Prince. In the darkness there was no way of ground-tracking the gelding; but he leaned forward and blew into the ear of the stallion. The surprised horse neighed in protest and the whinny of the gelding came back from the darkness of the slope up ahead and over to Kyle's right. He rode in that direction.

He caught the Prince on the crown of the hill. The young man was walking the gelding, reins loose, and singing under his breath—the same song in an unknown language he had sung earlier. But, now as he saw Kyle, he grinned loosely and began to sing with more emphasis. For the first time Kyle caught the overtones of something mocking and lusty about the incomprehensible words. Understanding broke suddenly in him.

'The girl!' he said. 'The little waitress. Where is she?'

The grin vanished from the Prince's face, then came slowly back again. The grin laughed at Kyle.

'Why, where d'you think?' The words slurred on the Prince's tongue and Kyle, riding close, smelled the beer heavy on the young man's breath. 'In her room, sleeping and happy. Honoured . . . though she doesn't know it . . . by an Emperor's son. And expecting to find me there in the morning. But I won't be. Will we, good Kyle?'

'Why did you do it, Lord?' asked Kyle, quietly.

'Why?' The Prince peered at him, a little drunkenly in the moonlight. 'Kyle, my father has four sons. I've got three younger brothers. But I'm the one who's going to be Emperor; and Emperors don't answer questions.'

Kyle said nothing. The Prince peered at him. They rode on together for several minutes in silence.

'All right, I'll tell you why,' said the Prince, more loudly, after a while as if the pause had been only momentary. 'It's because you're not *my* bodyguard, Kyle. You see, I've seen through you. I know whose bodyguard you are. You're *theirs!*

Kyle's jaw tightened. But the darkness hid his reaction.

'All right—' The Prince gestured loosely, disturbing his balance in the saddle. 'That's all right. Have it your way. I don't mind. So, we'll play points. There was that lout at the beer garden who put his hands on me. But no one would tell me his name, you said. All right, you managed to body-guard him. One point for you. But you didn't manage to bodyguard the girl at the inn back there. One point for me. Who's going to win, good Kyle?'

Kyle took a deep breath.

'Lord,' he said, 'some day it'll be your duty to marry a woman from Earth—'

The Prince interrupted him with a laugh, and this time there was an ugly note in it.

'You flatter yourselves,' he said. His voice thickened. 'That's the trouble with you—all you Earth people—you flatter yourselves.'

They rode on in silence. Kyle said nothing more, but kept the head of the stallion close to the shoulder of the gelding, watching the young man closely. For a little while the Prince seemed to doze. His head sank on his chest and he let the gelding wander. Then, after a while, his head began to come up again, his automatic horseman's fingers tightened on the reins, and he lifted his head to stare around in the moonlight.

'I want a drink,' he said. His voice was no longer thick, but it was flat and uncheerful. 'Take me where we can get some beer, Kyle.'

Kyle took a deep breath.

'Yes, Lord,' he said.

He turned the stallion's head to the right and the gelding followed. They went up over a hill and down to the edge of a lake. The dark water sparkled in the moonlight and the farther shore was lost in the night. Lights shone through the trees around the curve of the shore.

'There, Lord,' said Kyle. 'It's a fishing resort, with a bar.'

They rode around the shore to it. It was a low, casual building, angled to face the shore; a dock ran out from it, to which fishing goats were tethered, bobbing slightly on the black water. Light gleamed through the windows as they hitched their horses and went to the door.

The barroom they stepped into was wide and bare. A long bar faced them with several planked fish on the wall behind it. Below the fish were three bartenders—the one in the centre, middle-aged, and wearing an air of authority with his apron. The other two were young and muscular. The customers, mostly men, scattered at the square tables and standing at the bar wore rough working clothes, or equally casual vacationers' garb.

The Prince sat down at a table back from the bar and Kyle sat down with him. When the waitress came they ordered beer and coffee, and the Prince half-emptied his stein the moment it was brought to him. As soon as it was completely empty, he signalled the waitress again.

'Another,' he said. This time, he smiled at the waitress when she brought his stein back. But she was a woman in her thirties, pleased but not overwhelmed by his attention.

She smiled lightly back and moved off to return to the bar where she had been talking to two men her own age, one fairly tall, the other shorter, bullet-headed and fleshy.

The Prince drank. As he put his stein down, he seemed to become aware of Kyle, and turned to look at him.

'I suppose,' said the Prince, 'you think I'm drunk?'

'Not yet,' said Kyle.

'No,' said the Prince, 'that's right. Not yet. But perhaps I'm going to be. And if I decide I am, who's going to stop me?'

'No one, Lord.'

'That's right,' the young man said. 'That's right.' He drank deliberately from his stein until it was empty, and then signalled the waitress for another. A spot of colour was beginning to show over each of his high cheekbones. 'When you're on a miserable little world with miserable little people . . . hello, Bright Eyes!' he interrupted himself as the waitress brought his beer. She laughed and went back to her friends. '. . . You have to amuse yourself any way you can,' he wound up.

He laughed to himself.

'When I think how my father, and Monty—everybody— used to talk this planet up to me—' he glanced aside at Kyle. 'Do you know at one time I was actually scared—well, not scared exactly, nothing scares me . . . say *concerned*— about maybe having to come here, some day?' He laughed again. 'Concerned that I wouldn't measure up to you Earth people! Kyle, have you ever been to any of the Younger Worlds?'

'No,' said Kyle.

'I thought not. Let me tell you, good Kyle, the worst of the people there are bigger, and better-looking and smarter, and everything than anyone I've seen here. And I, Kyle, I—the Emperor-to-be—am better than any of them. So, guess how all you here look to me?' He stared at Kyle, waiting. 'Well, answer me, good Kyle. Tell me the truth. That's an order.'

'It's not up to you to judge, Lord,' said Kyle.

'Not—? Not up to me?' The blue eyes blazed. '*I'm* going to be Emperor!'

'It's not up to any one man, Lord,' said Kyle. 'Emperor or not. An Emperor's needed, as the symbol that can hold a hundred worlds together. But the real need of the race is to survive. It took nearly a million years to evolve a survival-type intelligence here on Earth. And out on the newer worlds people are bound to change. If something gets lost out there, some necessary element lost out of the race, there needs to be a pool of original genetic material here to replace it.'

The Prince's lips grew wide in a savage grin.

'Oh, good, Kyle—good!' he said. 'Very good. Only, I've heard all that before. Only, I don't believe it. You see—I've seen you people, now. And you don't outclass us, out on the Younger Worlds. *We* outclass *you*. We've gone on and got better, while you stayed still. And you know it.'

The young man laughed softly, almost in Kyle's face.

'All you've been afraid of, is that we'd find out. And I have.' He laughed again. 'I've had a look at you; and now I know. I'm bigger, better and braver than any man in this room—and you know why? Not just because I'm the son of the Emperor, but because it's born in me! Body, brains and everything else! I can do what I want here, and no one on this planet is good enough to stop me. Watch.'

He stood up, suddenly.

'Now, I want that waitress to get drunk with me,' he said. 'And this time I'm telling you in advance. Are you going to try and stop me?'

Kyle looked up at him. Their eyes met.

'No, Lord,' he said. 'It's not my job to stop you.'

The Prince laughed.

'I thought so,' he said. He swung away and walked between the tables towards the bar and the waitress, still in conversation with the two men. The Prince came up to the bar on the far side of the waitress and ordered a new stein of beer from the middle-aged bartender. When it was given to him, he took it, turned around, and rested his elbows on the bar, leaning back against it. He spoke to the waitress, interrupting the taller of the two men.

'I've been wanting to talk to you,' Kyle heard him say.

The waitress, a little surprised, looked around at him. She smiled, recognizing him—a little flattered by the directness of his approach, a little appreciative of his clean good looks, a little tolerant of his youth.

'*You* don't mind, do you?' said the Prince, looking past her to the bigger of the two men, the one who had just been talking. The other stared back, and their eyes met without shifting for several seconds. Abruptly, angrily, the man shrugged, and turned about with his back hunched against them.

'You see?' said the Prince, smiling back at the waitress. 'He knows I'm the one you ought to be talking to, instead of—'

'All right, sonny. Just a minute.'

It was the shorter, bullet-head man, interrupting. The Prince turned to look down at him with a fleeting expression of surprise. But the bullet-headed man was already turning to his taller friend and putting a hand on his arm.

'Come on back, Ben,' the shorter man was saying. 'The kid's a little drunk, is all.' He turned back to the Prince. 'You shove off now,' he said. 'Clara's with us.'

The Prince stared at him blankly. The stare was so fixed that the shorter man had started to turn away, back to his friend and the waitress, when the Prince seemed to wake.

'Just a minute—' he said, in his turn.

He reached out a hand to one of the fleshy shoulders below the bullet head. The man turned back, knocking the hand calmly away. Then, just as calmly, he picked up the Prince's full stein of beer from the bar and threw it in the young man's face.

'Get lost,' he said, unexcitedly.

The Prince stood for a second, with the beer dripping from his face. Then, without even stopping to wipe his eyes clear, he threw the beautifully trained left hand he had demonstrated at the beer garden.

But the shorter man, as Kyle had known from the first moment of seeing him, was not like the waiter the Prince had decisioned so neatly. This man was thirty pounds heavier, fifteen years more experienced, and by build and nature a natural bar fighter. He had not stood there waiting to be hit, but had already ducked and gone forward to throw his thick arms around the Prince's body. The young man's punch bounced harmlessly off the round head, and both bodies hit the floor, rolling in among the chair and table legs.

Kyle was already more than halfway to the bar and the three bartenders were already leaping the wooden hurdle that walled them off. The taller friend of the bullet-headed man, hovering over the two bodies, his eyes glittering, had his boot drawn back ready to drive the point of it into the Prince's kidneys. Kyle's forearm took him economically like a bar of iron across the tanned throat.

He stumbled backwards choking. Kyle stood still, hands open and down, glancing at the middle-aged bartender.

'All right,' said the bartender. 'But don't do anything more.' He turned to the two younger bartenders. 'All right. Haul him off!'

The pair of younger, aproned men bent down and came up with the bullet-headed man expertly handlocked between them. The man made one surging effort to break loose, and then stood still.

'Let me at him,' he said.

'Not in here,' said the older bartender. 'Take it outside.'

Between the tables, the Prince staggered unsteadily to his feet. His face was streaming blood from a cut on his forehead, but what could be seen of it was white as a drowning man's. His eyes went to Kyle, standing beside him; and he opened his mouth—but what came out sounded like something between a sob and a curse.

'All right,' said the middle-aged bartender again. 'Outside, both of you. Settle it out there.'

The men in the room had packed around the little space by the bar. The Prince looked about and for the first time seemed to see the human wall hemming him in. His gaze wobbled to meet Kyle's.

'Outside . . . ?' he said, chokingly.

'You aren't staying in here,' said the older bartender, answering for Kyle. 'I saw it. You started the whole thing. Now, settle it any way you want—but you're both going outside. Now! Get moving!'

He pushed at the Prince, but the Prince resisted, clutching at Kyle's leather jacket with one hand.

'Kyle—'.

'I'm sorry, Lord,' said Kyle. 'I can't help. It's your fight.'

'Let's get out of here,' said the bullet-headed man.

The Prince stared around at them as if they were some strange set of beings he had never known to exist before.

'No . . .' he said.

He let go of Kyle's jacket. Unexpectedly, his hand darted in towards Kyle's belly holster and came out holding the slug pistol.

'Stand back!' he said, his voice high-toned. 'Don't try to touch me!'

His voice broke on the last words. There was a strange sound, half grunt, half moan, from the crowd; and it swayed back from him. Manager, bartenders, watchers—all but Kyle and the bullet-headed man drew back.

'You dirty slob . . .' said the bullet-headed man, distinctly. 'I knew you didn't have the guts.'

'Shut up!' The Prince's voice was high and cracking. 'Shut up! Don't any of you try to come after me!'

He began backing away towards the front door of the bar. The room watched in silence, even Kyle standing still. As he backed, the Prince's back straightened. He hefted the gun in his hand. When he reached the door he paused to wipe the blood from his eyes with his left sleeve, and his smeared face looked with a first touch of regained arrogance at them.

'Swine!' he said.

He opened the door and backed out, closing it behind him. Kyle took one step that put him facing the bullet-headed man. Their eyes met and he could see the other recognizing the fighter in him, as he had earlier recognized it in the bullet-headed man.

'Don't come after us,' said Kyle.

The bullet-headed man did not answer. But no answer was needed. He stood still.

Kyle turned, ran to the door, stood on one side of it and flicked it open. Nothing happened; and he slipped through, dodging to his right at once, out of the line of any shot aimed at the opening door.

But no shot came. For a moment he was blind in the night

darkness, then his eyes began to adjust. He went by sight, feel and memory toward the hitching rack. By the time he got there, he was beginning to see.

The Prince was untying the gelding and getting ready to mount.

'Lord,' said Kyle.

The Prince let go of the saddle for a moment and turned to look over his shoulder at him.

'Get away from me,' said the Prince, thickly.

'Lord,' said Kyle, low-voiced and pleading, 'you lost your head in there. Anyone might do that. But don't make it worse, now. Give me back the gun, Lord.'

'Give you the gun?'

The young man stared at him—and then he laughed.

'Give *you* the gun?' he said again. 'So you can let someone beat me up some more? So you can not guard me with it?'

'Lord,' said Kyle, 'please. For your own sake—give me back the gun.'

'Get out of here,' said the Prince, thickly, turning back to mount the gelding. 'Clear out before I put a slug in you.'

Kyle drew a slow, sad breath. He stepped forward and tapped the Prince on the shoulder.

'Turn around, Lord,' he said.

'I warned you—' shouted the Prince, turning.

He came around as Kyle stooped, and the slug pistol flashed in his hand from the light of the bar windows. Kyle, bent over, was lifting the cuff of his trouser leg and closing his fingers on the hilt of the knife in his boot sheath. He moved simply, skilfully, and with a speed nearly double that of the young man, striking up into the chest before him until the hand holding the knife jarred against the cloth covering flesh and bone.

It was a sudden, hard-driven, swiftly merciful blow. The blade struck upwards between the ribs lying open to an underhanded thrust, plunging deep into the heart. The Prince grunted with the impact driving the air from his lungs; and he was dead as Kyle caught his slumping body in leather-jacketed arms.

Kyle lifted the tall body across the saddle of the gelding and tied it there. He hunted on the dark ground for the

fallen pistol and returned it to his holster. Then, he mounted
the stallion and, leading the gelding with its burden, started
the long ride back.

Dawn was greying the sky when at last he topped the hill
overlooking the lodge where he had picked up the Prince
almost twenty-four hours before. He rode down towards the
courtyard gate.

A tall figure, indistinct in the pre-dawn light, was waiting
inside the courtyard as Kyle came through the gate; and it
came running to meet him as he rode towards it. It was the
tutor, Montlaven, and he was weeping as he ran to the
gelding and began to fumble at the cords that tied the body
in place.

'I'm sorry . . .' Kyle heard himself saying; and was dully
shocked by the deadness and remoteness of his voice. 'There
was no choice. You can read it all in my report tomorrow
morning—'

He broke off. Another, even taller figure had appeared in
the doorway of the lodge giving on to the courtyard. As Kyle
turned towards it, this second figure descended the few steps
to the grass and came to him.

'Lord—' said Kyle. He looked down into features like
those of the Prince, but older, under greying hair. This man
did not weep like the tutor, but his face was set like iron.

'What happened, Kyle?' he said.

'Lord,' said Kyle,' you'll have my report in the morning...'

'I want to know,' said the tall man. Kyle's throat was
dry and stiff. He swallowed but swallowing did not ease it.

'Lord,' he said, 'you have three other sons. One of them
will make an Emperor to hold the worlds together.'

'What did he do? Whom did he hurt? Tell me!' The tall
man's voice cracked almost as his son's voice had cracked
in the bar.

'Nothing. No one,' said Kyle, stiff-throated. 'He hit a
boy not much older than himself. He drank too much. He
may have got a girl in trouble. It was nothing he did to
anyone else. It was only a fault against himself.' He swallowed. 'Wait until tomorrow, Lord, and read my report.'

"No!" The tall man caught Kyle's saddle horn with a

grip that checked even the white stallion from moving. 'Your family and mine have been tied together by this for three hundred years. What was the flaw in my son to make him fail his test, back here on Earth? *I want to know!*"

Kyle's throat ached and was dry as ashes.

'Lord,' he answered, 'he was a coward.'

The hand dropped from his saddle horn as if struck down by a sudden strengthlessness. And the Emperor of a hundred worlds fell back like a beggar, spurned in the dust.

Kyle lifted his reins and rode out of the gate, into the forest away on the hillside. The dawn was breaking.

The Garden of Time

J. G. Ballard

The nature of time continues to exert its fascination upon writer and reader alike.

There have been stories about journeys *forward* in time (Wells' *The Time Machine*), journeys *back* in time (see RAINBIRD and THE MAN WHO CAME EARLY), and stories of enormous conflicts raging across time and space (Leiber's *The Big Time* and Simak's *Time And Again*). But there has never been, to my knowledge, anything quite like THE GARDEN OF TIME: it eludes any attempt to categorize it.

J. G. Ballard was the first to encourage the view of sf as a genuine art form and the barriers that once separated the field from contemporary literature as artificial. Following his example, other writers such as Brian Aldiss, James Blish, Thomas Disch, R. A. Lafferty and many more have struck boldly away from the magazines and enriched our reading with their work. To many people J. G. Ballard *is* the future for sf.

Toward evening, when the great shadow of the Palladian villa filled the terrace, Count Axel left his library and walked down the wide rococo steps among the time flowers. A tall, imperious figure in a black velvet jacket, a gold tie-pin glinting below his George V beard, cane held stiffly in a white-gloved hand, he surveyed the exquisite crystal flowers without emotion, listening to the sounds of his wife's harpsichord, as she played a Mozart rondo in the music room, echo and vibrate through the translucent petals.

The garden of the villa extended for some two hundred metres below the terrace, sloping down to a miniature lake spanned by a white bridge, a slender pavilion on the opposite bank. Axel rarely ventured as far as the lake, most of the time flowers grew in a small grove just below the terrace, sheltered by the high wall which encircled the estate. From the terrace he could see over the wall to the plain beyond, a continuous expanse of open ground that rolled in great swells to the horizon, where it rose slightly before finally dipping from sight. The plain surrounded the house on all sides, its drab emptiness emphasizing the seclusion and mellowed magnificence of the villa. Here, in the garden, the air seemed brighter, the sun warmer, while the plain was always dull and remote.

As was his custom before beginning his regular evening stroll, Count Axel looked out across the plain to the final rise, where the horizon was illuminated like a distant stage by the fading sun. As the Mozart chimed delicately around him, flowing from his wife's graceful hands, he saw that the advance columns of an enormous army were moving slowly over the horizon. At first glance, the long ranks seemed to be progressing in orderly lines, but on closer inspection, it was apparent that, like the obscured detail of a Goya landscape, the army was composed of a vast confused throng of people, men and women, interspersed with a few soldiers in ragged uniforms, pressing forward in a disorganized tide. Some laboured under heavy loads suspended from crude yokes around their necks; others struggled with cumbersome wooden carts, their hands wrenching at the wheel spokes; a few trudged on alone; but all moved on at the same pace, bowed backs illuminated in the fleeting sun.

The advancing throng was almost too far away to be visible, but even as Axel watched, his expression aloof yet observant, it came perceptibly nearer, the vanguard of an immense rabble appearing from below the horizon. At last, as the daylight began to fade, the front edge of the throng reached the crest of the first swell below the horizon, and Axel turned from the terrace and walked down among the time flowers.

The flowers grew to a height of about two metres, their slender stems, like rods of glass, bearing a dozen leaves, the once transparent fronds frosted by the fossilized veins. At the peak of each stem was the time flower, the size of a goblet, the opaque outer petals enclosing the crystal heart. Their diamond brilliance contained a thousand faces, the crystal seeming to drain the air of its light and motion. As the flowers swayed slightly in the evening air, they glowed like flame-tipped spears.

Many of the stems no longer bore flowers, and Axel examined them all carefully, a note of hope now and then crossing his eyes as he searched for any further buds. Finally he selected a large flower on the stem nearest the wall, removed his gloves and with his strong fingers snapped it off.

As he carried the flower back onto the terrace, it began to sparkle and deliquesce, the light trapped within the core at last released. Gradually the crystal dissolved, only the outer petals remaining intact, and the air around Axel became bright and vivid, charged with slanting rays that flared away into the waning sunlight. Strange shifts momentarily transformed the evening, subtly altering its dimensions of time and space. The darkened portico of the house, its patina of age stripped away, loomed with a curious spectral whiteness as if suddenly remembered in a dream.

Raising his head, Axel peered over the wall again. Only the furthest rim of the horizon was lit by the sun, and the great throng, which before had stretched almost a quarter of the way across the plain, had now receded to the horizon, the entire concourse abruptly flung back in a reversal of time, and now appearing to be stationary.

The flower in Axel's hand had shrunk to the size of a glass thimble, the petals contracting around the vanishing core. A faint sparkle flickered from the centre and extinguished itself, and Axel felt the flower melt like an ice-cold bead of dew in his hand.

Dusk closed across the house, sweeping its long shadows over the plain, the horizon merging into the sky. The harpsichord was silent, and the time flowers, no longer reflecting its music, stood motionlessly, like an embalmed forest.

For a few minutes Axel looked down at them, counting the flowers which remained, then greeted his wife as she crossed the terrace, her brocade evening dress rustling over the ornamental tiles.

'What a beautiful evening, Axel.' She spoke feelingly, as if she were thanking her husband personally for the great ornate shadow across the lawn and the dark brilliant air. Her face was serene and intelligent, her hair, swept back behind her head into a jewelled clasp, touched with silver. She wore her dress low across her breast, revealing a long slender neck and high chin. Axel surveyed her with fond pride. He gave her his arm and together they walked down the steps into the garden.

'One of the longest evenings this summer,' Axel confirmed, adding: 'I picked the perfect flower, my dear, a jewel. With luck it should last us for several days.' A frown touched his brow, and he glanced involuntarily at the wall. 'Each time now they seem to come nearer.'

His wife smiled at him encouragingly and held his arm more tightly.

Both of them knew that the garden was dying.

Three evenings later, as he has estimated (though sooner than he secretly hoped), Count Axel plucked another flower from the time garden.

When he first looked over the wall the approaching rabble filled the distant half of the plain, stretching across the horizon in an unbroken mass. He thought he could hear the low, fragmentary sounds of voices carried across the empty air, a sullen murmur punctuated by cries and shouts, but quickly told himself that he had imagined them. Luckily, his wife was at her harpsichord, and the rich contrapuntal patterns of a Bach fugue cascaded lightly across the terrace, masking other noises.

Between the house and the horizon the plain was divided into four huge swells, the crest of each one clearly visible in the slanting light. Axel had promised himself that he would never count them, but the number was too small to remain unobserved, particularly when it so obviously marked the progress of the advancing army. By now the forward line had passed the first crest and was well on its way to the second; the main bulk of the throng pressed behind it, hiding the crest and the even vaster concourse spreading from the horizon. Looking to left and right of the central body, Axel

The Garden of Time

could see the apparently limitless extent of the army. What
had seemed at first to be the central mass was no more than
a minor advance guard, one of many similar arms reaching
across the plain. The true centre had not yet emerged but,
from the rate of extension, Axel estimated that when it
finally reached the plain it would completely cover every
metre of ground.

Axel searched for any large vehicles or machines, but all
was amorphous and uncoordinated as ever. There were no
banners or flags, no mascots or pike-bearers. Heads bowed,
the multitude pressed on, unaware of the sky.

Suddenly, just before Axel turned away, the forward
edge of the throng appeared on top of the second crest, and
swarmed down across the plain. What astounded Axel was
the incredible distance it had covered while out of sight.
The figures were now twice the size, each one clearly
within sight.

Quickly, Axel stepped from the terrace, selected a time
flower from the garden and tore it from the stem. As it
released its compacted light, he returned to the terrace.
When the flower had shrunk to a frozen pearl in his palm
he looked out at the plain; with relief saw that the army
had retreated to the horizon again.

Then he realized that the horizon was much nearer than
previously, and that what he assumed to be the horizon
was the first crest.

When he joined the Countess on their evening walk he
told her nothing of this, but she could see behind his casual
unconcern and did what she could to dispel his worry.

Walking down the steps, she pointed to the time garden.
'What a wonderful display, Axel. There are so many flowers
still.'

Axel nodded, smiling to himself at his wife's attempt to
reassure him. Her use of 'still' had revealed her own unconscious anticipation of the end. In fact, a mere dozen
flowers remained of the many hundreds that had grown in
the garden, and several of these were little more than buds—
only three or four were fully grown. As they walked down to
the lake, the Countess's dress rustling across the cool turf,

he tried to decide whether to pick the larger flowers first or leave them to the end. Strictly, it would be better to give the smaller flowers additional time to grow and mature, and this advantage would be lost if he retained the larger flowers to the end, as he wished to do, for the final repulse. However, he realized that it mattered little either way; the garden would soon die and the smaller flowers required far longer than he could give them to accumulate their compressed cores of time. During his entire lifetime he had failed to notice a single evidence of growth among the flowers. The larger blooms had always been mature, and none of the buds had shown the slightest development.

Crossing the lake, he and his wife looked down at their reflections in the still, black water. Shielded by the pavilion on one side and the high garden wall on the other, the villa in the distance, Axel felt composed and secure, the plain with its encroaching multitude a nightmare from which he had safely awakened. He put one arm around his wife's smooth waist and pressed her affectionately to his shoulder, realizing that he had not embraced her for several years, though their lives together had been timeless and he could remember as if yesterday when he first brought her to live in the villa.

'Axel,' his wife asked with sudden seriousness. 'Before the garden dies . . . may I pick the last flower?'

Understanding her request, he nodded slowly.

One by one over the succeeding evenings, he picked the remaining flowers, leaving a single small bud which grew just below the terrace for his wife. He took the flowers at random, refusing to count or ration them, plucking two or three of the smaller buds at the same time when necessary. The approaching horde had now reached the second and third crests, a vast concourse of labouring humanity that blotted out the horizon. From the terrace Axel could see clearly the shuffling, straining ranks moving down into the hollow towards the final crests, and occasionally the sounds of their voices carried across to him, interspersed with cries of anger and the cracking of whips. The wooden carts lurched from side to side on tilting wheels, their drivers struggling to control them. As far as Axel could tell, not a single member of the throng was aware of its overall direction. Rather, each one blindly moved forward across the ground directly below the heels of the person in front of him, and the only unity was that of the cumulative compass. Pointlessly, Axel hoped that the true centre, far below the horizon, might be moving in a different direction, and that gradually the multitude would alter course, swing away from the villa and recede from the plain like a turning tide.

On the last evening but one, as he plucked the time flower, the forward edge of the rabble had reached the third crest, and was swarming past it. While he waited for the Countess, Axel looked down at the two flowers left, both small buds which would carry them back through only a few minutes of the next evening. The glass stems of the dead flowers reared up stiffly into the air, but the whole garden had lost its bloom.

Axel passed the next morning quietly in his library, sealing the rarer of his manuscripts into the glass-topped cases between the galleries. He walked slowly down the portrait corridor, polishing each of the pictures carefully, then tidied his desk and locked the door behind him. During the afternoon he busied himself in the drawing rooms, unobtrusively assisting his wife as she cleaned their ornaments and straightened the vases and busts.

By evening, as the sun fell behind the house, they were both tired and dusty, and neither had spoken to the other all day. When his wife moved towards the music room, Axel called her back.

'Tonight we'll pick the flowers together, my dear,' he said to her evenly. 'One for each of us.'

He peered only briefly over the wall. They could hear, less than a kilometre away, the great dull roar of the ragged army, the ring of iron and lash, pressing on towards the house.

Quickly, Axel plucked his flower, a bud no bigger than a sapphire. As it flickered softly, the tumult outside momentarily receded, then began to gather again.

Shutting his ears to the clamour, Axel looked around at the villa, counting the six columns in the portico, then gazed out across the lawn at the silver disc of the lake, its bowl reflecting the last evening light, and at the shadows moving between the tall trees, lengthening across the crisp turf. He lingered over the bridge where he and his wife had stood arm in arm for so many summers—

'*Axel!*'

The tumult outside roared into the air; a thousand voices bellowed only twenty or thirty metres away. A stone flew over the wall and landed among the time flowers, snapping several of the brittle stems. The Countess ran towards him as a further barrage rattled along the wall. Then a heavy tile whirled through the air over their heads and crashed into one of the conservatory windows.

'Axel!' He put his arms around her, straightening his silk cravat when her shoulder brushed it between his lapels.

'Quickly, my dear, the last flower!' He led her down the steps and through the garden. Taking the stem between her jewelled fingers, she snapped it cleanly, then cradled it within her palms.

For a moment the tumult lessened slightly and Axel collected himself. In the vivid light sparkling from the flower he saw his wife's white, frightened eyes. 'Hold it as long as you can, my dear, until the last grain dies.'

Together they stood on the terrace, the Countess clasping the brilliant dying jewel, the air closing in upon them as the voices outside mounted again. The mob was battering at the heavy iron gates, and the whole villa shook with the massive impact.

While the final glimmer of light sped away, the Countess raised her palms to the air, as if releasing an invisible bird, then in a final access of courage put her hands in her husband's, her smile as radiant as the vanished flower.

'Oh, Axel!' she cried.

Like a sword, the darkness swooped down across them.

Heaving and swearing, the outer edge of the mob reached the knee-high remains of the wall enclosing the ruined estate, hauled their carts over it and along the dry ruts of what had once been an ornate drive. The ruin, formerly a spacious villa, barely interrupted the ceaseless tide of humanity.

The lake was empty, fallen trees rotting at its bottom, an old bridge rusting into it. Weeds flourished among the long grass in the lawn, over-running the ornamental pathways and carved stone screens.

Much of the terrace had crumbled, and the main section of the mob cut straight across the lawn, by-passing the gutted villa, but one or two of the more curious climbed up and searched among the shell. The doors had rotted from their hinges and the floors had fallen through. In the music room an ancient harpischord had been chopped into fire-wood, but a few keys still lay among the dust. All the books had been toppled from the shelves in the library, the canvases had been slashed, and gilt frames littered the floor.

As the main body of the mob reached the house, it began to cross the wall at all points along its length. Jostled together, the people stumbled into the dry lake, swarmed over the terrace and pressed through the house towards the open doors on the north side.

One area alone withstood the endless wave. Just below the terrace, between the wrecked balcony and the wall, was a dense, two-metre-high growth of heavy thornbushes. The barbed foliage formed an impenetrable mass, and the people passing stepped around it carefully, noticing the belladonna entwined among the branches. Most of them were too busy finding their footing among the upturned flagstones to look up into the centre of the thornbushes, where two stone statues stood side by side, gazing out over the grounds from their protected vantage point. The larger of the figures was the effigy of a bearded man in a high-collared jacket, a cane under one arm. Beside him was a woman in an elaborate full-skirted dress, her slim serene face unmarked by the wind and rain. In her left hand she lightly clasped a single rose, the delicately formed petals so thin as to be almost transparent.

As the sun died away behind the house a single ray of light glanced through a shattered cornice and struck the rose, reflected off the whorl of petals onto the statues, lighting up the grey stone so that for a fleeting moment it was indistinguishable from the long-vanished flesh of the statues' originals.

Afterword

No single volume could hope to do justice to the wide variety of science fiction now being published throughout the world. In *Beyond Tomorrow* I have brought together some of the finest contemporary writing from England and America, and combined it with a selection of Australian stories, demonstrating that there are a number of writers in this country already experienced in the difficult art of writing science fiction.

Recent years have witnessed an astonishing flowering of the genre in places as wide afield as Poland, Japan, Russia and South America, to mention only a few. Only a small proportion of this interesting new work has so far been made available in translation, and in some cases rights have proven difficult to obtain. These problems will be solved in time, and I like to think that future publications of this nature will include a representative selection of these important new voices.

The stories for *Beyond Tomorrow* were chosen with two main criteria in mind: fine writing and longevity. In most cases the latter attests the former: it is the particular quality present in the very best science fiction that renders it impervious to time. We can still read H. G. Wells' *First Men in the Moon* and *The War of the Worlds* and enjoy them as literature, even if time has exposed their original premise as wrong. Long-time science fiction readers are accustomed to placing such curiosities in an alternative time-stream of the mind, where all things are possible—a practice I feel sure Wells would have endorsed. I would like to think that the stories in this anthology will be read with equal pleasure fifty years from now. I believe they all have something that is timeless to say about the human condition, and such is the skill of the respective authors that they manage to get their point across without obscuring their narrative. This is a quality that science fiction can share with the classic fairy tale, and the large body of traditional fantasy writing from which it has only recently sprung.

If this book has served as your introduction to contemporary science fiction, then I urge you to seek out the excellent anthologies of such experienced editors as Damon Knight, Robert Silverberg and Terry Carr, to mention a few of the more prominent in the field. They will repay your attention handsomely.

Editing *Beyond Tomorrow* could have been a formidable task, had it not been for the whole-hearted and world-wide co-operation of authors and their agents. With only one or two exceptions, I was fortunate in obtaining the rights to stories I had selected, and I would like to thank all concerned with this endeavour for assisting above and beyond what would normally have been expected of them in such an enterprise.

Tony Thomas, Robin Johnson and John Foyster helped me with research. Alex Butler and Julie Anne Ford were helpful in enabling me to contact some Australian authors. Theodore Cogswell, Virginia Kidd, Andy Porter, Leslie Flood and Brian Aldiss helped me to locate overseas authors. Scott Meredith, Robert P. Mills and Henry Morrison acted promptly on their clients' behalf, and Mrs Genevieve Linebarger was especially helpful. Isaac Asimov responded to a request for a Foreword with a generosity that overwhelmed me, and for which I am indebted.

Finally, I would like to thank those close to me who gave help and encouragement when it was needed, and Dennis Wren for the opportunity to edit this historic anthology.

Lee Harding
Melbourne, Australia, 1976

Acknowledgements

RAINBIRD by R. A. Lafferty. From *Galaxy*, © Galaxy Publishing Corp., 1961, and R. A. Lafferty, 1972. Reprinted by permission of the author and the author's agent, Virginia Kidd.

NINE LIVES by Ursula Le Guin. From *Playboy*, © Ursula K. Le Guin, 1969, 1974. The substantially revised version reprinted here first appeared in *World's Best Science Fiction: 1970*, edited by Donald A. Wollheim and Terry Carr. Reprinted by permission of the author and the author's agent, Virginia Kidd.

IDIOT STICK by Damon Knight. From *Star Science Fiction*, © Ballantine Books Inc., 1958. Reprinted by permission of the author and the author's agent, Robert P. Mills.

THE ARK OF JAMES CARLYLE by Cherry Wilder. From *New Writings in Science Fiction* edited by Kenneth Bulmer. © Transworld Publishers and Sidgwick and Jackson Ltd, 1974. Reprinted by permission of the author and the publishers.

THE COMMUTER by Phillip K. Dick. From *Amazing*, © Ziff-Davis Publications, 1953. Reprinted by permission of the author and the author's agent, Scott Meredith Literary Agency Inc., 580 Fifth Avenue, New York, N.Y. 10036.

THE OATH by James Blish. From *The Magazine of Fantasy and Science Fiction*, © Fantasy House Inc., 1960. Reprinted by permission of the author and the author's agent, Robert P. Mills.

TAKEOVER BID by John Baxter. From *New Writings in Science Fiction*, © Transworld Publishers Ltd, 1965. Reprinted by permission of the author and the author's agent, A. D. Peters.

COMES NOW THE POWER by Roger Zelazny. From *Magazine of Horror*, © Health Knowledge Inc., 1966. Reprinted by permission of the author and the author's agent, Henry Morrison Inc.

LITTERBUG by Tony Morphett. From *The Magazine of Fantasy and Science Fiction*, © Fantasy House Inc., 1969. Reprinted by permission of the author.

LATE by A. Bertram Chandler. From *Science-Fantasy*, © Nova Publications Ltd, 1955. Reprinted by permission of the author.

MOTHER HITTON'S LITTUL KITTONS by Cordwainer Smith. From *Galaxy*, © Galaxy Publishing Corp., 1961. Reprinted by permission of the author's estate and Scott Meredith Literary Agency Inc.

A SONG BEFORE SUNSET by David Grigg appears for the first time. © David Grigg, 1975.

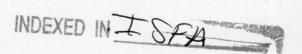